Also by Gail Godwin

NOVELS

The Perfectionists
Glass People
The Odd Woman
Violet Clay
A Mother and Two Daughters
The Finishing School
A Southern Family
Father Melancholy's Daughter

SHORT STORIES

Dream Children
Mr. Bedford and the Muses

VIRAGO
MODERN CLASSICS
486

Gail Godwin

Gail Godwin was born in Alabama, grew up in Ashev
North Carolina, and received her doctorate in English f
the University of Iowa. She has taught at Vassar College
Columbia University and has received a Guggen
Fellowship and the 1981 Award in Literature from the Nat
Academy and Institute of Arts and Letters. Her short st
essays, and articles have appeared in numerous magazine
newspapers and her highly praised books include *Th
Woman* and *Violet Clay*. She currently lives in Woodstocl
York.

THE GOOD
HUSBAND

Gail Godwin

Virago

A *Virago* Book

Published by Virago Press 2002

First published in the United States of America by
Ballantine Books, a division of
Random House, Inc, New York
First published in Great Britain by
André Deutsch Ltd 1994

Copyright © Gail Godwin 1994
Illustrations copyright © Prudence See 1994

The moral right of the author has been asserted.

Grateful acknowledgement is made to the following for permission to reprint
previously published material: Macmillan Publishing Company and Peters, Fraser
and Dunlop Group, Ltd.: Excerpts from *Memoirs of W.B. Yeats* edited by Denis
Donoghue. Copyright © 1972 by M.B. Yeats and Anne Yeats. Copyright © 1972
by Denis Donoghue. Reprinted by permission of Macmillan Publishing Company
and the Peters, Fraser & Dunlop Group Ltd.

The drawings that accompany the text are inspired by actual misericords that still
grace churches throughout Europe and the British Isles. In order of their
appearance these are: Title Page: *The Lovers*, Cologne Cathedral. Part One: *Mary
Magdalen as Penitent*, Saumur, Church of St-Pierre. Chapter Openings: *The
Wedding Band*, St-Jean-de-Maurienne, Cathedral of St-Jean-Baptiste. Part Two:
The Lovers, Church of St-Chamant. Epilogue: *Dragon, Apparently Asleep, with
Wings Expanded*, Wells Cathedral.

A CIP catalogue record for this book is
available from the British Library

ISBN 1 86049 913 9

Printed and bound in Great Britain by
Clays Ltd, St Ives plc

Virago
A Division of
Time Warner Books UK
Brettenham House
Lancaster Place
London WC2E 7EN

www.virago.co.uk

This novel is dedicated, in gratitude and affection, to the late Professor Wynn Reynolds, who taught me the importance of wit in his living and dying, and to Lynda Lyall, Wells Cathedral Guide, who instilled in me a fascination for misericords.

None of the characters in *The Good Husband* are portraits or sketches of any real persons, living or dead. Though I have taken the grace and dedication and sacramental quality of his daily living from one friend, the quiet beauty and composure from another friend, and the courage to die imaginatively from another friend, Francis, Alice, Hugo, and Magda are, I must admit, four stimulating but often puzzling parts of my own character.

ACKNOWLEDGMENTS

The author gratefully acknowledges Marie Duane for all medical research; Father Francis Skelly, C.Ss.R., for his help in sketching out Francis Lake's life in seminary; Sandi Zinaman for guiding me through the home birth of Alice Henry's child; Robert Wyatt for vital editorial involvement in the manuscript in progress; and my publisher and editor, Linda Grey, for her astute grasp of the narrative design and her inspired suggestions. Magda's ideas, though largely hers and expressed in her style, are also indebted to June Singer's *The Unholy Bible: Blake, Jung and the Collective Unconscious*, and the Rev. Janet Vincent-Scaringe's "The Ordering of Love in Dante's *Divine Comedy*."

PART ONE

Mates are not always matches,
and matches are not always mates.

—MAGDA DANVERS

CHAPTER I

Magda Danvers, the week before Christmas, returned home from surgery at Catskill Hospital and telephoned to her chairman she would not be meeting her classes for second semester. "It seems the Great Uncouth has taken up permanent residence inside me," she informed him. "Well, I always was a good student; now I must see what I can learn from my final teacher."

She had many visitors. This was during the first stage of her dying, when she still looked and spoke like her old self. Ray Johnson, the chairman of the English Department at Aurelia College, lost no time in disseminating her audacious remark around campus, and people wanted to go over to the restored Colonial farmhouse their prized teacher shared with her husband, Francis Lake, a devoted, self-effacing man much younger than herself, and see for themselves how Magda would go about learning from her final teacher.

During the remainder of deep winter, Magda held court in her snug upstairs study, crammed with all her books, surrounded by her beloved Blake reproductions. She reclined on the worn leather sofa in a baggy sweater and old tweed trousers and red velvet carpet slippers, an afghan spread over her, her famous mahogany hair floating loose around her shoulders rather than pinned up in its usual fat twist. A fire crackled in the small fireplace, tended by her husband. At regular intervals, Francis would poke his head around the door and ask, "How is the fire doing, my love?" If she replied, "We could use a couple more logs, Frannie," that was their signal that she was enjoying her visitor, and Francis would slip in unobtrusively and rekindle the fire. If she said, "I think we'll just let it burn itself out," that meant the visitor was not contributing enough to the precious time she had left in this world, and Francis was to return in three to five minutes and announce it was time for one of Magda's obligatory rest periods in the bedroom at the other end of the hall.

Her students came. Suzanne Riley brought Magda her map of the Mountain of Purgatory, Magda's last class assignment before entering the hospital. "I want you to have the original of this, Professor Danvers. I made a color photocopy to hand in to Professor Ramirez-Suarez. He'll be taking your classes second semester while . . . until . . ." The girl looked away miserably.

"It's okay, Suzanne," Magda soothed her. "We both know what you mean. But this is a gorgeous map. All the detail you put into these figures. I didn't even assign figures."

"Well, I *am* an arts major. At first I dreaded your assignment. You know. All that extra *work*. I mean, if you're going to draw a really good map, you have to read the stuff really carefully so you'll know what to draw. But then it was weird. I got really involved. I always know when I get involved while I'm drawing because my mouth begins to water. If that doesn't sound too gross."

Francis Lake poked his head briefly around the door. "How's the fire doing, Magda?"

"Oh, pile on some more logs," replied Magda cheerfully. "But first, come and look at this splendid drawing. I want to get it framed as soon as possible and hang it up with my Blakes so I can look at it in the time I've got left. A good map of Purgatory fits in *perfectly* with my present studies. Let's see, where am I on the Mountain? I'd like to be as far up as the Gluttonous cornice—the warm sins are better—but I'm probably still down in the lower Purgatory with the cold and proud. Where do you think I am, Frannie?"

"You're certainly not cold and proud," said Francis. "It *is* a splendid map. I'll take it down to the framers first thing in the morning, my love."

"First my grandmother dies, and then my girlfriend breaks up with me, and now I'm losing my favorite teacher," blubbered the young man, clutching at Magda's afghan. "This has been the worst year of my life. I'm like, wondering what's the point of living." He covered his face with a corner of the afghan, managing to tug it off Magda's knees in the process, and began to sob in earnest.

Francis Lake's slim figure materialized at once in the doorway. "How's the fire doing, Magda?"

"Oh, dying, like everything else in here," said Magda. "Could you give Rick a Kleenex so he can blow his nose before he goes?"

Ramirez-Suarez paid courtly visits. "We miss you, bright lady. My task this semester is to make Paradise as interesting as Hell. You would have done a much better job with your marvelous *viveza*. I have been entertaining them a little by reading passages aloud in the Italian. Oh, and I have had to supplement the text with my own notes, which I pass out to them each session. Magda, these young people have no receptivity to *allusions*. They don't know who Achilles was. They can't name the seven deadly sins. Their biblical references are almost nil. Would you believe it, many of them weren't familiar with the Sermon on the Mount."

Her husband, smiling, stuck his head in the door.

"Ah, Francis, I have stayed too long and tired out our dearest Magda," said the dapper little professor, leaping out of his chair.

"I'll be tireder if you *leave* me, Tony. Frannie just came to heap more logs on our fire. And then you'll have some tea with us. After you phoned this morning, Francis went out and bought those lemon squares you like."

"Oh, dear lady—"

"Sit *down*, Tony. Haven't you heard that invalids are always supposed to have their way? You know, I think we ought to propose a new course at Aurelia. A *required* course, and not just for liberal-arts majors, either. The catalog description would describe it as 'The very minimum of people, places, and things you'd better at least have *heard* of if you plan to pass yourself off as an educated person.' And we'd stuff it into them any old-fashioned way we could: forced memorization, pop quizzes, all the old dirty tricks. A two-semester course. We could call it Allusions One, and Allusions Two. . . ."

The chairman of English, Ray Johnson, dropped by regularly, his shining eyes behind the round glasses taking in the minute details of her decline so he could report back to others.

"Tony Ramirez-Suarez said he found you in excellent spirits the other day. You two were cooking up some amusing new course?"

"Allusions One and Two," said Magda. " 'Would you rather drink from the waters of Lethe, the Pierian Spring, or Parnassus's Waters? Why?' 'What did Circe do to men?' 'Why did Diana keep to the woods?' 'List the seven deadly sins and the four cardinal virtues and the four levels of meaning.' Just the basic stuff you need if you're going to read a poem rather than a balance sheet."

The chairman chuckled knowledgeably. Magda's mind definitely hadn't succumbed to the waters of Lethe yet, but her flamboyant dark red hair, he hadn't failed to notice, now sprouted an untidy inch or more of dead white at the parting. This shocking sign of the arrogant Magda's deterioration somewhat tempered his resentment of her for baiting him. He could get three out of four levels of meaning, but what the devil were the four cardinal virtues? Parnassus's waters rang a faint bell from somewhere in his academic past, but what the hell did you get from drinking them?

He changed the subject. "Poor Alice and Hugo Henry. They lost their baby."

"Oh, no! How?"

"He got tangled in the cord and the oxygen was cut off. Apparently it was going fine until the last minute, Hugo said. He seemed quite shaken when he came to school today. It was a home birth. That Dr. Romero all the mothers love and all the other obstetricians hate."

"Oh, poor lovely Alice. And she was so happy when I was with her at your party in early December. Oh, God, there we both were, laughing and talking together, her with her healthy baby inside her and me with my undiagnosed cancer inside me, both of us oblivious to our fates. . . ."

Francis Lake appeared in the doorway.

"Francis, Alice and Hugo lost their baby."

"When?"

"Last Thursday," said Ray Johnson. "But we didn't know about it until Monday, when Hugo came to meet his classes." The chairman then repeated the sad details to Magda's husband.

"Oh, I'm so upset for them," wailed Magda, clutching at her hair. "Francis, I must write them a letter immediately."

"After you've rested," Francis told her sternly. 'Ray, you won't mind waiting here until I get Magda settled in her room. Then we'll go downstairs and have some tea. If you can spare the time."

"Oh, I can always spare the time for one of your famous teas," said the chairman, laughing.

January's calendar flipped over into February, then on into March. Gresham P. Harris, president of Aurelia College, mounted the stairs behind Magda's husband.

"Last time, we went thataway," remarked the president lightly when Francis, at the top of the stairs, turned right, not left toward Magda's study with the nice fire burning.

"Magda is staying in bed today."

"Oh, I see," said the president, preparing himself not to show anything as he followed Francis Lake toward a room at the other end of the hallway.

"Magda, Magda," was all he said, when he saw his brilliant star lying gray and docile under the blanket in the big four-poster bed. She was *small*, she who three months ago would have been described by her aficionados as "statuesque," and by her enemies (for of course she had those, too) as overweight. Since his last visit to the house, she must have dropped twenty or thirty pounds. And the wiry white stuff bursting out of her scalp belonged to someone else. Some wild old woman . . . or man. The glossy dark red hair that had been distinctly hers, though everyone knew it came out of a package, still lay in straggles of its former glory on either side of her pillows. It had the look of having just been brushed out for his visit, probably by Francis Lake.

The president sat down in the chair Magda's husband placed for him on the right side of the bed. Left alone in the room by Francis in the direct range of the dying woman's penetrating gaze, he gained a few moments of respite by plucking at the knees of his perfectly creased trousers and surveying the neat lines of his black-stockinged ankles and the polished black wing-tip shoes below. He was a well-groomed, fastidious man who appeared younger than his fifty-eight years. He and Magda were the same age. Years ago, they had been graduate students at the same time in Ann Arbor, but they hadn't known each other. These days he also gave his smooth, dark hair a little help from a package. College presidents were expected to look younger now.

I, too, could be struck by cancer and waste away in a few months, the president suddenly realized. His gaze meeting Magda's snapping dark eyes at last, he had the distinct feeling that she had read his thought word for word. It made it easier for him to speak naturally.

"Well, Magda, this distresses me. I guess I was hoping for a miracle. Now that this Gulf War is over, I've rescheduled our Twenty-fifth Anniversary Alumni Cruise around the British Isles for August—our first cruise ever, to honor Aurelia's first graduating class of sixty-six. I had my heart set on your being the star lecturer. We thought we'd use a 'literary heritage' theme."

"I'd be honored, Gresh, if I weren't already booked for another journey."

"Are you in much pain?"

"It comes and goes. It has a life of its own. I've named it the Gargoyle. Every day its grin stretches wider at my expense, but of course from *its* point of view, I'm the impediment. *I'm* the thing in the way of *its* development and growth." She laughed weakly. "If it had a language, I wonder what it would name me." Then she grimaced in obvious pain.

That was the sort of remark that made her the popular and compelling teacher she was. He wished he had more like her. She hadn't come cheaply, of course, when he snared her five years ago. Better be glad she hadn't followed up on the meteoric early brilliance of that first book, or he'd never have captured her for Aurelia. There'd been chapters of its successor, spread out between long—too long—intervals in the quarterlies, but not nearly enough to show for twenty-five years of scholarship from the precocious author of *The Book of Hell: An Introduction to the Visionary Mode*. He still recalled how flattened with envy he had been, all those years ago back in Ann Arbor, when her outrageous young triumph had flashed across the academic firmament. His own age and already published. And from the same university. (Though at least he had been in a different field: he was doing history and poly sci.) Not only published, but her picture in *Time* magazine. "The Dark Lady of Visions." Her dissertation published before it had even been defended! Though later he'd heard that there had been some backlash by resentful professors that had delayed her degree for several years.

Her eyes were closed; she was focused on her pain. Her Gargoyle. An ovarian cancer that had gone too far. According to Ray Johnson, that champion disseminator of other people's business, the word was that she'd flat out rejected chemo when that new Indian doctor Rainiwari, who could be somewhat blunt, told her what her chances were . . . or, rather, weren't. "In that case," she'd told Rainiwari, "I'd prefer to spend the time I have left studying for my Final Exam, rather than studying my disease."

The president leaned forward and steadied himself with a hand on either of his charcoal-pinstriped knees. His first impulse had been to reach out and lay one of his hands on top of hers, which were clenched upon the blanket. But at present it seemed like an intrusion. The skin of Magda's hands had acquired a glossy, yellowish sheen; whereas her formerly high-colored face had been dulled to a powdery gray pallor. These mysterious details of an individual's dying: what would his own details be like?

He put his face nearer to hers. "We want to set up an endowed chair in your name," he murmured, moved as much by the sorrowful huskiness that had crept appropriately into his announcement as by the magnanimous gift he offered.

The eyes opened. Dark, receptive pools, though ambushed by pain. Then the cracked corners of her mouth tipped upward in an irrepressible smirk. Why, she was expecting it, thought the president.

"The Magda Danvers Chair of Visionary Studies, we were thinking of calling it," he continued. "I was talking to Ray Johnson. If we use the word 'studies' rather than 'literature,' we include the visual arts, which you've been doing all along anyway. It would leave things wide open for exciting linkups between departments. Our art chairman Sonia Wynkoop is having her Roman sabbatical, as you know, but I'm sure she'll be amenable to the idea when she returns. Maybe we'd include music and science as well. Colleges that stay in business these days are getting away from the old departmental isolation. Everyone's had their fill of the specialists, each keeping his acquirements to himself behind arcane jargons. The trend now is back to shared knowledge and cooperation. The Rounded Person."

"A trend whose time has come none too soon, wouldn't you say?" responded the smiling Magda, with a flash of that mocking insolence that many people, including President Gresham P. Harris, found disconcerting.

He rose, plucking at his trousers again to adjust their fall. "Well, you must rest. Keep up your strength for . . . for . . ." It was a rare occasion when he found himself at a loss for words.

"For my Final Exam," Magda helped him out. She reached up for his hand with one of her waxy, yellow ones. The grip was weak but sure. The hand was dry, and hotter than he would have expected.

"Thank you, Gresh. You've made me very happy about the chair." She sounded like a mischievous little girl who'd gotten exactly what she wanted and was trying to be demure. But she closed her eyes again before he could attempt to read them.

Though he had semicommitments elsewhere, President Harris let himself be talked into having tea downstairs with Francis Lake because the poor guy looked exhausted and lonely and had obviously gone to trouble preparing it. They sat facing each other at a small table in a cozy corner of the living room where the afternoon sun played attractively on the fronds of healthy hanging plants in the deep-set windows and brought out the various patinas in the woods of some rather good Early American furniture. Boy, wouldn't his wife Leora like to get her hands on that secretary.

Francis served him with attentive diffidence, making a little ceremony with all his paraphernalia: the strainer and the sugar tongs, the little silver pitcher of hot water. A soft-spoken, tranquil fellow, Magda Danvers's husband. Twelve years younger than she. The scuttlebutt was that, back in the sixties, Magda had stolen him out of a Catholic seminary somewhere up in the north of Michigan where she'd gone to lecture. He still had somewhat of the look of an aging choirboy. Now, that must have been an unusual courtship. But they seemed very contented in their domestic arrangement. Enviably so, his wife Leora believed. Once, at a faculty dinner party hosted by the president and his wife, Magda had made pointed innuendoes concerning their successful bed life.

"The forsythia will be out any day now," said Francis Lake, slicing a cake with fruit on the top and transferring a generous wedge to the president's plate. "I saw some buds this morning that were about to pop." He helped himself to a slice. "I hope she makes it to the lilac. Magda's favorite is that deep purple lilac." He motioned through the window at a very old lilac, whose convoluted branches were outlined in the liquid-yellow light of early spring.

"Let's hope she does," concurred the president. After a suitable pause, he added, "It's going to be a big loss for all of us."

"Yes," replied Francis equably, still gazing out at the old lilac. What on earth will he do with himself when she's gone? wondered the president. Ray Johnson said that Francis Lake had never even held a job. He'd been Magda's house husband, just as some women (though that model was getting phased out rapidly now) were never anything but housewives. Francis would have her pension, of course. Which would have been considerably more if she'd died at sixty-five rather than fifty-eight.

Whereas we will save, thought the president. But, damn it, whom could he get for the Twenty-fifth Anniversary Cruise? Had to be someone of star quality. Of course there was Hugo Henry, Aurelia's current novelist-in-residence, much more widely known than Magda, though not nearly as warm and engaging a speaker, his trusty spy Ray Johnson had reported. Hugo was truculent; short men often were. Nevertheless, he could do the job. His reputation would carry him. And people liked novelists, their creative aura. For the requisite bit of scholarly heft the president could get Stanforth from Columbia. Stanforth owed him several favors. But Hugo and his wife had had the disaster with their baby back in January and Alice hadn't been seen outside the house since. It was probably still too soon to decently ask Hugo to do the cruise.

But the publicity over Magda's endowed chair would be coming at a good time, for the twenty-fifth anniversary of the first graduating class.

"I wonder, Francis, would you happen to have a recent photo of Magda in profile? We've got plans under way to raise some big bucks for a Magda Danvers chair, and I want to have her tintype on the letterhead we send out."

"I was looking at some snapshots today. Does it have to be a profile?"

"Preferably. Profiles come out better on a tintype."

Already Francis had sprung up from his chair and was rustling through a drawer of the secretary. He returned with a bulging envelope of snapshots, which he emptied out on the windowsill and began to sort through energetically, passing his selections across the table with accompanying commentaries. "That was in Paris, the summer Magda was doing her symbols of apotheosis research. It's not very recent, but I think it's still extremely like her, don't you? Oh, now here's one. This is more recent, just before we came to Aurelia. Magda and I were accompanying the junior girls at Merrivale College on their semester abroad. I took this myself in Florence. You get a really good profile of Magda, though it's slightly blurred, because she moved just as I clicked the shutter. She was pointing out to the girls where Dante lived. . . ."

At this rate, I'll be here all night, thought the president. But he took another sip of tea, surreptitiously glanced at his wristwatch, and let Francis go on a bit longer. The poor man's face was animated with excitement and happiness. In his trip down memory lane (that old photo "still extremely like her"!), he had briefly forgotten the true state of affairs on the floor above.

A week later, Magda received a letter from the president, officially announcing the $400,000 fund drive for the Magda Danvers Chair of Visionary Studies.

"Well, at *least* that amount," remarked Magda to Francis. "Seeing as he's going to save almost that much on the salary I won't be getting for the next seven years." It was a good day, when she was relatively free from pain, though she stayed in bed all the time now.

Francis carried in the classical dictionaries and poetry books and reference volumes she requested and stacked them in piles on the bed, and for the remainder of that day Magda pounced and plundered and sizzled and revised until she had concocted a reply to the president that she deemed worthy of herself.

When she was done, she lay back exhausted on her pillows.

"My best allusions and conceits will soar right over his head," she told Francis weakly, handing up to him the untidy bunch of yellow pages which she knew would be deciphered faithfully and transformed into WordPerfect legibility on his computer.

"You know you didn't write it only for him." Francis laid the pages carefully on top of the pine huntboard near the door. Then he set about clearing her feverish work space back into a place of rest. The books he separated into piles conforming to Magda's esoteric system of arrangement. She could count on him to replace them exactly in the order she liked them on her study shelves. But for now, it gave her a weary satisfaction to see their familiar bindings stacked against the scrolled splashboard of the handsome piece of furniture which they'd bought in Charleston when she gave her Dante paper. Together they had created their own taste in furnishings, since neither had grown up among things they liked. Magda's mother's taste had been parvenu Empire. Francis's family had been too pressed for necessities to have settled on any style.

Whistling tunelessly under his breath, Francis gently lifted her head and rearranged her pillows so she would have a cool one on top. He folded the flat sheet neatly over the blanket, aligning the entwined monogram (MLF) with her exact midpoint. She had kept her own name when they married, but on all their household linens their first initials lay on either side of his surname. Not the way it was traditionally done, but in their marriage they had tended to make their own traditions.

"It's probably his best chance for immortality," said Francis placidly, continuing to fuss with her bedclothes. "A hundred years from now, people will open a book—*Survey of Great Twentieth-Century Prose* or something like that—and there, under 'The Occasional Writings of Magda Danvers,' will be your letter."

" 'Letter to President Gresham P. Harris, Accepting His Homage of an Endowed Chair in Her Name at Aurelia College, 1991.' " Magda took over from him. "There will have to be footnotes, explaining Aurelia College as a newish, middling, overendowed liberal-arts institution in the Catskills, with grandiose architectural facades and straining cultural ambitions, where every last toolshed bore the forgettable name of some donor. At least my name's not forgettable, but that's because I concocted it for myself."

She snorted gleefully at her exercise in malice, then paid for it, wincing. The Gargoyle did not like her to laugh.

The monumental effort of writing a mere witty thank-you letter, laced with a few frisky eruditions, had done her in. Not so long ago she could have knocked off six such letters in an afternoon and then scribbled out her lecture notes for the next day's classes, and still had plenty of energy left over to lead Francis a merry chase at dinner with her flights and probings.

"Are you feeling ready for some lunch? I got some more of that sliced turkey breast you liked. And there are fresh rolls."

Her husband's familiar, concerned countenance floated above her.

"No, thank you, sweet fellow," she said. "The Mental Traveller is packing it in for today."

Then she realized by the continued hovering of his face—was it her illness that had aged it so?—that she hadn't communicated anything aloud, had only heard her own inner voice. Lately this was happening more and more.

But for the life of her she couldn't summon the energy to try again.

CHAPTER II

Francis Lake gazed at the sky-blue screen of his computer. In it he could see reflections of the two small recessed windows of his study, as Magda insisted on calling his little room off the kitchen, and each window's contained vista of the shrubs outside. The forsythia was coming into bloom. But he had already forced a vaseful of branches for Magda's room.

Next would come the fragrant viburnum, the lilac in white and deep purple, the rhododendron, the mountain laurel. He would continue to fill the vases with blossoms, but on what day would she stop registering their identities? The daughter of a silk-flower manufacturer, Magda liked to tease him: "Before you came into my life, Frannie, I took it for granted all flowers bloomed at the same time."

She probably wouldn't make it to the rhododendrons.

Leaning forward on his elbows, he covered his face briefly with his hands, then removed them and gazed down at the choice of commands on the little printed template strip which lay along the top of his keyboard.

Cancel, he read. *Help*. *Save*.

Yes, please, all of the above. She was always telling her students that meaning lay behind everything. Some people had a natural instinct for recognizing the symbolic nature of their lives as they unfolded, but anyone who paid attention could learn to do it, she said.

List Files. Enter. Scroll down through accounts, budget, tax records, maintenance and capital improvements, all kept by him. She would neither balance a checkbook nor learn the computer. She refused to memorize any phone number but their own, joking that she already had too much in her mind.

Then Magda's essay files, Magda's speeches.

Past Francis's "Misericords" file: listings with short descriptions of the carved underseats in the choir stalls of the cathedrals and churches he had visited in his travels with Magda. An undertaking begun as a pastime one summer in Europe, while she was off researching her visionaries and he took to wandering in the cool interiors of old churches. And then continued more methodically on other trips to Britain and to the continent because it pleased Magda for him to have a scholarly project of his own. By now he had filled several boxes with photo slides, organized carefully by locations, date of carving, and subject matter. Some of the subjects were so touching and curious. Magda said there was a book in it, but he preferred it to remain his hobby, reminding her it was more important that he get on with *her* book, as soon as she had another scribbled chapter ready for him to type.

And there *it* was: DEVIL.01, DEVIL.02, DEVIL.03, part of DEVIL.04, *Of the Devil's Party: A Re-Visioning*, her long-awaited, now never-to-be-completed sequel to *The Book of Hell: An Introduction to the Visionary Mode*, which was responsible for the lecture tour that had brought her, an otherwise unlikely visitor, to his seminary on Lake Superior in October 1966.

Then Magda's Letters. Retrieve. Home, Home, down arrow. Already one hundred pages of her transcribed letters in one file. Time to start a new one, MLett.02?

Francis closed his eyes and took a ragged breath before acknowledging the fact that an MLett.02 file would not be needed.

March 23, 1991, he typed, on page 101 of the old file. Gregory the Illuminator, he once automatically would have added. Funny how the feast days stayed in your mind.

Dear President Harris:

Such an honor you have draped upon my reclining shoulders. Alas, it's too late for them to bear upright the heft of Elijah's Mantle, but I assure you they will carry the Mantle of Fidelity to Aurelia College proudly into whatever perpetuity awaits me. . . .

Francis paused and contemplated the sight of the azure screen filling with her words. How she had exhausted herself in the composing of this letter.

Lately, significances of the kind she was always encouraging people to look for in their lives would pierce his heart.

For instance, he had just thought: "I am seeing Magda out on a keyboard, just as I once summoned her into my life on a keyboard."

Not the kind of thinking he would have gone in for on his own. But living with someone like Magda for twenty-five years (twenty-four years and two months and twenty-three days, to be exact) encouraged a person to make such connections.

There hadn't been any computers or word processors at Regina Seminary up on Lake Superior in the fall of 1966. Francis typed for Father Floris several afternoons a week on an old Remington manual. He was proud of his touch typing, learned at the Catholic high school back in Alpena. Father Floris ran Regina's cultural forum. He had a network going with a dean over at Northern Michigan in nearby Marquette. Together they had discovered that interesting speakers might be better lured up into their wilds if they combined forces. Recalcitrant speakers were often gratified to boast they had two engagements in one city; some of them were actually intrigued by the idea of spending one of the nights at a seminary.

"Take a letter," Father Floris said to Francis, leaning back in his swivel chair, pressing his palms together under his chin, and closing his eyes. " 'Dear Jim. I'd like to override your veto on McLuhan. Though this book's not as electrifying as his last, he's a leading figure in this dizzying cultural revolution that's going on all around us whether we like it or not, and I want our students to have a crack at him. If one is apprised of each new "relevance" as it patters down on us in its hour, one is less likely to be swept away by the flood of change: that's our evolving directive over here, as you know. Nothing new, really: just a restatement of the old "wise as serpents" policy. We could kick in a bit more than our usual pittance for the occasion, and our rector, Father Birkenshaw, gives me leave to offer our distinguished speaker the founder's suite in our guest lodge for the evening of his visit with us here at Regina. It's where our superior general stays. You might mention to Mr. McLuhan that it's recently been redecorated and has a new tiled shower and a private phone line. We can also provide transportation to the airport at the crack of dawn or before, as our seminarians rise very early.' "

Sometimes trade-offs were made.

"Here we go, Francis. Ready? 'Dear Jim. Glad the plans for McLuhan's spring visit are progressing. Meanwhile, sure, we'll chip in our nickel for Miss Magda Danvers, this lady-scholar of visions that your colleague down at UM so enthusiastically recommends— that is, as long as the visions don't come out of a capsule or a bottle. In turn, may I offer your students what I can promise will be a fascinating evening with our excellent Sister Mary Joseph, member of our sister order. She has recently returned from a five-year tour of duty at our mission in Taiwan, and has much to say about the state of affairs in the Far East. We would be able to drive her over and back from your campus, and we'd be putting her up here, of course. . . .' "

Windows were washed by the seminarians twice a year at Regina Seminary. In October and in May. Francis was up on the stepladder, squares of old newspaper (neatly cut by the brothers in the kitchen) stowed in the pockets of his pea jacket, a bucket of warm vinegar water (at least it had been warm when it left the building) slung over his left forearm. The metal handle of the heavy bucket bit into his flesh through the wool sleeve. The cold wind coming off the lake chilled his fingers and whipped the skirts of his cassock against his jeans. But he was happy. During last year's novitiate up at North Lake House, his third year at Regina, the year set aside for discernment, discipline, and study of the rule, which the order liked to compare to the military experience, there had been some unhappy times. Having survived them, he felt practically on vacation back at Regina's main campus, where the beds were real beds and not army cots, the radiators worked, and someone wasn't trying to break your will from morning until night. Being back at Regina was like being a young man at college again. The only difference being that, unlike most college students of twenty-one, he already had taken his first vows toward living a certain way for the rest of his life. One of the more joyful benefits of the rigorous, humiliating novitiate year was that he was beginning to understand through his senses as well as by means of his indoctrinated will that a moment fully lived in service was a moment lived in God's time. So he was at the moment as happy as he had ever been, balanced on the stepladder under the cold blue sky, washing the fanlight beneath the round arch over the seminary's front door.

Composed of seven slender isosceles triangles of different-colored glass between radiating glazing bars, the fanlight was the only out-of-character adornment on this massive Romanesque pile of stone which had been built as a merchandising baron's country house in the late 1870s by H. H. Richardson himself. It was the opinion of Father Birkenshaw, the rector, who had studied to be an architect before joining the order, that this fanlight, suitable for the "lighter and more feminine" Georgian and Regency styles, had been a bitter concession to his client by the masterful Richardson, whose trademark was the strong, frill-free, rock-faced building.

"Depend upon it, a carved stone tympanum had been designed by Richardson to go under that arch," Father Birkenshaw never lost the opportunity to inform visitors. His brusque voice, rock-faced and frill free itself, seemed to cast some part of the blame for the frivolous fanlight on them.

The rector was just now approaching, on the gravel path leading from the guest lodge, with a large woman whom Francis at first assumed was a nun. She was all in black, from her voluminous wool cape, which swayed energetically about her calves, down to her stockings and shoes. She was tall, as tall as the rector himself, but she walked with her head lowered in a manner Francis first mistook for "custody of the eyes." The heels on her shoes were too high and spiky for a nun's, and her coiled and burnished hair too elaborately arranged, but everybody knew that nuns were in the process of drastically changing their image. Could it be their nun who'd just come back from the mission in Taiwan, the one who was booked to speak at one of Father Floris's future cultural forums?

"That fanlight, in my opinion, was a bitter concession," Father Birkenshaw, stepping along briskly in his well-fitting cassock, was saying to the visitor, who matched her strides to his as they approached Francis on the stepladder. She was carrying a bulky black briefcase, and as she raised her face to view the bitter concession, Francis saw that she was trying to keep an insolent smile within bounds. Not the nun, he decided.

"We haven't been able to locate the Richardson drawings for this place," continued Father Birkenshaw, "but depend upon it, a carved stone tympanum was designed to go under that arch."

The two of them had paused below the stepladder. Francis stopped wiping the glass and shifted his body to one side so that they could have an unobstructed look at the fanlight.

After a moment, during which Francis felt that he as well as the fanlight underwent scrutiny by the visitor, she asked Father Birkenshaw: "Is it the window itself you object to, or the colors?" She had a rich, low voice, with a touch of mockery in it that matched the smile she hadn't succeeded in repressing.

"It's not a matter of my objecting," responded the rector testily. "It's just not architecturally consistent. That's my point."

"Oh, if *consistency's* your point . . ." conceded the woman at once. She smiled collusively up at Francis, and her dark bright eyes seemed effortlessly to read his guilty heart. For, though the director had succeeded in intimidating the seminarians into believing that the fanlight was the one tasteless blight on their classic building, Francis clung to his secret pleasure in it. The colors reminded him of the ones in the LifeSaver packets of his childhood. In good taste or not, the fanlight made the old gray fortress sing for him.

She was, it turned out, the vision-lady Father Floris had invited to his cultural forum in exchange for Northern Michigan having his nun to theirs. M. Danvers was the name listed on her book, a study of the sources of creativity in certain famous prophetic artists, which had the provocative title *The Book of Hell*.

At dinner in the refectory, she sat at the head table between Father Birkenshaw and Father Floris. During a seminarian's reading, a meditation on Paul's Epistle to the Romans, "God does not change his mind about whom he chooses and blesses," she kept her head lowered demurely as she ate, so that it was impossible to see her expression. In honor of the visitor, there was dessert, baked apple, although it was a weekday. But the brother in the kitchen who was replacing their regular cook, who'd had a death in the family, had seasoned it oddly. After the first spoonful, Francis wordlessly offered his to a classmate who was always hungry and didn't appear to mind the peculiar taste.

That evening at the forum, Father Floris introduced their speaker as "Miss Magda Danvers, who, in the tradition of other celebrated ladies of the pen, chooses to remain genderless on her book jacket." The old priest's head waggled gaily as he provided this note of interest to the students, but Miss Danvers, waiting on the sidelines in an armchair, shot him an impatient look.

Though the lectern stood ready with its lamp switched on, she never so much as approached it. Instead she started stalking up and down the carpeted lounge. She carried not a single paper or notecard, delivering herself in a steady, confident, frequently amused tone. Once in a while she would slow down for a ruminative aside, or come to a full halt to scowl out of the window into the darkness, as if challenging the night to provide her with her next line. When pivoting around on one of her high spike heels for the return march, she would occasionally fix some member of the community with her insolent dark eyes. She still was all in black: sweater, skirt, stockings, shoes. He wondered if she had done it out of deference to the black cassocks worn by the teachers and professed novices. But the sweater did not hide the curves of her figure, and she did not give the impression of being a person who did much out of deference.

"Yes, Blake was thirty-three, that symbolic age. The very same age as a certain *other* troublesome person you may have heard of, when he was at the climax of his ministry to unsettle and remake the world. William Blake was thirty-three years old when he sat down to engrave the text and pictures for his highly subversive gospel, *The Marriage of Heaven and Hell*."

She was not the first woman speaker at the cultural forum. They'd had a black woman poet who wore a turban and native African dress and had sung and chanted in dialects, and they'd had a president of a woman's college who was also a renowned medievalist.

"Roughly the first half of Blake's life—he lived until the age of seventy and died singing—was turned outward toward the world he lived in. He was obsessed by the French Revolution and its implications—just as many of you are no doubt obsessed by the Vietnam War and *its* implications. However, I don't intend to draw any parallels between the French Revolution and Vietnam tonight.

"But now, at thirty-three, Blake had reached a point of despair. His concern for countries struggling against tyranny, his sympathy for the working people in his own England being sucked under by the machine age . . . these *outer* concerns paralleled a growing *inner* rage for liberation that was growing in him. You see, his personal life also had become a tyranny to him."

A loud belch exploded from the classmate who had inherited Francis's strangely seasoned baked apple. Several freshmen tittered; Father Birkenshaw turned them to stone with a look.

"What was going on in his personal life? you may well ask. I'm going to tell you. I *must* tell you, because I know that your order subscribes, as do the Jesuits, to the 'wise as serpents' policy of engaging with this world. You aren't afraid of hearing a few home truths about the multifarious ways the human psyche creates art, or you wouldn't have invited me here."

She spun on a spike heel and inclined her gleaming head toward Father Floris, who responded with a courtly nod.

"Therefore you will understand that art isn't made in a vacuum, any more than the vocations of each of you were. Those of you who really *have* vocations. What we feel *compelled to do*, whether it's making art or giving your life to God—I personally don't think there's any difference between the two—evolves out of the inner fabric of our lives, however disguised the patterns may be to us. The work, the vocation, is an attempt on the part of the would-be artist, or the would-be religious, to fulfill *in an inner way, in a symbolic way* what the outer world is failing to provide him with in the service of wholeness.

"So. Now are we ready to take a peek into Blake's domestic life?" Magda Danvers shot a challenging glance toward Father Birkenshaw, presiding in his wing chair.

"Blake was devoted to his wife Catherine, but she was a simple woman. She was his *mate*, but she was not his match. There's a big difference between the two. Mates are not always matches, and matches are not always mates. Many people in this world are mated to people who are not their match, just as, conversely, people who may be matches for each other should never have gotten together as mates. But regarding the first category, the mates who aren't matched, sometimes this can be a very happy arrangement, even though there are whole *realms* of mental existence to which the simpler mate cannot accompany the partner. The Mental Traveller must travel alone to these realms."

Francis thought of his parents, who would certainly fit in the first category. Neither his mother nor his father had gone beyond high school, yet his mother was an avid reader and liked to listen to the opera upstairs in the bedroom on Saturday afternoon while his father preferred his ballgames on TV with a few beers. Yet his mother had deferred to his father in all things, and they had been like sweet-hearts. Francis's older sister Jeannine once told him that if an ectopic pregnancy after Francis's birth hadn't resulted in their mother's having to have her tubes tied, they would have been a family of ten or more, because their parents couldn't keep their hands off each other until the day of their father's death. He'd had a coronary at fifty-one while operating his forklift at the cement factory. Francis had been a junior in high school. His mother still hadn't recovered from the loss. The only thing she had left to live for, she had confided to Francis before he left for the seminary, was the day she would attend his ordination into the priesthood.

"After Catherine found out she couldn't have children," Magda Danvers was saying, "she stopped having physical relations with Mr. Blake." Here she paused, as though deliberately to amplify the intake of seminarians' breaths.

"She didn't feel it was right," she continued smoothly, one hand reaching up to check on her elaborately coiled bright hair. "The sexual act by itself was wrong, Catherine Blake told her husband, if you couldn't bring children into the world."

Old Father Rolf, who taught moral philosophy and theory of sacraments, nodded drowsily in agreement from his armchair.

"Blake gave in, though he did ask his wife to let a girl live with them as Blake's concubine. But when Catherine put her foot down, he resigned himself, though he was still a man young enough to deserve the full experience of his sexuality."

Father Birkenshaw's high-boned face was a rock wall of cold courtesy.

"But Blake made the best of it. He taught Catherine to read and write and showed her how to color his engravings. He remained a devoted husband. The point is that Blake's longed-for experience of the feminine—the feminine that was *literally denied him*—forced him down into the regions of his unconscious, where he confronted the images he found, all of them male and female aspects of his warring selves, and made art out of them.

"But Blake was not a great prophetic artist just because he managed to solve his personal problems through art. Prophetic artists don't stop at the personal. What they do, you see, is *solve something for everybody* by making universally compelling images of their conflicts.

"Which brings us to Dante and Beatrice." Magda Danvers pronounced it Bee-a-*tree*-chay. "Now, you're going to love this story. Being about unrequited love, it's more suitable for seminarians. When Dante was out walking, he saw a little Florentine girl in a crimson dress and fell in love for life. They were both nine years old. He didn't lay eyes on her again until they were both eighteen. She spoke a courteous greeting to him in passing and that was it. She died at twenty-five. But this blazing visitation of love set fire to his poetic spirit. For him Beatrice was the Incarnation. Sometimes, suddenly loving someone can be like a flash of God. . . ."

Francis saw Father Floris cast a nervous look toward Father Birkenshaw, who remained rigid as rock, a cold, polite smile etched on his countenance. Old Father Rolf had dozed off in his armchair.

T he seminarian scheduled to drive Magda Danvers to catch her early-morning flight came down with intestinal troubles during the night and Francis was wakened at 5:00 A.M. by Father Floris, who brought him a Styrofoam cup of lukewarm coffee and a hard roll and informed him the job was his. "Not *quite* what we expected," the priest said gloomily of last night's speaker, "but we're still honor-bound to Northern Michigan to get her out of here. Poor Philip, his guts are in a complete uproar. I experienced distress myself during the night, and so, apparently, did others. The rector says that fool Brother Claude used liberal amounts of *cumin* in the baked apple instead of cinnamon. How about you, my boy? Feeling okay?"

Somewhat guiltily, Francis admitted he felt fine. Philip was the classmate to whom he'd given his baked apple.

"But I thought parts of her talk were extremely interesting," Francis said.

"Oh, you did, did you?" The habitually amiable Father Floris snapped up Francis's window shade rather violently and stood gazing out at the square of darkness, his hands clasped behind his broad black back. "Her plane goes at seven-ten. Be sure and get her there in plenty of time."

The speaker was waiting outside the guest lodge in her black cape, her bags and briefcase beside her on the sidewalk, when Francis pulled round in the station wagon. As the wan yellow of his headlights sprang upon her, she looked startled and defenseless and oddly disheveled. He hurried out to help her with her things, introducing himself. She did not appear to recognize him from yesterday, when she had passed beneath his stepladder.

"Weren't you cold, waiting outside?" he asked her when they were inside the station wagon.

"I welcomed the cold air," she replied in a low, exhausted voice. "Let's put it this way: my night was not exactly restful."

"You must have eaten the apple," he said, angling the wagon between the stone pillars and out onto the main road.

"Was that a theological remark, Francis?"

"Excuse me?" He turned to meet her eyes, glowing at him in the dim light of the wagon. She was smiling the same smile he had seen her trying to repress yesterday with Father Birkenshaw. The reason for her disheveled look, he realized, was that she hadn't put her hair up. Lying thick and loose around her shoulders, it made her look younger and more vulnerable. It came to him that she had thought he meant like Eve eating the apple of knowledge.

"No, I meant the baked apple at dinner. The brother who's substituting in the kitchen put in too much cumin."

"Cumin? Cumin doesn't belong in a baked apple. Even I know that and I'm certainly no cook."

"He mistook it for the cinnamon. He used a lot of it. Father Floris said many people had, well, difficulties last night."

She snorted. "I'll bet they did. Cumin is an emetic, isn't it? My mother would know. She's the world expert on bowel lore."

Francis couldn't think of any reply to this, so concentrated on the road ahead. Wraiths of mist from the lake floated up at his windshield out of the darkness.

"So that probably accounts for why I was up most of the night. I thought it was nerves. There was a good deal of resistance in my audience last night. I suppose I should have tempered my remarks more to the seminary setting, but they told me you were a progressive bunch, like the Jesuits, so I spoke the way I did at Northern Michigan. Though I never give the same lecture twice. Couldn't if I tried. Something new is always popping up."

"I liked your talk. You said some interesting things."

"Such as?"

He had expected her to thank him, not cross-examine him. "What you said about, well, vocation, for one thing."

"What did I say?"

Didn't she remember, or was she testing him?

"That it's a way to try to provide ourselves with some wholeness that the outside world isn't . . . I can't recall your exact words, but it made me stop to think."

"Was that good? Or not so good?" Again he felt her dark eyes burning at him from the dim interior of the wagon. Outside, the sky was beginning to lighten.

"Well, I suppose good. I mean there's such a lot I still don't know."

"Pardon my impertinence, Francis, but you're not in those skirts just to avoid the draft, are you?"

"To qualify for a Four-D? Absolutely not. I've wanted to be a priest ever since I was a boy."

She laughed. "But you're not much more than a boy now."

"I just turned twenty-one."

"You could have fooled me." A rough-and-tumble teasing had come into her tone that made him think of Jeannine, the older sister he got on with best. "What does the 'D' stand for?"

"In Four-D? Divinity."

"Ah. I should have figured that out. Have you ever had an experience of divinity, Francis?"

"Well, right now I'm still in the process of trying to give up my will so there'll be *room* for God to reveal himself."

"And how does one go about giving up one's will?"

"A lot of it's in the discipline. They have these ancient methods for breaking your will." Why had he said "they"? Hadn't he just taken his first vows to become one of them?

"Such as?"

He took a deep breath. Once she started on you, she wouldn't let you off the hook. "Well, for example, when I was doing my novitiate up at North Lake House this past year . . . ."

He was surprised at his ready flow of grievances. As if she'd only needed to press a button for them to come tumbling out.

". . . and then, well, there was this evening last spring. I was on dishwashing detail; you see, much of the novitiate is modeled after boot camp in the army. The novicemaster came up behind me at the sink and said I was slopping water on my cassock. He told me if I got any more water on it, I'd have to go and change before compline. I apologized and said I'd be more careful, but I guess he didn't like something in my tone, because he ordered me to kneel down and ask his forgiveness. There was a big puddle of dishwater on the floor, right where he was pointing for me to kneel, but I knew I didn't have a choice. I knelt down in the dishwater and asked his forgiveness. When I stood up again, he said, 'Your cassock is a disgrace, Francis. It has soapy water all over the knees. I'd better not see you in it at compline.' Then he looked at his watch and said compline was in seven minutes. There was no way I could finish the dishes and run up to my room, which was two floors up, on the far side of the building, and change my cassock and get back to chapel on time. And he knew it. He knew perfectly well it was a no-win situation."

"So what did you do?"

"One of the brothers smuggled me a soiled cassock from the laundry basket. It smelled terrible and was miles too big for me, but it was dry. When I got to the chapel, the novicemaster was waiting just outside in the corridor and he looked at the huge, smelly cassock and said, 'Surely you have the wings of an angel, Francis, if you managed to fly upstairs and change your cassock. That *is* your cassock, isn't it?' And I looked him in the eye and said, 'Yes, Father.' He knew I was lying, but he let me go in to compline."

"Why was that? I wonder?" She seemed really interested.

"Because he knew I'd have to confess it at Faults the next morning, and he could reprove me then. Meanwhile I'd have to pass the night knowing I lied, which was a punishment to my pride."

"If you ask me, I think boot camp would be a breeze, compared to your novitiate," she said after a minute.

Francis suddenly felt ashamed of his outpourings and the sympathy they had elicited. "But it's all part of the discipline," he hastened to defend the novicemaster. "Having to see myself as a cowardly liar was a lesson in humility. One of my worst faults, they taught me in the novitiate, was being proud of myself for being virtuous. My discipline with the cassock was, in a way, tailor-made for my particular fault."

"Wow, talk about casuistry! You're a budding *Jesuit*, Francis. Discipline is one thing, I'm a firm believer in discipline myself, it's got me where I am—though I'm not quire sure where *that* is, anymore. But egregious sadism . . ." She paused, grunted, then exhaled in resignation. She had obviously thought better of finishing what she had been about to say. "I've never had so much as a hello or how-do-you-do from the divine spark, myself," she went on, in a lighter vein. "But I'm fascinated by people who have. They're my specialty, as you may have gathered last night. I like to try and figure out what it was about their personalities and circumstances that made them . . . susceptible, you might say. I wonder if you will be one of the susceptible ones."

"I doubt it. I'm not in it for any big visions."

"What *are* you in it for?"

He was relieved to see the left-turn sign for the airport road. "Well, because . . . it suits me to serve other people's needs."

"Now *that's* an amazing statement for someone your age to make." She leaned over to peer at him more closely. "Hey, you're the pretty one with the pink cheeks on the ladder yesterday. When old Birkenshaw, or whatever his name is, was excoriating that Jezebel fanlight on your gloomy pile. You admire him, I suppose."

"Father Birkenshaw. He's our rector."

"I see." She laughed. "That was like my asking a buck private if he admires the general. Oh, but there was another thing I wanted to ask you: What about your own needs? Who's going to serve *them*, while you're off serving everybody else's?"

"I'm hoping God will," he said.

He was surprised at how this shut her up. He drove the remainder of the airport road in silence. Only when they were in sight of the airfield and small terminal did she groan, "I am exhausted, com-

pletely done in. Will I ever be glad to get home, or at least the purgatory that passes for home just now."

"Where is that?" he asked politely.

"University of Chicago. Drop by and see me if you're ever in
downtown Chicago. I have an adjunct lectureship in the English Department there. *Abject* lectureship is more like it. They get to pay
me slave wages and treat me like the typical leprous ABD. That
means 'All But Dissertation.' See? You have your Four-D, and I have
my ABD. We each labor behind our acronyms. Mine's a punishment
for going against my professors and publishing my book to notorious
acclaim before they approved it. So now they're making me write it
over to their old-fogey specifications."

"But how can they make you write it over when it's already
published?"

She reached across and took hold of his arm. "The same way
your novicemaster can make you kneel down in a puddle of dirty water and cover your clean young body with some fat old cleric's smelly
robe, and then go against yourself and lie about it. Because they've
got the power, and they want to make damn sure they keep their
power."

He carried her bag into the terminal, where half a dozen or so
sleepy people stood in line at the check-in counter. "Give me your
ticket, and I'll check you through."

"That's gallant of you, Francis, but it's really not necessary. I'm
used to doing these things for myself."

"Well, I'm here to do it for you this morning, so you might as
well sit down. You said you were exhausted."

She gave him a searching look as they confronted each other
face-to-face. She was as tall as he. "Okay, Friar Francis, I give in," she
said, smiling. She opened her large purse and rummaged around in its
ratty-looking interior. "Since it suits you to serve other people's
needs," she added humorously, handing him the envelope with her
tickets. A long red hair was stuck in its fold.

"You want me to check your bag through to Chicago?"

"No, I can carry it. Oh, what the hell, yes, check it. You see
how completely I have capitulated to your services." She sank down
in the nearest metal chair.

While he waited his turn in the line Francis stole several glances at her. How strange it was that this one person could be so many people in turn. First she had been a large, tall nun in a black cape, her eyes cast down as she marched beside the rector toward the seminary. Then that collusive look she had shot him when passing beneath the ladder. Reading his secret affection for the colorful fanlight in the gray building. Then she was the dangerous performer with her elaborate coils of burnished hair, ("not quite what we expected," Father Floris said), striding up and down the carpet in the spike heels, flinging provocative ideas like handfuls of colored jelly beans into their black ranks. Then the merciless intelligence beside him in the dark wagon this morning, cross-examining him, drawing all those things out of him, then making him feel they were *allies*, twin strugglers holding out against the superfluous cruelty of superiors. Though she herself was so superior. And now this woman, older by some years than his eldest sister, with her tired, vulnerable face and vivid hair flaming brazenly out into the grayish morning light of the terminal; this exhausted lady slumped in her black cape in the metal chair, toward whom he felt a sudden surge of protectiveness.

He hadn't even known her this time yesterday, except as a name in a letter he had typed for Father Floris. How strange to think that they were never going to see each other again.

CHAPTER III

Back in the Grand Union for the first time since the birth and death of her baby, Alice Henry found she had lost her ability to shop. One of those people who never troubled to make a list, she formerly had simply cruised up and down the aisles of the vast emporium, her practiced glance taking in what was fresh, what was needed, what would be relished at home, any outstanding Red Dot Specials it would be impractical to pass up—though she didn't have to be a bargain hunter, thanks to Hugo's generous salary as writer-in-residence at Aurelia College.

And about forty-five minutes later she'd be angling her full basket into a checkout line. However, during the latter part of her pregnancy, wanting to prolong the experience of presiding over so much amplitude, she would deliberately seek out the longest line of people with the fullest baskets. And there she'd loiter, in a state of blissful *particularness*, her full belly sticking out behind her full cart, not in the least tempted to leaf quickly through the new magazines to inform herself whose faces and clothes and books and movies had captured this month's glossy space. The passing events recorded by journalism had seemed substanceless to her. In her luxurious self-containment, there was nothing further out there that she needed. She had felt her taproot extending down, down into the ancient humus of humanity, touching other lives at their most elemental level. All these people swarming the aisles in their infinite variations enchanted her. An extremely reserved person by nature as well as upbringing, she would find herself smiling into the faces of the young sales help in their red uniforms whizzing by on roller skates to check a price or return a discarded item to its shelf, or she would seek to make friendly eye contact with a lonely-looking, well-dressed old man waiting in line to get a refund for his plastic sack full of bottles.

Every person in this store was some mother's child.

And in her final weeks, when her physical discomfort was offset by the amazing knowledge that the creature lurching and fidgeting and joggling around inside her would soon be a discrete entity out in the world, a complete small person setting off on his own important pilgrimage, she had played a game that gave her such a keen, aching pleasure she sometimes had to stop in the middle of it and catch her breath.

She would try to conjure up her own child, in fifteen, twenty, thirty years' time (she varied it), walking past her in this store right now. Which parts of herself, of Hugo, would she recognize in him? She already knew he was a boy. Would he be tall like herself, or short like Hugo, or medium tall, like Cal, the son from Hugo's first marriage? Would he move along in a cloud of self-preoccupation, or would he have eyes for everything around him?

Once she got as far as having his eyes meet hers.

But today, April 2, the Tuesday after Easter, she came out of a stuporous lapse of some minutes to find herself still standing at the entrance to Fresh Produce just inside the store, staring at bins piled dangerously close to toppling with red, green, orange, yellow, and pink fruit, unable to make the simplest decision of how many plastic bags she ought to tear from the dispensers stationed conveniently by, not to mention what she was going to put in them once she had them.

The spectacle of all this food, heaped, stacked, bulging, packaged, and arranged for mass consumption, was suddenly too much for her. It assailed her in an indiscriminate olfactory swirl: fresh bakery goods with deli salamis and roasted nuts; newly ground coffee with ripe cheeses and raw fish. It was nauseating. Yet she had never been put off by it when she was pregnant.

Tearing off a single plastic bag, she entered the Fresh Produce area. She would have to invent a new method of shopping for these new days. A pale, cool, unsmelling iceberg lettuce, already encased in its tight plastic wrap, seemed the least offensive beginning.

Then on, without stopping at lemons and limes. Hugo had left for Prague yesterday, so nobody would be drinking vodka tonics or martinis. On through cut flowers also. Nobody coming to dinner; nothing to celebrate. Though there were some nice irises, their long pale green stalks turgid in water.

Wheeling into the canned-goods aisle, she spotted Magda Danvers's husband up ahead. His profile was to her as he held a tunafish can at arm's length in front of him and squinted at its label over the tops of his glasses. Too vain to get bifocals, like Hugo? Though Francis Lake had always struck her as being the opposite of vain; in fact, you often got the feeling he was completely unaware of himself. He stood swaybacked and long-legged in his corduroys and old pea jacket, his feet in heavy brown lace-up shoes splayed outward, his mouth agape. A straight slab of graying sandy hair had fallen down over his forehead, and he looked baffled and exhausted.

Abruptly she reversed her cart, deciding to skip canned goods. She was sure he hadn't seen her; he'd been too absorbed in reading the tuna-fish label. She was ashamed she couldn't break out of her isolation and go up to him and ask about Magda. It would have been the decent thing to do. Magda had written them that wonderful letter, full of such vigorous compassion despite her own bad news. And Francis himself had shown up at the graveside service for the baby.

He'd been the only person there from the college, obviously having misunderstood Ray Johnson's information that it was to be strictly private. She and Hugo had been so embarrassed for him, but he carried it off well in his kind, unassuming way. Just stood there beside them quite naturally, his pale face bowed, while the Unitarian minister read the short burial service. The undertaker had found the minister for them, as neither of them went to church. Hugo had commented later that Francis in his black overcoat and solemn demeanor had looked like an extra clergyman himself. "But of course he was studying to be a priest once," said Hugo. "Ray Johnson told me. Then Magda went to his seminary to give a lecture and lured him away. We really must get over to see Magda. Ray says she's sinking fast."

But that was back in February and they still hadn't gone.

As Alice guiltily fled into the next aisle she nearly collided with Rhoda King, bouncing along in her lavender sweats and white aerobic shoes behind a basket already piled high with energy foods.

"I can't believe it! I was just *this very minute* thinking about you, Alice Henry!"

"How are you, Rhoda?"

"Oh, I'm good, I'm good. But how are *you* doing? That's the big question." Rhoda's brash eyes, heavily made up, bored unashamedly into Alice's grief and privacy.

"I'm doing pretty well, thank you." It serves me right, thought Alice, for running away from gentle Francis Lake.

"Did you get any of my messages about the program I'm putting together? I left them for Hugo at the college since you don't have an answering machine."

"I got them, but—" Alice could not finish.

"I know it's still very painful for you, but now with the news that the state board is trying to suspend Romero's license—it was in the *Record*, after the Bennetts lost their baby, too. You must have seen it in the *Record*."

"No, we don't always get the *Record*, unless one of us remembers to pick it up in town."

She and Hugo hardly ever picked up a *Catskill-Record*, before or after the baby's death, but people here got touchy if you didn't take an interest in their local media. Rhoda had her own radio show, "Issues at Noontime," weekdays on WCST, and took herself quite seriously. Her license plate had ISSUES on it, and she was notorious for taking double-parking advantages on the strength of her press decal. Hugo had been on her show last fall, reluctantly, ("Can Creative Writing Really Be Taught?"), under strong pressure from Ray Johnson, soon after they came to Aurelia College. "No use to get Rhoda's hackles up," Ray had said. "She's a pest and about as subtle as a bludgeon, but she's got a following in the community and she makes a formidable ally, or enemy, when she gets going on one of her trendy issues."

"The Bennetts have said they'd come on the program. I'm calling it *Home Births: Pros and Cons*. I also have a call in to several reputable midwives in the area, as well as some of Romero's satisfied clients who still swear by him. I want to get all sides. I think this could be of real service to women, Alice, while it's still fresh in the public's mind."

She said "the public" as if her listeners numbered in the millions. Directly above her glossy black curls, bobbing with the determination of her spiel, was a clever clothesline display of baby bibs: EASY EATIN' PLASTIC AND TERRY BIBS. The pink bibs said, *I Love My Mommy*, the blue ones said, *I Love My Daddy*.

". . . just say if you'd rather not," Rhoda was going on, "but I think your presence on the show would be invaluable, especially with Hugo being so well-known and all."

This is unbearable, thought Alice, powerless to speak or move. Then Francis Lake entered the aisle from the far end, sauntering along behind his cart. He squinted at a little piece of paper over the tops of his glasses.

"Oh, there's someone I really must speak to," said Alice, waving to get Francis's attention.

"Who?" Rhoda spun to look at the man who was heading toward them with the eagerness of a lonely person who has just been hailed by someone agreeable.

"Just an acquaintance who's been kind," said Alice, not volunteering the name. For she saw Rhoda did not recognize Francis Lake out on his own without his illustrious spouse. And Rhoda's rudeness was legendary when it came to having to talk to anyone who couldn't be of use to her.

"Well, I've got to run, or I'll be late for my meeting with the station manager. It's great to see you looking so well after your terrible ordeal. Will you promise to at least *think* about doing the program? I'll give you a call next week."

Off she bolted without waiting for an answer, escaping from a nobody.

"Hello, Francis, how nice to run into you."

"Well, likewise, Alice. It's been too long since we've seen you out and about."

"I know. But here I am, reentering the world. We appreciated Magda's wonderful letter so much. How is she doing?"

"Oh, she's holding her own, thank you. Her appetite's not good, but I do my best to find things she likes. Only, her tastes will change suddenly. For a while she was fond of this sliced turkey breast I buy here, but now she's gone off it. All she'll take at the moment is white tuna, with just a little mayonnaise mashed in, on a piece of bread with the crusts cut off. How is Hugo?"

"Hugo's in Czechoslovakia." The soothing comfort of this restrained, civilized exchange after the assault of Rhoda King!

"A book tour?" asked Francis Lake with interest, raking back the stubborn slab of gray-blond hair from his gaunt face. A pleasant-looking, boyish man, his own recent and ongoing ordeal had aged him noticeably.

"No, he's going as an American specialist for USIA, to talk about his work, and meet with other writers in the country. Several countries, actually."

"Czechoslovakia should be an exciting place to visit just now." He was examining the iceberg lettuce riding alone in her cart. "I hope you plan to make yourself proper meals while Hugo's away," he said.

Alice gazed down upon the anemic-green lettuce, sheathed in its tight wrapping *and* the plastic bag. It looked so antiseptic and prissy that she wanted to giggle. "This is my first time back in the Grand Union, and I seem to have forgotten how to shop," she confided to Francis. "Before, I never even used a list."

"Oh, I always have to have a list," he replied solemnly, contemplating his own basket, where the items were arranged in orderly fashion. There were two neat stacks of the tuna-fish brand she had seen him inspecting.

"I'd like to come and see Magda one afternoon. If she's feeling up to having visitors." Though she meant it in principle, she also hoped he would thank her and say he regretted Magda was not up to it. As soon as the offer had passed her lips, Alice knew that what she wanted most was to be out of the Grand Union and back under her satin comforter at home, where she had spent the major part of her days since January 10.

But Francis Lake pounced on her suggestion with pitiful eagerness. "Why not come this afternoon? Magda was asking Ray Johnson about you only the other day. She's always admired you."

"Well, I admire *her*," replied Alice, touched and flattered. "I've felt terrible about not coming, but it's just that . . . I haven't been going anywhere."

"We understood," said Francis kindly. "And perhaps you'd stay and have supper with me after you visit with Magda. If you don't have other plans. I was thinking of making a pot roast, only it seemed a waste, making it just for myself."

"Well, I—" She realized she wanted to go, after all. "If you're sure . . ."

"Could you come around five? She tires pretty early now."

"Five is fine."

"Great, we'll expect you then. It will give Magda something to look forward to, and it'll be a treat for me, as well."

They said good-bye, Francis looking more animated and cheered, and went off with their carts in opposite directions. After a moment's consideration, Alice doubled back to Fresh Produce, tumbled the iceberg back into its bin, and used the freed plastic bag to contain the dripping stems of a bunch of the lovely irises which she plucked from the bucket. She went quickly through Express Checkout with her one item.

"So Hugo is in Paris," murmured Magda from her pillows.

"Prague," said Alice. Though she'd expected to see a somewhat diminished Magda, she was unprepared for the startling change. In the few months since Alice had last seen her at Ray Johnson's party in early December, the high-colored, fleshy face had been replaced by a sharp-boned, yellowish, predatory one; the smaller, shrunken body under the bedclothes seemed to belong to another woman. Most shocking of all, somehow, was the untidy crop of white hair that sizzled for quite a few inches out of her skull before remembering itself and turning back into the glossy plumage everyone associated with Magda Danvers.

"Oh, *Prague*. Well, that's an entirely different matter." Her speech, though retaining its characteristic ironic cadence, was slower and slurred. "Francis, you told me Paris."

"I believe I said Prague," Francis corrected her gently, setting down a vase with Alice's irises on an attractive long table with a carved backboard.

"Okay, you said Prague." The brown eyes in the sharp yellow face danced at Alice collusively: let him have his way.

"I'll leave you two to visit while I see to a few things downstairs," said Francis Lake. "Is there anything I can bring you, Magda? How about some more of that liquid nourishment?"

"You know what I crave is a little mental or spiritual nourishment."

"Well, you call me on the intercom if you think of anything," replied Francis, though Alice saw a wounded look pass fleetingly across his face before he left the room.

Magda murmured something.

Alice sat forward in the chair Francis had placed for her beside the bed. "Excuse me, Magda, I didn't hear you."

"I said, I'm sorry for all you've been through."

"Thank you. Hugo and I appreciated your letter so much. You said just the right things. I'm sorry for what *you're* going through."

"Thank you," said Magda with a playful formality. "Actually it's not so bad as you might imagine. The pain's a nuisance, it distracts me from *thinking*, but I still have lots of good moments when I *can* think. I've always attempted to live my experience imaginatively rather than simply suffering what happens to me, so, in that sense, this is a rare opportunity. I'm thankful to be allowed in on my own closure. There's even a certain excitement in having some time to mull over what it's all been about."

"That's true," agreed Alice, thinking of her late parents and brother who had been allowed no mulling time at all. Magda had lost her robustness in looks and speech, but she engaged and stimulated the same as before. I wish I had come sooner, thought Alice, rather than hiding under my satin comforter. I wish I had known her better before she got so sick.

"But, now, *you* . . ." and Magda pointed her yellowish hand across the counterpane toward Alice—"you're still in the midst of things. What are you, thirty?"

"Thirty-four."

"You don't look it. I looked much older at your age. But at your age, I had published my first and only book and married Francis. My two accomplishments. I had planned to write *many* books and have *no* husband, unless I could find somebody as brilliant as Northrop Frye. But Frannie has his points. I torment him mercilessly, he can be so obtuse, but I would have been a lonely slob without him."

It was Hugo's theory that Francis would have remained celibate, or gone the other way, if he hadn't met Magda at a crucial juncture in his life. "They like women much older. Mother figures. Or else much younger, and preferably flat-chested like a boy. Though Magda's far from flat-chested." Hugo, who was unrepentantly homophobic, was also fascinated, in his belligerent, wary way, by the mystery of homosexuality.

"Did Hugo ever find a room he could write in?" asked Magda. "He was complaining of bad vibes in that house you're renting from Sonia Wynkoop when we talked at the Johnsons' party."

"He's set up his word processor in the downstairs bedroom," Alice told her, "but he still hasn't found his way into a new book."

She didn't say: in the downstairs bedroom where he sleeps alone now, because I can't bear to lie beside him anymore. She didn't say: in the downstairs bedroom where our son was born dead.

"It hasn't been a very good time for Hugo," she made herself add loyally.

"Well, *that's* understandable," said Magda. "I wonder what Sonia Wynkoop's got against furniture. Her bare house isn't at all what you'd expect of an *art* historian. And Renaissance art, at that. Strange cold bird, old Sonia. I wonder if I would have ended up like her if Frannie hadn't moved in with me. Maybe she equates furniture with commitment, something like that. Though I suppose some people might say we have too much furniture."

"Oh, I don't think so. I find your house very comfortable."

"Do you now?" murmured Magda, closing her eyes briefly, then refocusing on Alice with seeming effort. She was visibly fading. I ought to let her rest, thought Alice, but she sat on.

It was true, she did find the house comfortable. Aesthetically soothing, even. Though it was now a sickroom, the bedside table crowded with medicines, the invalid's bent straw in the glass, a little pad of paper with attached pencil on which doses were recorded, the room in which Magda lay was filled with solid, welcoming objects and warm touches of caring and color. The very opposite of the art professor's house she and Hugo were renting. On a sturdy chest of drawers with leaf carvings around the top and down the sides was a tall cut-glass vase containing sprigs of blossoming branches angled against one another in a satisfying way. The bed was one of those old-fashioned pineapple four-posters, high off the floor. Magda's tucked-in blanket was a rich plum color; the embroidered monogram on the white sheet neatly turned back over it was MLF. Had Magda taken his surname, then? But, in that case, the letter to the right of the "L" should be a "D." Alice's mother, a stickler for maintaining the proper forms, would have pronounced this monogram "most peculiar."

Alice sighed. Then realized Magda's dark eyes were intently watching her. She had the uncanny feeling the woman in the bed had been reading her life behind her silence.

"Well, so . . ." murmured Magda. A roguish grin sketched itself across the wan, hollowed face. "What next, eh?" The sharp brown eyes danced witchily on Alice for a moment before the heavy lids curtained down.

"Poor Magda, she was looking forward so much to seeing you, Alice, but she fades so quickly now. I would have come back to get you sooner if I'd known she'd fallen asleep. I thought you two were up there talking away. Magda loves to match wits with someone who can keep up with her, she loves nothing more than a good conversation. She's heard all my stories, and of course I've never been her match."

"We did talk, for a while," said Alice, wondering what Francis Lake's stories were.

"Oh, I'm glad." She was prepared for him to elicit specifics from her, as Hugo always did. ("You talked? What did you talk about?" Hugo would then go on to provide specifics for himself before she so much as opened her mouth: "She talked about her cancer, didn't she? She'd turn her disease into interesting analogies, that would be Magda's style.")

But Francis Lake merely went on serving her plate. Looking at Magda's husband across the small expanse of snowy tablecloth that separated them, she was liking him very much. He was sweet-natured, and peaceful to be around. Undemanding. The very opposite of Hugo. There was a gentle impersonality about Francis that both gave her room and took her out of herself.

The pot roast was delicious. She hadn't had such an appetite since before the baby was born. Everything on the table looked so pretty: the silverware gleaming in the soft spring evening light coming through the window beside the table, the colors of the vegetables shining through their coat of gravy on the platter. He'd even gone to the trouble of making an artful centerpiece of sweet-smelling narcissi and grape hyacinth in a small ceramic pitcher. Alice tried to recall the last time she had sat down to an intimate meal so carefully cooked and served by someone else, and couldn't. After she went to live with Aunt Charlotte, who was, as she would be the first to tell you, a Working Woman, their fare had been mainly frozen dinners. And even before Alice lost her family in the accident, her mother, who worked full-time at the public library, had been a last-minute cook: throw on the cuts of meat defrosted from that morning, and add a frozen vegetable, or a salad with the dressing out of a bottle. If Alice or Andy wanted the comfort of mashed potatoes, one of them had to peel the potatoes, and the other had to mash them. Only so much could be expected of a woman with a family and a full-time job.

"When Magda first came home from the hospital, she had so

much company," Francis said. "Too many people came, but she enjoyed them. Most of the time she did. We had a system. If she told me to throw another log on the fire, it meant she was enjoying the person. But if she said, 'Let the fire die, Francis,' I had to get them out. That was when she was still receiving visitors in her study. Things are much quieter now. I think it's because it's painful for people to compare her to the way she was. Of course, seeing her every day as I do, I'm not shocked so much by the contrast. But when I told her you were coming, she was especially pleased. She enjoyed talking to you so much at Ray's party in December. She mentioned it to me several times afterward."

"I'm sorry I didn't come sooner."

"Oh well, you were understandably . . . We were so sorry you had to go through what you did. But I hope you'll come again, when you have the time."

"Oh, I have the time." She was ashamed of the self-pity that had crept into her voice, but either he hadn't noticed it or kindly overlooked it. As he buttered his bread his face had the same quietly absorbed expression she'd seen on it at the graveside service to which he had mistakenly come, when he stood beside them in his black overcoat.

"People have their own lives to live," he continued, after chewing thoughtfully for a minute. "The students, they're busy with their courses . . . Magda was joking the other day that for some people she's already dead. President Harris had this stationery printed up for sending out letters to raise money for the endowed chair in her name. It has a tintype of her profile. . . ."

"Yes, we got one," said Alice. "Hugo already sent in our check. I thought it was very distinguished, the tintype, though it made her look a little staid."

Francis laughed. "That was her comment. She said they'd made her look noble but lifeless. Only she used better words than that. Oh dear, I don't know what I'm going to do without her. It's been such a privilege to share in her radiance. We've done such a lot together, these twenty-five years. Well, almost twenty-five. Our anniversary's not until the end of November."

The private happiness that broke over his wistful face as he spoke stung her with a yearning, bitter jealousy. But jealousy of whom? Yearning for what? Surely not jealousy of the dying woman upstairs. For Francis himself, then? Diffident, gentle Francis Lake, shortly to be bereft? Did she wish then to have for herself the kind of marriage Francis was describing: knowing yourself securely part of someone's "radiance," and feeling lucky in the partnership? Well, partly, though she'd always expected to provide her fair share of the radiance. But the bitterness came, she knew, from acknowledging that even if she and Hugo were to stay married for years longer, she could not imagine herself ever describing their union to someone in the heartfelt manner Francis had just described his. Francis Lake obviously was still in love with the woman he had been married to for twenty-five years.

For dessert there was peach ice cream and chocolate-chip cookies. "These were baked by Leora Harris. She's been so faithful, she brings us something every week. Magda won't touch sweets now, but I haven't the heart to tell Leora. Will you take coffee after your meal?"

"Only if you're going to make it for yourself."

"Oh, it's already prepared. All I have to do is press the button. Then I'll just run up and check on Magda."

He wouldn't allow her to help him remove the dishes ("I've developed my own system, our kitchen is so small. . . ."), so Alice sat tranquilly on in the fading light at the small round table in the corner of the living room. He and Magda always took their meals there when they were by themselves, Francis had explained. He'd considered clearing the big table in the dining room in Alice's honor—lately he'd been organizing all the hospital bills and Blue Cross correspondence on it—then he'd decided she wouldn't mind being family.

No, she hadn't minded at all, she of all people, being in someone's family. She heard him whistling under his breath as he set out cups and saucers in the kitchen, then his quick footsteps going up the stairs and down the hall to Magda. Alice glanced around the room, whose corners were filling up with darkness. Tall, interesting old furniture shapes took on added substance and seemed to advance infinitesimally forward to brood upon the new person in their midst. How sad that Magda and Francis would not face each other across this intimate corner table anymore, letting the lengthening spring twilight gather them in.

The feel of this room, with its green plants and intimate nooks and cared-for things, made her reluctant to return to the house she and Hugo were renting, where Sonia Wynkoop's impersonal, sparse furnishings gave off a desolate air of having been unlovingly acquired and then set down and forgotten. She and Hugo had always avoided the living room, preferring to go to bed early, in the time when they still slept together, or talking over dinner in the dining room—when they still enjoyed talking to each other. But Magda had put her finger on it: wasn't it bizarre that there should be no feeling of art, or of anybody's history, in the house of an art-history professor? Though, to be fair, nail holes in the white walls testified to absent pictures, possibly art too valued by their landlady to be left in the keeping of tenants. But there was no feeling of comfort or protection, either. The most protective place Alice had found for herself was in bed under her own satin quilt, now that she had moved upstairs again, and even that had its drawback, because she never forgot it was Sonia Wynkoop's bed in which she lay, the bed in which Alice had not been allowed to give birth to her baby.

Neither she nor Hugo had met Sonia, the woman Magda described as a strange, cold bird. Everything had been done through the college—though much later she had sent them that appalling letter from Rome, saying please not to have the baby in her bedroom. Was she one of those women like Aunt Charlotte, who was so busy Working that she couldn't be bothered with domestic comforts? As she grew older Alice wished she had insisted on saving more things from her parents' house when she and Aunt Charlotte had been dismantling it. But things hadn't seemed important then, when she was seventeen and had just lost all those people.

From the kitchen, the percolator gurgled and sighed, sending a nutty coffee aroma through the house. She heard Francis coming downstairs again. Immediately after coffee she must leave.

"Magda's mind goes in such strange patterns now," Francis Lake said, carrying in a tray with everything set out meticulously, down to small coffee spoons. "I wish I understood it better. The medications may be partly responsible. It's as if—do you take sugar? no?—it's as if there's no chronology sometimes. She's all over her life. The trouble is, I'm not always sure where. Sometimes we're traveling together. Yesterday she was angry with me when she woke up, and then, as she kept talking, I realized she thought I was her mother. Some of the things she says seem to be symbolic. I've never been much for symbolic thinking. In that way I've been a disappointment to her, I'm afraid. Just now, when I went up to see her, she opened her eyes and said—well, I *thought* she said, 'Go and find the miseries, my love.' "

"Go and find the miseries?" Alice repeated Magda's command, strangely moved by it.

"Yes. 'Go and find the miseries, my love.' I took it to be one of her symbolic remarks. I repeated it back to her . . . I always do that when I don't understand, hoping I can work it out in the meantime, but then she got very impatient and waved me away saying she had important research to do and would I *please* go find some miseries. But just now while I was in the kitchen, I realized she was saying *misericords*. It wasn't symbolic, after all. She thought we were on one of our trips abroad and she was sending me off to look at misericords so she could get on with her work."

"Misericords?"

"You know what they are, don't you?"

"They're something in cathedrals, aren't they?"

"In cathedrals or churches. They're projections on the undersides of the tip-up seats in the choir stalls. When you raise the seat flat against the wall, there's still this corbel, topped by a narrow ledge, that juts out and gives support to the person standing in the stall. So he can sort of half sit while he appears to be standing. They were called 'pity-seats' in the medieval Church, because in those days you stood to pray for ten or eleven hours at a stretch. I first learned about them back in seminary. Our rector gave us slide lectures on church architecture and iconography. The carvings on misericords are among the best surviving wood carvings we have from the Middle Ages. The reason I like them is they show sides of life you don't often get to see in the art or history of the period."

"What sides are those?"

"Oh, intimate, everyday scenes. Close-ups of plants and animals and people. There's one of two snails circling each other, it's among my favorites, though I never got a decent slide of it. *The Adoring Snails*, it's called: they can't keep their eyes off each other. But my favorite overall category—I have them arranged according to subject matter—are the ones of domestic life. They're like candid-camera shots from the Middle Ages. Domestic life with nobody looking, not at all idealized." Francis Lake's dim, weary face began to glow raptly as he elaborated on his hobby, and Alice believed she caught a glimpse of the youth Magda had plucked from the seminary all those years ago.

"You see, misericords weren't considered important because they weren't *seen* by many people, so the carvers felt free to carve what they liked rather than religious themes, your more exalted subject matter. I got interested in them when Magda and I started going abroad in the summers for her research. To pass the time while she was working, I'd go looking for them in the local cathedrals and churches. Magda used to get after me about making a book out of them, but I don't have the scholarly application. Finding ones I like and getting good slides of them has given me enough satisfaction. It takes patience to photograph misericords. They're so awkwardly positioned—I mean, people sat on top of them, after all—and they're almost always badly lit. And also, there's the problem of the tight fit. Medieval people were smaller than we are, and so there's very little space between the rows of stalls. At first, I took my photographs squatting or kneeling, but when I learned better, I lay on my back on the floor and tried to find the angle the carver worked from."

Alice could picture Magda's lanky husband cramped and crunched into odd positions between the stalls, his blond hair graying and his face growing older over accruing summers, completely enrapt by his quaint project.

"I could show you some now, if you like," he was offering.

"Well, I—I'd love to see them, but I ought to be going. I've been here since five."

"Please don't go on my account. Magda is sleeping, and I have to wake her at nine for her pill. I wouldn't mind looking at some of them again myself. It's dark enough now so we could project them on the wall above the mantelpiece."

"Then I'd really enjoy seeing them."

"Well, of course I won't show you *all* of them. They number in the hundreds. I have them arranged by category. Is there a particular category you'd like to see? Animals and plants? Domestic life? Or maybe you'd care more for mythical creatures or scenes from medieval romances."

"Domestic life," said Alice without hesitation.

As he left her alone once more in the company of the brooding furniture, she remembered that Hugo had said he'd try to reach her from Prague sometime early in the evening. Had he meant his time or hers? She wasn't even sure of the exact difference in hours between here and Prague. If he'd meant his time, she would have been at the Grand Union and missed his call anyway. If hers, he might be calling now. But she could hardly change her mind and disappoint Francis, who had gone off so happily to fetch his slides and projector. Yet an acrid resentment of Hugo stirred in her over the guilt he was causing her from halfway around the world.

"These are from a summer we spent in France. Some of the churches in the suburbs around Paris have wonderful representations of courtship and marriage and family life . . . I used to take buses . . . let's see, was it seventy-three or seventy-five when we were there? I have it marked on the slides, but it's too dark to see. *Sometime* around in there, when Magda was deep into her research of artists' visions of heaven and hell."

The machine's cooling unit made a steady whirring noise under Francis's nostalgic ruminations. Alice sat in one corner of an upright old sofa; he stood behind her, operating the projector from a high-legged table. In '73, I was sixteen and had a family, she thought, looking at the image of a dancing peasant couple frolicking on the wall. In '75, I was eighteen, and didn't. To me there was a universe of difference between 1973 and 1975. To him, the same time period is a swirl of travel with Magda, a "sometime around in there" when Magda was deep in her research of artists' visions of heaven and hell.

"Look at their clothes," said Francis, "the details of her head-dress and his hood . . . their funny upturned boots. And she's talking nonstop while they dance. Lecturing him a little, wouldn't you say? Don't you feel you know them? You can tell from their expressions that they've been married awhile. Imagine getting all that into a carving."

She and Hugo had been married less than two years. What was that: married? Lately it had become like one of those words that, said over and over enough times, sounds nonsensical. Or utterly foreign. You can tell from their expressions that they've been married awhile. What does that mean? Married awhile.

"Oh, now here are a pair of lovers. Aren't they sweet? Their faces nuzzling against each other. They look hardly more than children. Whereas, on this *next* slide . . . I like to put these two slides next to each other to show the contrast . . . *this* pair is more mature. They're obviously of higher rank . . . see the clothes, the elegant boots, something in the postures . . . they sit beside each other and lay their hands on each other, but with a kind of ceremonial dignity. They're not married yet, because there's no ring, yet it's obvious that she's . . . well, expecting."

She heard how his voice missed a beat before he forced himself to finish. He was probably remembering the last time he had seen her at the Johnsons' party, when she had been hugely pregnant.

"I like them, they're lovely," she helped him out. "I like their formal restraint, the way they're touching each other but not grabbing."

"Yes, their restraint. There *is* something appealing about their restraint, isn't there? And now, *here* . . ." With audible relief, he moved quickly on to the next slide. "This is one of my prizes. A young woman dressing. It's so natural, isn't it, the awkward way she's pulling on her step-ins. The way a person would, with no one looking. But there's nothing at all lewd about the carver's intentions, you can see that. She's put her dress on first. It was probably cold. And this next one's the companion to it, a man undressing. We can't tell his age, because he's pulling his shirt over his head. These are fifteenth century. They were carved on misericords next to each other in the same church, but now she's in a church in St. Cernin and he's at St. Illide. I came across them separately, and then found out their history later. Don't you find that interesting? They were meant to be together, but they got separated."

Alice thought of Magda upstairs. The sharp brown eyes dancing witchily at her out of the yellow, hollowed face. "Well, so . . . what next, eh?" What next, indeed. What was Francis ever going to do without her?

"Oh, now look at this one. A mother teaching her child to ride a tricycle. Look at its wooden wheels. Would you think they'd have had tricycles in the fifteenth century?"

Alice took in the mother and child and tricycle. So poor May Bennett had lost her baby, too. They'd been in the exercise class together, May Bennett coming in two months after Alice. May Bennett and her husband had agreed to be on Rhoda's program. And the state board was trying to suspend Romero's license. She wondered if Hugo had known about this, seen headlines in the *Catskill-Record*, when he was shopping for their food.

"Not only is the home birth more intimate and relaxed . . ." Dr. Romero's liquid, assured baritone, proselytizing in its fervor, still rolled over her at night. An educated man. Not a bloodletter or quack. A trained and certified physician whom many mothers swore by. A personable, caring man, father of four children himself, who happened to mistrust, as she did, much that went on in the terribly efficient modern-day hospital. ". . . but there is also the immediate bonding with your baby. And, most important of all, no separation after delivery."

"This one with the tricycle is in Belgium." Francis Lake's diffident voice, reinforced by happy memories, took on greater ebullience. "Magda was actually with me when we found it. She'd finished her research at the St. Genevieve Library in Paris, and we decided to take off and do a little sight-seeing on our own. . . ."

"Good," Alice had told Dr. Romero. "I've had enough separations in my life."

CHAPTER IV

Hugo Henry, no longer aloft in the floaty-euphoric stage of his jetlag, but in its gritty-eyed, dismal decline, continued to sit on in the restaurant of the Hotel Pariz, though it was late at night in Prague and he was not enjoying himself. He was drinking brandy with two men: a youngish one whose existence was immaterial to him, and the other his exact age, a writer from his own country whom he vigorously loathed.

The cultural attaché, Dick Pringle, was a clone of those who had hosted Hugo around at other posts in the past. The State Department seemed to have farms for cultivating these neutrally pleasant fellows with their interchangeable names, who could be counted on to speak informatively about your books—even if they hadn't read them—get you to appointments on time, and drive you to the airport when it was all over without burdening your memory with any lasting impressions of them.

But which of Hugo's evil stars had chosen to drop Joel Mark down into Prague with him—down into the same *hotel* with him—for the same three days? Joel Mark, that crafty literary politico and hack novelist, who fooled too many people far too much of the time.

Joel had just flown in from Belgrade. "Not because you *have* to go there anymore to spend your royalties, as Hugo here is undoubtedly aware of, but I've gotten quite attached to the place."

Since the Yugoslavs had pegged their dinar to the German mark last year, Joel Mark had been explaining (even though "Hugo here" must surely be informed of these developments), foreign writers could receive all their Yugoslavian royalties at home, if they wanted.

"The thing is," said Joel, boyishly ducking his cropped salt-and-pepper curly head and smiling mysteriously into his brandy snifter, "I've gotten into this nostalgic ritual of revisiting the countries that have always published my books. My Belgrade publisher and I always have our ritual dinner at the Dva Jelena . . ."

"Oh, the Dva Jelena," echoed Dick Pringle, with a respectful nod toward Joel Mark, "that's a wonderful restaurant."

". . . and then, I've made some good friends in Zagreb. You know how it is, Hugo, they start off being loyal fans and readers and then you realize they're pretty fascinating people in their own right. And Zagreb is such a fun place. I love the arts center there. The building alone, an old Jesuit monastery that's been beautifully restored, is worth a trip to Zagreb in itself."

"I'm fond of Zagreb myself," said the cultural attaché.

So Hugo's visit was tainted by the self-promoting machinations of Joel Mark before it had hardly begun. He had the choice of remaining silent on Yugoslavia, thus leaving the other two men free to deduce (correctly) that his novels had not been published there, or he could demean himself by remarking with affected sangfroid that actually no, he'd never been translated into Serbo-Croatian, though his books *were* translated into eleven *other* languages. Either way, Joel would have achieved his goal: to show himself the more internationally published writer to Dick Pringle.

Hugo chose to keep a dignified silence, staring into the amber depths of the brandy he could have done without after the long transatlantic journey and this afternoon's miles of euphoric walking (when he might have been wiser to take a nap), followed by a bland dinner at the home of bland Pringle and his equally bland wife.

He deplored this low level of survival-tactics thinking to which Joel Mark had succeeded in bringing him, when as recently as this afternoon, wandering elated through the curling, medieval streets of Prague, he had returned to what he considered his true mental rhythms for the first time in many months.

Too many months. He hadn't been operating on all his cylinders since they'd gone to Aurelia College and taken up residence in that sterile, grudging house of the art-history professor, and then everything but his teaching had been put on hold as they geared up together for the birth of the baby. And then the harrowing event itself. Jesus Christ, he'd think twice about visiting such a nightmare on characters in a novel. Particularly if one of them had already been given Alice's history of loss: it would seem like overdone punishment on the novelist's part.

But this afternoon, his mind had begun to *mesh* in its old exciting way, the way that had accounted for many of his happiest moments in life, as he had sat in that coffeehouse by the river and looked out and up through the tall, dirty windows at those Baroque villas and crumbly palaces and ruined gardens climbing and crowding one another until they culminated in the castle on the bluff.

Remote, archetypal Hradcany Castle, its ancient cathedral spires communing with the sky. A world in itself. Suggestive enough to contain whatever the human imagination chose to put inside it or make it stand for. The inspiration for Kafka's Castle.

He, Hugo Henry the writer, had begun sitting in the brownish interior of the Czech coffeehouse gazing directly up at the inspiration for another writer's masterpiece. And, yes sir, there were some invigorating connections to be made. Kafka wrote about K.'s obsession to get recognized by the Castle. Hugo wrote about the South Carolina poor boy standing on the golf course on a winter night, stabbed and bewitched by the superior pageantry in progress on the other side of the arched windows: the annual Christmas dance at the country club.

But it was the same story. There were only a few stories worth telling, which was why they needed to be told over and over again, until everyone recognized them as his own experience.

Sitting in the coffeehouse with the tall, smoky windows, he had rejoiced in his own moment of recognition as he gazed up at the monumental complex of Hradcany, which had overlooked a thousand years of changing fortunes in this city, and saw through its opaque windows, even though they were bronzed over with daylight from this angle.

He saw straight through the castle's multiple windows and into the innermost contours of the old Malvern Valley Country Club in Calhoun, South Carolina. Unlike Hradcany, the country club was no longer in physical existence, leveled back in the early seventies to make way for a shopping mall, but its chandeliered ballroom and card rooms and dining rooms now belonged to him forever because he had possessed them through his art.

So that he who was once denied its privileges could bring the old Malvern Valley Country Club to Prague and make it live again inside Kafka's Castle. Make all of it richer in resonances, including himself.

But that was this afternoon. Now he was smarting because he'd never been translated into Serbo-Croatian like Joel Mark. Whom they'd run into in the lobby as Pringle was returning him from the boring dinner. Pringle hadn't suggested any nightcap until Joel, dressed in killer-soft black leather and de rigueur stone-washed jeans, swaggered over with his tall man's buccaneering gait and *embraced* Hugo. Then Hugo and Pringle had to be introduced to Joel's friend the Czech poet, a smaller, stocky man, about Hugo's size and height, who wore a drab suit with enormous old-fashioned lapels and shoes of a very strange red color. And bland Pringle was saying with more enthusiasm than Hugo had thought him capable of: "I'm a great fan of yours, Mr. Mark, but I think my all-time favorite of your works is probably *Late-Blooming Flowers*. My wife and I must have given away at least fifteen or twenty copies to our friends."

"Please, just Joel is fine. I'll tell you something, Dick"— (appropriating the sleeve of Pringle's tweed jacket with his prehensile swarthy hand—Joel Mark couldn't keep his hands off people)—"I have a special place in my heart for *Late-Blooming Flowers* myself."

That was when Pringle himself had bloomed, for the first time that evening, and suggested they all have a nightcap in the restaurant. The Czech poet declined, having a train to catch to the suburbs. He spoke very precise English and regretted that a previous engagement would prevent him from attending Hugo's talk tomorrow at the embassy, which he was sure would be very informative.

"Oh, what talk? Can I come?" asked Joel Mark, looking from the cultural attaché to Hugo with boyish eagerness.

"I'll catch up with you two in the restaurant," said Hugo. If Joel Mark wanted to come to his talk, he couldn't stop him, but he certainly wasn't going to invite him. "I need to call my wife, she hasn't been well recently."

All the way up in the tiny, slow elevator, he simmered. *Special place in my heart.* If Joel Mark *had* a heart, it would be as counterfeit as everything else about him: ripped off from others, a trendy medley of better people's hearts reprocessed to promote his own glory. *Late-Blooming Flowers*, indeed. It wasn't enough to steal the *title* of Chekhov's early story of love across class barriers, a love realized too late. He had to steal Chekhov's story, too. Fashionably updating it, of course. And then the double-handed, self-serving Little "Afterword," in which he acknowledges his Russian master but also subtly *identifies* himself with him: that was Joel Mark down to the ground. The reviewers, of course, swallowed the whole thing like popcorn.

But, during this afternoon's euphoric mental flight, hadn't Hugo himself concluded that there were only a few stories worth telling?

Yes, but what was deplorable about Joel, what stuck in Hugo's craw the most, was his outside-in method. His eye always on the prize, Joel began by looking outside to see what others had done, to see what was coming, what would soon be "in." Joel studied the winners and the charts first, and *then* he wrote. The real writer started with the ache in his own soul and worked *out* from there, the way the Count of Monte Cristo dug himself out of prison.

Hugo had some difficulty getting past the hotel switchboard to an international operator. His connection finally having spanned the ocean, the phone rang and rang and Alice did not answer. It was, subtract six hours, five o'clock there. Where was she, who could hardly be prodded out of the house since January? They'd agreed she'd have to shop for herself while he was gone, maybe even take the big step of going back to the Grand Union. But five o'clock wasn't a likely time for her to be shopping. Unless she'd decided that, at that late hour, she would be less likely to run into anyone they knew.

"I'm sorry to hear Alice has been ill," said Joel Mark, abandoning the subject of Yugoslavian royalties now that he'd vanquished his competition. "Nothing serious, I hope?"

"We lost a baby back in January. It was very hard on her."

"I know what that's like," said Pringle, solemnly swirling his brandy. "Judy's had two miscarriages since we've been at this post."

"This wasn't a miscarriage. The baby was full term. He died during the birth."

"Hell, Hugo, I'm really sorry." Joel Mark leaned over and gripped his arm. He looked so genuinely stricken on Hugo's behalf that it was hard for Hugo to maintain the pressure of his hatred. "I won't presume to even *imagine* what it was like," said Joel Mark, shutting his eyes briefly and shaking his finely shaped grizzled head as though he were imagining it against his will. "How terrible for you both. But, I mean—I haven't had much experience in these matters, flyblown old bachelor that I am—isn't there some *warning* beforehand that things aren't going the way they ought to be? And then they do a C-section at the last minute?"

"It was a home birth. There wasn't time."

"Ah." Joel Mark fell back, defeated, in his chair. As if he had almost succeeded in going back in time and saving the little fellow, only to be routed by this last-minute revelation of their foolishness.

Thus Hugo found himself in the position of having to defend Alice's decision—a decision he himself had not at first shared in—to Joel as well as to the cultural attaché, who had also stiffened at the mention of home delivery. "He came highly recommended, this doctor. He was a very caring, reassuring man. Very convincing about how it was actually safer for the baby, less stressful . . . the way nature intended it. The women he'd delivered swore by him. We were new to the area, but Alice did her research, she's very thorough when she goes looking into something . . . especially something so important. She once had a bad experience with a hospital when her brother was dying. . . ."

He took another swig of the brandy he didn't want. Why was he here, at almost midnight, spilling his guts and his wife's secrets to people he didn't even like?

"Oh, Alice certainly *is* thorough!" Joel Mark exclaimed enthusiastically. Joel was always exclaiming enthusiastically, spraying you with fine droplets of spit in the process. To Pringle, who was looking mystified by his outburst, he explained: "Hugo's wife, Alice Questrom . . . I mean, *formerly* she was Alice Questrom, before Hugo here rode off with her into ■ the sunset, was one of the shining lights in publishing. My good friend Barney Kramer is still heartbroken that she won't be at Garrick to edit his next novel. You see, Dick"— another chummy squeeze of the cultural attaché's arm—"Alice was one of those rare *real* editors in New York. I'm not just talking about line-by-line stuff, which in itself is almost extinct now—editors are too busy 'acquiring' and promoting *themselves* as stars these days to be bothered with how a sentence is put together, or if a writer has used the same adjective five times on one page—but I'm talking about true literary comprehension. Barney says she's one of the few people he ever met who could lay hold of the hidden design in the text even when the writer himself has lost track of it. Doesn't she have a doctorate in comp. lit., Hugo?"

"No, no, just a B.A., from Princeton," said Hugo, finding it easy to resume full-throttle loathing for the enemy, though he was relieved Joel had diverted them away from the painful subject. But even in the act of letting you off the hook, wasn't Joel Mark subtly out to promote himself as a sensitive human being, as quick to pick up on a colleague's uneasiness as he was to appreciate the importance of the "hidden design" in the text? The "text": what typical consummate bullshit. And what did he mean about Hugo "riding off into the sunset" with Alice's "shining light"? More of his careless mixed metaphors—that was another thing that pissed Hugo off, Joel was such a damned sloppy writer: and got away with it!—or a subtle way to signal to Pringle that Hugo's career was waning, so for consolation he grabbed himself some bright young thing and dragged her off on his old limping steed.

"Ah, well, but Princeton," said Joel, his dark sloe eyes appeasing and challenging Hugo at the same time. Smiling, he hunched forward in his low chair, his long legs and arms forming a kind of angular bracketing around the brandy snifter clasped casually in the prehensile fingers. He gave the impression of positively glorying in his own arrangement of bones. "What will you talk about in your lecture tomorrow, Hugo? Or are you keeping it a secret?"

"Why should I keep it a secret?" said Hugo brusquely. Then felt obliged to add, in order to temper his hostility in front of Pringle: "Come and hear it for yourself, if you're interested."

"Of *course* I'm interested," effused Joel, with a coy duck of his head. "I was just waiting for you to invite me."

Back in his room, Hugo tried Alice again. No answer. He put on his pajamas and brushed his teeth, fretting over an unsightly crack down the middle of a top front tooth that had gotten more noticeable in the last year, and glowering at the loosening skin around his jawline: in about five more years he was going to be a dead ringer for his father's old pit bull Snafu. Joel Mark's sleek, swarthy face was as tight-skinned as a demon's; Hugo wouldn't put it past that perfidious bisexual narcissist to have had a face-lift. "Flyblown old bachelor," my ass.

He tried Alice again at 2:00 A.M.—still no answer; where could she be? He slipped a sweater over his pajamas, as the hotel room was chilly, and sat upright in a chair upholstered in a scratchy material, to prevent himself from dozing off while reviewing the typescript of the talk he would deliver at the embassy tomorrow. Or, shit, today.

The idea, when he was developing it back at Aurelia, had seemed both original and tailor-made for his audience. That there were important cultural similarities between Czechs and Southern Americans: they were both *wronged* people, as well as people of high courtesy and subtle codes of behavior, who had managed to transform their defeat at the hands of their brothers and neighbors into a proud sense of their own specialness. Which in turn prompted an impassioned quest for their own identity. Which made the practice of literature a vital necessity in their lives.

But scrutinizing his "text" from the viewpoint of Joel Mark, who would be preening himself, probably in the front row, tomorrow, Hugo was suddenly aware of the ingratiating and self-serving aspects of his lecture. ("Hey, c'mon fellas, read my books, they're not just stories indigenous to my neck of the woods, we're both so wronged and special!")

And wasn't his premise wobbly? What if someone—not Joel: straightforward attacks were not Joel's politics—but what if some pale, clever, high-boned Czech, who spoke precise English like that poet with the red shoes who wasn't coming to his talk ... what if someone like that got up during the question-and-answer period and politely challenged: "Please, Mr. Henry ..."—(or "Mr. Hugo." It wouldn't be the first time someone in an audience had gotten his name backward)—"could you explain please why it is only Americans from the *south* of your country for whom the practice of literature is a vital necessity? Why do you not include New Yorkers or Californians? Couldn't we say they are equally passionate in their quest for identity?"

Where could she be at seven, eight o'clock in the evening, her time? Out to dinner? With whom? Alice hadn't made any friends of her own since they had come to Aurelia last September. She had been so involved with the pregnancy, though she had liked a few of the others in her exercise class ... she had liked that Bennett woman whose labor pains the doctor had miscalculated, two months after Alice. That's when the whole nightmarish sequel had kicked in: that bitch Rhoda King, sniffing an "issue," had begun leaving messages at the college that she wanted them to be on her fucking program about home births! The Bennetts' baby had survived three days in the neonatal ward at the medical center. Ray Johnson had pointed out the story to Hugo a couple of weeks ago in the local rag, but Hugo hadn't been about to tell Alice. She was already remorseful enough. The state board was after Romero's ass. The popular doctor, resented by his more conventional colleagues, was having too many fuck-ups in too short a time (although, providentially, the Henrys hadn't been mentioned by name in the story). It was a third woman who'd blown the whistle on Romero: she'd been infuriated when the doctor, due to a last-minute positioning of the baby, had made her deliver in a squatting position. That was too much for the conventional doctors. Yet, ironically, she was the only one of the three who'd given birth to a healthy baby.

Could Alice be having dinner with the Bennett woman? Not likely. Support group wasn't Alice's style: let's pool our sufferings and have a good cry. Alice was one of the most reserved people Hugo had ever known. At first he had admired this, taken pride in it, what with so many people spilling their guts all over the place, but lately she'd given him cause to wonder if there was a point where reserve became pathological.

What the hell difference does it make to *us* if Romero loses his license to practice? Hugo thought bitterly, closing his eyes and leaning back against the scratchy chair in the Hotel Pariz. The birth scene on the late afternoon of January 10, which he had watched throughout, rose all too vividly in his memory: the preparations, the mounting elation, his own sensation that he was about to witness a miracle (he hadn't been present at Cal's birth; people didn't do things that way twenty-nine years ago), and then . . . just when they thought they were about to get their little guy . . . the awful, grisly climax. Instead of the lovely fellow with his life ahead of him, they had a bluish little corpse with a widow's peak just like Alice's.

Hugo's old, put-upon, redneck gorge rose in him, the way it always did when he felt rendered powerless by events. That meddler Ray Johnson had suggested in his oily undertone that Hugo and Alice might consider suing; it was rumored, Ray had told him, that the Bennetts were considering it. And their case would be considerably stronger if Romero lost his license.

But what victory is it for *us* whether the affable Romero loses his license, or whether or not we sue, thought Hugo, sick at heart. The money, if we won, if Romero hasn't used up all his insurance by then, wouldn't bring back the little fellow with the widow's peak like Alice's . . . in his casket the size of a cradle.

After failing to reach Alice at two-thirty—eight-thirty her time—he got into bed and tried to read. He was no longer sleepy. For the trip, he had brought along a new paperback reissue of Ford Madox Ford's *The Good Soldier*, intending to make his mind up about that provoking novel once and for all. He'd first tried it back in the late sixties, at the urging of Glendinning, an older writer who had befriended Hugo when he'd just moved to New York. Glendinning had been intent on copying it. On first reading, Hugo despised *The Good Soldier*, though he waffled with Glendinning because he liked him and was in awe of his greater reputation. But why all the literary genuflecting to the tale of these two dillydallying couples . . . four Edwardian fossils fucking their way around Europe on the eve of World War I? Well, three of them were fucking. No, actually just two. You kept having to revise your numbers because of the circuitous way the narrator, the cuckolded husband, told the story. This was called "the unreliable narrator method," his friend Glendinning explained to him excitedly. Glendinning was planning to have an unreliable narrator in his novel, too. Poor Glendinning, you didn't hear much from him anymore.

Some years later, when Hugo's marriage to Rosemary had soured and he had embarked one lonely summer in New York on a (subsequently abandoned) mean little tale of adultery, he had tried Ford's novel again, and been temporarily seduced by its craft and enigma. The whole way through the book, another novel seemed to shimmer at him from just behind the words he was actually reading: a novel that would use *The Good Soldier* as its beacon to lead Hugo through the murk of his own bafflements and duplicities that seemed to be part and parcel of erotic love.

This is the saddest story I have ever heard, Hugo began to read, under the cold, starchy sheets of the Hotel Pariz. What would he find this time? Would the brilliant book he might write next still shimmer enticingly from the adumbral realms beyond Ford's prose? Or was Hugo Henry simply following in the path of poor Glendinning, trying to piggyback his way out of creative senility on another writer's achievement?

"Where were you?" he demanded, when he finally reached Alice at half-past three.

"I went to visit Magda Danvers. And then I stayed and had supper with Francis. Have you been trying to reach me?"

Their connection was eerily distinct. He could pick up every decibel of withdrawal in her voice. She didn't like it when he was "gruff." But then she didn't like him most of the time anyway now.

Only every half hour for the last four hours, was on the way out of his mouth, but he made a supreme effort and switched into the indulgent, fatherly persona she had responded to best since January. "I was beginning to get a little worried. I couldn't figure out where you could be."

"I met Francis in the Grand Union. He asked me to come and see Magda and eat with him afterward. She doesn't come down for meals anymore."

Poor old Francis Lake was going to be a lost soul without Magda Danvers. He'd *already* looked like a lost soul back in January at the cemetery, when he'd gotten Ray's information wrong and showed up for the baby's burial in his black overcoat. "So you made it to the Grand Union. Good girl. How's Magda? Pretty bad, I expect."

"She looks so much smaller, and she tires quickly. . . ."

"Can she still talk? I mean, the way she used to. No, probably not."

"We talked some," she answered, after a pause. "She still says interesting things."

"Did you get a good dinner? You must have. He's always done the cooking over there. What did you talk about? He's not exactly a great conversationalist, is he?"

A longer pause. "*You* seem to be having a great conversation all by yourself, Hugo," she finally replied.

He'd been answering his own questions again. That was another thing she didn't like. He hadn't even been aware he did it until she'd recently informed him. "Okay, let's start over," he said with a brusque laugh. "Did you get a good dinner? What did you two talk about?"

"We had pot roast. It was very good. We talked mostly about Magda and her illness. And then he showed me some slides of his misericords."

"His what?"

She began describing, via satellite across the ocean that separated them, Francis Lake's slides of some carvings on the undersides of choir seats in churches. They sounded tedious and worthy, which was Hugo's overall impression of Magda Danvers's house husband. He had been going to tell her about Kafka's Castle, his epiphany in the coffeehouse with the smoke-grimed windows, but by the time she got around to asking him how his trip was going so far, his need to punish her had become stronger than his desire to share the experience with her.

"Hey, you'll never guess who of all my favorite people in the world the gods dropped down into Prague to spoil my trip."

Another pause. As if she was waiting to trap him into answering his own question. Well, if she was, she'd have a long wait.

"Am I supposed to guess?" she finally asked.

"Yes, guess. My favorite American writer."

"Joel Mark?"

"How well you know me." He began to laugh, but it was a forced, mirthless expelling of breath. Was this all that was left between them? So be it. He spent the rest of the expensive phone call—not covered by USIA—giving her a vitriolic account (leaving out the part where they'd discussed the birth) of his nightcap with bland Pringle and that literary pretender and prosehack, the globe-trotting, self-promoting Joel Mark.

CHAPTER V

"Francis?"

"What, love?"

"This isn't so bad. It's rather interesting sometimes."

"I felt useless last night. There was nothing I could do to make you comfortable."

"No, I didn't mean the Gargoyle. He's just an unmitigated pain who keeps me from doing my best work, but he seems to be giving me the morning off. I meant the other. The Big Other. What Henry James called the distinguished thing. 'Here it is at last, the distinguished thing': he actually heard a voice say that when he was falling to the floor from his first stroke. He told his friend Lady Prothero

6 5

about it later. It's commonly assumed those were his last words, but they weren't. According to Edel, they were most likely 'Stay with me.' Addressed to his sister-in-law, who was sitting at his bedside. I wonder what my last words will be."

"Oh, Magda. I wish you wouldn't."

"Wouldn't what? Talk about it? Talking and cogitating are the only pleasures I have left. Any day now, I'll wake up and not be able to make sense. Dr. Zeller said yesterday the cancer was 'disseminating.' I hate their soulless jargon."

"Dr. Zeller was here day before yesterday."

"See, I'm already losing it. Well, anyway, I still hate the way they hide behind their jargon. I prefer Dr. Rainiwari's visits, even if he addresses all his remarks to you because you're the man. I respect his dignified comportment. He knows he's the midwife of Death here. Zeller bores me with the plots of movies. Are you sure you don't want to send me back to the hospital?"

"Oh, Magda, how can you even tease about such a thing?"

"I'm not teasing. You look a wreck. All this running up and down the stairs when you should be out in the spring sunshine, doing your beloved yard work. I could do this just as well in the hospital. We've got beaucoup insurance."

"You'd hate the hospital, love. You wouldn't have all your familiar things around you. And think of all the jargon. . . ."

"But you could get some rest while I'm busy dying. Those were Goethe's mother's last words, by the way. 'Say that Frau Goethe is unable to come, she is busy dying.' "

"There will be plenty of time for me to rest later."

"Have it your way, then, but remember I offered. Goethe's last words were 'More light.' They say Beethoven's were 'I shall hear in heaven.' I wonder if those reports are apocryphal. Will someone report *I* said something far more interesting than I actually did? You, maybe, if you're with me at the time."

"I'm glad you're feeling better today, Magda, well enough to want to dig into me, but—"

"I'm not digging into you, Francis, I'm just projecting myself into your future via my mind, while I still have one. I can be with you longer that way. My imagining what happens at the end, and *beyond* my end, is my way of haunting you in advance."

"I won't mind if you haunt me. I hope you will."

"Well, I'll try my best," replied Magda, suddenly tired. "Now, do go out in the sunshine and rake some leaves . . . oops, wrong season. Mow the grass? No? Still too early for grass? Then take a walk, sweet fellow, while I take a little rest."

She closed her eyes, dismissing him, but continued to watch him through her ears as he moved softly about, finding little chores to postpone his freedom from her. He was afraid, he had admitted it to her, that she would give him the slip during one of his absences. She heard the soft scrape of branches against glass and the musical flutter of water as he repositioned some apple blossom he had forced in a vase, the thunk of her books being aligned against the back of the huntboard . . . books whose flights of words she could still follow with her eyes, like watching swallows skim across a field, but no longer trap for herself in blocks of meaning. The little purple morphine pills played hell with your attention span, but offered compensations. You could float down the stream of your life and simultaneously position yourself at various eras along the bank and watch yourself go by.

Left to herself, she would have been a lonely slob. (To whom had she said that, just recently? Was it someone in real life, who was visiting her in this room, or someone in a dream? That was another thing. You couldn't always be sure who was where.)

Francis had been the gift she would never have thought to imagine for herself. She knew what people said behind their backs: that Francis Lake was the perfect wife. But his steadiness and accommodation had provided a safe takeoff and landing field for her flights. Such as they were. The audacious ones were already over on the day he'd come to find her in Chicago, but she'd had no way of knowing that at the time.

He'd appeared in her office doorway at the University of Chicago at the onset of a November snowstorm. Just materialized in front of her eyes, in a very wet pea jacket and shabby jeans, his soaking hair streaming into his unhappy face. She didn't connect him at all with the serene boy in the black skirts who'd driven her to the airport in Marquette less than a month ago. But she wasn't connecting much of anything to anything on that dark, snowy afternoon. She was running a fever but didn't know it: she thought the research on her new book, *Evil in the Literary Imagination*—the book which was fated to die on her that very afternoon—was making her crazy.

Who was this who had suddenly formed in the center of her swirling fugue? Had she given this distressed boy a bad grade in her overcrowded survey course, evoking his march through a howling storm to challenge her?

Even when he spoke, she still didn't recognize him. The voice was both indignant and needy. "I've just been to my mother's funeral. She didn't even let me know she was sick."

A graduate student, perhaps, who hadn't been showing up for her Blake seminar and was now hoping to gull her with this outrageous excuse?

"I've just come from Alpena." He stamped his boots, then looked down in embarrassment at the puddles of snow forming on the floor. "I walked here from the bus terminal."

"The bus terminal? That's a very long walk."

"I was running low on funds. Father Birkenshaw gave me the money for my round-trip ticket from Marquette, and then my sister gave me some extra when I told her I wanted to stop by Chicago on my way back. You're right, it is a long walk. I hadn't realized it would be such a walk."

As soon as he named that arrogant divine, it had clicked into place. This soaked waif with the splotched, aggrieved face was Francis, the pretty boy who'd driven her to the airport, the boy who'd serenely said he expected God to satisfy his needs while he was satisfying those of others.

"Now, wait a minute. . . ." She wasn't thinking too clearly because of her fever (which she didn't know she had yet), but having spent years in Ann Arbor and ridden not a few buses herself, she did carry in her head fairly accurate shapes of the states of Michigan and Illinois. "How can you be 'on your way back' to Marquette when Chicago is at least eleven hours in the opposite direction?"

"Well, you said drop by if I was ever in Chicago." He explained it as if he were making perfect sense.

"You're telling me you took an eleven-hour detour in order to 'drop in' on me?" Already she was wondering what she was going to do with him. What was he *expecting* her to do with him? "How did you know where to find me?"

"It wasn't easy. But I kept asking. Nobody had heard of you in the first few buildings I tried." He sounded incredulous.

"That's not surprising. I'm small potatoes here, as I think I told you when we were having that interesting conversation on the way to the airport."

"Yes, you said we were each laboring behind our acronyms." He repeated her words back to her like a memorized lesson, while continuing to stand there dripping water on the floor.

"And are you still laboring hopefully behind your Four-D?" She strove for a jocular note because he looked so serious and miserable, and at the same time *expectant*, as though the effort of getting to this spot had exhausted all his funds, monetary and otherwise, and now it was up to her to take over.

"I guess I am. I mean I don't know. I'm not sure about hope anymore. Except that I was hopeful I'd be able to find you." He continued to stand before her, this orphan out of the storm, like some suddenly incarnated challenge to her charity. What was she supposed to do? What had he come eleven hours out of his way expecting her to do for him? She was feeling sicker by the minute, far too sick to expend energy on charities or challenges.

She was silently framing a humane dismissal. After all, his mother had just died, he was probably in shock. But *she* wasn't his mother; she hardly knew him. She might offer him money for a taxi back to the terminal and for the next bus out. Or an overnight on her sofa, to wait out the storm. Though Father Birkenshaw might not approve of his boy taking shelter with the whore of Babylon.

Then she happened to glance down at the jotting on her pad. *Evil = thwarted thread of plot*, she read. The letters wobbled and mocked. She had absolutely no connection to the clever person who had scribbled this obscure equation a few minutes ago. The room spun and her stomach responded with a sickening lurch.

"Excuse me, I must make a trip down the hall." She rose unsteadily from her desk. "I think I may be making myself sick with this research on evil."

"You look like you already are sick," he said. He advanced toward her, his long fingers, raw and red from going ungloved in the cold, already outspread to support her, his face already undergoing the transformation from grieving boy into her concerned caretaker.

Thus they had begun their life together as they were ending it: with him helping her get to the bathroom.

"Francis?"

"Yes, Magda?"

"Are you *still* here?"

"I'm just going down. To take my walk, like you said. Do you want something first?"

"I want to ask—"

"Would you like some water? How about a little of your liquid nourishment?"

"No, damn it, I want to *ask* you something!"

"Yes, Magda, I'm right here. But I can hardly hear you."

"Why did you come? You never told me why you came."

"Came where, darling?"

"To my *office*, idiot."

"You aren't in your office, Magda, you're in your room at home."

"No, dumbo, the snowstorm. What did you want from me? What did you expect I could do for you, before I collapsed over that evil equation in Chicago?"

"Oh, Chicago."

"Yes *Chicago*. You walked to my office through a snowstorm. To get what? What were you hoping for?"

"Well, Magda, I was hoping to find you. And I did."

"That's not what I mean, you knucklehead, and you know it!"

"Magda, it hurts me when you distress yourself like this—"

"I'm not distressing myself, I'm just trying to have something besides liquid nourishment."

"Are you sure you wouldn't like something before I take my walk?"

"Oh, obtuse oaf. Go take your walk and leave me to my snowstorm."

"Well, maybe that would be best, if you're going to get so agitated. If you're sure you wouldn't like me to bring you something before I—"

"Get out of here!"

W hy had he come to her? What had he told his sister, who gave him extra money so he could "stop by" Chicago—eleven hours in the opposite direction from his seminary? What had been his thoughts during that walk in the snow from the bus station? What had he wanted from *her* before her collapse turned him into her caretaker? In all their years of marriage, she had never succeeded in getting a satisfactory answer from him. He'd never been one for analyzing his motives. It had been the big disappointment in their life together, for her who believed, like Dante, that every act and choice, however small, is consequential in the pattern of a life. His refusal to assess or keep track of himself had thwarted her again and again: she, whose favorite sport was speculative thought about herself and those who interested her. (What he would call "digging into people.") For, though she had become thoroughly familiar with his physical habits, his surprising strengths as well as the endearing lacks, the manner in which he processed his feelings through his mind remained as much of a puzzle to her as ever.

"I remembered you said to drop by if I was ever in Chicago, and I wanted very much to talk to you again." That's as much as she'd been able to "dig" out of him in almost twenty-five years.

"About what? Your mother? Was it because she had died without even letting you know she was ill? You were very upset when you appeared in my doorway."

"Yes, I know I was."

"So? How would we have talked if I had been my well self you remembered from Marquette? What had you planned to say to me? How did you expect me to respond? Can't you go back and reconstruct the conversation we might have had if I hadn't been sick?"

"Magda, I just can't *do* that, my mind doesn't work that way. I can't reconstruct a conversation we never had. You *were* sick."

They were out on the Midway, the two improbable lovers-to-be, swept against each other like Paolo and Francesca in the flake-swirling winds. Taxis filled with fares hurtled by, yet he had manfully stopped one. She lay back against the seat, shivering and sweating inside her coat. Then they were somehow in front of her ugly building. "I hope you've got some money," he said apologetically.

"Take it out of my purse. If it isn't enough, tell the driver we'll be happy to walk back." This had seemed to her very witty at the time.

Her apartment was a funky shambles, but it didn't shame her to bring him in. She was still living out her rebellion against her bourgeois, house-proud parents. But she was mortified when she subsequently emerged from one of her fever fugues and realized she was in her dingy, smelly flannel gown.

To this day she had no memory of his undressing her. Pity. She'd had a good body then: large-framed, like her mother, but firm and unblemished. She had been one of those rare females who actually looked better without clothes. What a beguiling reverie it would be now, as she lay here dying, if she could only summon up the face of young Francis as it had looked when he had first seen her body, and then chastely put her to bed. Later he'd told her she'd been the first woman he'd ever seen completely naked. How could that be, she'd wanted to know, with two sisters in the house? "I guess we were a very modest family," was all he could offer.

He'd phoned the seminary and told them he was in Chicago, though she had no memory of that, either. How had he explained to old Birkenshaw that he just happened to have taken the Greyhound from Alpena south to Chicago rather than north across the bridge and back to Marquette? The rector had instructed him to spend the night over at Loyola with some Jesuits and take a bus out next morning. She *could* recall his anxious face behind over her, asking permission to take bus fare out of her purse to go to the Jesuits. "Now promise you'll take these aspirins and drink this. . . ." He'd filled an empty 7-Up bottle with water and placed it on a stack of books beside her bed, because there wasn't any table. "Is there anything else I can get you?" He seemed reluctant to leave her. "I'd like to stay and see you through this, but . . . but. . . I am under the vow of obedience," he had stammered apologetically as he was leaving.

Then the demons had her all to themselves. They played handball with her all through the night, smacking her against a cement wall until she broke into smaller and smaller pieces. That was the form it took: *that* part she could remember. Many of her sharpest memories *were* of inner events. The demons were out to get her; she was fair game. She had been poaching on their territory for months, gathering their secrets to use for her own professional aggrandizement, and they were going to show her a thing or two.

She awakened in the morning in sweat-soaked submission, her tight, hard, young brilliance (or it consoled her now to recall it as such) in shards. Her valiant jailbreak out of her parents' bourgeois prison, her name change, her academic strivings, her precocious success with the visionary book: all of it seemed to her, as she lay there in her defeated condition, simply a way to postpone meeting this lonely, smelly, middle-aged woman in bed.

Evil = thwarted thread of plot. Her own definition, which was to have been the linchpin of the dead book. Scribbled shortly before she was flattened by flu. A.k.a. her demons.

Had Francis been her fate, or had she, by succumbing to his stubborn desire to care for her, thwarted her own lonely plot? In agreeing to marry him at such a confused point in his young life, had she thwarted *his* plot? Or would Francis, being Francis, have been happy serving anywhere? "It suits me to fill other people's needs," he'd said on the drive to the airport.

After that early, easy, triumph with *The Book of Hell*, she had believed herself capable of anything. How many graduate students have their dissertations accepted for publication before they have defended them? An unforgivable act, according to her adviser. He felt she should have waited for his final blessing before submitting it to a publisher. She was outwardly repentant, but privately scorned him for wanting to hold her back, this teacher who had published no book himself. Ah well, he had gotten his revenge later; he and his cronies had made her wait for her credentials.

But first, the heady splash of notoriety, flying around the country like a minor rock star when the book came out. Performing her gig from university stages, stalking around carpeted student lounges without notes, spilling the love lives of the great visionaries. The arrogant young pedagogue dressed all in black, with her revealed scriptures of imagination and revolution—for which the zeitgeist was a pushover anyway.

M. Danvers, "Dark Lady of Visions," her bold broad face staring down the *Time* magazine photographer; Queen for a Day of the Lecture Circuit in her Halloween-witch black. The black chosen because it was arcane and slimming; the "M." chosen back in her obscurity, to befuddle those publishers who might reject unread a scholarly manuscript if they knew it was by a woman. In later editions, when the Women's Movement had made female authorship advantageous, she had "come out" with the Magda. Ah, formidable "M. Danvers," in all the swaggering glory of her thirty-three years. An age, she frequently reminded her audiences, significant for its human peaks.

Of course, the volatile sixties had been her most ardent ally. Casting off shackles with the exhibitionistic abandon of a stripteaser new to the business, wantonly embracing anything that promised "visions," the latter half of that decade would naturally be attracted to *The Book of Hell: An Introduction to the Visionary Mode*. The title alone was enough to guarantee it.

"You might want to reconsider that title," her adviser had warned her "jokingly," after she brought him the news that the manuscript had been accepted, and by a New York publisher. "I know it's catchy, and I know you're paraphrasing Blake, who believed all true poets, including Jesus himself, were familiars in the 'hell' of the subconscious, which is the source of all energy, but aren't you afraid some of the less enlightened are going to mistake it for a handbook on the use of hallucinogens?"

"Let them. After they buy it and take it home and read it, they'll realize their mistake, and be the wiser for it," replied the ungrateful protégé. Impertinent hussy. No wonder he had wanted to punish her.

The book *was* brilliant, she still believed it was as she lay here being munched on by the Gargoyle, squaring her accounts with herself in the blue book for her Final Exam. Her one and only opus had never gone out of print, it was a staple in college courses. But its brilliance was of the flashy, intermittent kind, the brittle twinkle of stars in a cold night sky. It couldn't provide a steady, nourishing light: that was what her unfinished sequel had been going toward: that unbroken, filling light that Dante the Pilgrim had finally reached.

But back in Chicago, when Francis, suddenly shorn of his certainties, had appeared in her doorway, she'd been embarking on something else altogether; on her doomed, foolhardy sight-seeing tour of Evil without a guide. It was to be her "I'll show them" project, a shockingly original little book produced in the miserable confines of her ABD servitude, to prove to her tormentors back in Ann Arbor that the *Book of Hell* had been no flash in the pan. She was going to rub their noses in the fact that she, Magda Danvers, ABD, was energetic and unrepentant enough to rewrite her published thesis to failed-old-fogey specifications *and* toss off an audacious new work at the same time.

God, the arrogance of herself at thirty-three. Had she really believed herself strong enough, *protected* enough, to toss off a survey course of types of evil in literature? Northrop Frye, with all his genius *and* his clergyman's training, wouldn't have gone near that one. (He had died this January, the great critic, also of Gargoyle complications.)

Blake himself had the sense to anchor himself to a tree root before letting the angel show him what was down in the abyss.

The flu. That's what you'd call what she'd come down with in Chicago if, like the medical profession, like Francis, you were symbolically illiterate. But she knew better. Her demons had broken her arrogant will into shards. Because, unlike the true visionaries, she had gone looking for dangerous secrets out of curiosity and ambition. And without protection. An Ariadne who forgot her thread. A Blake without his tree root.

Around midmorning, she was stumbling back from the bathroom when the doorbell rang. It was the seminarian, fresh-faced and clear-eyed again, his old beautiful self, en route back to the bus station after his night with the Jesuits. He'd borrowed money from them to return to her what he'd taken out of her purse to go to *them*. The snowstorm was over. The next bus to Marquette left that afternoon. "So I thought I'd come by and see how you were," said Francis. "Is there anything else I can do for you?"

The rest was history, as they say. But the details were still a mystery to her, as Francis's inner life, thanks to his inviolable obtuseness, was still a mystery. Though she had grilled him a thousand times about those strange November days culminating so surprisingly in their marriage, it looked as though she would shuffle off this mortal coil without ever learning what exactly had transpired inside him to make him want to stay.

"Look, there I was, a sick woman you hardly knew, leaning against the doorframe, hardly able to stand. I couldn't have been a great come-on in that smelly old nightgown. Did you see in me a chance to redeem your mother's sudden death, or—"

"Magda, you are nothing like my mother. I remembered I'd only left that one 7-Up bottle of water, and there was nothing to eat in your refrigerator."

"So I was an incompleted charity project you wanted to see to a satisfactory conclusion. But that still doesn't explain why you missed your bus back to Marquette. You went out and bought food. You stocked my refrigerator. You replenished my water supply. You sponged my face and arms with a wet towel, because I didn't own a washcloth. You spoon-fed me some delicious soup—"

"That was just canned soup. Campbell's vegetable beef."

"Don't evade the issue by escaping into the mundane. Even *after* you did all those things, there was plenty of time to make your bus. I went to sleep expecting never to see you again, and when I woke up, it was dark and you were still there."

"I'd been mopping your kitchen. I lost track of the time."

"Francis. Nobody can keep himself from himself that completely. What was going on in your *head* while you were mopping my kitchen and losing track of the time?"

"Magda, I can't remember. And then *I* came down with the flu. . . ."

"Not right away. Not for several days you didn't. In the interim you slept on the sofa and nursed me and cleaned my apartment from top to bottom. And made agonized phone calls back and forth with old Birkenshaw."

"I don't remember them as agonized. He was very patient and understanding . . . well, in his way. Those were unsettled times, novices and newly professed were leaving in droves. The Church was in flux, the whole world was. That Jesuit I stayed up talking with most of the night said it was all going to fly apart, and it would be a good thing. Then we could get out from under the sterile, medieval stuff and start caring for one another."

"Aha, that's the first you've said anything about a particular Jesuit. You've always just said Jesuits. What was his name?"

"I don't remember. He was small. Very neat and intelligent. He had a way with words, like you do."

"So, we owe our life together to cumin in the baked apple, your mother's unexpected death, my flu, and possibly the influence of a nameless Jesuit over at Loyola who had a way with words like I do. Oh well, I suppose some couples have done worse in assembling the pieces of how they got together. But mark my word, Francis, if you refuse to be *conscious* of how things happen to you, you're doomed to repeat your mistakes."

"Well, I certainly don't consider you a mistake, Magda. You're the best thing that ever happened to me."

"What's that, Magda? Love, I just can't *hear* you." Her weary caretaker's face was once again floating above her. She must have spoken aloud.

"What did—did—I say?" It took all her strength to separate the words until she made each one sound like itself.

"I thought something about a baked apple. Do you think you could eat a baked apple if I made it?"

"No, dodo. The *cumin* in the baked apple. That's why *you* got the job of driving me—"

"Sweetie, you're mumbling. Could you speak a *little* louder?"

"—to the airport."

"My love, you're ill, we can't go to any airport."

Oh God, he was weeping. She was making him weep.

Not making myself clear anymore, she said. Or only thought?

CHAPTER VI

"They were meant to be together, but they got separated. . . ."
Alice awakened out of her dream hearing these words, spoken in a quiet, masculine voice-over. She had been dreaming about her brother and lay stiff and tense, afraid that any movement would disperse the details, which were already fading. It was a strange dream, upsetting at the end, but she still counted any dream about Andy, who had been dead seventeen years now, as a gift.

In the dream they seemed to have been playing a quieter version of a game they'd played as children: pretending to be other people. They'd mince along the sidewalk in step, arms swinging, toes splaying outward like ducks, simulating the daily constitutional of an elderly couple down the block. Or Andy would walk his fingers stealthily across his scalp, as if in pursuit of some tiny crawly creature, in the exact comical manner of a chemist who worked with their father at the pharmaceutical lab. Or Alice would waggle her chin and scold noisy children in the guttural voice of the German woman who presided over the circulation desk at the public library where their mother was head librarian.

In her dream, she and Andy had been sitting side by side on a hard, high-backed bench, like a church pew, solemnly composing themselves in a tableau of some kind. They didn't cackle and egg each other on, the way they had as children. There was a high seriousness between them as they adjusted each other's limbs to "be" the couple they were imitating. But who was the couple? Andy sat inclined toward her so that one arm was around her shoulder and his other hand was on her knee. She covered this hand with one of hers, her other resting gently on his shoulder which inclined to her. It was a strange, formal, loving pose, with some very old deference behind it. They seemed to be being *directed* by someone in this tableau, though there was no one else present. Then Alice happened to look down at Andy's bare feet. They were the feet of an adult man, with dark hairs on the toes, not her brother's feet. Then had come the bad part of the dream, when she realized that Andy had grown up and become a middle-aged man and she had somehow missed all the intervening years with him. At that point, the quiet male voice had intoned: "They were meant to be together, but they got separated." The voice seemed remotely familiar, but she couldn't place it.

Another fair April morning was forcing its way through the beige mini-blinds of the art-history professor's bedroom in their rented house. Outside, birds took turns with their songs. Alice surveyed herself as if from above: a stiff figure stretched long and straight under an ice-blue satin quilt (wedding present from one of her authors), immobilized by an emptiness she had begun to feel more at home with than anything else.

In this bed she had spent many daytime hours since January 10, lying straight and still, feeling her body shrink and tighten back into the body of that other woman, a body that had never harbored a living child. In the ordinary course of things, she would have been pleased with the return of her "figure." But because things had turned out as they had, her resilience became an added source of sorrow. Every day that passed robbed her further of precious body-memories. The shrinking emptiness inside her was all she had left of a future life that would now never unfold.

That was probably what Andy's feet had been about in the dream. All the unlived years of the beloved departed. Her years in therapy had made her a good student of dreams. The psyche's kind gestures of displacement. For, to dream of the baby's feet as the feet of a grown man would have been too much.

Were losses supposed to teach you something? Did they eventually link up to meaning and growth? Or were they simply random occurrences in the planet's diurnal spin: so many infants don't make it through the birth journey, a certain number of families (minus the one who stayed at home) are extinguished in holiday traffic. Just as a certain number of seedlings perish before they can root, and some of those trilling birds outside will dash themselves against windows or be pounced on by the neighborhood cat before the spring is over.

Nothing more personal than that. This was probably what she had been environmentally conditioned to believe. Her father the chemist had found solace in the revealed truths of science, her mother the librarian had taken her cool pleasure in the systematized organization of books and people. Alice and Andy, eighteen months apart, had taken solace and pleasure in each other.

Whereas Hugo seemed to believe in an almost point-to-point destiny, with himself as its partner. This happened to me, which I made into *this*, which led to *that*, which I later was able to make into *this*. Also, Hugo was utterly, unashamedly, personal. He would be fifty in May, yet he retained a childlike belief in himself as center of the universe.

On the day she, as his new editor, took him to lunch at Lutèce, he had entertained her with stories of what it had been like growing up on the wrong side of the tracks in a South Carolina mill town. They were grim, humiliating stories, but he related them so amusingly in his rumbly melodic Southern voice that she couldn't feel sorry for him. His confident method of storytelling seemed to control his destiny in retrospect: there I was, then; here I am now. I made this out of those materials.

Then he'd snapped out some question to her about her own growing up. Whether it was because he came at her so fast, or because she already trusted in his writer's capacity to grasp things imaginatively, she found herself relating, in more detail than she usually went into, the events of that rainy night in her last year of high school. How she had been trying on clothes to impress her older brother, due home any minute from Yale with her parents. She had stayed behind with a bad cold, but the prospect of having Andy home for Thanksgiving had driven her from bed at the last minute. She couldn't stand the idea of his walking in and finding her languishing in a soggy nest of Kleenexes. Soon she was prancing back and forth in front of the full-length mirror, admiring her (two months') maturer self in a variety of different outfits through his eyes. Her cold dried up in the excitement. Then it got late and they didn't come. She sat around in her chosen outfit. Her nose began to drip again. She lay down on her bed, covered herself with a blanket, and fell asleep. Sometime past midnight the doorbell rang.

"It was a state trooper. All he said was that their car had been hit, exiting off the expressway. When he found out I had no way to get to the hospital they'd been taken to, thirty miles away, he offered to drive me. I asked if any of them had been badly hurt and he said, 'Everyone was, in both vehicles.' Then he added something about visibility being practically zero in this downpour and wouldn't look at me."

"Damn. All of 'em gone, just like that?"

"My brother lived four more days, but he never regained consciousness. I wanted to stay with him in the hospital. I was convinced that if I could stay beside him round the clock, I could *make* him come back because I needed him so much. We were very close. But it interfered with their routines and procedures. I've hated hospitals ever since. The routines and procedures come first; people are secondary. Then Aunt Charlotte, my mother's sister, came. She said I'd never forgive myself later if I didn't go to my parents' funeral. Andy died while we were burying them."

"And then you went to live with Aunt Charlotte?" They had gotten through the Pouligny Montrachet, although they were not quite finished with their main courses. But Hugo Henry was an important enough author for her to charge a second bottle.

"No, she came and stayed in our house until I went away to college. There was enough money for everything because of . . ."

"The insurance," finished Hugo. Completing her sentences for her even then. But she hadn't resented it then.

"It was hard for her because she liked to live by herself. Aunt Charlotte was a very independent woman."

"Don't tell me *she's* dead, too." The writer glowered at her from under his shelf of grizzled eyebrows, as if she'd heaped on one too many deaths to be believed.

"Yes, she had a heart attack at fifty-two. She collapsed and died at her desk at the insurance firm where she worked."

"Like poor Saunderson," said Hugo gruffly. "That's what you women get for wanting to compete with us in the marketplace: you get to drop dead early like us, too." He was careful to wink so she'd know he was only kidding.

He was her first famous author. And he wouldn't have been "hers" if the legendary Saunderson hadn't dropped dead at his desk several months before Hugo Henry was due to turn in *A Month with the Manigaults.*

Where had they come from, those images of how you fell in love? The stranger across a crowded room, the instant "somehow I knew." Because when did it ever happen that way? Elizabeth Bennet's first impression of Mr. Darcy was overhearing him insult her looks at a dance. It took many chapters of despising him, tormenting him, and even the satisfaction of rejecting his first proposal before love was realized on her side. And this only after she had seen his property in Derbyshire. Great writers were always clear-eyed when it came to the mixed motives of human beings.

When Alice Questrom took Hugo Henry to Lutèce, she was still missing her boyfriend, who had been transferred by his securities firm to Dallas. They had lived together for five years. Neither had been the great love of the other's life, but they had been bedmates, contemporary professional strivers, and good friends. They had shared a Water Pik and the rent and taken turns stir-frying supper. Wasn't that as much as most modern marriages aspired to? For months after he left, he'd phone from Dallas and they'd talk enthusiastically about their jobs and then complain about the dearth of suitable partners. He'd taken up country-and-western dancing so he could meet women, and was considering the drastic move of going back to church for the same motive. "But no one tempting has appeared on my scene, yet," he'd said one night. "No, no one on mine, either," she'd answered cheerfully. A silence followed, during which both knew that they cared more about their jobs than each other. If that hadn't been the case, she might have given up hers and gone to Dallas. She was thirty-two and wanted children, but that in itself wasn't enough to justify marrying.

Or was it?

On the day of the lunch at Lutèce, she hadn't remotely considered Hugo as an eligible partner. She had never been much attracted to older men. Also she had assumed he was still married to that sleek, dissatisfied-looking wife in the strapless silver gown she had seen him with at the Book Awards ceremony two years before, when his book was nominated but didn't win. There had also been a grown son in black tie, extremely striking like the mother, but sullen. Hugo Henry, short, shaggy, and tense in his formal clothes, had strained between them like a testy circus lion led in on his choke collar by two bored keepers.

She became involved with the writing before getting involved with the man. When she learned she was to inherit Hugo from Saunderson, she read his seven published novels in chronological order. Some of them she had admired before, the way you admire someone from a distance, but this time around it was different: he was going to be her author. From now on—or at least as long as he stayed with Garrick Press—she was to be his appointed truth teller, the reader whose job it was to take his development most to heart. She went through the novels with poised pencil, like the honors student

she had been at Princeton, those fragile years when devoted application to literature had kept her from flying to pieces. She wanted to be
on intimate terms with Hugo Henry's patterns, his themes and obses-
sions. Also his frailties and foibles. Were there any besetting flaws?

His early work suffered some from what she termed cock-of-the-
walk syndrome, a common affliction of young male writers, she privately believed. They strutted the confidence they wished to feel and
spread more verbal feathers than necessary to achieve their effects.
But by book three he had calmed down. Wanting to pursue his people
and their plots had now taken priority over needing to prove he was
an original. The language was less flashy and more direct, but the energy still throbbed steadily behind it.

His strong suit was the way he saw people. He didn't cut corners with their complexities. Even his minor characters gave you the
sense that they were borne along on the deep streams of their personal histories. He could be very funny about them, but seldom
stooped to cheap shots. His chronic fault was that he rushed, or could
not sustain, or grew impatient with his endings.

A week after the lunch, the manuscript of Hugo's new novel, *A
Month with the Manigaults*, was hand-delivered by agent's messenger
to Alice's desk. She took it home that same evening and read it
through.

It was his funniest, most engaging book. That boy: the dazzled
poor boy, haplessly serving out his term as summer victim to a family of shabby Southern aristocrats on their Carolina island. You
writhed at the tortures that came so naturally to the condescending
Manigaults to inflict on their eleven-year-old summer guest from the
wrong side of the tracks. But you also kept erupting into outraged, incredulous laughter. Reading the book made you realize that laughter
itself was far from a simple response. And how right the author had
gotten it, how secure you felt, after the first few pages, that he would
continue to get it right: the awed boy's mounting desire to please his
tormentors as his torments increased, his slavish devotion to "Lady"
Manigault, as everybody called her, a vain, capricious drunk.

And the layers of coded behavior these people went in for! Besides being achingly funny, the story had subtlety and tension. It

combined the best aspects of a novel of manners with a psychological mystery. What gave them their power, these Manigaults? How long would it take the boy to figure it out? How long would it take the *world* to figure it out: that was the wider question implicit in Hugo's tale of one poor boy's summer woe.

And he had done the thing that the best writers do. He had given each and every one of them their autonomy. Not just the underprivileged boy-protagonist. Any number of "sensitive" writers could have aced *that* viewpoint—and relegated the remaining cast to caricatures. But the dipsy hostess, putting the captive summer urchin through long afternoons of "deportment lessons" in her pink satin bedjacket (while sipping her "medicine" from an iced-tea glass in bed); the mill owner Manigault with his mastiff cheeks and complacent fat man's waddle and monosyllabic put-downs; the gap-toothed twelve-year-old monster and heir who applies his own special "torturability criteria" when selecting pets and summer guests: how every one of them *lived* in all their vivid particulars.

"I fell in love with your writing first," Alice would tell Hugo later.

Yet she had felt something lacking at the end of *A Month with the Manigaults*. The book failed to complete some expectation. It wasn't only that you wanted to know whether the man the boy grew into ever made peace with the Manigaults' shabby hearts. You had the feeling Hugo hadn't fully come to terms with them either.

But it was touchy, questioning an author's ending. Any author, let alone a star. How would Saunderson have handled it? Yet obviously he hadn't, because the earlier works suffered from the same precipitate wrap-ups.

Self-doubts reared their ugly heads. She wouldn't *be* Hugo's editor if Saunderson were still alive. And she might not be his editor if she challenged him. Writers a lot less admired and gifted than Hugo Henry had taken violent umbrage when their endings were challenged. She knew that from experience.

Her job was her life, her reason for getting up in the morning. Yet her profession was daily growing more fraught with the strains put on it by the need for profit making. For their mistakes, editors far more glamorous and "indispensable" than herself had been told on Friday that their desks must be cleared out by Monday. Could she afford to offend Garrick's important author?

It was finally the very precariousness of her position that made her stubborn. She had already lost so much she cared about. Shouldn't that mean she should cling all the more fiercely to what she still had? And she still had her artistic standards.

So she wrote Hugo Henry a letter, which she revised many times. Starting with the praise, then respectfully but rigorously addressing the flaw. She had her secretary call to see if he was at home, then messengered the letter to his apartment downtown.

He was on the phone to her almost before the most intrepid of cyclists could have reached his building.

"I want to get one thing straight, before we go any further," rumbled his ice-cold voice. Not bothering with a greeting.

"Fine," she said, heart thudding.

"Does this mean you turn the book down if I refuse to change the ending?"

"I don't have that power," she replied truthfully. "And I didn't say change it. I believe I said it needed development."

Why had she said "I believe I said . . ." when she knew exactly what her words had been? She hated herself for even this much backing down. I can live without this job, she thought. I'll go back to school, apply for a fellowship; in graduate school, you can question writers' endings to your heart's content; you can make an industry out of second-guessing the way the greatest writers put their books together. A strong sense of her brother permeated her office. In times of stress she still called on Andy's support to give her courage. "It needs more development," she repeated firmly, with no qualifications.

"Your people were counting on this book for their fall list." She picked up perfectly on the way he wielded his choice of pronouns to separate her from the interests of the house.

"I don't see that there has to be a problem there. What I'm suggesting could easily be done in a few days."

There was a pause. She could feel his hostility beating at her through the telephone line.

"Just what do you have in mind by 'development'?" He pronounced it like an obscene word.

"There was something unresolved. I wanted to know whether Woody ever comes to terms with the meaning of the Manigaults."

"Oh, if you want a sequel . . ." he drawled nastily.

"No, a resolution. It needn't take lots of pages. Just a certain fine-tuning of his perception, after he's grown, that we could be party to. It wouldn't compromise your point of view. You've already framed your narrative inside his adult memory."

"You know," began Hugo Henry in a menacing singsong, "you nonwriters just floor me sometimes. 'Just a certain fine-tuning of his perception, that we could be party to' . . ." He raised his tone to the pitch of a silly female's as he mimicked her request. "Do you have any idea what you're asking?" The voice deepened to a belligerent growl. "You think we creative types can just hop in the saddle and, 'easily, in just a few days,' "—the high-pitched silly-female voice back again—"knock out a couple of pages that will 'resolve' your expectations without altering the whole *integrity* of the work." He stopped, choked with his own indignation. "It just doesn't work that way, little lassie. . . ."

She bridled at the "lassie." In fantasy she gave herself the satisfaction of retorting, "Hardly *little*, Mr. Henry, when I'm a head taller than you."

"Well, would you give it some thought at least? I'll get back to you in a few days, we'll talk again."

She could tell from the impacted sputters that here was a man who did not take waiting gracefully. "No, I'll get back to *you* when I'm ready," he drawled in the ominous singsong. "Meanwhile I'll ask you to send me back my manuscript. I'm an old-fashioned writer. I like to work from the original."

"Of course. I'll just make a couple of copies so Val and the art director can start reading."

"Nope, no copies. I don't want anyone else at Garrick looking at it until I've . . . *given it some thought*."

His voice didn't rise to the silly-female pitch this time, but she was sure he was flogging her with her own phrase.

"You'll have it within the hour," she told him. "I'll wait to hear from you, then."

S he waited.

"He's still doing a little tinkering with the ending," she told Val Kellerman, the new president of Garrick.

Kellerman didn't seem too perturbed: the deadline was still a few weeks away, and he'd heard from his staff that Hugo Henry was an author who always met deadlines. "I wish you could get him to change the title," Kellerman told her. "People will go into the stores and won't be able to remember the family's name. And if they do remember it, they won't be able to pronounce it. I can't pronounce it myself."

"They can just ask for the new Hugo Henry novel, then. He loves the title. He likes its alliteration."

Val Kellerman gave her a mildly hostile look. Was it possible he didn't know what alliteration was?

"Also, Val, their name is so entrenched in the plot. It's part of the family's mystique. If the book lasts, and I believe it will, people will be going around saying 'Manigault' as easily as they do 'Karamazov,' or 'Karenina,' or 'Père Goriot.' In fact, Manigault practically rhymes with Goriot."

"Okay, Princeton. I'm only a toy man myself." After the junking of Garrick's last president, who had overspent on the company's move downtown, Kellerman had been wooed away from a toy company whose profits had tripled in the decade he was its CEO. Finding ways to sell this new product, a book, whose assets were partly intangible ones, seemed to humble and antagonize him in equal degrees. Which probably accounted for his mixed demeanor of gloomy self-put-down and smart-ass contempt, and for his pet habit of nicknaming editors by their academic affiliations while at the same time baiting them with their ignorance of marketing techniques.

"Far be it from me to mess with a literary author's title," said

Kellerman acidly, "but *A Month with the Mangos*, or however the hell you pronounce it, doesn't shout big book to me."

"Maybe we shouldn't think big book. Maybe we should think small masterpiece and be grateful."

Another week went by. The beginning of another. On Wednesday, she returned from lunch to find the manuscript of *A Month with the Manigaults* back on her desk. There was a new last chapter called "Final Deportment Lesson."

The covering note began without any salutation:

Well, here it is, your fine-tuning. Woody still hasn't made his peace with their shabby hearts, as you called them, and he never will. *He will always be attracted to them: they've left their mark on him forever.* That's the secret you, as reader, were waiting to have revealed to you. Surprised? I was, somewhat, myself. So here's a final visit with Lady Manigault, unchastened as ever, despite the fact her entire universe has collapsed around her shapely ankles. But isn't it just like her to give our hero *another* deportment lesson, though he's now the reigning prince of the hour? She still sees him as her personal summer urchin. Unregenerate old snob. And though he sees her as she really is, he's still in awe of her, he still wants to please her, and you know what? I *like* him for it. If he felt smug about seeing her as she really is, he'd be insufferable. One more hardened, sapless Success who's murdered his squirming boy-parts so as never to make a fool of himself again. Keep Woody squirming! That's my motto. Nevertheless, I sulked mightily before unleashing this addendum and sent you some ungallant thoughts.

As ever,

HH

She read the new ending. It was all she had wished for. It was more. "Final Deportment Lesson" ordered all the tensions, even those that must remain forever unresolved. It caused the bitter, brutal funniness of the preceding chapters to be embraced by a larger perspective. You laughed some more, but this time your laughter was mixed with compassion. You had to admire the old bitch for keeping up the show, and you loved the man Woody for having remained tender to his boyhood idol.

She picked up the phone and called him. He answered warily.

"It's great," she said, not bothering with a greeting.

"You like it, huh?"

"I love it. I love *you* for being able to write it."

It had just slipped out of her mouth. That was the kind of ending the new ending was. It made you ashamed of protecting yourself. It dared you to risk something emotional, even if the risk lay you open to making a fool of yourself.

"Let me take you out to dinner," said Hugo Henry, chuckling confidently, "and you can tell me more."

She *had* fallen in love with the work, but had she ever truly been in love with the man?

During the production stages of the novel, when almost every week brought some new sign that the book was blessed, she had been flattered by his grateful reminders that it was she who had "brought out the best in Woody and me."

She had felt indulged by his gallantries: flowers on her desk when *Manigaults* was made a book-club main selection, when it got the boxed review in *Publishers Weekly*. He took her to dinner in intimate places downtown, always holding doors for her and pulling her chair out and standing protectively behind her until she settled herself and then pushing her securely in until her knees brushed under the tablecloth. His quick mind rushing to meet hers made her realize how lonely for a mental companion she had been. He had an old-fashioned man's habit of taking charge, of taking possession without bothering to ask permission, which she had found erotic at first.

But would she have married him so soon if she hadn't gone on that weekend visit to her college roommate, and been knocked dizzy with envy over Anna's three-year-old son and eighteen-month-old daughter?

And then there had been her battle with Val Kellerman ("Now, don't be greedy, Princeton. You've already had your small masterpiece for this fiscal year") when she had wanted to buy the Emily Osborne novel and he forbade her to go a penny over fifteen thousand. So the competition had gotten it for fifteen-five.

Shortly after had occurred the brutal firing of a beloved senior editor, the one Kellerman called Stanford-Oxford, followed by a well-publicized protest of authors and editors, and Kellerman's equally well-publicized rebuttal, suggesting in his humble-flip style that in today's publishing game the old-fashioned function of editor may have become as obsolete as the old-time caddy on the golf course.

Mixed motives. Circumstance. Happenstance. Were the same forces at work behind everyone's marrying story?

But there had been attraction, hadn't there? Certainly there had been attraction to the virile, vigorous sweep of Hugo's gestures and mind, the way he took hold of you and held on. And the child at the core of him, still so curious and easily wounded, made you want to delight him and protect him in equal degrees.

But he also needed more reassurance than any person she had ever known.

If she was to be scrupulously honest with herself, she had to admit there had been aversion, too, from the very beginning. To his sudden explosions of anger, to his self-pitying career sulks, the diatribes against competitors, his tendency to create worst-case scenarios and overlook the good things taking place right in front of him, right now. Hugo had very little aptitude for living in the present, she had discovered this very early on, so she couldn't say he deceived her. They'd been walking toward a favorite restaurant one lunchtime, on their way to celebrate his boxed review in *PW*, when he surprised her by sinking into a black depression. He knew he was going to be slighted by the *Times*, he said. She'd first thought he'd heard something through the grapevine, but no, he was simply indulging in a worst-case scenario. "But, Hugo, this is today," she'd told him. "We're celebrating your boxed review in *Publishers Weekly*." "So we are," he'd replied rather sheepishly, pulling her toward him as though he'd just remembered the good things in his life. Nevertheless, it had dimmed the festive mood.

And his chronic impatience, his tendency to rush everything, hurrying you through stores and past pictures in museums, finishing your sentences for you. Even in bed he tended to rush.

In many ways, the house they were renting from the art professor had exacerbated her aversions: Hugo's telephone voice as it echoed through the sparsely furnished rooms, with its "staying on top of things" arsenal of tones: belligerently self-assured, vigorous, semibullying, the singsong harangue of an evangelist preacher for hammering a point, the whine of the misunderstood child when he was losing ground, the cordial treacly rhythms of the South Carolina gent when he was getting what he wanted again. All those thrusting, demanding, manipulating Hugo-voices that still needed so much from the world.

And the thud of his feet, his fast aggressive walk through the jarringly resonant house. Slamming his heels down. Even in his socks, he could make the house shake. Always in a hurry. Coming in from teaching or conferences with his students. Rushing out for his squash game with Ray Johnson. Making himself a sandwich. *Thud, thud, shake. Bang, clatter.* Even the muted *ticky-tack-tick* of his word processor was amplified by the barren house. Not that he was writing anything these days. But there were always the letters—to his agent, to the bureau who set up his speaking and reading engagements, to readers who wrote to him about his books, to his son Cal, to a few fellow writers he could tolerate. He even wrote to his ex-wife Rosemary, mostly about twenty-nine-year-old Cal's lack of initiative in finding a job.

All that remained of Hugo now, it seemed to Alice as she lay on in bed on this fair April morning under her satin quilt, trying to sort through the tangle of motives and happenstance that had landed her here, was his negative, unlovable aspects: the thudding, resentful, belligerent Hugo, jealously guarding his reputation or promoting it, snapping at other contenders for the bone. (Joel Mark, of all people, had been the passionate topic of both Hugo's phone calls from Prague. Why let a third-rate writer and blatant self-promoter like Joel Mark enrage you so? Alice had wondered with growing distaste as Hugo had worked himself up on the phone. Why demean yourself?)

The Hugo she now had as a husband was a bit like Snafu, that dog from his childhood he loved to talk about, the pit bull who went around growling and protecting his territory and had once shaken a neighbor's chicken to pieces in the front yard while Hugo's father laughed.

Where was the Hugo she had found attractive? That Hugo seemed to have gotten buried with their baby.

Some of it was her fault. She hadn't been easy to live with since January 10. If Hugo, for her, had been stripped to the essence of pit bull during the last three months, then she, for him, also had become reduced to a negative distillation of her former self. She even knew what the distillation was, because Hugo, never short on words, especially when he had a grievance, had told her. She was turning herself into a ghoul, he said; she preferred the company of the dead to the living. She was more in love with death than him.

Well, maybe so, why not? She lay there almost smugly, in the upstairs bedroom of Sonia Wynkoop's house. If it *was* so, then there was nothing more to hope for, or be hurt by, was there? Wasn't there a definite consolation in that?

This was not the same bedroom where her child had been pulled, still warm with his recent life, from her body. That bedroom was downstairs, where Hugo now slept. Last November they had received an arch-apologetic note from their landlady on sabbatical in Rome:

I hear from Ray Johnson that you two have decided on a home birth. Would you mind *terribly much* not using my bedroom upstairs? It's probably just old-maid fastidiousness on my part, but there it is. You will understand, I hope. And the downstairs room does have its own small bathroom right next door, so I don't think there should be any inconvenience when the time comes. Anyway, all best wishes. You two must be getting so excited by now!

"Ray Johnson and his big mouth," Hugo had exploded. "Well, fuck the bitch, we'll do what we like."

"No, I'd rather not, if she feels that way," said Alice.

"Why not? It's our bedroom while we're renting this house. Besides, who has to know which room we use? We're not going to be charging admission to the event. We're not going to offer Ray Johnson an orchestra seat."

"No, I'd rather not. I want to keep everything clean and true." All her life she had been scrupulous by nature, but she had become positively Zen-like in those countdown months before the birth. The preparations must be worthy of the event. The birth of this baby was to redeem all that had been lost.

N ow the art-history professor would not have to return to her house and sleep in a bed where a life had been snuffed out before it could catch its first breath of air. "I'm so glad I wrote that letter!" Alice could imagine her confiding to colleagues. "Of course at the time I felt perfectly *stupid*, but something in me must have *known*. . . ."

After the burial of the baby, they had come back to this house and she had sat down on the floor, just inside the front door. There seemed to be no point in going a step farther. Hugo had put his hands under her armpits and lifted her, supporting her up the stairs and into the art-history professor's bedroom, where they had been sleeping once more since the birth downstairs. He helped her undress and get into her nightgown. He was the taking-charge Hugo she had always known; he was also the partner in this terrible loss. Then she had begun to leak milk and he had bound her breasts with the soft cloths recommended by the doctor to minimize the aching fullness until the milk dried up naturally. And as she had stood, holding her nightgown around her neck while Hugo tied up her breasts with two of his own undershirts, torn and then knotted together to make a sort of bra, she began to recoil. What a grotesque scene they must make. And afterward, when Hugo kicked off his shoes and lay down beside her on the bed, as if it was the most natural thing in the world for him to be doing, she was overcome by revulsion and she showed it. His presence beside her like this, all bound up like a leaking mummy, was loathsome to her. She hurt for him when she saw the effects of her violent recoil register on his rumpled face—as always, he had been supersonically quick to sense rejection—but the thing in her that wanted him out of the room was much more powerful than her pity.

He had taken his shoes and gone downstairs without a word.

Since then they had slept apart. She in the squeamish art-history professor's bed, Hugo downstairs in the bed where their son, a healthy, sturdy little boy, had struggled valiantly against the tangled skein of flesh that bound him to his mother and which ultimately had choked off his breath.

She'd had to go to the hospital after all, she who had been determined to stay in control, to avoid their impersonal routines. They scraped out the remaining bits of her connection to her son, and fed her antibiotics through a vein in her arm, and everyone was subdued and efficient and very kind.

"*Well, so ... what next, eh?*" Magda Danvers had challenged, the witchy brown eyes dancing in the yellow, hollowed face. Had Magda been referring to her own "next," or Alice's "next"? Or maybe she had meant both of them. Or everybody's "next," who could tell? What next indeed? It would soon be over for Magda, and as she had so engagingly remarked to Alice, she was thankful to be allowed in on her own closure. "There's a certain excitement in having time to mull over what it's all been about," Magda had said.

Call it ghoulish if you liked, but Alice envied the dying woman. To lie there, still cognizant, going over your life story, *was* a privilege. I did this, then this, then this. That happened, then that, and that. And then to see if you could put together what it meant. Magda could lie there and review the work she'd done, the ideas she'd had, the book she'd written, the articles and essays, the people she'd known, the students she'd taught, her marriage with Francis, their life together, the good meals, their comfortable home, their travels, his devoted love—even if she had called him obtuse.

Whereas I'm still in the middle, thought Alice, and don't have any idea what comes next, though as recently as January 9, the day before the birth, there seemed a straight, clear path. If someone asked me to sum up my story so far, what would I say? She grew up with two strict, hardworking parents and was close to her brother. Then they all died. She lived with her hardworking aunt and went off to college and then the aunt died. Then she had a breakdown and did therapy for a while and went back and finished college. Then she got a good job and was hardworking herself. But she wanted to marry and have children. She got married to a well-known writer, somewhat older. Then she gave birth to a dead son, and could no longer stand her husband.

And then? That was the problem. She hadn't the remotest inkling of what *could* follow. She couldn't even formulate what she'd *want* to happen next. Her imagination abdicated from her own enervating predicament and flew across town to the more stimulating one of Magda Danvers lying there working on the meaning of her life story, which would soon be completed.

I wish I had known her better before she got so sick, Alice thought. There were things I might have asked her, things I never felt I could ask my mother, because she probably wouldn't have answered them. Magda seems the type of person who might have enjoyed answering them.

Maybe she would go and visit Magda again today. She kicked off a corner of the comforter and stuck out a long, pale leg. The skin was dry and flaky from lack of care, and a soft cropping of light brown hairs had been allowed their natural growth. For the first time she noticed a blue vein below the skin, threading its way across her shinbone. That must be from the child, she thought. Her heart lifted oddly. The vein was like a message that he had really been there.

She reached for the phone beside the bed, then realized she didn't know Magda's number. The phone book was down in Hugo's room.

Her own passage through the bare house reverberated around her like the movements of a loud ghost. Down the stairs and through the dining room, and past more white walls, then turn right into the room.

The bed neatly made. No sign of the bloody struggle its history now contained. Hugo's word processor and printer wearing their plastic hoods.

The phone book. There it was, in full sight, with its cover photograph of the reservoir surrounded by autumn colors. But first Alice moved toward a metal filing cabinet, as she had known she was going to do, and extracted a certain folder containing printouts of Hugo's correspondence, which he kept organized by dates. Simplifying the task of his future biographer, he joked; only they both knew he was serious.

She knew exactly which letters, to his son Cal, to his ex-wife Rosemary, contained what she wanted. She had done this before, though her nature and upbringing revolted against it. You didn't read other people's correspondence, even if you knew they were saving copies of it to be published eventually in a book. But her need was stronger than her scruples, just as her need to get Hugo out of her bed had been stronger than her pity for him. Was this need a form of sick consolation? A kind of séance? Or a harmless route out of grief? She didn't know or care. All she knew was that there was precious life still to be found in passages of certain letters.

. . . One of the pleasures of expecting this baby is how my lost memories of you as a baby return to me, Cal. Prior to Alice's pregnancy, I could remember nothing much about you until you were two or three years old. Now it comes back. Of course, not *everything* is pleasant to recall: the projectile pissing, the mustard-colored poop, the lack of sleep. But there was something so blissful about smelling the top of a baby's head, like becoming clean and new again yourself, getting a chance to do it over. . . .

. . . Oh, did I tell you? We're pretty sure our baby is a boy. While our doc is an advocate of home birth, he recommended an ultrasound viewing at a diagnostic center. You and I had no such viewing opportunities of Cal in utero. Well, it was markedly apparent that it was either a boy, or a girl with a penis. Under those circumstances, I hope I won't be accused of sexism if I admit to hoping for a boy.

But what an amazing invention it is, this ultrasound! What you see first is a void, then a galaxy of Milky Way appearance, then an isolated heartbeat (with no apparent body containing this pulsing heart). It's the heart that locates you and gives you your bearings. Because often the fetus is standing on its head, or swimming lengthwise. And then ... and then ... like an entry into a science-fiction world, there is suddenly A FACE. This face is so shockingly human, so complete; yet at the same time it is not exactly a human face—not at sixteen and a half weeks. The sockets for the eyes are larger than human eye sockets; the mouth gapes. It's such a fierce little face! Defiant, territorial. (Just like Hugo, I can hear you saying.) But we're going to name him Andrew, Andy for short, after Alice's late brother, from all reports a prince of a young man whom I'm sorry I never met. I trust *that* will civilize our fellow a little.

Though Hugo hadn't found his way into a new book yet, his writing energy pulsed as vigorously as ever through the outlet of his letters. Wasn't it odd that she could still be fond of the Hugo behind the fence of his prose, though the flesh-and-blood man had become too much for her?

She replaced the letters carefully according to their proper dates in the file. Then she looked up "Danvers" in the phone book. No listing. She looked up Francis Lake.

He answered raggedly on the first ring.

"This is Alice Henry, Francis. I hope I'm not calling at a bad time."

"Oh, Alice, how nice ... no, I ... it's ... I was just wondering whether ... I'm down in the kitchen. Magda said something about a baked apple, at least I think that's what she said. This has been a very trying morning."

"I was calling to ask if I might come by and see Magda later today, but it sounds as though I'd better make it another time."

"No, today would be ... I think she would welcome a visitor. She's getting impatient with me. You see, I can't always understand her and she gets very angry. She'll say things and I won't know what she means. She's in some part of her life that's perfectly clear to her, but it usually takes me a while to figure it out, and by then she's given up on me and I feel so bad when I've let her down. But she *mumbles* so, which doesn't help matters. And sometimes she *does* get confused—for instance, a while ago she wanted to go to the airport—but, yes, please do come, Alice. She doesn't always make sense, you'll have to make allowances for that, but I know she'd be very grateful for a visit from you. She's getting so fed up with me."

He sounded thoroughly beside himself.

It suddenly came to her that the odd tableau she and Andy had been trying to enact in her dream had its source in one of Francis's misericord slides. That one of the medieval lovers with their formal restraint, even though the woman was pregnant; only in the dream she hadn't been pregnant. And the quiet man's voice-over had been Francis Lake's gentle travelogue-ish drone.

"What time would be a good time?" she asked.

"Well, let's see, Magda's due for another morphine pill at three. She's brightest just after it takes effect. . . ."

"How about three-thirty?"

"Oh, that would be good, Alice. Thank you. See you then."

CHAPTER VII

"It's the hair."

"What, Magda?"

"My *hair*. It's why people don't come anymore. My appearance puts them off. Even my faithful Tony Ramirez-Suarez hasn't been lately. I look like someone playing a witch in a sloppy costume production. My real hair's sticking out at the bottom of my fright wig. Only in this production everyone knows that the real hair *is* the fright wig. No wonder people stay away, except for Ray Johnson, who comes to keep track of the damage."

"Leora Harris came yesterday."

"She comes for you."

"Oh, don't be silly, Magda. And Alice Henry's coming this afternoon."

"Well, I *know* that, dummy. Why did I ask you to bring me the hand mirror? Oh, this is disgusting. Why didn't you tell me it had gone this far?"

She was becoming distressed, Francis could see. As long as he'd known Magda, she had hennaed her hair, first to give a mahogany sheen to what she called her "unimaginative brown," then, as the years passed, to cover up the gray. Magda's hair—its thick, burnished aliveness—had been the thing she liked best about her looks and it made him wretched as he watched her unhappily examining herself in her hand mirror. Lately, it seemed to him as if some boundary had dropped and he often *was* Magda.

The dead-white frizzle that had taken over the top of Magda's head did look like a fright wig slammed down on her old hair. But what was to be done?

"What we really ought to do is shave my head. I'd be bald by now anyway if I'd gone in for chemo."

"Perhaps we could trim it a little, neaten it up."

"No, I think we ought to cut it quite short and leave *only* the fright wig. Let's do it now. Make a clean break with the old Magda."

"Don't you think we should wait? You don't want to tire yourself out for Alice. I could brush it back—"

"No, I want to get rid of these old . . . *leftovers* . . . now. But I'm not sure I have the strength to sit up for you to . . . do it." She was close to tears.

"Well, I . . . let's see. You could stay as you are, and I'll tuck a towel under your head so I won't get hair cuttings on the pillow."

"Maybe you should just cut my entire head off and be done with it." Magda laid the hand mirror facedown on the bed.

Francis went off to collect his implements. He had cut Magda's hair as long as they'd been married, but this was going to be different, and he had never felt sadder. Magda always used to henna her hair on a Saturday morning, and then would go around for several hours wearing a sort of turban fashioned out of aluminum foil. It trapped the heat and helped the color take better, she said. The first time he had seen her come into a room like that he had been startled, and she had laughed and called herself "the Woman from Mars." From then on, every six weeks or so, and then every four weeks as she got older, or sooner if she had an important speaking engagement, she would examine her hair in the mirror and announce, "I think it's time for the Woman from Mars." Now yet another of their many domestic rituals had come to an end; there would be no more Saturday visitations from the Woman from Mars. Now she wanted him to crop her head and "make a clean break with the old Magda." What had she meant by that? Magda always meant several things at once.

When he came back with the scissors and bath towel and her brush and comb, she was waiting expectantly, her hands folded on top of the covers, a quizzical smile on her face.

"I've got it all planned," he said, gently easing the towel under her head and lifting up her back hair. "I'm going to brush it out around your head and then cut in a semicircle."

"Like a halo," she murmured, smiling. "My apotheosis."

He brushed the hair out into a fanlike effect and made a first tentative snip. Then paused, feeling choked up.

"Don't be chicken, Francis. Get all the old color out."

"But that's going to be awfully *short*, love. It's going to be a very big change."

"Good, it will prepare for the larger change to come."

Reluctantly he began to cut at the line where the color stopped. He was not as easy about this as she seemed to be as she lay trustingly below him, her eyes closed, smiling slightly. It was going to be so *short* . . . as short as the haircuts currently in fashion for men.

"I like Alice. I'm glad she's coming. Tell me again what happened to her baby. Sometimes I get mixed up now and say the wrong thing."

"It died during the birth. It was what they call a cord accident. And there were further complications about the shoulders being in the wrong position. The undertaker told me that."

"Oh, that's right. You went to the funeral . . . uninvited."

"It wasn't a funeral. Just a graveside service. They were very kind about my mistake." As Francis combed and snipped he was careful to keep a lookout for bits of hair that had fallen on Magda's face or neck and brush them lightly away.

Magda mumbled something angrily.

"I couldn't hear you, love?"

" . . . not *your* mistake. That blabbermouth Ray Johnson got it wrong."

"Well, it doesn't matter." He stood back for a moment, to survey his progress. "Alice thanked me for coming, and I think she really meant it. She looked terrible that day. Understandably."

"I like her, or did I say that? You ought to go after someone like that after I die."

"I wish you wouldn't talk that way, Magda."

"Talk what way? About the fact you'll soon be a widower? You'd better be prepared, Frannie, you're going to be mobbed. A forty-six-year-old male who's been broken in by a good woman, and kept his hair and figure and teeth, and has a nice house? And you'll have a decent income, too, with my pension and social security and the investments from my parents' silk-flower factory, and the steady little dribble of royalties from *The Book of Hell*."

"Please, sweetie."

"We might as well have some fun over it while I'm still here to enjoy it. Now, I don't think Leora is for you, although she keeps you knee-deep in baked goods and can't stop patting you while she dispenses her platitudes of encouragement to me. God, I've never seen a woman with so many pastel outfits . . . sets and *sets* of pastel pants and tops. Do you think she buys them in bulk? The Pastel Patter, I think I'll call her. Not that the Pastel Patter will be among the serious contenders for your hand. She likes her position as president's lady too much. But she's probably slavering for your body because of what I intimated that time at her house. Serves her right for treating us all like trapped kindergartners at her dinner table: 'Now I want each of you to share your most enjoyable experience of the last twenty-four hours.' I settled her hash, didn't I?"

Francis laughed sadly. "You certainly did." As he plucked a stray cutting of the dashing red from Magda's collarbone, he was surprised at how hot her skin was: she must be running a fever again.

"We might as well have *some* fun over your future while I'm still here to enjoy it with you."

"But I don't enjoy imagining life without you."

"But, I told you. My imagining it with you now is a way of keeping company with you after I'm gone. You were saying only last week that you hoped I haunted you."

"I said that this morning."

"Ah, well, time whirls differently for old Morphine Magda."

"I do hope you haunt me, but imagining other women ... I don't want to do that."

"Why not?" Her dark eyes were fixed intently on him.

"Well, because ..."

"Because what?"

"Because I'm married to you."

"Okay, Prince Humdrum, you win this round." She snorted with exasperation and closed her eyes. Francis continued to clip steadily on, his attention completely engaged in the close-up aspects of his task: cropping away the brilliant red, leaving only an inch and a half or so of the white.

When at last he finally did step back to survey his handiwork, he looked with awe and dread upon the new Magda his scissors had sheared into focus. His wife's countenance, less fleshy since her illness and deprived of its habitual animation, possessed a stern, remote majesty. It was like having a preview of what it would be like to look on her dead face.

Alice Henry arrived promptly at three-thirty, and Francis took her upstairs. They found Magda propped up on her pillows, studying herself in the hand mirror.

"Oh!" exclaimed Alice, taken aback by Magda's new appearance.

Magda put down the mirror and inclined her magisterial thatch toward her visitor. "I can't decide whether he's made me look like Julius Caesar or an old Talmudic scholar," she said, her dark eyes glittering with the recent dose of morphine. "What is your impression?"

"It's imposing," said Alice, "It's very—"

"Talmudic scholar, I think," Magda continued, before Alice could finish. "After all, I am Jewish."

"Here, Alice," said Francis, "let me move that chair forward for you. The caster on the front leg can be tricky."

"That is, I was born Jewish," Magda went on, as though Francis hadn't spoken, "but we never practiced any formal religion at our house."

Alice sat down in her graceful, quiet way, smoothing her skirt along the sides of the chair.

"In my last year of high school I changed my name, my complete name," continued Magda. "My father was furious. 'What's wrong with Danziger?' he said. 'It's a very old family name. Our ancestors came from Danzig since the fourteenth century.' " Magda was doing her father's heavy German accent. " 'There's nothing *wrong* with it,' I told him, 'but I want to apply for colleges under the name *I* chose to represent the person I am going to be. I want to create myself afresh.' 'But your name comes from the city of your ancestors,' he said. 'But the city's changed *its* name, too.' I said. 'It's Gdansk now, isn't it? Why don't you and mother change your name to Gdansker?' That infuriated him, but he retaliated by saying I'd just be changing my name again when I married. 'Oh, no I won't,' I said. But they let me do it, though my mother persisted in calling me Marsha for the rest of her days."

Magda must like Alice especially, thought Francis. She didn't tell this story to many people.

"How did you happen to choose the name Magda Danvers?" Alice asked. She had a manner of lacing her fingers across her lap in an indrawing, self-protective way, yet inclining her body forward in an attitude of interest in what Magda was revealing. Francis had been struck by this odd contrast of gestures the other evening, when they'd been having supper downstairs. She seemed to hold herself back in a private realm of her own, yet focus intently *out* from it on the other person.

"Well, of course you know who Magdalen Danvers was," Magda challenged. "With your degree in comp. lit. from Princeton."

"No, I'm afraid I—the only Danvers I can think of is that sinister housekeeper in *Rebecca*."

"No, not her," said Magda, "though I found Mrs. Danvers fascinating. She's the most vivid person in that novel. She's also the real creator of the character of Rebecca, though I have my doubts that the author realized it."

"I always loved that book," said Alice.

"So did I, but as I tell my students, or *used* to tell them, don't ever let the line between good and best become smudgy, or you're abetting the return of the Dark Ages. *Rebecca* is a scrumptious read, but it's not *Jane Eyre*, and you and I know the difference."

Magda's voice had suddenly slowed and dropped. Alice inclined forward to be nearer. "So who was Magdalen Danvers?"

"Well, when she was a widow of forty, John Donne wrote her a birthday poem:

> No *Spring*, nor *Summer* Beauty hath such grace,
> As I have seen in one *Autumnall* face. . . .

Does that give you a hint?"

"That's 'The Autumnall'. . . ."

"*That's* right," crooned Magda, nodding her stately thatch encouragingly at Alice. Magda loved to coax things out of people, thought Francis, watching the scene. She missed her teaching.

"But I'm afraid I still can't place her," said Alice.

"She was quite a woman. Cultivated, intelligent . . . very beautiful. She was friend and hostess to the best scholars and poets of her day. At the time Donne wrote that poem, her name was Magdalen Herbert . . . she was George Herbert's mother."

"Oh, of course," said Alice Henry, smiling.

Magda nodded, pleased with the little pedagogical exchange she had initiated from her bed. "As I said, Donne wrote the poem for her fortieth birthday. And that same year she remarried, after she had gotten her ten children settled at universities and schools and so on . . . can you imagine? Ten children, at the age of forty? I couldn't even imagine *one* child. Francis and I didn't even try for one, though we still could have . . . I was still thirty-three when we got together . . . how old are you, thirty?"

"Thirty-four."

"Oh dear." Magda looked puzzled and unhappy. "I must have asked you that before, because I remember you said thirty-four. You'll have to excuse me . . . it's the medicine." Then she brightened, as if remembering something important. "Didn't *you* have a child recently?"

"Madga, love, you remember they—" Francis sprang to the rescue, but it wasn't necessary.

"I did, but he died," Alice said quietly. Her fingers remained laced composedly on her lap, though the color had drained from her face.

"Oh, God, of course he did, I *knew* that! Sorry, sorry, sorry. Francis, you *should* have cut my head off."

"Please, Magda, it's all right." Alice reached over and captured one of Magda's flailing hands in both of hers. "You were telling me about Magdalen Danvers, remarrying when she was forty. . . ."

"Oh, dear, oh, dear . . ." moaned Magda. "I just can't . . . did you say remarried? Oh, right, of course." She laughed ruefully. "I was telling *you* the story, wasn't I? She married a man twenty years younger than herself. John Danvers, a nobleman. They say he was so handsome people stopped to stare at him on the street."

"Oh, my," said Alice. The color had come back into her face. Stroking Magda's hand, she gave Francis a reassuring smile.

"You know, I've often thought it was downright prescient of me," said Magda, having regained her confident momentum, "to name myself in *high school* after this woman who married a much younger man. Of course, I was only thirty-three and Francis was twenty-one, there wasn't such a huge difference. And though he was handsome, he looked like an archangel when I first met him, I don't recall people ever going so far as to stop and stare on the street. . ."

"Alice, can you stay to tea?" Francis asked suddenly.

"Thank you, I'd like to," she replied, still stroking Magda's hand.

"He can't abide personal talk," taunted Magda. "Well, you *were* beautiful, Frannie. The first time I saw you walk across my apartment without any clothes on—"

"I'll go down and start the tea," blurted Francis. Bolting from the window ledge on which he'd been half sitting, he fled the room.

"Poor love, I've embarrassed him," murmured Magda with a little croaking laugh as Francis's footsteps faded down the stairs. "But he was . . . oh, he was. You should have seen him in his prime."

Magda's hand clung stubbornly to Alice's. Though the position was becoming uncomfortable to her, Alice didn't want to be the first to let go, so she sat straining forward so their entwined hands could rest together on the blanket.

Magda said something too low to be heard.

"What, Magda?"

"I said I never had any beauty at all . . . I was the despair of my mother. I had a certain flamboyant presence, which has served me well enough, but . . ." Magda's eyelids were drooping.

Alice heard the faint kitchen noises of Francis making tea. She found herself constructing images of Magda's husband "in his prime." It was not difficult to imagine a ruddier, blonder, younger version of the man who had just blushed and fled the room. He was still so agile and graceful. She could imagine the same agility and grace in a younger Francis . . . crossing a room without any clothes on.

Her hand was suddenly squeezed hard, then released. Alice saw dark eyes glittering at her through the half-closed lids.

"So?" commanded Magda. "What next?" That same ambiguous question from last time! But whether because of the rather daunting new face beneath the cropped white head, or because of something that had shifted in her own perceptions, the question now seemed addressed specifically to Alice.

"I don't know," Alice replied simply.

"Ah." Magda nodded approvingly, as if this had been the correct answer. Her eyelids briefly closed, then, after a visible effort, fluttered up again. "One *does* know, eventually. I am beginning to know."

"Know what, Magda?"

"What matters and what's . . . garbage. Lots of garbage."

"And what does matter?" pursued Alice, straining forward although her hand had been freed.

"Things you've loved. People . . . some you never met. Ideas. You love certain ideas. What finally matters is . . ." Her voice sank again.

"What? What matters?" Alice was embarrassed by the sound of desperation in her own voice.

"Ordering your loves."

"Ordering . . . ?"

"Not like you order somebody around. The other kind . . . putting in order. I wrote a paper on it once. Published somewhere . . . I forget. . . ." Her yellow hand made a pounce and claimed Alice's again. "But, mark my word, it will be the big question on the Final Exam."

CHAPTER VIII

They should pay you to fly these days, thought Hugo, jammed midcenter into a row of strikingly repellent fellow creatures, westbound from London on a filled-to-capacity jumbo jet. Only two rows forward from the smoking section (where the smoke, blown forward, was consequently thickest), he felt a surge of fury at the prospect of being trapped in his place for the next seven hours and having little or no control over his comfort or destiny. This wasn't traveling, this was being packed and shipped.

The person on his left (eyes closed, earphones clamped to his skull) had been tapping drum fusillades on his laptop computer ever since they'd taken off from Heathrow; the person on his right, having thoroughly ravished the two trashiest London dailies, stuffed them messily into the seatback pocket in front of him so that they crackled against Hugo's knee if he crossed his leg. Each of them had an elbow planted firmly on one of Hugo's armrests.

Having a hangover didn't improve the situation, and it seemed to Hugo he'd had one for most of the trip. What of enduring value to himself or his work was he bringing home from his exhausting stint of cultural ambassadorship? Except for that euphoric first afternoon in Prague, when the bronzed reflections on the castle's windows had flashed meaning back into his life for an hour, it had been two weeks of grainy-gray loneliness, low-boiling resentment, and rock-bottom self-esteem. Last night's civilized dinner on Gloucester Avenue with his publisher, Dornfeld, had somewhat redressed things. But only somewhat.

When Hugo had first agreed to this trip, it was to have lasted six weeks. He was to have visited a post in each of the European countries that published his books. But then came Alice's pregnancy, and he'd told the USIA officer in Washington he didn't want to leave his wife alone with a new baby for six weeks. Most understanding, she had pared his trip down to "essential posts": Prague, because cultural programs were in hot demand since Havel's election; Stockholm, Oslo, and Copenhagen, because his books did well there; and London because he wanted to see Dornfeld. The trip was canceled when things were heating up for the Gulf War. The birth-death of their child occurred soon after. Then the war was suddenly over and the same itinerary was offered to Hugo again in March. By then he wasn't in the mood, but things had gotten so bad between him and Alice that he thought the separation might give them both a chance to reassess things. And perhaps a drastic change of scene might jump his creative batteries. *A Month with the Manigaults* soon would have been out two years. Two years. Always before, Hugo had been well into his next novel by the time its predecessor had been out a year.

"So, when do I get my first peek at the new Hugo Henry novel?" Dornfeld had asked last evening. Downright sporting of him, to inject that amount of eagerness into his voice, after the money he lost on my Manigaults, thought Hugo. But Dornfeld was too much of a gent even to allude to that disappointment at his own dinner table, and

Hugo, surprisingly restored to goodwill toward himself by the sooth-ing dinner, along with the low-pitched, cultivated voices of people so well disposed toward him, and the excellent wine with which Dornfeld steadily but unobtrusively kept refilling the glasses, cer-tainly wasn't about to bring it up.

"It's a little early yet," said Hugo about the new novel. The novel that hadn't had its inception yet. "Elizabeth, this is the best lamb I've ever tasted. It has this soothing quality."

Dornfeld's wife laughed. "It's actually mutton, not lamb. One doesn't normally serve one's guests mutton, but we love it. As a fam-ily, we consider it a special treat."

"And since we consider *you* close to family . . ." Dornfeld inter-jected pleasantly. "it does have a soothing quality, doesn't it? Though that's partly due to the bread sauce, don't you think? When our boys were small, they used to fight over the bread sauce. That's why Eliz-abeth always makes double the recipe. What is to be the subject of the new book, Hugo?"

This was asked with such assurance that there really was a new book, that Hugo, assisted by the wine, did an emergency dredging of his depleted waters. "Love," he said, dropping his gaze to the white tablecloth as he presented his timeless fish.

"Oh, super," exclaimed Elizabeth. "I've been longing for a good love story. A really responsible love story. I hope you'll give married love a go. Or is such a thing a . . . oh, drat, what's that word I want when two things are opposite? Do you find yourself losing words yet, Hugo?"

"He's still a young man," Dornfeld gallantly interjected, though he was only five years older than Hugo. "Oxymoron's the word I think you want, Elizabeth."

"*A Month with the Manigaults* is of course a masterpiece of its kind," said Dornfeld, after the two men had retired upstairs to the library, with Dornfeld's extensive collection of first editions. Hugo's English publisher was one of those rare readers who could ap-preciate Lawrence and Joyce equally, never running down one for lacking the very different strengths of the other. In the library, over a very smooth cognac, Chaliapin's Boris Godunov resonating gloomily over the CD speakers, Dornfeld sucked on his Havana cigar and held forth in his leisurely way on how certain good books, like certain good wines, simply didn't travel. In itself a fascinating discourse—if Hugo's own novel hadn't been the subject of it.

"Yes, *Manigaults* is a superlative example of its kind of thing," reiterated Dornfeld, narrowing his eyes at Hugo over a sinuous plume of smoke. He pronounced "Manigault" exactly as a Charleston blueblood would have: heavy Southern trochee on the "mani," French on the "gault." "It's absolutely on the level with *Tonio Kroger* . . . or Musil's *Young Törless*, an abiding favorite of mine. Yes, your *Manigaults* is just what one hopes for in a good *künstlerroman*: the budding artist struggling out of an inhospitable environment into an awareness of his mission. And the manner in which the hostile environment sometimes actually *feeds* the young creative spirit. What makes your book superb is the tension you maintain right to the end between the charms of your marvelously snobbish Manigaults and the emerging values of young Woody. But you don't parody the Manigaults or make villains of them. You allow them to keep their attraction. People who don't have to strive *are* damned attractive, whether we like to admit it or not. They're the nearest thing we have to gods and goddesses—or our poor tottering Royal Family. They aren't always *nice* or even exemplary, but they inflame us, they focus our desires. That's why artists have always needed them, in whatever local guise they are lucky enough to find them."

Boris, gasping, asked that his shroud be brought. Dornfeld, taking an ecstatic draw on his Havana, turned up the volume. Chaliapin's great voice, preserved by digital technology, filled the room. Though the smoking of cigars made Hugo's throat so sore he had forsworn them, he relished the aroma of a good one. It made him nostalgic, he didn't know why. His father hadn't smoked them, he had smoked Lucky Strikes or chewed tobacco; and even if he had, he could never have afforded cigars like these. Maybe the nostalgia was for some ideal father who, instead of punching his son at the least provocation, spitting brown quids into his wife's meager flower beds, and cursing the world for making him a mill hand, would have been able to invite Hugo into a book-lined study, where, over cognac, with a great masculine voice surging toward his death aria in the background, they would have had important father-son talks. A powerful, influential father, but not a snobbish bully like old Mr. Carteret (a schoolmate's father on whom "Mr. Manigault" had been based). Maybe someone similar to Dornfeld.

On the subject of father-son talks, Hugo had decided it was high time he had one with Cal. He would phone his nonearning offspring when he arrived at Kennedy tomorrow and invite himself over to that slum warehouse he shared with some fellow social worker who paid the rent for both of them. Hugo had nothing against social work, and to be fair, Cal had stopped asking him for money, but he failed to see why his son, a twenty-nine-year-old man with a college degree in history, shouldn't have his own paying job instead of just helping a friend with his. Cal said he didn't want to leave New York, he had grown up there, and it stimulated him. Well, it wasn't the end of your world to leave New York if it meant a job. Hugo himself had left New York for a job. Though lately things had seemed to be moving steadily closer toward the end of Hugo's world as he had wanted it.

Dornfeld sensuously released another smoke plume and pressed the off button on the CD player. "Magnificent," he said, with the same relish he had pronounced his wife's dinner magnificent. Drawing ruminatively on the dwindling Havana, he had then returned to his subject of nontraveling novels.

"Now, why the British reading public couldn't make the transatlantic equation between the enduring delights of, say, someone like Lady Catherine de Bourgh in *Pride and Prejudice*, for example, and the enduring delights and *abiding narrative necessity* for a 'Lady' Manigault in the Southern United States, I simply cannot explain. Quite honestly I had assumed they were capable of it. But I had a similar case in reverse several years ago. A brilliant first novel by a Yorkshirewoman. She got everything perfectly. An unerring and *unsparing* rendering of conflicting class values playing themselves out in the young heroine. The Americans wouldn't touch it. After it was short-listed for the Booker, I had a single piddling little bid from an American publisher, and I told him where he could stuff it.

"However, her *next* book, not nearly as rich or subtle, was auctioned off at a quite decent price and did well on both sides of the Atlantic. Middle-aged Englishwoman, upper-class spinster, on a walking holiday in Wales meets middle-aged Welsh widower: working class, but self-taught. After an initial rebuff on the part of the lady, and a few subsequent misunderstandings necessary to the plot, love conquers all. There's been a stylish BBC production just made of it. The actor playing the widower has a beautiful singing voice, I'm told. Which greatly assists a romance, I would expect." Dornfeld laughed, extinguishing the stub of his cigar. "What lesson does all this teach a publisher? You tell me, Hugo. Of course now I'm looking forward enormously to *your* love story, whenever I'm permitted a peek. It seems there's always room for one more of those, on either side of the Atlantic."

Rattled off to his Mayfair hotel via old-fashioned London taxicab charged to Dornfeld's account, Hugo had sunk back on the spacious seat in a rapture of good digestion and literary talk. Thank God for the Dornfelds in publishing, he thought, transported through Regent's Park. Trees made black shapes against the pink glow of London. Though Dornfeld belongs to a vanishing breed. He knows I'm the real goods, damn it, he know where to place me. Look at poor Lawrence's sales figures in his lifetime, look at Joyce's. Alice, who also lives by Dornfeld values, once told me I was a national treasure, and that was before she even loved me. Well, I'll make an effort and revive her love. Let her finish grieving, then I'll win her back. We'll have another baby if she wants. And I'll talk some ambition into Cal tomorrow. He liked me when he was little, we just got estranged during all those years of Rosemary's and my great nuptial war. It's natural for a boy to side with his mother, I did the same thing myself. I'll buy some duty-free cognac before boarding the flight at Heathrow and show up in true fatherly elegance at that slum of his. I'm too old to go looking for the father I wanted, but I can try and be that father. Also it's time to stop sulking over my misunderstood Manigaults and start a new novel. Just toughen up and start something. Ford Madox Ford began *The Good Soldier* on his fortieth birthday. Maybe I'll begin mine on my fiftieth birthday next month. A love story's not such a bad idea, the Dornfelds certainly seemed keen on it. I'll get Alice involved, reading it chapter by chapter. Poor girl, she hasn't had enough to do, that may well be a big part of our problem. I wonder what Elizabeth Dornfeld meant by "a really responsible love story." Mine will be a *maturer* treatment of love than Ford's because I'm ten years older, it will embrace a wider range of human desires. "A Tale of Passion," Ford subtitled his. If I were a parasite like Joel Mark, I'd subtitle mine that. Maybe I will . . . hell, no. It'll stand on its own. People will recognize it for itself, not because it piggybacked on another writer's masterpiece. I can write my own damn masterpiece. It will be my fiftieth birthday present to myself and the world. Irresistible on both sides of the Atlantic. It'll be translated into fucking Serbo-Croatian.

But now, homebound aboard the packed jumbo jet, wedged between the drummer and the tabloid reader, Hugo had taken a hundred-and-eighty-degree turn on the confidence scale from last night's taxi rapture. Both head and stomach were in different moods, and he read his publisher's remarks in a much less flattering light. Dornfeld had compared *A Month with the Manigaults* to *Törless*, which most people had never heard of. Well, okay, he'd compared it to Mann's novella, too—Alice was always telling Hugo he tended to stress the negative side of people's remarks about his work—but why had Dornfeld not so much as alluded to his precious Joyce's *Portrait of the Artist as a Young Man*? The very prototype of the *künstlerroman*. Or why not his precious Lawrence's *Sons and Lovers*?

Feeding time. Choice of chicken or beef, the menu said. Hugo chose chicken as the lesser of two evils, but when the flight attendant reached their row, she announced they had just run out of chicken. As she glowered down on them like a prison matron, he was sure he detected a note of glee in her voice. Her blouse had pulled loose from her too tight pants. Hugo was old enough to remember when all stewardesses, as they were then called, were trim, impeccable, and flirtatious, and treated the lowliest male aloft like a king.

Now the airlines saved the svelte, attractive women for first class. The male gender was no longer king, but money still ruled.

There followed the gymnastics of airborne consumption: keeping your elbows pinned to your body while tugging your utensils and dinner free from their plastic wrappings. So that you could eat more plastic. Canting his neck forward like an old geezer, Hugo, guiding a forkful of mystery-mush to his mouth, tried not to see out of the corners of his eyes that both the drummer and the tabloid reader exactly mirrored his gesture. They had all three chosen to begin with the mystery-mush, which tasted remotely like gluey potatoes au gratin.

Then the scramble for toilets before the movie started. Once you achieved a cubicle, better not look anywhere but straight into the aquamarine-tinted water—that is, if the person before you had bothered to flush. And watch where you stepped.

The movie was third-rate swill, with car crashes and unshaven punk actors he'd never heard of, so he kept his light on—a tiny beacon of literacy in the surrounding darkness—and continued his rereading of *The Good Soldier*. He neighbors on both sides took turns shooting him murderous glances, and he derived no small degree of gratification from knowing his little ray of light was preventing their complete immersion in the swill.

He had reached Dowell's dark little discursus on the impossibility of believing in the permanence of any man's or woman's love or passion.

Why had Ford chosen such a neutered character to be the mouthpiece for such intense views on love and passion? Had Ford really liked sex? He never wrote explicit sex scenes, but that could have been an artistic preference. Hugo himself had cooled toward the nuts-and-bolts school of bedroom writing after admitting failure in his early novels. You couldn't render the subtler shades of human passion through engineer-precise descriptions of characters' anatomical joinings. Despite his legendary philandering, poor Ford may simply have been after some sublime ideal of emotional intensity all along.

After the bitter process of divorcing Rosemary, Hugo would gladly have taken a vow against emotional intensity for the rest of his life.

After finally extricating himself from his wife—or, facilitating Rosemary's extrication from him would be the better way of putting it—he had been sickened at the mere prospect of ever again opening his closet door and finding a woman's clothes hanging alongside his. His marriage to Rosemary, as well as his subsequent forays into adultery as the marriage declined, had convinced him that women as a species just weren't decent anymore. Perhaps they never had been, but he'd been raised to believe the fair sex was "nobler," and he had wanted to continue believing.

So, for close to twenty-two years he kept telling himself that beneath all Rosemary's layers of guile and subterfuge and discontent, there surely did beat some variety of a steady and loving female heart. Even now, when they talked on the phone about Cal, Hugo found himself listening hard to hear the "better" Rosemary, whom love from the right man (not Hugo) and enough material goods (more than Hugo could supply) might finally have freed into being. What he heard was her same husky, confidential, Southern siren-voice, but no echo of any new loving woman behind it. If he heard anything more clearly, it was the harsh insistent throb of her voracious will, insatiably bent on getting whatever it wanted at a particular moment. He could hear it more clearly because he no longer had to see her. Rosemary had been, and still was, a poignantly beautiful woman. Even after their marriage soured, Hugo's heart would still catch in his throat at certain glimpses of her. And the torment was that those beautiful glimpses still held out hope for the existence of the Rosemary he longed to believe was there.

As for the other women, a few had angled valiantly to make him divorce Rosemary and marry *them*. They were sheer delight to be with—as long as they thought there was hope of acquiring him. They were paragons of thoughtfulness and charm, devising the most imaginative ways to make an evening perfect. But once the ultimatums were issued and he demurred, the lovely masks dropped, and guess what? There was his old friend Voracious Will again. He might just as well have stayed home with Rosemary.

Then there were the younger ones he'd met during the course of his teaching and lecturing stints to pad the family income. This new crop had been emancipated by the efforts of their older sisters, the Women's Libbers of Rosemary's generation. Not that Rosemary had ever gone in for Women's Lib. ("What do I need it for? I can get what I want without organizing. Besides, women are treacherous in groups.") The young ones wanted him to read their manuscripts and worship their young bodies—there was no coy pretense about him being the first lover, or even the only lover of the moment—and then lie gratefully beside them afterward, catching his breath, the Middle-aged Man of Letters, assuring them of their talents and their futures. They didn't want marriage, but they did expect him to find them a good agent.

With the young things, Voracious Will was much closer to the surface. It was as though within a single decade there'd been an evolutionary change. Often Hugo could glimpse Will's grim and feral presence not even bothering to conceal itself from him beneath the contours of a fresh young face.

Yet he hadn't seen himself giving up women altogether, he wasn't heroic enough for that, so he had resigned himself, during the divorce proceedings with Rosemary—talk about Voracious Will in its element!—to go on playing the game with Will behind its assortment of beguiling faces and bodies but never to get domiciled with it again. There would be the occasional makeup kit (blushes to cover Will's naked aggression) hogging the back of his bathroom sink, but no pretty dresses—no pretty pantsuits, either—sharing his closets on a permanent basis.

Then Alice Questrom took him to lunch at Lutèce. What an unexpected revelation of womanhood she had been. He had spoken to her several times on the phone, was somewhat reassured by her low, straightforward voice with no discernible feminine wiles and not a trace of the prevalent New York hysteria that set him on edge in so many publishing voices. But he was still in shock over Saunderson, only three years older than himself, checking out at his desk like that. Also he was miffed that they'd shunted him off on a woman editor: that meant he'd probably have to explain all the army stuff in the flashforward section dealing with Woody's basic-training ordeal, as well as the nautical lore without which she couldn't fully appreciate the scene where Manigault father-and-son take Woody out sailing and humiliate him.

Then he was led upstairs to her table at Lutèce, and there she sat waiting for him: neat, upright, unaffected, and calm, hands crossed one upon the other on the white linen cloth. That rarest of creatures in grabby, grubby, hyper-contemporary New York: a lady.

Walking back to his sublet in Gramercy Park where the un-packed boxes for his bachelor life awaited him, he couldn't have told you what color her eyes were or what she had worn. He did remember that when she had stood up to shake his hand, she had been *tall*. Professional success had made him less nettled about his five feet five inches, but he still registered it every time an attractive woman looked down on him.

That hadn't mattered much the day they met, because he hadn't yet perceived her as a woman capable of agitating his heart; he was hardly thinking of her as a woman yet. Her clean-cut lines would do equally well on a young man. In fact, her long, slim build, dark wings of hair, and milk-white skin had much in common with his son Cal's physical type. She was a composed, friendly intelligence sitting across the table from him, interested in what he had to say and willing to relate experiences of her own. She was agreeable to look at and interesting to talk to, but his nerves remained unfraught because he hadn't found her sexy.

Then had come her letter about the *Manigaults*, each judiciously worded paragraph piling up more doubts and pressures in his mind. First came the outrage ("Who the hell does she think she is?"), then despondence ("Goddammit, I thought I was *finished* with this book!"), then sullen vengefulness ("Let her wait. Let them all wait. They won't love her for it over there if we miss the fall list.").

A couple of days passed after his phone call to her, instructing her to send back the manuscript. He unpacked his boxes. His ex-wife had taken him to the cleaners with the divorce, partly because it had given him a superior satisfaction to play the gent with Rosemary and her sharpie lawyer, but mostly because he was in the final throes of two years of intense involvement with Woody and the Manigaults. Their destinies being played out in the South Carolina of his youth were far more real and absorbing to him at that time than the sordid, petty, day-to-day haggling over who would get which possessions from the busted-up domicile on Riverside Drive. Rosemary seemed to want every steak knife and throw rug in the place, and Hugo's attitude at the time had been: who cares? That she would eventually walk off with the very chair in which he sat typing never occurred to him, and if it had, it wouldn't have mattered a whole hell of a lot: he was in thrall to his characters. Everything in his real life, including his instinct for self-preservation, was put on hold for them. He'd even thought it unusually decent of Rosemary to let him remain in the apartment on Riverside Drive until he finished the book.

A week after the decree, she announced she was going to marry a real-estate mogul she'd snared while staying with her parents down at Hilton Head. ("Please be happy for Randall and me, Hugo. You were a *very* difficult person to live with, you know.") She'd had this Randall waiting in the wings until every chair and toaster oven she hankered after had been consigned to her keeping. Decent old Rosemary. She'd been right about the Women's Lib: what did she need *it* for? She could get what she wanted with her guile and subterfuge—assisted by her good old ally Voracious Will.

In his new bachelor quarters he indulged in a minor orgy of misogyny. Women were destroyers, no exceptions. Only their styles varied. His mother had been a passive destroyer, giving in without a peep to his father's bullying; Rosemary was a born sneak and taker; the others, the recent ones, were a streamlined new breed of heartless destroyers.

And behind her comely facade of straightforwardness, Alice Questrom was as conniving and crooked as the rest of them. Engaged in the power games of the "Professional Woman," that scariest of critters, she obviously thought it would win her points at work to "stand up to" an established writer like himself. She was out to destroy him, too, the bitch.

He called her a few other things in passing, then—also in passing—picked up his copy of A Month with the Manigaults and leafed through the final chapter. Pretending he was someone else, just a careful reader who had enjoyed the rest of the book so far.

Could she be right, damn her? Had something failed to happen that needed to happen? Oh groan, oh blasted, fucking *hell*: more work!

As he got to know her better during those prepublication months of *A Month with the Manigaults*, with its new last chapter, he realized that she herself was a lot like good writing. A thing of clean, true lines. When you were with her, you felt you were with *her*. No posing or coy manipulations to conceal a lack of direction and depth. What was there was there, and it was more than ample. Despite all the things he'd called her during his tantrum after the letter, he discovered no signs of Voracious Will. If anything, her libido might have benefited from a dose of Will's lusty forwardness. At work, she was pure focused editor, sparing no energy or determination when it came to her books and her authors; but outside of work, there was a passivity about her, a lapsing quality. It was the dark side of her poise and her calmness. Unlike the other women he had taken out, she didn't make a move on him. Yet she seemed happy in his company. She looked at him with affection. She told him straight out that she liked and admired him. She'd even said she *loved* him the day she'd called about the new last chapter.

But still he'd been suspicious. Maybe she was making the ultimate old-fashioned play for him. Borrowing an older generation of female strategy: withholding your body until the sucker's pledged his life. Yet she hadn't tried to pass herself off as untouched goods. She'd told him early on about the live-in boyfriend who'd moved to Dallas. Later she confided in him about the serious breakdown she'd had in college.

The night she'd confided about the breakdown, they'd been having supper at her apartment, and he took her to bed. It wasn't the pyrotechnic madness of the old Rosemary days, but there was rapport and trust. Maybe he'd reached the era of his life when rapport and trust was more suitable than pyrotechnic madness. He found himself wondering if Alice might marry him. To wed such a congenial intelligence would be a little like marrying your own muse. Was there too much of an age difference? He knew that she wanted children. Well, he could give her children. He had expected he and Rosemary would have more than one, but Rosemary had loathed being pregnant and equipped herself soon after Cal was born so as never to have to repeat the experience.

Shortly after this, they were having lunch and Alice had told him confidentially that she was going to resign from Garrick Press.

"But you love your work," he protested.

"I love my work, but I don't love going to work at Garrick anymore. I wake up angry every Monday morning, and I don't like to begin the week that way. But don't worry, I intend to see your book properly launched before I go."

"But what will you do?"

"Probably look for another job. I'm also attracted to the idea of going back to school. I like reading and studying. There's still money from Aunt Charlotte. I'm not about to give up books, Hugo, just Val Kellerman and what he's doing to Garrick."

"I'm not about to give *you* up," said Hugo, deciding to seize the moment. "I want to bind you to me for life as my editor. Why don't you marry me, *and* get another job, or go back to school, whatever you like, and read my manuscripts. We could also have a couple of kids. You're a modern woman, you could handle all that, couldn't you?"

"Well, I . . ." She sat facing him, hands calmly crossed one upon the other in her characteristic way. He could see from her face that he'd startled her.

"You don't have to answer now. Think it over," he tacked on brusquely, fearing a turndown.

"But I *want* to answer now, if you'll give me a chance," she said, smiling. "What I was getting ready to say before you answered for me was, I'd like to try to . . . to do all of those things."

"You mean you'll have me?"

"I'd like very much to have you."

"I'll be waiting to hear from you, then," she'd said last night when he'd phoned from his London hotel, still flying high from the dinner with Dornfeld, to tell her of his plan to drop in on Cal in New York, before heading up to Aurelia on Amtrak. Her voice had been perfectly friendly, indicating willingness to pick him up at the train station anytime he chose to arrive. Same woman, but different voice from the one that had said, two springs ago, "I'd like very much to have you."

The intimacy was lacking. She might have been his secretary. Now, Rosemary would have faked it; even at the end she would have faked it. Rosemary would have considered it a point of honor—if it wasn't ludicrous to ascribe honor to Rosemary—to *sound as if* she'd missed him and couldn't wait to have him back. When your husband is returning from abroad after two weeks, you owe it to the tradition to put a certain little promissory lilt into your voice even if you've grown to hate his guts.

But Alice didn't "put" things into her voice. It was there if she felt it, and it wasn't there if she didn't. She didn't fake things. The first time they'd gone to bed, he hadn't known quite what to make of it. Of course he'd been nervous, he already knew she was important to him and was worried that he might let her down. But she had wrapped her long limbs about him and welcomed him so good-naturedly that after a moment of recalcitrance on the part of his body, it proceeded in complete accord with his desires. She seemed to be right there in the moment with him, but in utter silence. Rosemary had writhed and undulated and uttered little feline screeches of pleasure—or fake pleasure, as the case may be. Later on in the marriage she had thrashed and slapped and egged him on with commentaries laced with obscenities and dirty jokes. The young things had been partial to sitting on top of him (they had no bad angles yet), rocking back and forth and talking shop about writing or their careers. The women of Rosemary's age who wanted to annex him to themselves had by and large treated the act as some holy ritual, complete with baths and massages and slave-girl foreplay, followed up by extravagant compliments on his performance, the whole thing culled from those How to Satisfy Your Partner manuals. (To his mortification and disgust, one short-lived paramour had confessed she'd learned all she knew from an article hoarded from an old *Cosmopolitan*, "What Men Really Want in Bed," a piece he himself had perpetrated under a pseudonym some years back when he was heavy into journalistic moonlighting to pay Cal's college bills.)

Lying beside Alice afterward, that first time, he had felt obliged to ask, as he always had in the past, if everything had been all right. She had replied something affirmative, almost *polite*, he forgot her words, but he could remember feeling his question had torn a slit in the intimacy they had made between them. It hadn't been a comforting moment for his pride, but it added to his regard for her. She was a new kind of woman for him.

Not that she'd ever been what you'd call "passionate." But he'd taken her willingness to have him, the trusting way she snuggled into him, as proof that her feelings were true. There had been a very short wanton interlude on her part just after she'd learned she was pregnant. But the wantonness was conducted in complete silence. She seemed to be teaching herself more about love by possessing his body in new ways. The interlude had been extremely pleasant while it lasted.

Maybe he'd been deluding himself that her physical withdrawal from him had been brought on by the baby's death. Maybe she'd simply taken less time than Rosemary to conclude he was too difficult to live with. But whereas Rosemary in her disenchantment had simply upped the ante on her bitching, Alice retreated into herself. Of course she wasn't silent on the subject of his flaws, either, but she expressed sorrow rather than spiteful pleasure in having to mention them. She seemed sad for them both over her having fallen out of love with him.

His muse appeared to have fallen out of love with him, too.

In the months following his marriage to Alice, he hadn't tried to begin anything new. They'd gone over to London, Paris, Frankfurt, and the Scandinavian countries for the novel's publication in each of those places, and rambled about on their own for several months after. During these travels, he'd jotted down ideas for possible future novels in the pocket-sized leather notebook that Alice had given him for this purpose. Oh, he had felt rich during those months, so contented with his life that he had abandoned his chronic writerly modes of retrospect or anticipation and actually lived smack in the middle of the day he was passing through, a feat both Rosemary and his son, in different ways, had declared him incapable of. Rosemary often said he spent all his time either living in a past that had never been, or imagining or dreading some future that would never turn out that way. Cal accused his father of "making people into what *you've* decided they are, like characters in your novels; you never consider that the real people might be up to something entirely different on their own."

Well, they should see me now, Hugo had thought on his combined honeymoon-book tour. He had been a happy man, and perceived himself as such in the eyes of others as he traveled with his lovely young bride, promoting the novel he was satisfied with, and in his spare moments dashing off provocative nibbles in the little leather notebook that fit snugly inside his hip pocket. Except in England, *Manigaults* did well, though it didn't explode over the literary horizon the way he'd secretly hoped. It toted up more accolades than his previous works, but failed, as the others had, to get any of the big prizes. But as Alice kept reminding him, it wasn't an explosive book. It was one, she said, that wormed its way into your heart and stayed there. "Which would you rather have?" she'd asked him, and he'd drawn her close and nuzzled her sweet-smelling white neck and answered, "I have everything I want." And meant it most of the time in those happy months.

But those nibbles that had looked so promising when dashed off between book signings, or scribbled in quiet, uxorious elation aboard a train with Alice asleep on his shoulder, had turned flat or incomprehensible once the travels were over, and he was left alone with them in the cozy writing alcove Alice had set up for him in a corner of her living room.

This underlined, starred Swiss entry, for instance: *For Possible Development.* ***: "At the bar tonight in the Duc de Rohan, waiting for Alice. Talking to an American—late sixties. Ball turret gunner in WWII, plane shot down over Stuttgart, pilot made it to Lake Constance in neutral Switzerland. He was interned there for 7 mo. and so was his wife's brother. His wife's brother stayed a year and thoroughly enjoyed the people and the skiing; he got bored out of his skull and escaped via the underground."

What was the "possible development" that had rated three

stars? The way the men handled their confinement? That must have been it, but now, without two malt whiskeys under his belt and the influence of the big, hearty, self-loving raconteur sitting next to him at the bar, it left him cold.

Or what the hell was this in the notebook? "I think I have inherited my father's *sehnsucht* for a place I have never been and am not likely ever to see." What had inspired *that*? Who was *speaking*? Someone he'd met or made up? The entry said Bern, but where were the visual and visceral accoutrements that went with the phrase he himself had penned?

Whereas other entries—"Had to bite the bullet over my absence from the shelves," for instance—were all too clear. That simple phrase brought back to him, in *too much* detail, his morose snit in the downstairs English section of the bookstore in St. Gall, when he couldn't find any of his books. He had fumed and sulked afterward at lunch until Alice told him he had spoiled the day. It had been the first time she'd ever flat out criticized him, and he had only to scan that phrase in the notebook to bring back the visceral woe of their walk back uphill to their hotel, not touching or looking at each other. The phrase memorialized her first spoken disenchantment with him. Yet, if he'd been given the chance to go back and do that day over, he would have repeated his behavior. That was the terrible thing. His bitterness at not finding himself in the bookstore in St. Gall had taken precedence over every other concern at that moment, even his wife's happiness.

They'd chosen Alice's apartment to start their married life in because it was larger and far more habitable than his. She enrolled in a graduate program at Columbia and did some free-lance editing at a desk in their bedroom. He'd had to forfeit two months' rent to get out of his Gramercy Park lease.

When Aurelia offered him the writer-in-residence, he first said no, then called them back two days later when they learned Alice was pregnant. In these new circumstances, the money was too good to turn down.

Once settled into their rented house near the campus—as much as the old-maid art professor's barren spaces allowed them to settle in—he'd made several attempts to squeeze some mileage out of some other entries in the notebook. After all, he was here as the resident novelist, and novelists were expected to be writing, weren't they? But none of the honeymoon teasers would budge out of their anecdotal stage. If anything, they mocked him for his barrenness and lack of invention. And as the winter came on, and Alice's pregnancy advanced, he would sometimes look at her and feel a baffled resentment. *She's* developing all right, he would find himself thinking. She's getting what *she* wanted, but what the hell's developing here for me?

After he cleared Customs at Kennedy, he impatiently waited his turn for a pay phone. He was half hoping there would be no answer from Cal's current place of residence with the social worker in lower Manhattan. Drained by his seven hours in air freight, Hugo was not feeling up to playing role model to his laid-back, critical son. What he really wanted was for one of these uniformed chauffeurs to step forward bearing a sign with his name on it, relieve him of his bags, and speed him upstate in the roomy backseat of a limo. He felt slighted. Who were these other men being claimed with such respect, having their garment bags and briefcases whisked solicitously away from them, while he, who had just come back from serving his country abroad, from representing *art*, should have to drag his three pieces of luggage, plus the unwieldy duty-free shopping bag with the cognac for the "father-son" talk with Cal?

He stood wedged between other callers at the bank of pay phones, punching in Cal's number, followed by his credit-card number. He felt a moment of humble gratitude when he heard the nonhuman operator thank him for using AT&T, thus "approving" his right to charge the call. The old bitterness rose in Hugo's throat: whatever I've done, it's still not enough. I still haven't made it, somehow. If *Joel Mark* had been in my place, he would fucking well have wangled a limo and who knows what other perks I'm not even aware of out of USIA. He wouldn't have traveled steerage, either. He would have pleaded his "long legs" and made them send him business or first.

"Hello?" answered a hearty male voice. Surely not Cal, who

tended to sound distant and morose over the phone. Must be the roommate.

"This is Hugo Henry," shouted Hugo, to be heard over the competing callers on either side of him. "Is my son Cal there?"

"Dad! This *is* Cal."

"You didn't sound like yourself. You sounded—" Hugo broke off. You sounded happy, he had been about to say.

"Where are you?"

"At the airport. I thought I might drop in on you, if you're not busy."

"You mean, right *now*?"

"If you'd rather we make it another time, that's fine with me." Hugo bristled.

"No, Dad, now is fine." Was Cal laughing at him? "If you don't mind the mess. I'm in the midst of making two hundred sandwiches for the shelter tonight. I've been hoping you'd call. I've wanted to talk to you. Are you coming by taxi? I'll put on some coffee—"

"Don't bother with the coffee. I've got something much better for us."

"Now, Dad, when you get to our building, what you have to do is take the elevator to the third floor and then walk back *down* a flight of stairs. You can't miss our door. It's blue and it's the only door. The elevator doesn't stop at our floor because there's a wall there. This building's been completely renovated, it used to be a furniture dealer's warehouse back in the thirties, then there was a fire—"

"Okay, okay . . ." Hugo broke in. Wasn't that just like Cal, to want to tell you the entire architectural history of the place when you were calling on a pay telephone. "I should be there in about a half hour, depending on traffic."

He gathered up his burdens and went outside to the taxi rank to stand in line, or "on line," as people seemed to be saying these days. It was too much to expect Cal to have proper cognac glasses like Dornfeld's; Hugo would settle for any kind of glass. For all he knew, Cal and his social-worker friend drank all their beverages from cracked mugs. Two hundred sandwiches for a shelter. At twenty-nine years old, with a perfectly good degree in history. Oh, well. Hugo prepared himself for the probable scene that awaited him: too young do-gooders squalidly living together, dirty socks thrown in a corner, un-washed dishes in the sink. He knew the type of place: some of his artist and writer acquaintances had succumbed to the lure of these cavernous lofts. They bought all that space and then spent years making one or two habitable corners to cower in. He and Cal would probably have to sit on the floor. Let's hope there'd be cushions, at least. But, here for the best of reasons, Hugo would lift his glass, or cracked mug, as the case may be, and propose his toast and hope for a miracle. "To your best life, Calvin. To your best *work*. A man's best life *is* his work, son. It's the one thing that never lets you down. Peo-ple fall short of our expectations, but if you've found the work that suits you, you'll always wake up with something to look forward to. That's why I think you ought to consider seriously getting a real job, a job that meets the needs of your—"

"Whoa there, buster," said Hugo to a suntanned sharpie edging past him to the front of the taxi rank line. The interloper wore a rak-ish tweed trilby and vicuña sport jacket, and carried a spotless trench coat folded over one arm with its Burberry lining ostentatiously showing. He was blatantly commandeering the taxi that had drawn up beside them. "That's my cab," said Hugo, tugging at the vicuña sleeve.

Stepping off the curb and opening the rear door of the taxi, the man turned to leer at Hugo contemptuously before tossing in the first of two expensive-looking leather bags. Beneath the suntan he had pockmarked skin. *Thump.* In went the second bag. "Well, it's mine now, *buster*," he snarled back. "This is New York. We're busy people here. You were standing there daydreaming." The folded Burberry fol-lowed the bags in with a smart plop.

"New York or not, friend, it's my cab. So if you'll kindly get your stylish crap out of there, yours will be along shortly." The man's whole slick, crass aspect—the rat who had won the race and wouldn't be caught dead without his designer clothes—reminded Hugo of Rosemary's sharpster lawyer.

With an insolent shrug, the man stooped to duck into the taxi. Hugo's swift fingers, obeying an instinct that descended directly through his father's contentious redneck protoplasm, reached out and snatched the rakish trilby off the man's head. Off it sailed across the busy thoroughfare, above the multicolored roofs of cars and taxis.

"Why, you little ... fuck."

Hugo's fists were ready for combat, but his victory was better than he anticipated. Scalped of his headgear, the enemy's baldness was revealed to the world. In a flash the exposed sharpie made his choice. Already he was weaving desperately through the honking sea of vehicles in pursuit of the trilby, but not before having aimed a vicious kick at Hugo's leg. Narrowly missing, he got the customs bag instead. Hugo heard the cognac bottle smash as it fell to the pavement.

He removed the expensive suitcases from the taxi and set them on the sidewalk, draping the Burberry over them. Tossing his own possessions into the contested cab, he left behind the capsized bag of smashed Rémy Martin. He would drink Cal's coffee, after all.

The taxi merged into the traffic jam out of Kennedy. A sullen, dark fellow—Hugo guessed Arab from the name on the hack license—the driver was either oblivious to the entire transaction that had just occurred over his cab, or else indifferent. Or maybe his English simply wasn't good enough. Hugo had to repeat Cal's address several times and even then he wasn't sure it registered.

Eventually they achieved the parkway and jolted on worn shock absorbers into the city, which looked meaner and dirtier than ever. Hugo's excited blood thudded triumphantly through his veins. On the brink of his fiftieth birthday, he felt pride in his quick reflexes, though shorn of any lasting victory. It wasn't even something he could make into an anecdote for Cal. Cal disapproved of all forms of violence. How could he explain about the "something much better" he had promised to bring? Well, he would just have to say he'd had some nice cognac but it had gotten smashed in transit and let it go at that. Cal wasn't much of a drinker, anyway.

CHAPTER IX

S oft rain fell steadily through the end of April and into the first
week of May. The lower slopes of the Catskills could be seen
greening through the mist, though the peaks still clung to
their tweedy mixture of winter and bud. Driving to the college in
early morning, President Harris waved from behind his glass to the
Aurelia professors who had rushed out to reseed lawns in the perfectly modulated downpour. In their catalog-ordered slickers they
returned his greeting exultantly: his tenured league, who were
confident of staying awhile and thus had an investment in the
growth of their grass. The gentle, steady rain aroused a *tristesse* in
him, a not unpleasant swirl of regret, wistfulness, and some alluring

third thing, which, if he'd had more time to think about it, he might have enjoyed uncovering in himself. But college presidents had no time to be transported into sweet or sorrowful self-starring reveries, though this mesmerizing green wetness certainly was an incentive.

The rain was a college president's ally in that it would enhance Aurelia's already spiffy grounds for the May 18 graduation. Which was more beneficial to his $46.5-million capital campaign drive than the fact it was at this moment adding to the water damage over at the Jeff B. Smith Humanities Building, which had leaky skylight flashings. Trustees, alumni, and PBDs (his own humorous coinage for Potential Big Donors) were bullish on appearances, on the overall *impression* of the physical plant. Their checkbooks would open more readily at a recent memory of a plump squirrel nibbling complacently on a lush green sward of campus than at the assurance that all hidden flashings and gaskets in the buildings were watertight. Splurge on surfaces and publicity, skimp on the invisibles: that was his (private) motto during a capital campaign drive. If an institution looked and sounded prosperous, everyone wanted to jump on board; admit a leak or a deficit, and watch the rats abandon ship.

Speaking of ships, it was down-to-the-wire time for a press release about the upcoming Alumni Literary Heritage Cruise around the British Isles in August, listing the names of the illustrious lecturers. Stanforth from Columbia had promised to do three talks (Joyce, Yeats, Wordsworth, Hardy, whatever) in exchange for passage for himself and his unhappy thirty-nine-year-old daughter, who had just divorced again. For the famous writer, Stanforth had suggested he dare to approach the eminent, though rather ancient, Giles Rodman. The English novelist, whom most alumni could be counted on to have heard of, even if they hadn't read him, was teaching a semester of creative writing at Columbia and might welcome the inducement of a free passage home at the end of the summer, Stanforth hinted. But after playing Harris like a trout for almost two months, Rodman had just abandoned him for a larger catch: a summer residency at Lake Como, all travel expenses paid and no lectures to give: all the old fart had to do was heft his doddering body into first class on a jet to Italy and, once there, shuffle picturesquely around the paths of the colony and allow himself to be looked upon by lesser, struggling artists.

That meant Ray Johnson was going to have to pop the question to Hugo Henry no later than today. After all, he'd done the State Department trip, and Alice was going out more now: Leora had met her over at Magda Danvers's house last Friday. Poor Magda, the general consensus of everyone who still visited her, except for the loyal Ramirez-Suarez, was that she was gaga most of the time now. Ray said Francis Lake had to send her back to the hospital by ambulance this past weekend . . . intestinal blockage. Devoted, long-suffering Francis Lake. I wonder if my spouse would preside as devotedly over my disintegration? he wondered briefly, then moved on to more consoling speculations. There was still so much he desired to accomplish. He didn't want to go out of the race as president of Aurelia College, not even its most visible and successful one. Stanforth said there were rumblings that Columbia might be looking for a new president in a couple of years. College presidents became disgruntled faster these days. Columbia. Now, *that* would be a worthy last entry for one's curriculum vitae. What was needed was one preposterously big proof of superior helmsmanship. Aurelia's endowment had almost doubled since he took over, but something splashier was required to get the attention of the big guys: a coup, a masterstroke. And he was ahead of the game in that he had one in mind, as well as a living, breathing local PBD capable of funding it. His dream was a culture center. Housed at Aurelia, but extending its influence out into the public sector. If he could get *that* set up, the arrangements made, the architect's blueprints in hand, his name inextricable from the concept in all the publicity ("The far-reaching vision of President Gresham P. Harris"), then the big guys' attention would be snared and he could swim out of these backwaters, pleasant as they were, and into the main stream. In a more perfect world the center would be named after him, but at least he wouldn't have to stick around to see his dream unveiled as the Elbert Elmendorf Culture Center. When the Widow Elmendorf paid for something, she named it what she pleased. Recently she'd bought her eleven-year-old granddaughter away from an indigent son-in-law somewhere out west and renamed the child Elberta, after the lately deceased Mr. Elmendorf, the industrial-laundry-service tycoon. If Mamie Elmendorf would do a thing like that to her own grandchild, there wasn't a straw of hope that she was going to shell out fifteen million for a Gresham P. Harris Culture Center.

He must remember to ask his wife to spend more time courting little Elberta, a lonely, ill-at-ease, homely child. Just because Leora's imagination had been captured by Magda Danvers's deplorable rotting away and the exemplary behavior of Magda's house husband, now was not the time for her to neglect her duties to their own future. Something in his imagination was suddenly moved by the thought of being bought and renamed by a wealthy grandparent. The dramatic disorientation, the adjustments required of the relocated child . . . but there would be such opportunities, too. Opportunities he himself had never been given.

He would very much have enjoyed pursuing this line of thought, with himself as the rescued child, but there was too much on his schedule to continue this sort of reverie. The president accelerated and his black car cut purposefully through the mesmerizing rain toward his present place of proving himself.

Hugo Henry, standing at his office window between fiction-writing "tutorials," as they were called at Aurelia, could spy down on students through the Jack P. Fishman Library's tall Palladian windows across the narrow strip of lawn that seemed to be greening even as he watched. They were so *young*: their faces barely emerging from puppy fat. Yet when he'd been nineteen, twenty, he was sure he'd believed his face and the faces of his friends to be fully completed and adult.

But whatever the individual funk or fantasy going on behind those puppy faces, every single one of them still believed in himself or herself as the indisputable protagonist of the story.

What would happen to a novelist, Hugo asked himself, whose forte has been the hero's forging of the autonomous self, if that novelist suddenly lost his belief in any such thing as "the autonomous self"? What, for that matter, would happen to the person who stopped trusting in any reality, if it came "merely" refracted through his own point of view?

Hugo had felt very "mere" since his return from abroad. First, the incredible outcome of his impromptu visit to Cal. And then resuming his life with Alice. If their circumspect, courteous sidestepping of each other—this stately dance imposed by her—could be called living a life with anyone.

("Son, I find this whole thing unreal," Hugo had admitted to Cal when they were at last alone together in the "warehouse" he shared with the "social worker." "But it's real to me, Dad," Cal had replied, smiling. "Maybe it's because you hadn't imagined it for me ahead of time that it's not real to you yet.")

What do I really know about anything or anyone? Hugo wondered, rocking back and forth on his heels in front of his office window, his fists in his pockets, gazing down through the soft rain at those impossibly young, self-absorbed faces over there behind the Palladian windows. And if I no longer believe in myself as someone who knows things, what the hell kind of book can I write?

Francis Lake, not bothering to put on a slicker, went out with clippers and harvested a great heap of purple lilac. The rainwater streamed in runnels down his face and mixed in with some tears. By the time he'd clipped the stems and arranged all the branches in vases, then dashed upstairs to change his shirt, jeans, underwear, socks, and shoes, hastily toweling his soaking hair on the return trip down, the supervisor from the nursing agency was ringing the doorbell.

Alice Henry, who, sometime during the month of April, had regained her aptitude for grocery shopping, was putting two packages of veal shanks in her cart at the Grand Union when Rhoda King accosted her.

"I tried to call you several times, Alice, but you weren't home. Why don't you get yourself an answering machine?"

"We don't need one, Rhoda. Hugo gets his important messages at school, and I don't need one for myself."

"I can't *imagine* my life without an answering machine."

I'll bet you can't, thought Alice.

Today the hostess of WCST's popular noontime talk show was wearing cerise sweats with *Issues* stitched in large, loopy silver above a pert right breast.

"Oh well," said Rhoda, shaking her glossy black curls and giving Alice the once-over, "it's just as well we didn't set something up about that home-births idea of mine, because my boss vetoed it. He said we were getting into litigious waters. Romero may be in trouble with the state board, but that doesn't mean he can't still sue the station. Just lately, you know, I've been doing my series on date rape. Of course we have to be careful there, too, but this is *really* in the forefront of people's minds. Have you been listening?"

"I caught part of one program on the car radio," said Alice. She had immediately switched to another station.

"Isn't it just incredible how our consciousnesses have been raised? I mean, all of us can remember a time when somebody went farther than we wanted with us, but *we* felt guilty. You know, for 'leading them on.' All those old jocks' tales about men's impacted juices, and stomach cramps, if they were denied . . . poor things! Well, today we call it by its right name: rape! Just pure and simple *date* rape. The dean of students at Aurelia has been fantastically cooperative. Of course we had to sign all these papers about not revealing any names, but voices can convey a *lot*. I mean, voices are what my media's all about."

Your *medium*, corrected Alice silently. She was pleased with the fresh, pink color of the veal shanks for the big pot of osso buco she planned to make as soon as she got home. These days she thought of meals she could cook for four. Or, actually, three. Magda ate hardly anything anymore, Francis said. But he had lost interest in cooking for himself, and Alice had begun dropping by with suppers for him two or three times a week.

"I mean, you yourself have probably had the experience, if you look back into your past," Rhoda King was saying.

"Pardon me?"

"I said you yourself have probably endured the experience of date rape."

"No," said Alice, "I have never been raped, on a date or otherwise, I'm thankful to say."

"Well, aren't you the lucky one," said Rhoda King, rather sourly. Then bounced on to another topic. "Ray Johnson said Magda Danvers is back in the hospital; she had some kind of blockage in her intestines, didn't she?"

"She's home again now."

"Ovarian cancer's the silent killer. Most women don't even know they have it until it's too late. Now it's all over her, Ray said. Magda told him it was her husband who discovered it. He felt this growth on her abdomen while they were lying in bed one night. Isn't *that* something?"

"I really don't know," said Alice, refusing to meet Rhoda's eager glance or rise to her insinuation. "We've never discussed it." But an image rose in her mind of Francis Lake lying naked next to his wife and running his hand tenderly along her abdomen.

"That's right, you go over there a lot, don't you? But she's out of her head most of the time now, Ray says. Such a brilliant woman, what a pity."

"She still has wonderfully lucid periods. And even when she's what Ray Johnson calls out of her head, she makes more sense than a lot of people. At least, that's my opinion."

Well, pardon *me*, thought Rhoda King, wheeling away her cart of yogurts, greens, and grains. I just realized, I don't like you very much, Alice Henry. Your holier-than-thou, aloof face looking down at everybody from its stalk of a neck and your whispery, elitist voice that makes other people feel like they're shouting, and those uptight folded hands on the handle of your cart while you're condescending to converse. I'm sorry you had to go through such a horrible experience, I am a woman, after all, but, I mean, who do you think you are?

You don't even have a *career*. You're just a writer's wife, without an answering machine, with so much time on your hands that you visit a dying woman out of her mind practically every day.

Magda had endured Ray Johnson's lying to her about how well she looked. Now she was enduring his "patience" with her as he sat benignly beside her bed, his round, gleaming glasses focused diplomatically on the vase of purple lilac, awaiting her suggestions for the core syllabus for the proposed Visionary Studies program which was to outlive her and bear her name.

Somewhere here on the bed was the list she had scribbled in preparation for his visit. Now, where was it? Her hand . . . was that yellowish claw her hand? . . . scrabbled over the crisp white bedspread. Poor Francis had changed all her linens again this morning. Since her accidents had started, he had to change them every day, sometimes twice in one day. The yellow claw plucked up the nearest paper and passed it to the chairman. "Read it back to me, will you?" she croaked at him majestically.

Ray took up the paper, adjusted the round glasses on his short nose, and after raising his eyebrows as he scanned through its contents, obediently began reading aloud:

Dear Magda Danvers,

    I am wondering if you received my last letter about my desire to tape a *brief* and *to-the-point* interview with you at your home. On the phone your husband told me you were ill, and I would certainly not want to tire you. But, as I explained in my follow-up letter, an hour with you would be of inestimable value to my thesis, *The Scripture of Magda Danvers: The Role of Poet as Prophet*, which I hope to complete by next fall. As I offered in my first letter, I would be glad to send you some sample chapters. Your work has meant a great deal to me, and I think you would find my homage to it not altogether lacking in value. I hope to hear from you soon. After May 30, my summer address will be . . .

Ray looked up politely. "Do you want me to continue, Magda?"

"Whoops, wrong piece of paper. Sorry, Ray." She tired to grin at him, but her lips stuck to her teeth. Her mouth was so dry and icky. Lately there'd been a foul taste. The Great Uncouth working its way up into her throat. She should have stopped Ray sooner, but she'd gotten sidetracked during his reading. It wasn't her notes for the syllabus, only the latest dot-matrix imposition from a graduate student called Mira Dooley, an indefatigable pest from Ann Arbor. Would I have pestered a dying scholar for some last words to enhance my dissertation? she had been wondering as he read the letter aloud. And gone off on a sidetrack, as was her frequent wont these days.

Now where in hell was that syllabus she had so painstakingly scribbled out this morning? Or—God, awful thought—had she only scribbled it in her head?

The "scripture" of Magda Danvers, oh dear me. She could picture Mira Dooley perfectly: an earnest Irish-American version of her own earlier grad-grind self. (Had Mira Dooley, whose initials were the same as her own—everything seemed to have significant congruences these days! Which was some compensation for the nasty mouth, the accidents, etc.—had Mira Dooley ever toyed with the idea of changing her name to something more glamorous and prepossessing: Mary Davenport. Minerva Dumas?)

Would I have pestered a dying scholar for some last words to enhance my dissertation? Let's say, let's say I had been writing my dissertation on the contribution of Northrop Frye to the understanding of visionary literature, and his wife had informed me he was very ill . . . would I still have persisted in trying to storm his sickroom with my tape recorder? No. No way. Never. I just wouldn't have dreamed of it.

But if he had been a *woman*, I might have.

Now, that's the most demoralizing thought I've had all day.

"Crap, it's got to be here somewhere," said Magda, groping for the piece of paper with her syllabus.

"Don't you love the sound of that gentle rain," remarked Ray Johnson, who looked so fucking *pleased* with himself for not showing impatience with her. "Early this morning I sowed some rye grass in the bare patches of our lawn. Waved to Gresh as he drove by. It's the perfect rain for seeding, you hardly feel it."

" 'I shall not see the shadows, I shall not feel the rain,' " murmured Magda. Ah, note the elegant balance of those incantatory lines!

Then realized, from the look of embarrassment and pity that came over Ray Johnson's undistinguished countenance, that the chairman of the English Department had no idea she had been simply quoting Christina Rossetti, but took her to be lamenting her own imminent extinction.

"There are some things I liked about this piece of writing, but it's not a story yet," Hugo told the scruffy young man slouching in the chair to the left of his desk. "Maybe you should think it through some more."

"What makes you say it isn't a story?"

"Well, because nothing happens. What you've got here is basically just a meditation on . . . on a son's anger at his father. But, now, the zoo details are good. . . ."

They weren't very good, but Hugo felt obliged to offer *some* encouragement. The more hopeless a student was, the kinder he tended to become.

"I wouldn't say the son was *angry*. He's more, like, *disillusioned*. And I don't agree with you that nothing happens. I mean, this person has gone to the zoo, trying to recapture important lost feelings from his childhood, and who does he run into at the gorilla cage but his father, playing with the back of some woman's *neck*. He discovers his father has a *mistress*. Are you saying *that's* nothing happening?"

The boy's voice rose, aggrieved far beyond the pitch necessary for defending his slight effort. He narrowed his dishwater-colored eyes at Hugo: slits of impotent wrath. This boy actually did see his father at the zoo, fondling the back of some woman's neck, thought Hugo, and it's the most important awful thing that's happened to him so far. And I'm the stand-in for the perfidious father as we sit here for the next twenty minutes and discuss it as a literary problem.

"No, no, no. By nothing happening, I mean . . ." Hugo cracked his knuckles, an old bad habit when stalling for time. He wished he were more facile with this technical talk: it was one thing to feel your way through your own fiction; another thing entirely to describe where you felt someone else had gone wrong. "Look, I'm not saying the son needs to stride around to the other side of the gorilla cage and punch his father out."

The responding flicker of jubilation in the boy's sullen face was not lost on Hugo.

"Or, to go to the other extreme, I'm not saying that the father and son and mistress all have to go off and eat ice-cream cones together and come to respect one another's points of view. I don't mean that, either. When I say nothing happens, I mean nothing happens to the reader. The *reader's* feelings haven't been moved, or his perceptions changed, because he hasn't been given enough to work with. Now, a more skillful writer would be able to take the same incident and move or shake the reader through, oh, any number of techniques. Sheer evocative language alone, if you happened to be that kind of writer . . . vivid descriptions . . ."

The dishwater eyes were fixed morosely on something, or nothing, on the mostly empty shelves behind Hugo. Hugo hadn't bothered to impose his persona on his office, tape little jokes on the door, bring in the books that expressed him (or that he wished others to think expressed him), because he had considered this writer-in-residence appointment at Aurelia to be strictly a one-year stint, even though his contract had a three-year renewal clause. Then he and Alice and the baby were to have taken his fat earnings and gone off to a South Carolina island for him to finish his novel. The one he hadn't yet started.

Now if it had been *Joel Mark*, here on even so much as a *three-week* stint, you could bet your ass he would have lost no time in plastering advertisements for himself all over the walls of his office: laminated good reviews, blown up large enough to be read from the hallway . . . his collected works in all translations, including the

Serbo-Croatian . . . photographs of himself posed intimately with celebrities.

". . . Or, if you were another kind of writer, what you might do is find connections within the information you've already given us and then set about making them resonate. Create a little string quartet of meanings."

The boy clearly wasn't listening, but Hugo forged ahead anyway, perhaps in the hope of working out some of his own problems.

"For example, you mention in passing the sad, mangy old gorilla. Well, you might take that demoralized old gorilla and use him as an emotional focus on the boy's part. It's too early in life for the boy in your story to sympathize with his father, that won't come till years later, if at all; perhaps not until he finds himself in the same circumstances as his father one day. Now, that might make *another* story."

As Hugo paused to laugh appreciatively at his own comment, the boy came out of his funk long enough to shoot him a surly look of disgust. "But meanwhile, what I'm saying is, you could get more mileage out of that gorilla. You could use the mangy old fellow mammal as a sort of safe-deposit box for the boy's growing ability to empathize with other creatures outside himself. Establish a mood between the two unhappy creatures, trapped in circumstances not of their own making, if you see what I mean."

Hugo labored on, feeling like a psychoanalyst posing as a creative-writing teacher.

At the same time he was imagining a parallel tutorial in which he, Hugo Henry, was the surly, belligerent apprentice. A wiser presence sat perpendicular to *him*, seeing his misery from a larger perspective and offering tactful hints of revision.

What would that "wiser presence" prescribe, say, if Hugo had handed in a story about a father paying a visit to his son in what he assumes is going to be a slummy warehouse in a big city, a residence which the nonworking son shares with a social worker. A story about a father having his world turned upside down in a matter of a few minutes.

"There are some things I liked about this piece of writing," Hugo's Wise Tutor might begin. "The element of surprise, for one thing. My goodness, you certainly do pile on the surprises. And what a slew of stereotypes you've slain in this short visit! But it's not yet satisfactory as a *story*."

"Well, hell, if you ask me, there's more than enough 'story' here for anyone to swallow," a prickly Hugo might retort.

"Oh, the *incidents* are there, all right, but your protagonist hasn't enlisted our sympathy. That's why it remains on the level of anecdote. Why should we care about this man? Why shouldn't we shrug and say, 'Serves him right, he had it coming to him. We know plenty of men like *him*.' "

"Damn it, whose side are you on, anyway?"

"When the story is done right, I'll be on his side. I'll also understand more than I do now about the other two characters."

"Are you saying that I have to make the father *happy* that his son is . . . ?"

"No, but you have to give us a perspective large enough to contain the tensions. What you've given us so far is a list of surprises and the father's inability to absorb them."

"Well, damn, could *you* absorb them?"

"That's not the issue. There are things you're not using here because you're not seeing them yet."

"Like what? What am I not seeing? Give me a clue. Look, I just gave this hopeless boy his gorilla to work with. Can't you give *me* some specific image like that?"

"Let's see. How about the elevator?"

"The elevator?"

"The elevator in their building. It's as good a place as any to start. Its strength as an image is that when the father is going *up* in it, he has certain preconceptions, and when he comes *down*, an hour later, they have been displaced by realities he couldn't imagine on the trip up. Go up in the elevator again. The elevator that won't stop at the second floor because it can't, because there's a wall where the doors would open. Ride on up with it to the third floor, as your son instructed. Then walk back down the flight of stairs to the floor where your son lives. By the time the father rings the bell beside the blue door, we need to know who he is and what he expects from his son and what he expects to find on the other side of the blue door.

And then, when you've done that, go in and face what's behind the blue door."

"I don't know if I ever *can* face what's behind the fucking blue door. If you knew how I *felt* when I . . ."

"Well then, when the blue door opens, put the father's feelings aside. From now on, just describe what he sees. We'll have learned a great deal about him on the elevator if you've done your usual good job. You've always been good at narrative summary, it suits your impatient temperament. So go on now, have him ring the bell, and here come quick footsteps, and then the usual rustle and rattle of New York locks and chains, and now the blue door is opening. . . ."

The scruffy boy who had seen his philandering father at the zoo was straggling to his feet, showing no evidence of enlightenment, Hugo's gorilla-gift notwithstanding.

"I wonder if you could tell me what my grade is going to be," he asked Hugo accusingly.

"Oh, Alice, you're so good to us," said Francis. "What have you brought this time? Poor Magda probably won't eat it, she eats scarcely anything, but I'm very grateful to have something in the evening. I hardly know where the days go. Early this morning I did laundry. I wanted to have everything fresh for Ray Johnson's visit. They put their heads together about the syllabus earlier this afternoon, you know. We timed it so it would be just after her pill. Oh, and the supervisor from the nursing agency came to look us over. She said we were going to need a hospital bed, so I called the medical-supplies place and they're delivering one tomorrow morning. She seemed a very efficient, capable woman. Oh, and she also suggested I get one of those tables on wheels that fits over the bed, like they use in the hospital, so I ordered one of those, too. What do you think of all this rain?"

Francis Lake, neatly dressed as always but more haggard and drawn in the face than three days ago, when Alice had been here last, followed close behind her into the narrow, rather dark kitchen, keeping up his constant stream of lonesome man's prattle as Alice set out plastic containers along the counter. Francis was a totally different breed of man from Hugo. Alice could not recall having known another person like him. She felt completely at ease with him, yet she also felt she didn't know him at all, despite having been over here many times during the past month. On some days he seemed infinitely more mature than she: a serene man, twelve years her senior, who apparently didn't think about himself very much, and was content to be where he was, doing whatever needed to be done at the moment, even if it meant taking care of a dying wife. At other times, she felt as if she were the much older one. Today, for instance, his trusting, mundane prattle as he hovered so close behind her she kept stepping on his feet, brought out all her motherliness.

"That smells wonderful. I can smell it through the container. What is it?"

"Osso buco. All you have to do is heat it until it bubbles."

"Until it bubbles," he echoed obediently.

"The salad's in here, and the vinaigrette is in this little jar."

"I never could make a satisfactory vinaigrette. You know, Alice, I haven't exactly figured out how to organize this bed switching tomorrow. Will the men delivering the hospital bed from the medical-supplies place resent it, do you think, if I ask them to help me move our old bed into a spare room?"

"I don't see why. They must get this request all the time."

"*That's* true," he acknowledged, as if she had been the source of a great enlightenment. "And I'll be able to help them, of course. I'll get Magda settled comfortably into a chair, only she's never really comfortable sitting up now. . . ." As he puzzled out tomorrow's maneuvers his soft gray eyes behind the glasses dwelled on Alice's forehead, as if he were reading his directions there. He raked at his hair in that helpless clearing-away motion she'd first noticed in the Grand Union. One swatch kept flopping down again, and several wispy gray-blond strands remained sticking straight up, but he was oblivious of it. Again she imagined him lying beside his wife, running his hand knowledgeably over her familiar body just before he found the cancer, and she looked away in confusion from his earnest gaze.

"Shall I go up and see Magda, or is she done in from Ray's visit?"

"She's tired, but she'd be very disappointed if you didn't go up,

Alice. You've become her favorite person." He touched her arm diffidently as he confided this.

"I should think *you'd* be that."

"Oh, no"—he laughed tiredly—"I'm just second nature to her by now. I'm hardly a separate person anymore, we're such an old couple."

He had that same look of private contentment that had filled her with envy and yearning when she'd been having supper with him that first time and he had said, "It's been such a privilege to share in her radiance."

"I wish I understood more about marriage," she said suddenly.

"Well, shall we go up?" He gave no sign of having heard her previous remark, and she felt rebuffed.

"Can you stay and have tea with me afterward?" he asked, following right behind her up the narrow stairs.

It had come over her, as it did some half a dozen times a year, how much she could still miss her brother. She would probably never share with anyone the kind of talks they'd had about everything. Andy would be thirty-six this year. He'd undoubtedly be married, too. Probably with children. She would be Aunt Alice to one or more people. She and Andy would meet for drinks or tea or dinner without their respective spouses and talk about anything they wanted. *He* would talk to me about marriage, Alice thought.

It was tempting to punish Francis for his lack of response by saying she couldn't have tea with him, but she said yes because she wanted to stay. She liked being here in this house, even though Magda was dying in it. In a strange way, Magda's dying and letting her be a part of it was becoming a source of unexpected happiness to Alice.

Magda was dozing. The short white hair looked fluffy and freshly washed; Francis must have found time to do that along with everything else. Even after only a few days, it was always startling for Alice to see Magda again. She altered so drastically from visit to visit.

Alice sat down in her accustomed chair beside the bed. Then she saw Magda's dark eyes glittering at her from beneath heavy, purplish lids. Her dry, chapped lips stretched into an eerie smile. Her teeth seemed to have grown yellower and sharper.

"I've just come to sit with you awhile," said Alice. "Please don't try to stay awake."

Magda mumbled something.

"Excuse me, Magda, I didn't hear you," said Alice, leaning closer.

"Working, not sleeping."

"Go ahead, then. I just want to sit here beside you."

Magda inclined her head sagely, as if approving the wisdom of Alice's desire. Then the eyes closed again, but the mouth remained ajar. Alice picked up the foul whiff issuing from it.

But the scent of the abundant lilac in the room was fortunately stronger, and Alice folded her hands in her lap and gave herself over to the hiss of soft rain outside the windows.

Of course, if Andy were alive today, the others would probably also be alive. The natural deaths of her mother and father would still be in the future. In the natural order of things, it might be another decade or two before she would be watching at the bedside of a parent, the way she was watching now with Magda.

INTERDEPARTMENTAL MEMO
FROM: Ray Johnson, Chairman
TO: Blum, Darling, Fagen, Ramirez-Suarez

Me again, folks, with one more request to stress you out in the hectic countdown before finals and graduation. Deadline for copy for the '91–'92 catalog is breathing down our necks. I need your input pronto for syllabus and course description for Magda's course. I was over with her earlier today and I'm sorry to report the news isn't good. She thought she had prepared a list of texts, but it never materialized. She had confused it with a letter someone had sent her.

Also, as I mentioned at our last get-together, we will all have to take turns wearing Magda's hat until the first Magda Danvers Professor of Visionary Studies is appointed, which may not be until the '92–'93, or '93–'94 academic year. There's still time to work out our strategies (team teaching is an attractive possibility), but meanwhile we have to get something in the new catalog. I'm counting on you guys!

Hugo had finished his last tutorial. The girl, or young woman, as you were supposed to call them now, had presented herself smugly for her appointment, no doubt expecting high praise for her bold excursion into the exotic world of the lower classes: a "story" about a couple living in a single-wide trailer and having a marital crisis because the local sawmill has shut down and the husband is reduced to staying home and doing the laundry and minding the kids while the wife works. Lots of writers these days had taken to this kind of slumming . . . not really stories, but a kind of market research into the lives of the poor.

In the girl's story there was plenty of filthy language and more-or-less-accurate redneck talk, but without the ring of conviction: more of a voiceprint from a world she knew nothing about firsthand. She had dished up a nasty climax—no, better use "culmination," to avoid the pun—in which the man pins his exhausted wife facedown across the clothes dryer and rapes her up the ass. Meant to show that she could "write like a man"? A gauntlet flung down at her conventional middle-class upbringing? (Her father was a bank manager in town.) Or was it supposed to be a statement of some kind about poverty—or what the girl thought poverty was all about: that if you were poor and powerless, you had to take your consolations where you could find them, even if it meant up the ass?

If she had been his first "tutorial" of the day, before he got wrung out by trying to separate the personal subtexts from the "art" in these unformed young utterances, he might have let her have it. He knew about being poor, and he knew how rednecks really talked. Also, there was the logistic problem with the final scene. If the wife is lying haunches up across the top of a standard-sized clothes dryer and the man is standing behind her, there's no way to get the requisite nuts and bolts together unless the man stands on something. Unless, of course, he's six-foot-eight, in which case the writer had better mention it earlier in the story.

Probably fortunate he *had* been wrung out and had simply told her it was an adventurous effort but he "hadn't warmed to it"—that old cop-out of editors who don't want to buy your story and are too lazy to think up a critical reason for their antipathy. He told her that the people weren't convincing, she needed to work on the dialogue. "Go hang around the diner over in Fisher's Hook and listen to some real talk," he'd advised.

If I'd *had* the energy left to tackle her on that dryer scene, thought Hugo, tilting his chair back and crossing his feet on his desk, the Writer Scorned might be scurrying off to accuse me of sexual harassment on campus this very minute. I would have been the next "Noontime Issue" on the Rhoda King show.

Closing his eyes, lulled by the soft, monotonous rain, he was not at all surprised to find his Benign Tutor patiently waiting for his return.

"Well, Hugo, how's the revision on your story coming?"

"I can ace the elevator stuff. You're right, I do narrative summary easily. And it's not as if I don't know the father, is it, ha, ha? If you want to know the truth, I'm getting a little tired of the father. I think I'm ready to take a stab at that nonfeeling technique you mentioned. When we go through the blue door."

"Then . . . let's go."

"This may be a little rough, at first."

"No feelings, remember?"

"No, I meant the *technique* may be a little rough. The way I describe things. I may have to inch along."

"That's permitted in a first draft. Describe it any way you can."

The door opens. There's Cal. Looking fit and somehow . . . glossier, pinker. Like there's more blood being stirred up in him, or something. Looks the father in the eye . . . then hesitates . . . then uncharacteristically embraces him. The father is embarrassed, they've never gone in for this. . . .

No feelings, remember?

Sorry. While in his son's embrace—the son is taller, so the father has to look around him rather than over his shoulder—the father takes in the pleasing surroundings spread amply before him. Also he sees that there's another person watching quietly from the middle distance of this loft filled with beautiful things. Now, don't expect me to describe the *decor*. I can't, without doing my research. I can't tell a Duncan Phyfe from a Chippendale. . . .

Blatant narrative intrusion, Hugo.

Sorry. Anyway, it's beautiful, the father, with his limited knowledge of furniture and interior decorating, can see that—somebody around here has *money*, money and taste: all this stuff's so *confidently settled* into this huge space. And I mean, it's so artfully done, there are alcoves and arches and carpets alternating with shining floors, and custom-built bookshelves to the ceiling, with several of those movable ladders . . . there's even a grand piano, with music on the rack. The only out-of-context thing is the huge trestle table set up in the middle of the room with all the loaves of bread and gallon jars of peanut-butter-and-jelly sandwiches on it. Charity in its basic operations plunked down in the centerfold of *Antiques* magazine. And then this other person in the room is coming forward, an elegant, gray-haired black man. I have to say black, or even probably African-American now, but in actual *color* he's really more of a copper—

Intrusion, Hugo!

Sorry. An elegant, gray-haired, copper-skinned man, somewhere between fifty and sixty, comes forward and cordially shakes the father's hand, introducing himself as Laurence, Cal's roommate, and welcoming the father in a warm modulated voice—just a cultivated Middle-American voice, no regional accent. He says he's read some of the father's work, that he particularly likes—

Could we hear him say it!

"Old Manigault," he says, pronouncing the name exactly right, "now, he was just plain scary. I *know* the man, you got him perfectly. But you didn't get vindictive and lose your control, you just coolly laid on the details of him and let us shudder for ourselves. Not many writers can do that with their villains." Meanwhile the son is looking on proudly, eagerly, as if he collects every word that issues from

Laurence's mouth. That's when the father gets his first uncomfortable feeling that—

No feelings, Hugo.

Okay. Then the father found himself being seated in one of the
comfortable alcoves, and presto, out comes the coffee in little blue-
and-gold cups on a tray—no cracked mugs here!—with a nice assortment of cookies, and Hugo is being questioned abut his trip by both
of them, and then they volunteer what *they've* been doing. Laurence,
it turns out, has *founded* a network of charities in the city, only one
of which is this shelter they've been making the sandwiches for.

Laurence sat facing the father on a backless settee with rolled
arms, his graceful copper hands dangling loosely from his knees. His
long thin legs in rumpled chinos were parted and the father couldn't
help but see the outline of his cock. Cal sat catty-cornered to both of
them and the father ... the father ... oh, shit ...

Go on, don't interrupt the narrative flow.

The father watched his son as he sat looking from one to the
other of them. Cal looked at Laurence with a barely concealed rapture, the way a girl in the presence of her father might look at the
man she's crazy about and wants her father to appreciate.

Soon after, Laurence rose and said, "If you'll excuse me, Hugo,
I have to go to my office and write some grant applications," leaving
Cal and his father alone.

Cal spoke first. "Dad, I'm so glad you finally decided to come
and see how we live. Mom's been terrific about it, but I couldn't be
truly happy until you're okay, too."

"I'm not sure I *am* okay," said Hugo, not yet able to meet Cal's
eyes. "Son, I find this whole thing unreal."

"But it's real to me, Dad. Maybe it's because you hadn't imagined it for me ahead of time that it's not real to you yet."

"This gentle rain is conducive to forty winks," said a suave
voice from the doorway of Hugo's office, "or are you simply recollect-
ing in tranquility?"

"Oh, hi, Ray, come in. I've just had my weekly tutorials. Seven
of them, back-to-back this afternoon."

"You might consider spreading them over a whole week," suggested the chairman congenially, easing himself into the chair facing Hugo and crossing an ankle over one knee. His sock was too short to cover his hairless shin. He casually clutched a batch of curly new faxes. "Oh, I know, I know. You creative people like to have your mornings, when the juices are running high. At least you come to your tutorials sober, which is more than I can say about your predecessor, who shall remain unnamed." He suddenly leaned forward complicitly. "Hey, just between us, Hugo, can anyone *really* teach another person how to write?"

Hugo knew that Ray Johnson, being Ray Johnson, had asked this question dozens of times to dozens of "creative people," with the identical spontaneous overture. Hugo also knew perfectly well who his predecessor was, and knew Ray Johnson knew he knew: the notorious aging bad boy, McKenna, who hadn't been able to finish his second novel in twenty years. Hugo had done a joint reading with him several years ago at the 92nd Street Y: McKenna, who was three-sheets-in-the-wind already, read first. Refusing the microphone, he swaggered back and forth across the stage in his white suit, pink shirt, cowboy boots, and string tie, incoherently intoning an endless, rambling excerpt from the novel-in-progress. As he finished each page he dropped it nonchalantly on the floor, so that when it was Hugo's turn to come onstage, he'd had to pick his way across the snowfall of McKenna's pages.

"I can't teach anyone how to see, or feel, or pick up on what's crying out in their lives to be given shape to," said Hugo, after a pause—a pause as disingenuous in its way as Ray's "spontaneous" overture, for Hugo had been asked this question at least as many times as Ray Johnson had sprung it on others. "But there are a few tricks of the trade I can teach them. Things *I* learned the hard way."

"Such as?" Ray's "interested" eyes gleamed at Hugo behind their round glasses.

"Simple mechanics. How to get a character out of a room, or into a car, or off to another city . . . or into the next month or year of his life. You'd be surprised how many beginning writers get a hand on a doorknob or a key in the ignition and then bog down in despair at all those *motions* ahead of them that they think they have to chronicle faithfully."

"Ah," said Ray Johnson, eyes twinkling with enlightenment. I know what it is that unnerves me about this man, Hugo realized. It's that he's *playing* being someone called Ray Johnson. What he thinks "Ray Johnson" should be. So everything he does or says has this once-removed quality about it. There's no connection to any real center.

"Or how to ease into a flashback without sandbagging the reader," Hugo went on. "Or when narrative summary is your best device. That's when you want to flat out *tell* your reader some important information about a character without a lot of coy pussyfooting. For instance, oh: 'John Smith had been playing at being a man called "John Smith," for so long that everything he did or said had a once-removed quality about it.' "

"Now, that's an intriguing one," said Ray Johnson appreciatively. "Don't you love the sound of that rain? This morning I went out and sowed rye seed in our bare patches. I could practically hear the grass growing. Oh, and I was over to see Magda. Quite a shock. He's given her this butch haircut, you know. She's totally white now, all that famous dye job chopped off. It's appalling how much her mind's deteriorated. We were going to plan a Visionary Studies syllabus. She was supposed to have prepared a list of texts, but instead she made me read aloud this letter she *pretended* was the syllabus. Some student doing a thesis on that one book of hers. My guess is she wanted me to know she's not totally forgotten yet. Her ego certainly hasn't deteriorated."

"I've got to get over there myself and see her. I always did enjoy sparring with Magda."

"I wouldn't expect much sparring if I were you. *He* dissimulates about how well she still functions. That's what threw me off. Otherwise I never would have asked her for that syllabus."

"Poor Lake. Alice says he's nothing short of an angel. She's been going over fairly regularly, taking food."

"So Leora says. Very good of her."

"She says she likes going."

"Now *that's* happy news. Aurelia's dance card hasn't been the same without you two. Susie was saying to me just the other night she'd like to have you and Alice, maybe one other couple, over for dinner. Of course, after your ordeal it was only natural for you both to want to have a little time to yourselves. But now *you're* back on the transatlantic celebrity circuit, and your lovely spouse is out and about again. . . ."

"Well, not totally out and about yet," put in Hugo quickly, to forestall an immediate invitation. "But she's coming along."

"You let us know when," said Ray Johnson smoothly. "Oh, I wanted to show you these." He spread out the curly sheaf of faxed pages on Hugo's desk.

"What are they?"

"First proofs for the brochure for our Twenty-fifth Anniversary Alumni Cruise in late August. We just got them from the travel agency in New York. You can't tell much, because they're in black-and-white, and then this malodorous smell. Reminds you of those old thermofaxes back in the early sixties, doesn't it?"

President Gresham P. Harris and the Alumni of Aurelia College Invite You to Join Us Aboard the Galatea *for a Literary Heritage Cruise of the British Isles and Ireland.* Hugo made out in elaborate Gothic lettering superimposed upon what could either have been a ruin of a castle or a monastery outlined against the sea.

"I'm sure Gresh must have mentioned this to you back last fall. It's been the bee in his bonnet for about a year now. All the leading schools and cultural organizations have educational cruises these days, and you know his motto: If the best of *them* have it, why the hell haven't *we* got it?"

"I thought it had fallen through because of the Gulf War."

"Well, he put it on hold. But when things had stabilized over there, he sent out query letters to the first graduating class of sixty-six, and would you believe it, he got back forty-two firm commitments. They're rearing to go. They're prosperous, loyal alumni, on the doorstep of their fifties, and they *want* their anniversary bash. Some of them sent in deposits as a kind of *pledge*, can you beat that for loyalty? But Gresh's biggest piece of luck was getting the *Galatea* at a slashed rate because another college group canceled back in February. They couldn't get enough people to sign up because of the war. He was born under a lucky star, I guess."

" 'An exclusive voyage aboard the privately chartered *Galatea* August nineteen to thirty,' " Hugo read aloud slowly from the smudgy proof to gain time. He had some idea of where this conversation was leading.

"We got an incredible deal, because the *Galatea* was between itineraries and you know they have to pay their staff and crew whether there are passengers or not, so they grabbed our offer. They'll break even just with our forty-two passengers. But now Gresh has been negotiating with the agency some more, and if we can sign up forty or fifty *more* people—a hundred and thirty will fill the ship—we can offer this cruise to individuals in the community for practically a steal. The agency that owns the *Galatea* will make a profit and we'll be building local cultural credit. That's very important to Gresh. With all his connections, he can easily lay hands on the master lists that really count . . . the Restoration Society folks, the Philharmonic crowd. Who knows, if we all work our butts off, we may even manage to lure some PBDs aboard!"

"Are we all supposed to go out and sell tickets, then?" asked Hugo innocently, still stalling for time.

"Those of us without the greater gifts will be expected to drum up business, but in your case Gresh is hoping you'll consent to be our star literary attraction. You're his first choice, you know."

"I see."

"The challenge is to make sure they have a wonderful time. Dancing to the music of their eras while the *Galatea* plies its nighttime course between ports. They'll get five-star meals—we've been promised the chef is first-rate—and drink their hearts out and recapture their youth in shipboard flirtations. But we also want them to come away injected with a healthy dose of culture so they'll realize that culture and the arts . . . represented locally by Aurelia College . . . depend on their continued support. That's where you come in. Stanforth of Columbia will do the pedantic gig—he's the Wordsworth scholar, but he'll do the other guys for us as well. You'd just be yourself, the renowned Hugo Henry, standing before them in person, sharing a few secrets about the novelist's creative process. We pick up the tab, of course, all travel and accommodation paid. Deluxe cabin for two, for you and the lovely Alice. A second honeymoon. Wish Susie and I could go but I have to stay behind and supervise the Elderhostel program on campus."

Sharing a few secrets about the novelist's creative process, thought Hugo bitterly. Cabin for two . . . second honeymoon. When my fiction-making muscle's gone impotent and my wife and I don't even sleep in the same room anymore.

"I'm flattered," he told Ray Johnson, staring fixedly down at the faxed proofs. No matter what part of the world our ancestors came from, we all share a common literary heritage in the British Isles. . . . "Please tell President Harris that I'm very honored that he thought of me. But I'm not sure if Alice . . . she isn't completely . . . I would have to ask Alice. . . ."

He would put the burden of his refusal on her. She owed him that much. He had no intention of being a part of any "literary cruise" for affluent illiterates, even if he miffed "Gresh" and had to sell pencils on the street next year. In his present circumstances, such a travesty of a journey promised only further variations of failure and pain. Alice wouldn't mind being his nay-sayer. She said no to so much else to do with him these days.

"Well, of course you do!" crowed the chairman, rolling up the proofs with the dispatch of one who had gotten what he came for. "*All* us married blokes have to ask the boss. Even Gresh admits he is run by Leora."

"I'm getting . . ." Magda rolled her eyes at Alice in exasperation, dropping her voice to a whisper on the last word. It sounded like "unnerved."

"You're getting what, Magda?" Alice had learned it was better to ask her to repeat, even at the risk of Magda's ire, rather than pretend she heard and then be mistaken. Magda hated that even more.

"A *nurse*. She's coming tomorrow. Or, no, the bed is coming tomorrow, then the nurse is coming after that. Every *morning*!"

"But that will be a great help, won't it?"

"For *Francis*. Not for me."

"But why not?"

"I do my best work in the morning . . . mind is clearer. She'll bustle her self-important ass around . . . interfere. I'm in the midst of my Final *Examination*, for Pete's sake. Not that *he* cares. All he cares about is washing the fucking sheets and replenishing my liquid nourishment. Who the fuck needs *liquid* nourishment?"

Her breath wasn't the only thing that was growing fouler.

". . . If you'll pardon my French," added Magda, who often showed an uncanny ability to read your thoughts. She grinned her yellow grin and reached a wasted hand across the counterpane to clasp Alice's, like a naughty child wanting to be forgiven. She squeezed Alice's hand. "I have a question for you."

"Yes, Magda?"

"Do you know why Blake died singing?"

"No, why?"

Magda cackled triumphantly. "Don't ask me. That's what I'm trying . . ." Then her face twisted into a expression of angry disgust. "Oh, get out. Get *out*!"

"But what—"

"Get out. Get my husband. Do as you're told. Get the hell out!"

Stunned, Alice fled downstairs.

She found Francis in the kitchen, placidly spreading cream cheese on dark bread. The crusts he had cut off lay in a neat pile on the counter.

"Magda wants you. I seem to have upset her. We were talking and she suddenly got very distressed and ordered me out."

Francis put down the knife at once. "Oh, dear, I think I know. . . ."

He was already brushing past her in the narrow kitchen. She heard his swift, light sprint up the stairs. She wasn't certain what she should do. Mortified by Magda's sudden animosity, Alice was strongly tempted simply to slip out of the house and be gone from here. Francis hadn't even looked at her when he brushed past her to go upstairs. Was she making a nuisance of herself, coming over here so much? Perhaps her desire to be with them was a ghoulish self-indulgence, having nothing to do with friendship or charity.

From above came sounds of Magda's angry expostulations, fol-

lowed by repetitive soothings from Francis. To the right of the sink
Alice spotted a notepad with a grocery list dashed off in the small,
scatty, elliptical script she recognized from Francis's postcript to
Magda's sympathy letter after they'd lost the baby. Upstairs, the toilet flushed. There was a pencil attached with string to the grocery
pad. Alice was about to tear off a page and leave a note explaining
she'd thought it best to go, when Francis reappeared with an armful
of bed linens.

"Alice, I may need your help in a few minutes. Magda's had a
little mishap. This is something we were told to expect, but it's very
upsetting to her when it happens."

The smell coming from the bundle in Francis's embrace left no
doubt about the nature of the mishap.

"What can I do?"

"I may need your help in lifting her when I remake the bed. I
hurt her just now. It really takes two people. Unless you're trained at
this—oh, I'll be so glad when that nurse comes. Though it will only
be for four hours every morning."

"Do you need help with those sheets?"

"Oh, no, no." He seemed appalled at the question. "Just . . . if
you would go upstairs and wait nearby while I load these into the
machine. If she calls out or sounds distressed, would you come to the
basement and get me? But don't go in the room yet. Go into the little
room next door, it's the one opposite the bathroom. You can hear her
from there, it's where I sleep now. I've got her cleaned up and covered
with a blanket, but she would want to have a gown on before we try
to move her again, and her other good gown's still in the dryer downstairs. She's so fastidious about her dignity. She was afraid she had repelled you."

"But I didn't even know anything had happened. She must have
ordered me out the moment she realized—"

"That's exactly what I told her," said Francis, a delighted smile
breaking suddenly over his drawn face. Then he opened a door and
clumped down basement steps with his armload, and Alice went quietly back upstairs, hurting for Magda and deeply ashamed of her own
mistaken supersensitivity.

She entered the little room across from the bathroom. It was long and narrow, with a single window at the end. Even though he had instructed her to wait there, she felt shy about crossing the threshold. This was where he slept now. That must mean they had slept together until Magda's illness.

There was just space enough for a single bed and a spindly-legged bedside table, a chest of drawers and a straight-backed chair. Clearly he hadn't been expecting visitors. Damp jeans hung from their muddy knees over the chairback; a rumpled blue cotton shirt, one she recalled from several previous visits, shared the seat with a balled-up wad of underwear. White socks were slung over the cross-bar of the chair, and an array of boots, shoes, and a pair of house slippers walked in different directions on the wide painted floorboards. The bed was neatly made, with one of those old white cotton bedspreads with a raised pattern.

On the table there was a small digital clock, a notecard in Francis's scatty handwriting listing times for Magda's dosages. One was for three o'clock in the morning. There was a single book: *Clinical Care of the Terminal Cancer Patient*, stamped *property of Catskill Hospital Medical Library*, with a marker halfway through it.

Alice stood unmoving in the middle of the little room. Raindrops made soft plops on the dense leaves of a massive gray-barked shade tree whose nearest branches all but touched the window. Occasional growly protests were audible from Magda's room next door, but none of them sounded distressed enough to warrant fetching Francis from his chores in the basement.

Alice's tenderest sympathy went out to Magda's loving husband as she pictured him lying in this narrow bed at night, studiously paging his way through the ominous textbook borrowed from the hospital library, alert to every utterance coming from the room next door. ("I'm hardly a separate person anymore.")

But it was the intimate proximity of his damp, cast-off clothes, and all those shoes—muddy work boots, worn sneakers, cordovan Rockports, the old pair of backless brown slippers—walking in their separate, mateless directions on the bare floorboards as though they were lost, that suddenly and convulsively gripped her heart.

CHAPTER X

INTERDEPARTMENTAL MEMO
FROM: H. Rodney Darling, Associate Professor of English
TO: Ray Johnson, Chairman

Why don't we just go with Magda's old syllabus and the course description she herself wrote for the catalog? After all, it was her creation. To be frank, I've never been exactly certain what "visionary" studies are, but Virgil, Dante, and Milton—and to some extent Blake— are certainly known quantities and I'll be happy to pitch in and do my share in the interests of team spirit. Though as a rational eighteenth-century man, I can't promise to deliver her degree of excitement about them.

INTERDEPARTMENTAL MEMO
FROM: Morton Blum, Jacob D. Vanderkill Professor of English
TO: Ray Johnson, Chairman

Why should any strong work be called more "visionary" than another strong work? What criteria are we using when we accept a poet's pet trope as spiritual evidence? What is the distinction between spiritual evidence and transcendental self-deception? Why the Bible and not Beckett? Why Blake and not Wallace Stevens? Why not just "Western Literature from the Old Testament to Samuel Beckett" as our catalog rubric, which leaves each of us free to perform his own pet softshoe dance when his turn comes to wear Magda Danvers's hat, not that any of us will ever be able to match that colorful lady's plumage? (Could it not be that her *performance* was *her* pet trope?) I know these cavils of mine contradict in essence the whole idea of "Visionary Studies," or an endowed chair for them at Aurelia College, but there it is. Or there I am. I'm perfectly content to be the Jacob D. Vanderkill Professor of English here in these lovely Catskills; why shouldn't someone else be equally as happy to come here as the Magda Danvers Professor of English?

INTERDEPARTMENTAL MEMO
FROM: Gennifer Fagen, Assistant Professor of English
TO: Ray Johnson, Chairman

Sorry, Ray, here I go again, but there is not a single work on Magda Danvers's reading list written by anyone other than a dead white Western male, unless you count Augustine (on the supplementary list) and most people think of him as white. I know Magda was a wonderful personality and brought glory to the college, and I'm sorry she's got cancer and is going to die, but I really think her elitist position is extinct as the great auk. Let's get some *women* on this list! Let's get some Afro-Americans and Native Americans and some Buddhists (I should think Buddhists would be *very* visionary!) and some Arabs. Sure, keep the Bible, but have the Koran and the Kabballa (sp.?, sorry, I've still got forty more freshmen rhetoric final themes on my desk to grade, or I'd look it up). And what about the Indians and the Chinese and the Japanese? Confucius and Tao and some Hindu writing—surely *they* are visionary? I mean, visions are the property of the whole human

race, not just a small exclusive stag party of Western male suprema-
cists.

P.S. And while I'm on the subject, Ray, I have to say I really resent it
when you address us all as "guys" in your interdepartmental memos.
Let's have some equal time here, please! How's about if I start addressing all of *you* as "gals" for a change?

INTERDEPARTMENTAL MEMO
FROM: Anthony Ramirez-Suarez, Professor of English
TO: Ray Johnson, Chairman

Dear Ray, how sad that we are losing our enchanting Magda. I will never
forget the fascinating class of hers in which I participated last October
when she asked me to read parts from Juan de la Cruz's *Noche Obscura*
and *Ascent of Mount Carmel* in my Castilian Spanish. She was very flattering about my somewhat rusty performance—I have not spoken the
language with anyone since my mother died—and her students seemed
captivated by her presentation of the material: Juan de la Cruz came
alive in that hour: the handsome, swarthy head, the tiny body, his abso-
lute imperviousness to Santa Teresa's emotional charms! Why, you could
practically hear the swish of their horses' tails as they rode around Spain
together founding covents and monasteries! A most *empathetic* teacher,
her peer will be difficult to find. Meanwhile, I will certainly do my part
in filling the great gap she leaves behind. Not only will I be glad to read
Juan de la Cruz in my rusty Castilian again, but I will even recite Dante
in the original. (I became quite proficient in spoken Italian during my
Fulbright year in Rome.) Regarding the syllabus, my feelings are, why
shouldn't we honor her by keeping it "as is," as well as the course description she herself wrote when she first came among us? That is, let us
keep it so for the time being, until the first Magda Danvers Professor of
Visionary Studies is appointed. That would be my respectful suggestion.

"Francis, would you read me that letter again?"

"Which letter, Magda?"

"From that girl. That pest we won't let come here. *You* know.
The one who's doing her thesis on me."

"Mira Dooley?"

"No, she changed her name. It's something else now. Something more glamorous."

"I don't think so, love. I think you may have confused her with . . . with someone else."

"Have it your way, Mr. Obtuse, but I know what I know. I know because her new name has the same initials as my name."

"Well, but . . . so does Mira Dooley, doesn't it?"

"Oh, *crap*, Francis, stop trying to *win* every time we have the simplest exchange, and—"

"I'm not trying to win anything, Magda. All I want is—"

"All *I* fucking want is for you to bring me that letter so I can fucking answer it!"

"Please, Magda, the nurse is on her way up. You don't want her to hear you talking like that, do you?"

"That's all I need. Big Broad-butt hustling around, preventing me from doing my work. Crap, crap, *crap*!"

"Magda, love, please—good morning, Diane."

"Good morning, Mr. Lake. What kind of night did we have?"

"Well, it was—"

"I'm still alive over here, Diane. I can answer for myself. Francis, for the last time: go get that letter."

"Good morning, Mrs. Lake. I'm glad to see you're feeling perky."

"I'm glad you're glad, Diane, but I'm not Mrs. Lake. You may call me Magda. A first name will be more than enough at this stage. Where I'm headed, I won't need any name at all."

"No problem, Magda. Would you like me to raise your bed?"

"Yes, please. My husband's just off to fetch a letter I mustn't delay answering any longer. A young scholar doing her dissertation on me."

"That's nice. Can you just raise up a little, Magda, and I'll plump up your pillows."

"At least you're not rough. *He's* so rough. Even if you do interrupt my work."

"I'm sure Mr. Lake doesn't mean to be rough. He's very devoted to you."

"Oh, yes, devoted. Here comes the devoted Mr. Lake. Is that the letter, Francis?"

"Yes, Magda."

"Well, dummy, haven't you forgotten something?"

"What have I forgotten now, Magda?"

"When people are going to answer a letter, they generally need pen and paper. . . ."

"Oh, Magda—"

"Oh-Magda what?"

"Magda, you know you haven't been able to read anything, much less write anything, for many weeks now. You're very ill."

"Why do you *cross* me, Francis? And Hustle-butt here was just saying what a good husband you were. Boy, I could tell her a few things. What are you two whispering about over there?"

"I'll . . . get you the pen and paper, love."

"Well, there's no need to cry about it. You tell me to watch my language in front of the nurse and then you go and *cry* in front of her."

Dear Mira Dooley, of Ann Arbor, Michigan, for some time I have had your latest request for that hour with me that would be of inestimable value to your thesis. It perches now, your entreaty, atop the shifting calms and swells of my death journey, implacably riding the bedclothes kept sweetly fresh by my long-suffering husband (though now assisted by a part-time nurse). If you should ever find yourself in my predicament, you couldn't do better than to have secured for yourself—preferably some years before so he will have come to know your every need—a good husband like mine.

However, getting yourself the right husband to see you through such an unlikely event as your own death (when I was your age, or the age I assume you are, based on the earnest, striving tone of your letters, my personal death was unimaginable) is probably the last thing on your mind. Or maybe you already have a husband, maybe Dooley is your husband's, not your father's, name. Perhaps both of you are graduate students, divvying up the dreary space of some rented domicile for your respective scholarly pursuits, and, I hope, finding some unscholarly delight in snuggling up against each other at night. There is a great deal of creaturely comfort to be derived from proximity to a body your body happens to like.

I wander, as I do quite a bit now. As my agenda detaches itself from its old goal-oriented leash, my interest tends, like the wind of the Spirit, to blow where it listeth. . . .

So.

Having recently downed one of my little purple "pain management" pills, I have a limited time to flash my diminishing light your way.

First of all, Mary? Minerva?—he wouldn't tell me what you changed your name to—it's too late in the game for me to be able to read "sample chapters" from your thesis, *The Scripture of Magda Danvers: The Role of Poet as Prophet*. I can't retain blocks of prose anymore. (I do hope you have chosen the word "scripture" with exactitude and haven't just snatched at the titillation angle. I'll make a confession: in the light of its quarter century of public exposure, I admit I would now think twice about calling *my* thesis *The Book of Hell*. Irresistible as it was to me at the time, for its irony, its flashy little war cry of rebellion, it has resulted in many a misguided preconception.)

I don't know what questions would have been on your list for that "*brief* and *to the point*" interview we are not going to have, the interview which you say would have been of inestimable value to you. But here are some snippets of inestimable value to me as I lie here constructing a little obituary of my soul history. Soul history as opposed to case history. The *sub specie aeternitatis* version rather than the *Who's Who Down Here* version. Do you know the difference yet, Mira-Minerva?

I was foremost a teacher, a tracker of people with vision. Up until a few months ago, I could lead small expeditions of impressionable young minds to the interesting stuff. I was not myself a visionary, or a poet or prophet, or even much of a public personality except for my two or three years in demand on the academic lecture circuit before the hoopla surrounding *Book of Hell* wore off.

My best ideas of recent years have been delivered orally and peripatetically, hoofing it up and down classrooms and letting the day's testament—wherever I was at the moment in relation to my heroes—spout forth from my lips. All unrecorded, except, of course, whatever synoptic traces found their way into my students' notebooks. (You might want to keep this in mind, should you reconsider your use of that word "scripture," whose original meaning, after all, is simply "anything written.")

Although *The Book of Hell: An Introduction to the Visionary Mode* has become a useful primer—perhaps the best little summary of its kind (she murmured modestly)—my true work, my maturing work, that grew as I grew (this is something I've only recently figured out for myself as I lie here taking my Final Exam), the work that will go unrecorded in dissertations and theses like yours, has been in the line of *arousing*. I have been successful, theatrically successful, if I may say so, in infecting receptive young minds with a desire for wholeness. (I sometimes think this is what initially attracted my husband to me, though he has never said so himself.)

I have shown them some pointers toward the wholeness, led them on day-trips toward it, but I haven't provided the wholeness myself. That is art's purpose. It may be the only way we can get what we strive for in this life. The human condition is notorious for its lack of wholeness.

So I was basically an arouser, not a fulfiller. It gives me comfort to have figured this out about myself at last. For years I fretted about not fulfilling my quota. I asked myself the same question others did, the question you no doubt would have slipped in tactfully at some point in your interview. You know: What happened to Magda Danvers? She had such a brilliant start, then fizzled out. Why did she not just buckle down, put her nose to the grindstone (fill in your own cliché), and complete her promised sequel, *Of the Devil's Party: A Re-Visioning*, alluring tidbits of which appeared from time to time in the proper quarterlies?

The source of my sequel title was Blake's *Marriage of Heaven and Hell*, in which, I am sure you know—I certainly harped on it enough in my book—"Devils" are the original geniuses, those who are familiars in the "Hell" of the subconscious, which is the source of all energy. The "Devils" are contrasted to the "Angels," who, in

Blake's mythology, are the restricting spirits of conventionality. According to Blake, all true geniuses were "of the Devil's party," though some of them, like Milton, were unaware of it. Others, like Jesus, Blake believed, were perfectly aware of it. Blake, for that matter, was aware of it about himself.

Of the Devil's Party was going to be the amplification of my youthful opus, an inclusive stretching-forth of my thesis. But I slowly came to realize as I got less youthful (I realized it also by the way my energy flagged each summer when there were no teaching duties to come between me and the writing of it) that even if I should finally finish it one day, it would be only a restatement of what others—the mighty Northrop Frye, primarily; some of the Jungian analysts with a literary bent: Marie-Louise von Franz . . . Barbara Hannah . . . June Singer, to name the best—had set forth. Now, that's a dangerous thing for a scholar to realize. Just as well for the grinding presses of academia that not many of them ever achieve such humility!

On the other hand, think of poor Mr. Casaubon in *Middlemarch*. If he had realized his *Key to All Mythologies* would add nothing to the world's enlightenment, might he have relaxed a little on his Roman honeymoon and learned to delight in his young bride?

Poor Casaubon. I have been there. I have *been* Edward Casaubon, except I knew better than he how to delight in my young spouse. All those summers in interesting places, and Francis and I would have breakfast in our pension or hotel, and then I'd watch him meander off down some winding cobbled street in his fresh clothes, foreign sunshine in his floppy hair, and off I'd go to my dusty library or museum to "tie in" mandorlas in old mosaics with symbols of apotheosis in the writings of Virgil and the Acts of the Apostles, or some such project, so I'd have material to crank out another chapter to send off to the journals and keep the publish-or-perish policemen away from my office door a little while longer.

My husband's hair, when he was younger, was a gossamer reddish gold. It flopped when he walked. Well, it still flops, but the ethereal glow has gone out of it. When he sauntered off into those foreign mornings, with that light, swinging gait of his that proclaimed he had nothing ahead of him but serendipitous discoveries, he looked like a cross between a gigolo and an archangel. As I watched him disappear around a corner, his vanished loveliness would catch in my throat and I'd feel as if I'd somehow bewitched him into staying with me and wonder if this might be the day he'd come to his senses and simply not return.

But there he'd be back again every evening, and by the middle of dinner my amazement that he actually seemed to have missed me more than I missed him had worn off. Even though I was starting to realize I had nothing new to add to the world's enlightenment by way of a sequel to *The Book of Hell*, that didn't mean I wasn't carried away by my research during the course of a day. I *loved* finding out things, making the connections, jotting down notes to whet my students' appetites. ("Now, if you ever get to Santa Maria Maggiore in Rome, you'll want to compare for yourself the mosaics of *Abraham and the Three Angels* and *The Stoning of Moses*. In Abraham, the mandorla represents the aura of holiness, in Moses, it serves as a protective shield. . . .")

But I digress, what was I . . . ? Oh, it was about Francis's glow I was telling, his weightless hair, his supple body in light shirt and trousers disappearing around the corner of a cobbled street, his aura of loveliness . . . did I once confuse it with holiness? Possibly. Who was it, St. Anselm, I think, who carefully listed the qualities of the transfigured bodies of the elect? Let's see: beauty, agility, strength, penetrability . . . now, that's a peculiar one . . . penetrability and . . . there were seven in all . . . sorry, Mira, my purple-pill agility is fading, time to pack up your tape recorder and return to Ann Arbor.

My Francis would sit across the table from me at dinner, rambling on about his serendipitous findings of the day. Everything pleased him. His lack of discrimination, of method or *plan* in his evening recitations, used first to relax me, then bore me, and finally exasperate me. How could I be married to such a simpleminded man? Then later, when we were cuddled up in bed—neither of us could have made it into the sexual Olympics, but over the years, Mira, we took solace in each other's bodies, and right up until my recent illness, we have kept going between us an amazingly consistent flow of mutual creaturely appreciation—I'd repent and ask myself wasn't I just jealous of his freedom? *He* had no sequel to write, he had no career agenda. He could wander at will, delighting in whatever he came across, without having to *account* for it. Perhaps it was sheer spitefulness on my part that made me suggest he ought to take his misericords seriously. They were the nearest thing he had to an interest outside of my welfare. Search them out and make a project of them, I suggested. Get out of the sunshine and lie bunched up in strange positions in the shadows between choir stalls and photograph the little carvings under the seats. Label them. Categorize them. Cross-reference them. Maybe eventually publish a monograph about them! (How's that for curbing a sweet fellow's serendipitous nature?)

Go find the misericords, my love.

Hang on ... I've got all seven:

Beauty
Agility
Strength
Penetrability
Health
Delight
Perpetuity

The seven qualities of the transfigured bodies of the elect.

How about that, Mira-Minerva? The Gargoyle hasn't *quite* chewed up my memory and spat it out. May you perform as well on your Final Examination.

May 9, 1991
Dear Ms. Dooley,
My wife, Magda Danvers, has asked me to reply to your recent letter. I'm afraid an interview would be out of the question at this stage.
She also asks me to tell you that she regrets she will not be able to read sample chapters of your thesis. Due to the medications prescribed for her pain, she now tires very quickly, and needs to save what energy is left to her for her own work.
She says if you are in the final months of completing your thesis, you will no doubt be familiar with her three published chapters of *Of the Devil's Party: A Re-Visioning*, the proposed sequel

to *The Book of Hell: An Introduction to the Visionary Mode*, and that those chapters should be of help in your overall assessment of her work. (Chapter I, "*Discrezione* and the Ordering of Loves in Dante's *Divine Comedy*" can be found in *MLQ* 31 (1970); Chapter II, "Blake's *Four Zoas* as Mimesis for the Poet's Struggle for Wholeness," appeared in *PMLA* 91 (1976); and Chapter III, "Discernment of Symbols and Imaginative Truth," appeared in *Kenyon Review*, Spring 1980. Though parts of Chapter IV, "The Drama of the Soul's Choice in Visionary Art," exist in draft form, that chapter is unlikely to be completed.)

I join my wife in wishing you all best success with *The Scripture of Magda Danvers: The Role of Poet as Prophet*. I hope you will send us a copy when it is finished.

Sincerely yours,
Francis Lake

CHAPTER XI

"Will you lift up his body with these bare hands and lower it with me?"

The tall, red-haired Antigone in the college production stalked menacingly toward Ismene. As she stretched out her hands and flexed her fingers at the smaller, mousy actress, her purple-and-gold draperies parted at the shoulders, baring rock-solid pectorals. She probably pumped hours to get those on the Nautilus over in the Dave E. Lowe Gym and is very proud of herself, thought Hugo, who was put off by the Amazon look cultivated by many females nowadays. He was sitting dutifully in the audience of the Marvin C. Buttermore Auditorium along with the rest of his colleagues. Aurelia faculty members were expected to turn out for student productions. President Harris and his wife, that overgroomed Barbie doll couple, sat two rows ahead. The president's fastidiously barbered neck was in Hugo's direct line of vision, and as the stage action shifted from left to right and back again, "Gresh" and Leora's two pert heads swiveled, tennis-match style, to follow it, setting a good example for all. The smug ambience of the college roused Hugo's ire more than usual tonight. He had just renewed his contract with Aurelia and felt trapped in its bountiful second-rate hamlet, unable to begin serious work on the reversal of his crumbling destiny for another year.

Alice was beside him. Tonight they were making their first public appearance as a couple since the death of the baby.

Ismene, pleading rules and regulations, shrank away from her muscular sister's invitation to bury their brother and embarked on a recitation of their dire family history to date. Our father, reputation in ruins, gouges out eyes; his mother and wife, both in one, hangs self; our two brothers dead in a single day. Oh boy, the Greeks. The girl playing Ismene was as tepid as the red-haired Antigone was overwrought. Furtively Hugo squinted down at his program. "Following the Ancient Greek custom, tonight's production will be continuous, with no intermission." Oh Christ, how long *was Antigone*? In the old days, when he was still sure of Alice's regard, he would have leaned over without hesitation and whispered, "Hey, honey, how long is this thing, anyway?"

But that was the old days. Now such an act would simply earn another check mark next to one of her staple grievances against him. Too impatient and too critical of others. Too quick to reject things out of hand and fly off the handle. Too tense. He was altogether too much. He was too much *himself*, that was really the problem, wasn't it? If you didn't love someone anymore, his besetting characteristic became faults, right?

What was going to become of them he couldn't imagine. His son Cal accused him of imagining ahead of time what everybody's life was going to be like and leaving no room for alternative realities. Well, this time he was truly stymied. He couldn't begin to imagine his and Alice's future. If they were to have one together.

He didn't even know where they'd be living in a month. Their landlady was returning at the end of June from her Roman sabbatical. Ray Johnson had left a list in his office mailbox of new sabbatical rentals coming up, but living in someone else's house was not an experience he cared to repeat ever again if he could help it. Spirits of absent owners became part of the air you breathed. This year his and Alice's air had been infiltrated by the barren, ungenerous, old-maidy molecules of Sonia Wynkoop. Could some measure of their problems be ascribed to her influence?

A possible idea for a story? Newly married couple, much in love, rents house of a cold-blooded spinster. Take out plot complication of wife expecting child, also remove the action from an academic setting, many people were put off by academic settings. Just concentrate on the ... *haunting*, as good a word as any.

The Haunting of the Harpers. Hell, people *were* haunted, even in these times. Maybe more than ever in these times. Modern life contained a whole spook show of specters out to sap your soul: miasmas in the air you breathed, the water you drank; alien counterpoints in the background noise, in the emotions of all the people who bumped against you during the course of a day; the corrosive influences of advertising—hell, you couldn't open a magazine anymore without being assaulted by ten perfumes; the deadweight of too much information crowding in on you faster than you could process it ... no wonder the average person was deranged.

But the twist would be, this newly married couple, much in love, decides to flee all the miasmas of modern life in a city, take a year off, and go somewhere quiet and simple. (Why? So the husband could write a novel? Hell no, stay away from that!) Anyway, for whatever reason, to be thought up later, they rent an isolated house for a year to escape modern miasmas and find themselves neck-deep in a sinister, *old-fashioned haunting* that threatens to destroy their marriage. (Will it? Won't it? The story as it comes to be written will decide that.) Of course, the old spinster's personality, as it reveals itself through her haunting of the couple, is a grab bag full of all the things that kill a marriage. *That* will be where the art comes in.

Thus Hugo occupied himself with this possible story—the first idea to arouse him since his ill-fated birthday attempt to actually write the story about the father visiting his son—until the entrance of the old men of Thebes. Three youths in white robes and stuck-on beards sidled across stage in white socks and Birkenstock sandals, thumping their canes in unison and hitting you broadside with more Information Necessary to the Plot. The shameless Greeks, blissfully ignoring the whole "show, not tell" maxim which had been pummeled into his own generation of writers.

He stole a look at Alice, who seemed completely wrapped up in the play. It had come to that: he now "stole" looks at his wife, for fear of intruding on her space.

She had talked him into going on the Twenty-fifth Anniversary Literary Heritage Alumni Cruise in late August.

"Wouldn't it be the political thing, Hugo? I mean, since we *are* going to be staying at Aurelia for another year?"

"Who wants to waste valuable writing time preparing lectures for a bunch of illiterate hucksters on a boat?"

"Well, but"—he knew she was thinking, *but you aren't writing anything now,* but wouldn't say it; that wasn't Alice's "ladylike" method of attack—"didn't Ray Johnson say all you had to do was talk about how you write your novels?"

" 'Share a few secrets about the novelist's creative process,' was his highly original way of putting it. As if I had any secrets to share."

"Well, but perhaps the experience might give you an idea for a—"

"The good old timeless theme, huh? The ship as agency of change and destiny, the voyage as crucible for all our disparate little yearnings to knock around together in until they form new patterns and alliances. More than one writer has been lured out into *that* treacherous ocean, my dear. Katherine Anne Porter would have done better to have stuck to her Texas short stories."

"I didn't mean necessarily write about a *ship,* Hugo—" He had watched her struggle to suppress her impatience with him (bad old Hugo, finishing her sentences for her in order to inject his negative scenarios) so she could pursue her point—which was, of course, getting him out of her sight on any occasion that she could manage. With such phrases had she nudged him off on the USIA trip back in April.

Out of pure spite then, he had dipped her a gallant Rhett Butler bow, and said in the Southern-gent voice she used to claim she loved, "Well, come go with me." By God, he'd flush her out of her ladylike blind.

"Oh, I—no, Hugo, I'm not—I've never been much for the ocean. Once Father took Andy and me out deep-sea fishing on a charter boat. It was supposed to be a big treat, but I spent the whole time throwing up over the side. Father said I was a poor excuse for a Norwegian. Whereas Andy reveled in it—"

"Ray Johnson said the *Galatea* travels at night, when the passengers are asleep. People don't get seasick when they're lying down. And daytimes, we're going to be in port, sight-seeing. Also, there are these very good patches you can get for seasickness." He said this to goad her. At this point he knew he was going to give in and go on the cruise, make Ray Johnson and "Gresh" happy, smooth his path as writer-in-residence for the coming year; and having decided to go, he knew it would be better for him to go alone. Given the present state of their union, it would be downright masochistic on his part to put it to the test of that shared cabin, deluxe or otherwise.

But he hadn't been able to resist rubbing her nose in how bad things were between them. It would give him satisfaction to make her abandon that distant gracious-lady stance, force her to wail flat out, with a disappointment to match his own: "Oh, Hugo, in the shape we're in, how can we possibly share a cabin?"

But she only lowered her eyes and repeated in that resolutely amicable, quiet voice, "No, Hugo, I really think—I think it would be best if I stay here and get us settled into our new house, or apartment, or whatever it will be. Really, I'd prefer it, getting us organized for the coming academic year. When you come back, ready to write, I'll have everything unpacked and set up. Your books on the shelves, my spices on their rack . . ."

"What the hell about *your* books? I seem to recall you've got thirty-two boxes of your own. That's more than I have. What is this spice-shelf shit? Is it meant to be some kind of message to me that I've shrunk you down to a mere modest housewife?"

"Hugo, please don't pick a fight." Turning her face away on that aloof long neck, a gesture that used to intrigue him but had come to exasperate him, as her ladylike ways, which he used to admire, had come to infuriate him. They used to talk for *hours* about *everything*. But now whenever he dared to probe their present sorry state of affairs, the thing that ought to be the most pressing topic of conversation for them both, it was "picking a fight."

"And I really couldn't think of going off anywhere while Magda's over there dying. Going to see Magda has become very important to me."

"I know it has." He couldn't resist a final goad. "But she'll be scattered to the wind long before August rolls around."

"Yes, but"—still the resolutely quiet and amicable voice, the lowered eyes—"it just wouldn't feel right, saying yes to go on a cruise when she's still alive."

Next day, he'd told Ray he'd do the cruise, but that Alice preferred staying home, putting their new domicile in order. When they found one.

"Well, you can still have the deluxe cabin for yourself," Ray said. "That was part of our deal."

"Why don't you give it to some deserving PBD and spouse? I'll be perfectly happy with a single, as long as it's not down in steerage." He did not relish the mockery of that deluxe cabin for two. Besides, he thought, not without some self-pity, ultimately each of us travels alone.

"There *is* no steerage on the *Galatea*." Ray Johnson chuckled. "But that certainly is showing team spirit, Hugo."

He bitterly glimpsed a possible future (the only possible one?) for them. Might their marriage still warm itself from some embers of fellow feeling if he managed to stay gone most of the time? If he became one of those sad gig writers, always on the road, swaggering from one podium to the next to read from novels published years ago. Consoling himself with groupies afterward.

Perhaps that was one reason he had said yes so fast to the phone call from that lady, Mrs. McCandless, on the library board in Calhoun, S.C., asking him to be the keynote speaker at the dedication of the library's new building in early June. "We know you must be in constant demand, Mr. Henry, and we can't even pay much of an honorarium, but I got up my nerve and called anyway because it would be such a special thing for us all down here. Because you do belong to us, you know. Why, you're our claim to fame." All the right words and nuances, spoken in exactly the right voice. Though he'd never set eyes on her, he knew this Mrs. McCandless from her frosted hair tips and twenty-four-inch single strand of pearls down to her long narrow black shiny pumps. If he'd met her prototype on the streets of Calhoun forty years ago, she would have looked right through him because he *didn't* belong. Yet he hadn't been able to ignore his rising elation as her soft-consonanted contralto flattery trickled into his telephone ear. That drunken mill hand Wayne Henry's son was being begged to come to their exclusive dance at last.

For his fiftieth birthday last week, Alice had taken him to a French country restaurant on the other side of the river. Made the reservation days ahead and neatly written down the travel directions given to her over the phone by the proprietor. She had driven them there in the early-evening light, though he was the one who customarily drove. She didn't know why, she said, but today she felt in the mood to drive, and he had tried not to read anything ominous into this innocently expressed wish. He sat docilely strapped into the passenger seat, holding the little piece of paper at arm's length so he could read her the directions when she called for them. A couple of times he jumped the gun, and even though it was his birthday, the exasperation slipped into her voice. "Not *yet*, Hugo."

Her sudden wish to drive them made him feel old. Well, he *was* old now, wasn't he? That had been his first thought when he woke on the morning of his birthday: now I am old. and he was going to get *older*. Whereas Alice was sixteen years younger than he and always would be. If they stayed together, the day would probably come when she had to drive him everywhere. You saw such couples every day: the ancient husband being peeled out of the car in some parking lot by his forbearing junior spouse, already a senior citizen herself; the frail old coot in the supermarket shuffling gratefully alongside wife and cart, happy as a child to be taken somewhere. "Can't we buy these hot sausages, Mother?" Hugo had recently heard a plaintive codger whine to his better half in the Grand Union. "Don't be ridiculous! They'd kill you in a minute," snarled the blue-haired dragon, snatching the packet out of his fingers.

His son Cal had sent a card with a warm message. (The picture on the card was Monet's *Cliffs near Dieppe*—had Cal and Laurence chosen it together? Were the rock-solid gray cliffs and the stony beach supposed to represent Hugo, being "softened up" by the surrounding atmospheric pinks and blues? The way they perceived he had "softened" after his visit to the beautiful loft?)

> Many happy returns, Dad, on this special birthday, and I do love you very much.

The friend with whom he had found happiness must have freed up Cal to say such things to his father. Cal's elegant friend, Hugo reflected with fresh confoundment each time it hit him again, was seven years *his own* senior. Laurence (spelled with a "u"; Harvard; Rhodes scholar; plus eight more lines of philanthropy and civic awards—Hugo had gone over to the Jack P. Fishman Library twice to brood upon his son's friend's *Who's Who* entry) was fifty-seven years old.

Rosemary, now married to Randall the developer, had sent Hugo a manila envelope from Hilton Head, stuffed with various goodies. The scrawled note inside one of her typical "funny" nonfunny birthday cards ("Congratulations! Now you're a geezer!") baited him in the grand old Rosemary style. "So glad you've at last put your seal of approval on Cal's way of life——it means the world to him." Wait just a damn minute here, thought Hugo, I haven't "put my seal of approval" on anything. I may have accepted the inevitable, but some aspects of it still turn my stomach. And wasn't that "at last" just pure Rosemary—signaling that she, the understanding parent, had been in on it much longer. There was also a cache of pamphlets and booklets from PFLAG, the organization for parents of gays which she'd just enthusiastically joined. ("Can We Understand?" "Why Is My Child Gay?" "About Our Children/Acerca de Nuestros Hijos/Au Sujet de Nos Enfants"/also in Chinese and Japanese.) "It's a wonderful organization," her upbeat-sadistic note went on, "you wouldn't believe how many nice people I've met at Hilton Head whose children are gay! Interestingly enough, most of the members in my group are the *mothers*."

If you have the choice about when to tell your parents, advised the little green-and-white booklet *Read This Before Coming Out to Your Parents,* "choose a time when they're not dealing with such matters as the death of a close friend, pending surgery or the loss of a job."

How about the loss of a parent's new child? Or the demise of a parent's creative powers? Or the death of a parent's new marriage? Though to be fair, Cal hadn't known about the latter two items.

O n the morning of his birthday, Hugo has awakened warily into birdsong in the downstairs bedroom where their dead son had been born, and where he had slept by himself since the day they returned from the cemetery. He first did a quick physical inventory on himself, as though turning fifty might have robbed him overnight of some sensory or motor capacity. No, everything seemed to be okay, he just didn't feel much like getting up, that was all. But he did get up, showered and shaved and made himself coffee and toast (it was before seven; Alice was still asleep) and closed himself back in the room where the dead child had been wrestled out of Alice while he watched. He removed the plastic hoods from his word processor and printer and turned on the current. Though his personal life might be falling to pieces, he was going to begin his fiftieth birthday by practicing his craft. He was a writer, wasn't he? If he'd been a farmer whose personal life was falling to pieces, he would have still gone out and plowed his fields, wouldn't he?

Ford Madox Ford had begun *The Good Soldier* on his fortieth birthday.

Hugo began describing the father riding up in the elevator to visit his only son. He had saved the idea so he'd be sure to have something to start on his birthday, novel or not. The father got out of the taxi and entered the elevator. First surprise: he'd expected a mess of off-putting graffiti; there was nary an obscenity or a single squiggle on its walls, which were clean and gray.

The father pressed button 3. There was no 2. Due to an anomaly of this converted warehouse, the son had explained on the telephone, you had to ride to the third floor and . . .

Hugo, suddenly losing all interest in the father, had found himself unable to go on. He had switched off the machine without saving anything, and gone out for a walk.

The boy playing the Sentry in *Antigone* was reporting the offstage action to Creon in an aggrieved Brooklyn accent: somebody had disobeyed Creon's edict and covered Polynices' body with a light cover of road dust, given it proper rights.

A snotty reviewer had once taken Hugo to task for too much narrative of past events—too much offstage action and not enough present "rendering." Said even Faulkner's writing would have benefited from more present action, and Hugo wasn't Faulkner. Also, continued the reviewer, warming to his demolition task, Hugo's present-time scenes were "too tenaciously sustained" for the modern reader used to living in "short, elliptical 'takes.' " Mr. Henry's scenes would profit greatly from the techniques of splicing, montage, cutting back and forth: "It's as if he's been totally uninfluenced by *film*," sanctimoniously whined the reviewer, whose name was Michael Murdoch. This was back in the early seventies, when the trendies were advocating that novels take on the characteristics of moving pictures or else bow to instant obsolescence.

Hugo had fantasized knocking on Murdoch's door (he knew he lived in the Village, it wouldn't be hard to find out where) and punching him out. Then a more fruitful idea struck him: the next time he had need of a despicable minor character, he would name him Michael Murdoch.

However, as his next novel (to be a stylish little send-up of a marriage of two cynical adulterers) began to emerge from the typewriter, Hugo caught himself working in a new way: cutting back and forth, leaving plenty of little white spaces between episodes, as many of his fashionable contemporaries had begun to do. There *was* something fulfilling about those chunks of white space: it got you through your page faster and at the same time gave you the illusion of having gone somewhere. Also, you were operating from a position of power: your *readers* had to supply the missing connections for themselves.

He also found himself breaking up his "tenaciously" lengthy scenes into sequences of shorter once, capable of bite-sized ingestion by the busy modern reader who lived in short, elliptical "takes."

And so, before "Michael Murdoch" as despicable character ever made his first appearance on a page, Hugo had ingested the real Michael Murdoch's aesthetics. When his cowardice dawned on him one morning, he abandoned the novel in disgust. It had begun to bore him anyway.

That had not been a good time for anybody. Rosemary had taken eleven-year-old Cal and departed for ocean breezes and summer dalliances with old boyfriends at her family's Myrtle Beach cottage. This was before her parents bought the condo at Hilton Head. He had sweated out the summer alone in their apartment on Riverside Drive, listening to the Watergate hearings and doing one of his moonlighting magazine pieces, for a lucrative fee, on high-class hookers. He dallied some himself, with "nice" girls, not the hookers he interviewed, though a few of them were quite classy.

One of his summer sleepovers stole some of Rosemary's jewelry, along with a considerable portion of Cal's obsessively treasured comic-book collection. That took some explaining. Rosemary, who had been far from an angel herself over the summer (and had taken her good jewelry with her) eventually forgave him. But Cal didn't. Probably still hadn't. ("And then, when I was eleven, one of my father's floozies slept over and stole my comics . . . all my old Marvel comics, can you believe it?" Lying next to the elegant dark man, old enough to be his father, with who knew which parts of their anatomies joined, spilling out grievances about his disappointing male parent.)

Antigone, dragged in by the Sentry, admitted her crime. Yes, she did it: she covered her dead brother with dust and gave him proper rights. Ismene tried to horn in on the credit. Creon ordered slaves to remove both women from the stage. The three old Birkenstock geezers thumped their canes in unison and gleefully predicted the ruin that had already been set in motion.

Am I embarked on my ruin, then? wondered Hugo, sneaking another look at Alice, whose raptness for this amateur production bordered on the catatonic. She hadn't moved since his last covert glance
her way.

Did *I* set it in motion? When? What unforgivable act or attitude
of mine first tripped the switch?

"—and one generation cannot free the next," gaily chanted the
geezers from Thebes.

Well, I can tell you one thing, thought Hugo, setting his jaw. I'm
sure as hell not going to do what everybody *else* is doing these days,
blame it on my folks. Though my old man . . . the unregenerate old
bully . . . God rest his cringing, cowardly soul . . . probably deserves
to take *some* of the rap.

A lice felt Hugo's belligerent stiffening beside her and, distracted
by it from the play, looked down at his hand in the act of
clenching the arm between their seats. Out of the side of her eye she
could see his jaw begin to work in that way that set her on edge. It
made him look like an old redneck gumming tobacco. But when she
angled her face away to remove him from her side glance, she
couldn't see all of the play. She put her hand up to the left side of her
face, making a blinker for herself to shut him out, awkward though
the gesture was. She abandoned it after a few minutes when she realized she had been concentrating so hard on blocking Hugo out of
her consciousness that she had missed everything that had transpired
on the stage.

Never lose your sense of judgment over a woman, Creon was exhorting his son Haemon. Spit her out like a mortal enemy.

Though she could hardly bear Hugo's clenching, belligerent,
jaw-grinding proximity, she felt she could follow some of his
thoughts and associations during the play. Another of marriage's little
paradoxes? She was sure that during Creon's exhortation to his son to
spurn his traitor-financée Antigone, Hugo was making remorseful
parallels to his own situation: if only *he* had been granted the luxury
of warning his son Cal off a *fiancée*!

This, in fact, would probably be one of their "coming together" things to talk about after the play. They worked hard to find them, unvolatile topics of conversation that could get them through time together without touching directly on the unhappiness of each with the other. They were both practically prostrate with unhappiness, though neither of them knew what to do about it. They were allies in their disillusionment over their marriage, if allies in nothing else.

Yes, best to rehash Cal's interesting situation some more. Poor Hugo: though she could see the poetic justice in the homophobe's discovery that his son was gay, she did feel sorry for him. He had been taken by surprise and brought low by it. It had hit him at a bad time, when so much else was going wrong for him. The least she could do was to read the PFLAG pamphlets with him and accompany him on the treadmill of why's and when's and how's.

After all, it wasn't as though his son was dead—or, worse, dead by his own hand, as Creon's son was going to be very soon. Cal actually was much friendlier since Hugo's milestone visit to the loft shared with the philanthropist. He phoned frequently now and, if she happened to answer, encouraged her to stay on the line. Their roles had reversed. The cold voice who used grudgingly to ask, "May I speak with my father?" and resist her attempts at drawing him out now seemed determined to win *her* over. As though, in the fullness of his own happiness, he was ready at last to grant her the right to be happy with his father.

But there were painful ironies, too. A surly Cal had greeted the news of their engagement with, "But she's only five years older than I am." A chilly but scrupulously polite Cal had graced their wedding reception at the Lotus Club on Hugo's stern orders, dutifully downed a single glass of champagne, and slunk off as soon as the cake was cut. Cal's response had been one of edgy forbearance when an ebullient Hugo, after the ultrasound, had informed him he would have a little brother. When the baby was born dead, Cal wrote them a prompt note of condolence which arrived in the same mail as Rosemary's. Later he sent them a second note, somewhat warmer, but still in the dutiful mode, in which he volunteered news about his satisfying work for a privately funded consortium of charities, and

announced he'd moved into a renovated warehouse with a friend connected with these charities.

But now that his own flagrant happiness was secured and out in
the open, both parents and stepparents submissively consuming their
shared publications and having dinner discussions about his sexual
orientation, he seemed magnanimously bent on hearing all the domestic details of their lives which would assure him that they were
as equally delighted with *their* partners as he was with his.

"What are you two having for dinner?" he would demand in his
new expansive voice when he phoned now. "Oh, hello, Alice, what
have you all been up to?" Or, "Where are the two of you going to
take your vacation this year? Laurence and I are going up to Wellfleet
for a couple of weeks. But we don't want to be away from here too
long, with the new shelter opening and all." He was surprised and
rather disapproving when he heard that Alice would not be accompanying Hugo on the Alumni Cruise in August. "But it sounds like exactly what you two need: a total change of scene, after what you've
both been through you need to get away *together*."

When he phoned Hugo on the morning of his fiftieth birthday,
he told his father that he certainly hoped they'd try to have another
child soon, because he thought he would make a wonderful big
brother, "especially since I won't be having any children of my own
now."

Creon gave orders for Antigone to be buried alive, and the actress, though overexcited in her delivery, launched into the
farewell speech that, for Alice, was the heart of the play. Antigone
proclaimed she would never have gone to so much trouble for a
husband, or even for the children of her own body, as she did for her
brother Polynices.

> A husband dead, there might have been another.
> A child by another too, if I had lost the first.
> But mother and father both lost in the halls of Death
> no brother could ever spring to light again.

Though the actress didn't do justice to the lines, Alice experienced them profoundly. It was a speech she had discovered for herself while reading *Antigone* during her first year at Princeton. The sentiments of these lines, though in another translation ("But, sire and mother buried in the grave,/ A brother is a branch that grows no more. . . .") seemed to have been written for someone with her exact situation in mind. After reading that speech of Antigone's, she had understood in a thoroughly conscious way where her own deepest family allegiance had lain. That was perhaps the first time the saving/healing powers of imaginative writing had struck her with the full force of personal application. Yes, she'd had a brother and with his branch lopped off she'd go on growing, but she'd never be the same tree. But the loyalty and the love were still there, alive as ever. She would be faithful to Andy's memory, try to incorporate his excellence, all those wonderful qualities lost to the world now, into her own being. And this resolution of hers, inspired by some lines in a play written in 441 B.C., gave her new energy and a larger-than-personal kind of mission that went a long way toward subsuming her grief.

But then there was the later time, after Aunt Charlotte's disturbing family revelations, when these remembered lines in Antigone's farewell speech caused pain and bitterness and an *emptier* feeling of loss than ever before.

"My sister would have wanted you to know, I feel sure of that," said Aunt Charlotte, sitting across from Alice over one of their inveterate frozen dinners. It was the summer between Alice's freshman and sophomore year in college. They had sold her parents' house and she was sharing her aunt's Hartford apartment.

Aunt Charlotte dropped her bomb. "You were my sister's only birth child."

"What do you mean, Aunt Charlotte?"

She knew already from the way her guardian was watching her that she was about to hear news that would rob her of something precious. Aunt Charlotte had the zealot's gleam in her eyes as she prepared to Do Her Duty.

"Andy was adopted. Hazel and Paul adopted a little infant boy because they didn't think they could have any children. They'd married late and were eager to start a family, and then nothing happened. And then, a year and a half later, here you came out of the blue. That often happens, you know. When a woman stops trying, she relaxes and conceives."

"But then Andy and I—" She felt she was about to mouth words from some tawdry melodramatic script that had lain in wait for her ever since she was born. She couldn't finish the sentence.

But Aunt Charlotte had no problem finishing it for her. "That's right, dear. Andy wasn't your real brother."

"But—why are you telling me this now?"

"It seemed the right thing to do. I'm sure it's what my poor sister would have wanted. She always planned to tell you both when you were older, but she kept putting it off. 'They're so close, Charlotte,' she told me, 'they're closer than most *real* brothers and sisters. I don't want to rupture something prematurely.' 'I wouldn't leave it too late,' I advised her, 'the longer you leave it,' I said, 'the harder it's going to be.' But Hazel was always one to put off anything confrontational. She liked people to stay quietly in the background, neatly arranged on their shelves like her library books."

"But, why are you telling me this *now*, Aunt Charlotte? I mean, why not before? My brother . . ." She had felt almost sick as she pronounced the word for the first time with the new separation between them. "My brother's been dead almost two years. . . ."

"Because you're mourning too much for him, dear. It isn't natural for someone your age after all this time. I thought it would be healthier for you to know that you weren't even related. I didn't want you to be weighed down by a burden of kinship that never existed. I hope I've done the right thing. It cost me some sleepless nights, I can tell you."

In the fall, she had been eager to return to Princeton. Though her guardian was scrupulous about allowing Alice her freedom, Aunt Charlotte just wasn't by nature a hands-off person. She was so interested in Alice's comings and goings from their "bachelor girls" apartment, as she liked to call it, so eager to offer the loan of "the right" silk scarf or a designer handbag for a special occasion, so avid to hear all the details of the occasion—often waiting up late for her niece at the desk in the living room on the pretense of catching up on office work.

One October afternoon of her sophomore year, Alice was called out of a lit. theory class and informed that her aunt had suffered a fatal coronary that morning at work.

She took a week off from Princeton and drove up to Hartford to make funeral and burial arrangements. Her competence in organizing these matters came as a surprise to her. It all seemed effortless; through all the proceedings she felt enveloped in an airy calm. She regretted that her aunt had not been a happier woman, but on her own behalf felt nothing but a weightless, superior remoteness as she went about her chores of disposing of the dead woman's goods. She recalled certain times of closeness they'd had, the evening they'd gone to the ballet in New York, for instance, but this was done as a kind of memorial exercise. In the same spirit she forced herself to make keepsakes of Aunt Charlotte's favorite silk scarves and a cherished Louis Vuitton carryall. With one of her aunt's friends at the insurance company, she dispersed possessions to various acquaintances and charities. The capable lawyer in charge of the estate finagled a nice compensation in return for the two remaining years of Aunt Charlotte's lease on the apartment because the landlord was impatient to turn it into a co-op. Alice was informed that her aunt's investments were more substantial than anyone might have guessed.

"She was a careful woman," the lawyer told Alice smugly, as if all of it had been his doing. "As her sole beneficiary, you shouldn't have to worry."

"I'm not worried," Alice replied calmly, resting her hands loosely upon her lap, and hearing her voice as well as the lawyer's coming from a very great distance.

Her airy remoteness seemed to offend the executor, who was, after all, presenting her with news of her good fortune. "At least not for a *while*," he had added in a less friendly tone.

On the drive back to Princeton, Alice talked to Andy. In all but body, he was definitely in the car with her. "We're going to be fine. We're going to be perfectly fine. We always were, and we always will be. Even when we were little, we always stuck together." She spoke to him in a gently repetitive, reasoning croon, the way he used to speak to her when she was uncertain or scared. Only now she was the older one, because she had lived in the world two years longer than he, and she was therefore . . . it made perfect sense as she figured it out while she drove . . . half a year older. "If we stick together, I promise you, we're going to be fine." As long as she kept talking to Andy, she moved forward imperviously through traffic. The miles between Hartford and Princeton were only dream miles.

Only when she had reached Princeton, and had parked and locked her car, and stood alone and silent, watching a windblown piece of scrap paper dance madly in circles all by itself on the pavement, did she began to tremble violently from head to foot.

She was hospitalized briefly, and took the rest of the year off from college. A chunk of Aunt Charlotte's windfall went toward her residence in a plush facility in Connecticut, all arrangements made by the helpful lawyer who was no longer miffed by her remoteness now that he knew its source was a mental breakdown rather than any feelings of superiority toward him.

For seven months she absorbed various medications, with positive and negative effects, and talked to a variety of doctors and interns about herself.

One doctor had his heart set on her remembering that she and her brother had been lovers, since that would account ideally for the *timing* of her breakdown. Could it be that, upon learning from her aunt that there was no blood relation between them, *therefore no taboo*, she would have had to reexperience the loss from an entirely more troubling perspective? Was it possible that, in the months immediately following Aunt Charlotte's revelation, the terrible thought had been rising into her conscious mind that *all along she'd wanted to marry her brother*. Could it be that, after her aunt's death and burial, that noxious thing that had been threatening her on the drive back to Princeton was the unbearable realization that, had Andy been spared in the accident, she might have been able to fulfill this secretly cherished wish?

Another doctor saw religious significances. Her brother Andy as Christ figure. In the absence of any family orientation toward religion, compounded by the distant parenting of the scientist-father and the crisp, professional librarian-mother, the worship-need as well as the love-need in Alice had fastened upon the person of her brother, especially after he had been sacrificed. This doctor did not believe the breakdown could be blamed on Aunt Charlotte's revelation that Andy had been adopted. A brother was a brother, if you had grown up *believing* him to be your brother, was this doctor's opinion. "So he will always remain your brother in the deepest part of your psyche," he assured Alice.

Immediately, as if to challenge this doctor, Alice began having erotic dreams about Andy. They were high-school lovers in the backseat of a car who couldn't get enough of each other; they were a couple on their honeymoon, tenderly mating and vowing to love each other always; they were a young pharaoh and his sister-wife, performing a series of ritual sexual acts on a mattress-barge that floated ceremoniously down a dark, narrow river while crowds bearing torches watched from the banks on either side. She became disoriented and violent and had to have her medication changed.

A young resident psychiatrist urged her to look deeper into her relationship with her mother. Had Alice felt her mother *resented* her? Alice had mentioned that her mother had been a brisk, business-like woman, cold in temperament, never showing much affection to her husband or children, hating housework and resenting it if you got sick and she had to stay home and take care of you. Wasn't there a possibility that the mother had ambivalent feelings about Alice being a blood daughter and Andy being an adopted son? Tried not to show favoritism for the blood child and therefore overdistanced herself from both of them? "While you wouldn't have known the *reason* for this distancing, you would have picked up on it. Perhaps you ought to look into this."

Alice began looking into it, exactly as a good student embarks on her next assignment. She was feeling more like her usual self again, and had begun to regard her residency in the plush Connecticut facility as a kind of alternative education year, which she had paid for out of her inheritance and therefore should make the most of. Only, instead of English and biology and European-history courses, she had been taking courses in dreams and feelings and family history. But for the first time she could see to the end of her stay, as someone toward the close of an intense school year finds herself remembering the upcoming summer.

Dreams about her mother promptly came (patients at the facility always dreamed what their doctors told them they were going to dream about; she had discussed this with some of the others) but the mother-dreams were curiously lacking in feeling and intensity. They weren't half as interesting as her other dreams. They had no "affect," as she had learned to say here. Even the young resident looked bored when she related them to him. He became increasingly distracted in the sessions, though he seldom took his eyes off her.

Then one day he told her he wouldn't be meeting with her anymore. He had developed too strong a countertransference, and he and his training analyst had decided it would be unproductive for him to continue with her. "You see, you remind me of my sister. She died at nineteen, of anorexia. You bear many resemblances to her: your low voice, your physical build, the poised way you carry yourself. I have many unresolved feelings about her. But, in a professional capacity, I would advise you to continue pursuing your feelings about your mother until you get some affect."

She left at the end of May, having pursued her feelings far enough to know that she had gotten all she could from this place, that she was glad to have learned that psychiatrists were just as vulnerable to family fallout as anybody else, and that she was eager to get back to the study of the world outside of her immediate family and personal circumstances. "You've still got work to do, Alice," the director of the clinic told her at her discharge, "but in my opinion, you're definitely one of our summa cum laudes."

She spent the intervening summer teaching swimming and crafts at a camp for overweight kids. (The helpful lawyer to the rescue again: both his children attended this camp.) In the fall, she started her sophomore year over again, taking the train to New York twice a week for therapy sessions with Dr. Anita Starling, recommended by the Connecticut doctors. For three years her alternative education progressed alongside her academic one. She studied late into the evenings, producing term papers on the *künstlerroman* tradition in German literature, or the "necessary angels" of Rilke and Stevens, or travel as an instrument of emotional enlightenment in the heroines of Henry James and George Eliot. Then she turned out the light and plunged obediently into her "night courses," filling pocket-sized spiral pads with dreams penciled hastily just the other side of sleep next morning to deliver to Dr. Starling. Among her fellow students, she had the reputation of being poised, disciplined, and rather shy. Her women friends told her she was calming to be with and that she was a good listener, who seemed really interested in what they were saying. She tried to develop this technique, because it furnished her with a sociably acceptable front for her natural reserve. She was the one they all wanted to fix up with their boyfriends' roommates, or their brothers, if they had them. Men her age admired her, but after taking her out a few times, the majority of them seemed to find her old-fashioned poise and reserve a strain and sought more relaxing company elsewhere.

"You'll always be fragile, Alice," Dr. Starling told her at the end of their intensive therapy, "but it's not the brittle kind of fragility that shatters like glass and can't be mended; it's more like . . . well, you've seen long-stemmed flowers after a heavy rain, how they bow all the way down to the earth. But unless their stems got broken, they rise again when the sun dries them out. Yours is that resilient kind. It goes *with* nature, not against it. You've been brought low by the elements, and you've certainly had your share of elements! But you've snapped back. I'm confident that if *more* elements conspire to bring you low, thanks to all you've learned about yourself, you'll bow down again, but you won't break. You'll just lie low for a while."

It was all a matter of education, then. Most people concurred that it was a good thing to educate your mind, but not everyone understood that it was also necessary to educate your feelings.

If you knew the reasons behind, say, the French Revolution, you'd better understand the principles of all revolutions. You would be able to spot incipient revolutions in the making.

But if you didn't know that certain configurations of traits in another person matched up pretty well with traits of someone you longed for, or never got enough of, or feared, or loathed, in childhood, you'd be setting yourself up for repeated "actings out," as they would have said in Connecticut. The traits of the new persons became "hooks," as they would have said in Connecticut. Just as she had become the "hook" for that young resident psychiatrist who still had unresolved feelings about his sister.

Over and over again, you'd get "hooked" and be doomed to *react* to the people you meet, based on whom they reminded you of, rather than perceiving each new person and responding to who was actually there in front of you. You'd be doomed to expect each new person to give—or withhold—what X, or Y, in your early life, did—or did not—give you, rather than accepting what Z, who was now standing in front of you, could offer.

That was what therapy had taught her, but there would always be more to learn. Part of her life would always be a mystery to her. Fortunately Dr. Starling had been a wise woman and had warned her in their farewell session that she'd never be finished with the education of her feelings.

"You never graduate, Alice, you keep taking the courses. But what I hope we've done together is lay the groundwork for your continuing education."

So, here she was: brought low by the elements of last winter. ("And what elements, Alice!" Anita Starling surely would have said.) Yes, she had bowed flat to the ground and lain low for a while.

And now? Was she rising once more, beginning to lift into the sunshine? Here she was at the theater, slimmed back from her last burgeoning public appearance before Christmas. Here she was, "recovered" from her pregnancy and its awful outcome, sitting beside her gruff, respected, famous-writer husband, taking in the play.

The only trouble was, in her "recovery," she could no longer stand her husband. Was it Hugo she couldn't stand, or some configuration of a past person's traits that, having awaited its hour to surface, now repelled her?

But she had never met anybody like Hugo before. She had responded to Hugo for himself, for his own qualities: because he was such a fine writer, because he had inclined his shaggy head and listened to her with a lively attention that made her feel he knew who she was, because he had taken charge in that old-fashioned masculine way women were were all supposed to have had enough of. He wasn't a bit like her absentminded father, or remotely like her "prince of a brother," as Hugo liked to refer to Andy. (After they decided to marry,

Alice had told Hugo about Aunt Charlotte's adoption story, adding, as she always did, when she told close friends about her life, the opinion of the psychiatrist who said her brother would always be her brother in the deepest part of her psyche, if she had grown up believing him to be. "Well, of course," snapped back Hugo with belligerent tenderness, capturing her hands in both of his. "Of course he is always going to be your brother."]

Then which was it? Had she married the wrong person and slowly discovered it, or had some inner shifting in herself turned him into the wrong person for her now?

The private happiness that had broken over Francis Lake's face when he confided that evening over the pot roast that he had lived all these years in the radiance of the right partnership and didn't know how he would go on without it: what jealous yearning it had roused in her; still did.

Tiresias was exhorting Creon that it was not too late to mend his errors. She glanced at her watch: a few minutes before nine. Almost time for Magda's next pain pill. Alice was there in the room with them. She could see the familiar standbys on Magda's tray table that had been rented along with the hospital bed: the small notepad with attached pencil on which doses of medications were recorded in Francis's scatty script, the plastic glass (half-filled with juice, or Ensure) and the bent straw, the lemon swab-sticks with which Francis had recently began cleaning away the dried secretions that now gathered at the corners of Magda's mouth, the folded washcloth, scented with verbena cologne, with which Francis sponged Magda's face and arms when she was feverish.

When she was not actually there, their house was the present place in Alice's life where she most consistently existed in her thoughts. An evening breeze fluttered the sheer white linen curtains that Francis washed and ironed himself. The last of May's lilacs scented the room, still stronger than the encroaching scents of death. The lamplight made gold etchings in the leaf carvings on the chest of drawers facing Magda's bed.

Under a monogrammed sheet, fresh from today's laundry load, a woman with a thatch of very short white hair lies still as a corpse, her eyes closed, the jutting contours of her emaciated face trapping the shadows.

Enter the husband, treading softly past the huntboard stacked with today's paper, mail, books (though she can't read them anymore, Magda still likes their familiar shapes in her range of vision). He pauses to adjust a drooping lilac in its vase.

Now he's bending low over her face. A slab of his graying hair slides into the path of lamplight and momentarily becomes a youthful reddish blond. His face is tense, concerned, his body weary from the exertions of the long day. But then her eyelids flutter and this restores him. A faint smile lifts the corners of his mouth as he shakes a purple pill from the little plastic vial, gazing on her face all the while. He lays the pill to one side of the tray and studiously notes the dosage on the little pad. *Morphine*, 30m. 9:00 P.M.

"Madga, love, time for your medicine."

No response.

"Magda? Do you think you can sit up for a minute? Then there's a better chance you'll have a restful night."

Still no response, but he has seen the eyelids flutter. She's still alive, still with him. He still exists in the radiance of the partnership.

"I'm going to slip my arm under your head, Magda. I'll try not to hurt you. Can you raise your head just a little?"

The lids rise to half-mast. Angry dark orbs regard the stooping, solicitous figure with resentment.

"I know you hate to be disturbed, love. I don't blame you a bit. It seems so silly, I know. Me having to wake you in order to feed you a pill that makes you *sleep*. It's almost as bad as the hospital, isn't it?"

He keeps up this prattle while supporting her head gently in the crook of his left arm. He places the purple pellet on her coated tongue. Then quickly reaches for the glass and guides the bent straw between her parched lips. More of the foul, dried stuff has gathered at the corners of her mouth. He'll have to swab again with the lemon sticks. "This is juice, Magda, that apricot nectar you like . . . I diluted it with a little water so it will go down better. Can you take a sip of it and wash the pill down? Then you can go right back to sleep, my love."

The lights went up, the student performers collected their curtain calls and bunches of flowers, and Hugo, worn-out from his strenuous thoughts during the course of the play, stood up feeling debilitated and mean, wishing only to be whisked directly to bed, already in his pajamas, without having to drive through the night or say another word to any person, including Alice. The play's last lines, chanted by the gleeful doomsayers, about the mighty blows of fate at last teaching us wisdom, did nothing to improve his mood. He stood aside to let Alice go first up the aisle. Let *her* run the gamut through the chitchatters.

Oh, fucking hell, she was letting herself be stopped by that gallant Latino jackass Ramirez-Suarez.

Ah, Alice, you are looking so lovely, how wonderful to see you again, we have all missed . . . okay, that's enough. Finish kissing her hand, Tony, and get a move on. Ah, Hugo, what did you think of the Fagles translation? Isn't it a fine translation, English so fresh and direct, yet willing to subdue itself in favor of the original Greek. That's right, let's stand here blocking everybody in the aisle so you can get your rocks off about the original Greek, Tony. We know everybody at Aurelia speaks original Greek at their breakfast tables. Okay, okay, enough. Oh, *now* we have to do a medical update on Magda Danvers. Over there yesterday, oh, you, too, Alice? . . . yes, isn't it sad, but she still has these lucid moments . . . and isn't *he* wonderful?

Oh boy, now isn't this my lucky night, here comes Leora Harris to get in on the act. Our poor dear Magda . . . it *can't* be much longer now, can it? . . . but *he's* so loving and so patient, though anyone with eyes can see he's exhausted. Okay, okay, we get the point, he's a fucking paragon and he's exhausted. What about me, I'm exhausted, too.

"Let's get going, Alice."

■ ■ ■

The chill in the parking lot wasn't from the night, which was quite warm. It was coming from Alice.

"Shall I drive, or do you want to? I might as well."

"Well, why *ask* me, Hugo, if you've already decided."

"Just trying to be friendly."

"You weren't trying to be very friendly in there. You hardly spoke to Tony and you didn't even acknowledge his wife."

"Why don't you drive? Maybe it'll put you in a better mood."

"Me! I'm not the one with the mood. But thank you, I will drive."

She accepted the keys from him and took her own sweet time in going around to unlock her side, then fussing with the driver's seat to accommodate her longer legs. At long last she condescended to remember he was standing out there in the dark and, reluctantly, it seemed to him, leaned over and unlocked the passenger's side.

As a hermetic container for hatred, a car is much more potent than a house, thought Hugo, being driven by his silent, reproachful wife through the play-toy streets of Aurelia, the pressure building between them block by block. He saw the academic hamlet in which they were to be trapped for a second year as an airtight pressure chamber for all their smaller pressure chambers: Sonia Wynkoop's barren house, their jointly owned car, any other enclosed space that might happen to come along and enclose them together. Containers within containers, squeezing out all hope of escape. With this pressure, he would never make a start in reversing his plunging fortunes. That boy-thespian playing Creon, in his gold-and-white tunic from the costume shop, crying out at the end of the play, "Whatever I touch goes wrong!" Someday, son, thought Hugo, those words may actually mean something, if your life turns out to be anything like mine.

"Hey, why are we going this way?" Alice had turned down the wrong street. "This isn't the way to our house."

"Oh . . . sorry. But this will get us there as well."

"Yes, but not the quickest way."

There was a pause. Then she said in a cold voice, "Well, Hugo, what's the rush? I mean—" she exhaled a small choking gust of what reached him as pent-up loathing. "I mean—" she repeated, then left another pregnant pause before releasing her final volley: "what wonderful thing awaits us at home?"

I am becoming monstrous, thought Alice. This marriage is turning me into a cold, sarcastic bitch. But how dare he treat people with such offhand contempt? He was rude to Tony, and ignored Mrs. Ramirez-Suarez's existence completely, and gave Leora such a sneering look when she was saying how good Francis was. And then it's "Let's get going, Alice," as though he owns me.

She drove down the familiar residential blocks, then turned into a more rural road with fewer houses: the roundabout route she had known she was going to take when she suddenly decided to accept the keys from Hugo. It was her small treat, her reward to herself for enduring the long evening. No, it was more than a treat, it was a lifeline.

Magda's room was dark. Their whole house was dark except for a single light burning in that little room where Alice had recently waited in the presence of Francis's damp, cast-off clothes, and all those forlorn shoes. Was he in bed, reading that book on terminal care? What did he wear to sleep in? Pajamas, or something else?

"Oh, we're going past Magda's," said Hugo, adding with a brusque, mirthless laugh: "I guess you've been going over there so much the car just naturally turns into their road."

"That's exactly what must have happened," said Alice, laughing at herself for Hugo's benefit. Not only cold and sarcastic, but I'm becoming a liar as well, she thought. Yet, having had her little glimpse of light, she felt strangely calm and happy.

CHAPTER XII

Francis was alone in a foreign city. He was searching for Magda, but couldn't remember where their hotel was.

He approached a cathedral and went in to look at the misericords. He walked purposefully toward the choir stalls, toward his secret carvings nestled in the darkness beneath the seats, but was disappointed to find a crowd gathered there. He usually had the misericords all to himself.

When he got to the edge of the crowd, he asked a tall, forbidding-looking priest why they were all clustered around one particular misericord. Silently the priest moved aside with a frosty smile and yielded his place to Francis.

Francis saw that the crowd was attentively watching a solemn ceremony on a tiny television screen embedded in the misericord. It was a Mass of some kind, perhaps an ordination. "I was going to have an ordination once," he heard himself say aloud.

"Shush," said somebody angrily. "This isn't an ordination. It's Magda Danvers's funeral."

Francis awakened with a sob. There was a pale silvery light in the spaces between the dense leaves of the old sycamore tree just outside the window. Holes were visible in some of the leaves. He hoped Brian the tree man would remember to come and do the second spraying for gypsy moth.

The green numbers on the digital clock beside the bed changed from 5:03 to 5:04 as he watched. From the edge of the woods a cardinal piped three long notes, and after a pause, three more identical ones. Then came the mourning dove's throaty sigh from very close. Probably from the upper branches of the sycamore. When he had first pointed out to Magda that they had a sycamore next to the house they'd bought, she had laughed and said, "So *that's* what one looks like! All *I* knew about sycamore trees was that the ancients believed that the birds who lived in them were souls of the departed. See how I depend on you for my mundane life, Frannie?"

He listened for her sounds. Nothing. He hastened barefoot into their old room. His first thought on most mornings now was that she had given him the slip somewhere between her 3:00 A.M. pill and the dawn.

He put his face close to hers. There was a shallow, raspy breath, then another. He had grown used to the smell coming from her mouth. It was not a nice smell, but on the other hand it meant that she was still here with him.

She had kicked off her covers and lay with her legs splayed. They were so thin now, a smooth, waxen, yellow color. Almost like someone else's legs. The ankles and feet were swollen. Her gown had hiked up, and on the sheet, between her legs, was a small compact stool. It was composed mostly of dried blood. He was able to remove it successfully without disturbing the catheter tube taped to the inside of her thigh.

Should he save the stool to show Diane? No, he was sure if he simply described it she would know what it meant. And today the doctor was supposed to come anyway. He hoped it would be Dr. Rainiwari.

Had she been awake he would have cleaned her up a little, but it seemed cruel to interrupt her rest. Last night she'd been in such pain he'd had to rub her back for a long time until she finally fell asleep. She was having trouble swallowing even that little morphine pill now. He would have to ask Rainiwari what they could do about it. If it was Rainiwari today.

He covered the strange, pitiful legs lightly with the top sheet and went downstairs and made himself coffee. He ate one of Leora Harris's blueberry scones. Leora brought so many baked goods so often now that he had taken to freezing them.

People had been extremely kind. Last week, Tony Ramirez-Suarez had given Magda a beautiful filigree crucifix belonging to his late mother. It had been blessed by Pope Pius XII. Tony had put the crucifix in Magda's hand and closed her fingers around it.

"Tell me, Tony," Magda had said, "do you think heaven will be anything like Dante's description?"

"Dear lady, of course it will. Where do you think Dante's ideas came from?"

After he left, Magda told Francis, "Be sure and return this to Tony after I'm dead. With one of your appropriate notes."

They had discussed briefly what should go in the note.

"Father Birkenshaw used to say he believed in the sacramental power of things when they were given or received in the right spirit," Francis remembered.

"Yes, yes," said Magda happily, "put that in, Frannie. Tony will eat that up."

It was so disorienting. He already lived part of his time in a near future when Magda would be gone. Then the wrenching poignancy of it would hit him: she's still here.

After breakfast he did some dusting and straightening and watering of plants, running up to check on Magda from time to time.

She still slept. It was a beautiful morning, but he never took his walk until after the nurse arrived.

Diane came promptly at eight, bringing them some flats of lobelia. She was always bringing them presents, even though he knew she lived frugally with her mother. The two women were raising Diane's little girl. Diane was a single mother. Francis admired her for her cheerful steadiness and strength. She was such a help. She never got ruffled by Magda, even when Magda was being her worst. Whereas sometimes lately, he found himself slipping into despair. It seemed he could do nothing right anymore in Magda's eyes, yet the minute he was out of the room she was calling for him again.

They got Magda cleaned up together, and stripped and remade the bed, though it wasn't easy. She yelled obscenities at them, though her yell was scarcely above a whisper now, and accused them of deliberately trying to hurt her.

Hoping to distract her, Francis described the lobelia flats that Diane had brought them. "They're those dark blue ones with the white centers. I always liked the ones with the white centers best."

Magda rolled her eyes at them and smirked nastily. "Scones and flowers, scones and flowers," she chanted in a rasping whisper. "What did I tell you, Frannie? They're lining up . . . and my ashes not even sprinkled yet." Francis was mortified, but Diane seemed not to catch Magda's insinuation. At least he hoped she hadn't.

When he made his second trip to the basement to transfer the sheets from the washing machine to the dryer, he discovered that the machine had overflowed. There was sudsy water all over the floor. He reset the dial to spin, but there was a lot choking and sputtering and no water drained.

He hauled out the cold, wet sheets, transferred them into a plastic garbage can (after he had first rinsed it under the faucet of the laundry sink), and then ran upstairs to put in a call to the plumber. He was good at most household things, but hopeless when it came to machines.

Brian arrived in his natty green van to do the second spraying for gypsy moth.

"This frankly isn't an epidemic year," he told Francis, "but you naturally want to cherish and safeguard your young birches and important shade trees, like that venerable old sycamore."

Brian had degrees in forestry and horticulture from Cornell. He also had a way with words, like Magda. His son Mack was with him, a stocky, self-confident little boy. When Brian put on his mask and began spraying the sycamore tree, Mack sat on the porch steps with Francis.

"Do you know where a polar bear keeps his money?" asked Mack, kicking the undersides of the steps with his high-topped white shoes. They reminded Francis of spaceships with elaborate, colorful trim.

"No, I'm afraid I don't," said Francis.

"In a snowbank!" Mack cackled so hard that Francis found himself shaking with laughter, too.

"Why didn't the skeleton cross the road?" cried the boy triumphantly, invigorated by his success.

"I don't know," replied Francis.

"Because he didn't have the guts!"

"That's enough, Mack," Brian called to the boy from behind his mask.

He probably thinks the skeleton joke is painful to me because of Magda, realized Francis.

Diane appeared behind the screen door. "Magda's asking for some blue book, Mr. Lake. I wouldn't have bothered you, but she seems pretty agitated."

He hurried upstairs. Magda was sitting up in bed. He hoped the plumber would come soon, as they were down to their last set of clean sheets.

"I don't ask much of you, Francis," Magda said, glaring at him furiously, "because I know your limitations. But how could you, *how could you*, let me run out of blue books at a time like this?"

"Blue books, Magda?"

"*Examination* books, dummy. What do I have to do to impress on your thick skull that I'm running out of time?"

She meant the blue books teachers hand out for final examinations. Her Final Examination was how she thought of the time she had left to lie here and account for her life. But now, poor love, she must think she needed a real blue book. Or rather several.

"There may be some in your file cabinet," he said, playing along. "Maybe in that file where you keep your old exams from graduate school?"

"Well, go and get them. I don't have all day."

"How many . . . um . . . should I bring?" He knew this was a symbolic request she was making, but was determined to satisfy her. What almost always happened was that she would soon drift on to another, completely different subject: that was the way her mind worked now. She'd be onto something else by the time he returned with the blue books. Or he hoped she would.

"Two . . . no, wait, better be safe and bring three."

If she thinks she needs three exam books, how much real time does that translate into? he calculated to himself. As he set off down the hall he met the nurse laboring up the stairs.

"Everything okay now, Mr. Lake?"

"Well, she wants . . . something from her study." He didn't like to betray Magda, even when she was being unreasonable.

Diane achieved the stairs, puffing heavily. For such a young woman, she was very stout. But he did wish Magda wouldn't refer to her as "Broad-butt" in her hearing.

Still catching her breath, the nurse put herself directly in Francis's path and waylaid him by placing the flat of her hand against his chest. "You're a wonderful person, Mr. Lake," she said in an emotional voice. "And I want you to know that I admire you very much." This last was uttered rather angrily. Then she released him and bustled on past to Magda's room.

Entering Magda's study, he was struck by its abandoned, moping quality. The empty grate without its fire looked so black and shrunken and cold. The lovely magenta color in the Turkish carpet they had bought from that trusting rug man across the river, who had urged them to take it home and try it before buying it, seemed to have faded since Magda's illness to a disconsolate mauve. Magda's poor unconsulted books huddled together in dusty blocks along the shelves. They had ordered those shelves out of a catalog, expecting them to arrive fully assembled. Instead, several flat packages had arrived, and he and Magda had exchanged words of frustration over his slowness in putting them together. But afterward, when all the books were organized on the shelves, she had praised him and called him her "unearned gift."

Francis straightened a Blake print in its blue-and-silver frame that hung awry on the wall above Magda's sofa. It was *Queen Katherine's Dream*, her favorite. They'd bought it together at the National Gallery in Washington and spent too much on having it framed (this was long before the days of her Aurelia salary) because she said it was important that the frame be worthy of the picture. Even the figures in the Blake prints seemed to have lost some of their airy radiance without Magda's appreciation to enliven them.

And there was Suzanne Riley's *Mountain of Purgatory*, in its place over the file cabinet. The last thing he and Magda had hung in the study. After it came back from the framer's, Magda hadn't had long to enjoy it from her sofa. Despite its nice frame, the student picture looked a little amateurish without Magda's enthusiasm to bring out its qualities.

Would he keep this study as it was, as a shrine to her? Dusting the books and straightening the prints and airing the Turkish carpet twice a year, while remembering all sorts of things about their life together?

He went down on his knees to open the bottom drawer of her file cabinet. In this drawer were her oldest files, herself preserved as student before she began to teach others. Here were her old exams, the exams of the Magda he had never known. The young Magda with the brilliant mind. After the flu he had nursed her through in Chicago—and then come down with himself—she had lost the cutting edge of her brilliance, she often reminded him: her mind had never been as sharp again. He'd never quite believed this, but if it *were* true it was probably just as well for him that she'd lost that edge. How could she have endured him all these years if her mind had been any sharper?

He took three blue books from one of the file folders, and returned to Magda, who was sipping juice and watching him avidly over the top of the plastic drinking glass being held by Diane. He saw from the impatient, beckoning motions of Magda's fingers that she hadn't forgotten what she had sent him away for, and she wanted the books *now*.

As he slipped them beneath her hand he intercepted an intense look being directed his way by the admiring nurse. Turning away in confusion to look out the window, he watched sun-browned Brian in shorts and singlet moving professionally along the edge of the woods, spraying the young birches.

"Oh *God*, you fool!" came Magda's hoarse cry.

There was the clatter and bounce of the plastic glass hitting the floor.

"Now she's done it," said Diane. "Looks like it's sheet-changing time for us again, Mr. Lake."

He turned to see apricot juice puddled on sheets and blanket and splattered across the front of Diane's smock and trousers. Magda of the sizzly electric hair brandished the examination books in her fist and trained upon him a look of black rage.

"I ask him for something I *need*, and he brings me these ancient old things with *writing in them*. With fucking *writing* in them! Oh, Death, deliver me from Simple Simon here. Who's going to let you bring blue books with *writing* in them into an examination room? I ask you! And when you think I could have had Northrop Frye."

The doorbell chimed. Francis looked out the window again and saw the plumber's truck parked behind Brian's green van.

"Mop up the best you can," he said to Diane coldly. "There are no more clean sheets anyway, until we get the machine fixed." He fled, Magda howling curses after him.

He took the plumber down to the basement and explained the problem. It was not their usual man. He was rather curt when Francis was explaining what had happened, and he had whiskey on his breath.

Brian had finished spraying, and was walking slowly around the edge of the lawn with Mack, looking up at the trees.

"Things are looking good, Mr. Lake. I'll come back for one more application in mid-June. That okay?"

"Sounds good, Brian." Francis wondered if Magda would still be alive in mid-June.

Brian, who knew the state of affairs inside, seemed to read his mind. "How is your wife doing?" he asked in that respectful way people ask when someone is definitely dying.

"We're taking it a day at a time," Francis told him.

"That's pretty much what Mack and I are doing, too," Brian replied with a bitter laugh.

Brian's wife had left him to go off and live with a ski instructor in Colorado when Mack was two. "I try not to think about her," Brian had once told Francis, "but when I wake up every morning and look at Mack, how can I help it?"

Francis settled the bill with him. "Saves me a stamp," he said, though he knew Brian was glad not to have to wait for the money. These single young parents, it couldn't be easy for them. Diane with her little girl. Brian and Mack.

The plumber came out of the house and reported the washing machine to be functioning again. "Clogged drain was all it was."

"Well, you've certainly saved our day," Francis told him gratefully.

The plumber shrugged. "Not a major job." He gave Francis a surly look as he departed.

Francis went back to the basement and transferred the wet sheets from the garbage can back into the machine and began again.

He was sipping some cold coffee in the kitchen and jotting down the things he wanted to ask Dr. Rainiwari, if it was to be Rainiwari today, when Diane came downstairs.

"She's dozing again. I mopped things up as best as I could." The nurse's smock was damp where she had sponged off the juice and Francis could see the outline of her brassiere. "I could help you set out those lobelia while we're waiting for the sheets to dry. No sense disturbing her until we've got the replacements ready."

"That would be nice," said Francis, not knowing what else to say. "I'll go and get the trowel. Where do you think they ought to go?"

"Oh, that's up to you, Mr. Lake. They're yours to do as you like with."

"How about those old terra-cotta planters on either side of the front steps? I think they'd look nice there. We could fill in with something else later, impatiens perhaps."

"Yes, I'll bring some impatiens flats tomorrow," she offered immediately. "We'll fill in with those."

Francis realized Diane thought he had meant herself and him when he said "we," whereas he had meant, of course, himself and Magda.

While they were planting, the nurse got progressively happier and friendlier. She asked Francis if he had been named after St. Francis. He said no, for his great-uncle Francis, his mother's favorite uncle, who had been a priest. "Though, he was probably named for St. Francis. Or else, whoever *he* was named for was named for St. Francis. . . ."

She laughed as though he had made a very clever joke, and went on to tell him she had seen this wonderful movie about St. Francis, and that he reminded her a little of the actor. Only she thought Francis's features were finer.

He was feeling hungry and tired by the time they'd planted the lobelia, and put clean sheets on Magda's bed, over Magda's profanity and protests, and Diane had gone home at noon to relieve her mother, who worked afternoons in a meat market.

Although Magda hadn't taken solid food for many weeks, he liked to mark the occasion of their old lunch hour by bringing up his sandwich on the tray along with her Ensure, and having it in her company. Often she just continued to doze while he sat in the chair and ate and read the newspaper. Sometimes if she were awake, he read aloud items he thought might interest her.

But after her attack on him some weeks ago, he had thought it best to discontinue this practice.

"So? Who cares?" She had interrupted him in midsentence while he was reading to her from page one. "What if they *do* discover that the Reagan–Bush campaigners made a deal with the ayatollah? What difference does it make *now*? Carter is out . . . Reagan is out . . .

soon Bush will be out. And then whoever follows Bush will be out. We'll all be out, sooner or later, in the newspaper sense. If you want to entertain me, Francis, tell me something of real interest. Tell me the story of a young seminarian. He's twenty-one and he's taken his first vows and he's been given permission to go home for his mother's funeral. He didn't even know she was sick. He goes home to the funeral. But *then*, instead of getting back on the bus and returning to his seminary in Marquette, he asks his sister for money so he can go in the opposite direction, and 'drop in' on this woman in Chicago. I want to hear the *inside* story before I die. The story of this young man's thoughts and fastasies as he rides eleven hours south on that bus. What is he expecting to *say* to this woman in Chicago? What does he expect her to do for him?"

"That was twenty-five *years* ago, Magda."

"But wasn't it a significant trip? Didn't it change your life?"

"You know it did, but I can't remember my thoughts from twenty-five years ago."

"You could if you'd paid attention to them at the time. If you'd been a hero in a novel, those thoughts would have marked the end of one of your chapters. They would have been the significant bridge to your *next* chapter."

"But I'm not in a novel. I'm certainly not anybody's hero."

"There you go. Your Mr. Modesty act. Well, it won't get you off the hook. It's *sinful* not to try to keep track of who you are. You'll suffer for it yet, mark my words."

"I knew I wanted to see you, and lucky for me I found you. I didn't plot and fantasize, I just went *toward* you because . . ."

"Because *what*? That's what I want you to tell me before I die."

"Well, Magda, because I wanted to see you again. I wanted to talk to you again. You've always *complicated* me too much, Magda. I'm not introspective like you."

"Oh, *bullshit*. You're just afraid to face the rest, that's all."

"Face *what* rest?"

"That's what I want you to tell *me*."

"There isn't any more, Magda."

"Of course there's more. You just refuse to take responsibility for knowing about it. And you've denied it to me all these years, you chicken."

"Magda, I would give you anything I have, but—"

"Anything you have but *that*. And that's what would be of real interest to me as I lie here dying, Francis Lake. Not some warmed-over political plot out of a fucking newspaper."

N ow he let the newspapers pile up downstairs, hardly glancing at the headlines before throwing them out.

This day was so beautiful, and Magda had been so awful through the first half of it, that he considered having his lunch outdoors. But how would he feel afterward if she were to choose that moment to die?

He made himself a tuna sandwich, from one of the many cans left from that time when she wanted tuna on a roll every day, and carried it and a glass of milk upstairs on a tray along with her Ensure. She was still dozing, thank God. He left the Ensure on his tray to keep from waking her, and sat down in a corner chair beside the huntboard and ate his lunch slowly, almost dozing off himself several times in the act of chewing.

Compared with now, when he had to raise her in the hospital bed and coax her to take even a sip or two of liquid nourishment, those earlier days when she would sit up by herself in their old four-poster and chew and swallow her tuna on a roll seemed like an impossibly healthy bygone era. Yet at the time he'd been deploring how far she had declined from those *earlier* days when she still sat across from him at meals downstairs and robustly put away several portions of everything he cooked. She had gained more weight in the year or so preceding her illness. That's probably why they hadn't found the tumor until so late. Then one night last winter while they were watching "Masterpiece Theatre" in bed, she had taken his hand during a slow part—it wasn't one of the better programs—and placed it on her lower abdomen on top of her gown.

"Something in there has been making these nasty twinges,

Frannie, and my back hurts a lot. Can you just poke around and see if you feel anything ominous?"

At first he didn't feel anything. That was when he was still expecting his fingers to hit a certain kind of hard, discrete lump, the kind he always dreaded coming across when Magda periodically would imagine she had breast cancer like her mother and make him examine her breasts. But then he realized that her whole left side was distended.

"How long has this been like this?" he asked, lifting her gown and moving his hand back and forth on the bare skin, comparing sides.

"How long has what been like what?"

"This sort of . . . swelling on the left side."

Her hand was on top of his, following the terrain. "That's obesity, dummy," she scoffed. "All your good cooking has taken its toll, and I was never what you'd call a sylph."

"No, it's . . . feel . . . the left side has this swelling that the right side doesn't. Does it hurt when I press down?"

"No. It hurts when *it* decides to hurt. Forget it. If you don't feel a definite lump, I'm not going to worry."

"But I'll worry."

"Oh shit, Frannie, make an appointment then."

She had moved away from him angrily, almost as though he had *caused* something to be wrong inside her by saying he felt it there. They'd lain side by side without touching, staring stonily ahead at the rest of the program—a slow-moving drama of Irish aristocrats at the turn of the century in which nothing much happened.

He'd made the appointment with the gynecologist. Then came the tests. Then the referral to the surgeon. Then Magda's surgery. After which Drs. Zeller and Rainiwari, the oncology team, were called in. Magda was exasperated with Francis during this whole period. She behaved to him and to all the medical people like a grand personage being forcibly restrained, even to the point of being *cut open*, by nitpicking inferiors who wanted to keep her away from important work.

Then came their talk with Rainiwari while she was still in the hospital. Francis hadn't liked the way the Indian doctor had outlined her prospects. He seemed so unfeeling and remote; he hadn't even looked at Magda, addressing all his remarks to Francis, the husband. He spoke as if he were describing some sort of Star Wars going on inside Magda that only he could see.

Yet the strange thing was how Magda perked up as Rainiwari, looking at Francis, not at her, recounted in his oddly inflected English this saga of invasions and intercellular junctions and satellite tumors. She was like a child listening to a fascinating bedtime story. But when Rainiwari got to the point of describing how neoplastic cells (the bad ones) had a capacity for mutation that allowed them to develop a resistance to radiation and chemotherapy and furthermore permitted them to replace the sensitive (good) population that had been killed by therapy, Magda held up her hand almost cheerfully and stopped him.

"Dr. Rainiwari, I am going to opt for going home as I am. I would rather spend what time I have left studying for my Final Examination than studying my illness. Interesting though it is, I confess I find myself more interesting. Even in my present condition."

That had been one of the rare times Dr. Rainiwari had looked at her and bowed. He approves of her fatalistic decision, thought Francis, feeling shut out. He felt they had both abandoned him for some attractive, higher, inscrutable region where he could never follow.

While Francis was still eating his lunch and watching Magda doze, he heard a car pull into the drive. He ran down. It was Rainiwari today, whom Magda approvingly referred to as her midwife of death, and not Zeller, who annoyed her by jollying her along with plots of the newest movies he had seen.

Francis walked beside Rainiwari to the house, describing recent developments: the stool this morning, composed mostly of blood; the increasing caked stuff at the corners of Magda's mouth; her increased difficulty in swallowing. "Several times lately she's choked on her morphine pill, and I've had real difficulty getting it down her. But she's still so active in her *thoughts*, Doctor. Of course, I don't know what's going on a lot of the time now, but it seems to make perfect sense to her. This morning, for instance, she wanted more blue books for her Final Examination. You know how she refers to this time she has left as her Final Examination?"

Rainiwari nodded in a way that could have meant "yes," or simply "please continue." His smooth brown face, as always, was impossible to read.

"Well, I humored her. To tell the truth, I was hoping she would have been onto something else or maybe dozed off by the time I got back with some old blue books from her files. But she was waiting for them, just as alert as you please, and when she discovered they were filled *with writing*, she blew up at me. She knocked her juice all over the bed, and all over the *nurse* . . . you should have seen her . . . the energy! She said, 'Who's going to let you bring blue books with *writing* in them into an examination room?' She said some more things, too, but I won't repeat those."

Francis started laughing in a gasping, helpless way, and found he couldn't stop. What would Dr. Rainiwari think? He made an effort to pull himself together, staring hard at the lobelia he and Diane had planted earlier in the terra-cotta pots on either side of the walk. Providentially, a clear memory of Father Birkenshaw's stern face, exactly as it used to look when quashing unseemly hilarity in the seminarians, flashed through his mind and dried the laughter from his lips like a cold wind.

"I just hope," said Francis, recovering himself, "I just hope, Doctor, that she'll keep her mind right up to the end. It's so important to her. She's always been such a worker. Even now, while she's . . ."

"Blood in the stool," echoed Dr. Rainiwari in his odd emotionless singsong.

"Well, actually, it was *mostly* blood," said Francis. "It was like a very dark blood clot . . . about so big." With his thumb and forefinger he measured a small space in the air between them.

"Mostly blood is to be expected at this stage," Rainiwari said. "As for the residue at the corners of the mouth, continue to use the lemon swab-sticks as often as necessary. She may experience bouts of choking. You should be prepared for that. I am going to send over the nursing supervisor with a pump to suction the fluid that gathers in the mouth. She will show you how to operate it. It looks a little daunting at first, but it's quite simple. To replace the pills, I will prescribe a liquid medication, Brompton's Cocktail. It's an elixir of morphine and cocaine in a flavored syrup. In Britain they are still using heroin because of its greater water solubility, but the morphine is just as effective in controlling the pain. This mixture will increase her alertness for several hours each time she takes it. Unfortunately, the effects wear off in about two weeks. The patient quickly becomes tolerant to the stimulant. But for your wife, perhaps the two weeks will be enough."

Here, for the first time ever, Rainiwari smiled bleakly at Francis, who stepped aside to hold the screen door open for the doctor.

CHAPTER XIII

Hugo, feeling sociable, had taken a break from the speech he was writing for the opening of the new library in Calhoun, S.C., and was lounging against the doorframe of the kitchen of their rented house—the house they would be leaving soon to move who knew where—watching Alice pull meat from the bones of chicken pieces. The scene had the quality of a domestic idyll: a lovely woman in a chef's apron, framed in the year's new green foliage outside the open window above the kitchen counter, quietly intent on preparing food. Though her back was to him, her gold wedding band that he himself had slipped on her finger flashed intermittently into view as she plucked away at the still-steaming chicken.

Under the influence of the moment, the art professor's sterile house seemed almost negligible. Who knew? Maybe they could have exorcised its malaise if they'd lived on in it a second year. Hugo was suddenly feeling hopeful. The first paragraphs of his speech, which he had dreaded beginning this morning, struck him as having achieved just the right modest, witty tone for a down-home boy returned as famous writer to grace a local reaffirmation of literacy. Maybe the process of composing this speech would be the very thing that would restore his old momentum.

"That's a lot of chicken," he remarked cheerfully.

"Not all that much," Alice replied defensively, as if he'd been finding fault with her, when all he'd been doing was making conversation—sort of commenting on the *abundance* of the scene.

"What are you making? Chicken salad?"

"Mmm-hmm."

"I love chicken salad. But shouldn't you wait till it cools off so you won't burn your hands?"

"I'm not burning my hands, Hugo. I thought I'd go look at those two houses for rent, and I want to take some of this to Francis when I stop off. I phoned over there a while ago."

"Oh. Maybe I'll go along. I'd like to see Magda."

Alice did not reply, but began shredding one of the hot chicken pieces into a glass bowl. He could see it was burning her fingers from the way she handled it, but would say no more on that subject.

Yet he did want to see Magda. He had left it rather late, but better late than never. And he had the time now, since classes were over at Aurelia. Of course, people could argue that *others* had gotten over to see Magda while classes were still in session, but Hugo had learned to make allowance for his own low tolerance for social overload. He had *wanted* to go see Magda long before this, even though Ray Johnson said her admirers exaggerated how compos mentis she still was, but if he had dragged himself over there after his classes, or those blasted "tutorials," he would have been practically as much of a vegetable as she, and what good would that do anybody? Besides, hadn't Alice represented them both on her frequent visits? With all this food-kitchen stuff, she'd been doing more than anyone else. Even President Harris, whose spouse had been a regular Lady Bountiful to Magda and Francis, had remarked on "the Henrys' " extraordinary kindness to the couple.

"What time are you planning on going?" he asked, since Alice, her back to him, still had not said anything. "We'd drop by on Magda first and then go look at the houses, right?"

"Actually, I'd planned to look at the rentals first, and *then* go on to their house," she replied in a clipped voice, plucking a chicken breast to pieces.

"Oh, okay. That's fine. It's a beautiful day out. Who knows, maybe today will be our lucky day with one of these houses."

She didn't answer. After a brusque wipe of her hands on a dish towel, she snatched up a bunch of celery and ripped off a stalk. As she slashed away at the strings with a paring knife, he glimpsed the deep red of her fingertips from the hot chicken.

"Just let me know when you're ready to leave," he said. "I'm going to see if I can squeeze out another paragraph of my library speech."

As he crossed the house to his bedroom-cum-study at the other end, he was aware of the loud slapping sound the leather soles of his loafers made on the bare parquet floors. Maybe their next house would have wall-to-wall shag carpeting; there were always hopes. Or to rephrase that: he had not yet abandoned all hopes.

Though Alice hadn't answered him, and though he could tell she hadn't been overjoyed about his decision to go along, she hadn't said he *couldn't* go. She hadn't said, as she might have, "Actually, Hugo, I'd prefer to go alone." That's one of the bonuses of being married to a civilized woman, he thought bitterly, she may hate your guts, but she's not going to come right out and *tell* you she'd rather do without your company.

He sat down in front of his word processor again and, after down-arrowing through his opening paragraphs on the screen, lost all desire to go on. He saved what he had, switched off, and gazed out the window into a neighboring yard.

A memory from his childhood floated up: himself on a summer afternoon standing behind his mother in the kitchen of their small, hot house in the mill village, asking if she'd take him to the lake to swim. Sometimes she said yes, more often she said no, and frequently she didn't answer him at all. But he had learned to read, in the set of her shoulders, in the varying moods of her silences, what his chances were. On the days he sensed there was no chance of their going, he would kick the table legs and fly into a tantrum, thus justifying her refusal to take him anywhere and getting himself a smack as well; but on the days when he sensed there was definitely *hope*, he would stand there quietly for a minute or two after his plea, and then in his gentlest, most winning voice, say, "Well, I'll be out back," just as he had allayed Alice's possible rejection just now. He'd tiptoe outside, being careful not to bang the screen door, and sit in an agony of impatience on the back stoop.

He hadn't thought of that lake in years. Your feet sank into squishy layers of mud and decomposed leaves as you entered, and just when you had forgotten to think about it, your leg or arm would encounter what might be either a long fish or a small snake swimming beside you. But it was all they had and it must have been passable, because mothers from the mill village took their children there. The only other swimming places in Calhoun were the recreation park, which charged twenty-five cents a head, even for small children, and the Malvern Valley Country Club, remote and unattainable to the likes of him as some legendary Shangri-la.

Over one summer, the last summer he retained an image of his mother as a strong and effective person, she had taught him how to swim, holding his wriggling body aloft in those brownish waters. It was the summer he was five. She instructed him to do the impossible: move his arms *and* legs in totally different ways, put his face down and up in the water, and through all this, *stay on top*. Once, he got so frustrated by her demands that he kicked at her, and she lost her balance and fell back clumsily into the muddy shallows. Two women rushed to help her, as if she'd been sick or something. When they helped her to her feet, he noticed for the first time how heavy and ungainly she had become. "Why, you're *fat*!" he had cried. The three women had exchanged a look that excluded him, and then his mother had laughed nervously, almost apologetically, and insisted they go back to his swimming lesson.

At the end of that summer she had gone to the hospital and come home with a baby girl, who lived less than a week. In later years, as she grew more passive and apathetic, and shrank in size, as if her body were expressing her diminished expectations, she would often cast a blighting glance on her surroundings, or on his father when he had just committed some brutality, or sometimes on Hugo when he had crossed her or disappointed her. And then she would gather herself up and make the withering little speech that she must have treasured as her last weapon: "I'm glad my little Lorena had a hole in her heart because at least she didn't have to stick around to be a part of *this*."

The first house they looked at was a sabbatical rental, two blocks over from their present house. Alice and Hugo picked their way over toys and children. The wife had the radio tuned loudly to a station that seemed to broadcast only commercials. She showed them through the cluttered rooms of the rambling Victorian two-story and never stopped talking. Her professor-husband, whose specialty was marine biology, was to do a year's research by himself in Florida while she and the kids went to stay with a sister with kids in Iowa. "There's a good Quaker school there. Sis and I will take them there in the morning, and have the days all to ourselves. I'll miss Dick, of course, but I'm old-married enough to be looking forward to it." She laughed meaningfully. "You two are still too newlywed to understand *that* yet."

The second house, an older frame bungalow, sat isolated by itself on a slightly hilly rise at the dead end of a street of newer tract houses. But inside the thick stand of evergreens that shielded it from its neighbors, it had a charming, woodsy intimacy. The realtor, decimated by hay fever, had trusted them to go alone with a key and look at it for themselves. Hugo and Alice walked thoughtfully through its few small bare rooms, all on one floor. It smelled musty because it had been on the market for over a year. The owner, a divorced working woman with a son who would be entering college this fall, had now decided she had no choice but to opt for the rental money, the realtor explained.

"The Victorian job is nice and spacious, it would be all right in itself," Hugo remarked afterward as they were driving on to Magda's. "But *in itself* is just what we'd never get. That clutter would be lurking behind every closet door, it would be omnipresent in the molecules of the air. As well as all their noisy *vibes*."

"From old-maidy-barren vibes to old-married-clutter vibes." Alice laughed, sounding almost like her old self.

At least we still share some problems, thought Hugo: like looking for a roof to cover our heads.

"I liked the fireplace in the little bungalow," added Alice regretfully, after a moment.

"And that stream out back, wasn't *that* a surprise?"

"You could have had the back room looking out on it for your study," Alice said.

"Yeah, too bad the place wasn't a little bit bigger."

"Oh, it was *much* too small," she agreed with alacrity. "It would never have done."

"Nope, never."

There had been only the living room, eat-in kitchen, bathroom, and two small bedrooms. Even in the first intimate year of their marriage it would have been too small for their life. They could have managed the cuddling-up part, in a double bed in the one small room, allowing Hugo to have his workroom in the other, the one with the view of the stream. But even then, it would have been a curtailment for Alice: what about *her* books, *her* desk, *her* workroom?

Not that she had one in their present house. Of course, this past year she had been thinking of the baby coming. And if the baby had lived, he would have taken over Hugo's present work space in the house they now occupied.

"This has not been a good year for us, by any means," he said. "But at least that gives us room to hope for improvement."

He had half expected she might take him up on this, but she looked out the window on her side and didn't respond. She was being his passenger today. Ever since they'd set out together from the house, she had been compliant and agreeable, but—except for that one moment just now when she had laughed almost like her old self—he felt the wall was still between them, whatever the hell it was composed of now. Surely she should be recovering from the baby's death by now. He was accepting it more as each week passed, and it had been his baby, too. If she'd been Rosemary, he would have guessed a new affair. That's how he'd always known with Rosemary, she became evasive and dreamy and withdrawn. But Alice's only life outside the house, he was sure, consisted of going to visit Magda, or what was left of her, and occasionally staying afterward to chat with devoted, dull Francis, who—even if all his energies hadn't been taken up with a dying wife—wasn't what Hugo would call affair material. And anyway, Alice was too straight and decent to sneak around and have affairs. If she fell in love with someone else, she'd tell him. He could picture how Alice would look, breaking such news to him, but he couldn't for the life of him picture the man. This ought to have given him more consolation than it did.

Francis Lake was hurrying out the door and down the walk to greet them before Hugo had even switched off the ignition. Though he was smiling and neatly dressed as always, he looked terrible, his face a drawn grainy gray, his always trim body so wispy now you'd be afraid to sneeze in his direction for fear of blowing him away. The poor guy was being sucked dry by his own devotion. If I got cancer, would Alice waste away in caring for me? wondered Hugo. Funny enough, he was sure she would make a noble attempt at doing so, even if she no longer loved him. This thought gave him as little consolation as his being unable to imagine the outlines of her potential lover.

"Hugo, what a nice surprise," said Francis, shaking his hand.

"We probably should have phoned, in case Magda wasn't up to more than one of us," Alice apologized as she removed the food basket from the backseat.

"Oh, no, Magda will be so pleased. You'll get the benefit of her new medication, Hugo, and who better than you for her to try it out on? It's this wonderful new . . . she was having trouble swallowing her pills, so Dr. Rainiwari prescribed this liquid when he was by earlier today. Ramirez-Suarez was kind enough to pick up the prescription at the drugstore so we could start her on it right away, and since about a half hour ago, she's been her old self again. I'm so glad you two have come, so she'll have someone worthy of her . . . she always enjoyed matching wits with you, Hugo. Oh, Alice, I can tell you've overdone your kindness again."

"It's just some chicken salad, and a few other things," murmured Alice, following behind them with her basket as Francis, lightly grasping Hugo's elbow, talked them happily up the walk and into the house.

"Magda asks about you often, Hugo, we keep up with all your activities and travels through Alice. Now we understand you're off to South Carolina to give a lecture. Magda once lectured in Charleston, at a Dante festival at the college there. I went with her and we had a great time. We took a horse-and-carriage ride around the Battery and toured through some of those lovely old houses and ate ourselves silly . . . there was this delicious crab soup, we had it every chance we got. . . ."

They went through a sunlit room full of objects and plants and old furniture. Too full and fussy for Hugo's taste. Alice excused herself, saying she'd quickly unpack the things and join them presently, and nipped into a shadowy kitchen. She certainly acted at home here.

Francis, cheerfully calling out, "Magda, love, I'm bringing Hugo Henry up," went first up the narrow flight of stairs and led Hugo down a hall to a room at the end.

Oh Jesus, thought Hugo, catching his first glimpse of Magda since last December. "Her old self?" What had the poor man been thinking of?

"Magda, here's Hugo, back from his travels abroad, and now off again to South Carolina to give a lecture. Like you did that time in Charleston. What lecture *was* that, love? Was it that one on the ordering of loves in Dante, or—" As he kept up this one-sided banter he was pulling up a chair for Hugo, positioning it much too close to the motionless wizened thing in the hospital bed. "Please watch the caster on this chair, Hugo. It's okay, as long as you *roll* on it, but don't try to lift it up."

Taking a deep breath, Hugo sat down.

The brownish-yellow face with dead-white frizz all over its head opened its mouth and uttered a whispery crackle.

"I'm afraid you'll have to speak a little louder, love," coaxed Francis. "What was your subject that time in Charleston?"

"Horse dung and she-crab soup," the crackly voice pronounced audibly. Bruised eyelids suddenly snapped open and Magda Danvers's dark eyes glittered collusively at Hugo. "That's all *he'd* remember of it anyway. You were in Paris?"

"No, not Paris," said Hugo. "First I went to Prague, and then up to Oslo and Stockholm and—"

"*He* told me Paris."

"I believe I said Prague, love," interjected Francis somewhat sadly, hovering to readjust the bedspread so it would cover the partly full piss-bag that hung inches away from Hugo's right knee.

"What are you ... writing?" Magda asked Hugo, as if Francis had not spoken.

"Well, right now I'm putting together a speech for the opening of the new library in my hometown down in South Carolina."

"You know speeches don't count," said Magda, with a wink.

My God, thought Hugo, perhaps she still *is* her old self under that ghastly visage.

"This hasn't been a good year for the real writing, Magda." He decided to level with her. Why not? What did he have to lose in this room with a dying woman and her exhausted husband, who, probably to appear unobtrusive, had lifted aside a thin curtain and stood half-turned away from them, looking out of the window.

"The years fly by," taunted Magda, parting her lips at him in a ghastly, yellow-toothed smile.

"I know, I know," replied Hugo glumly, cracking his knuckles, then stopping himself. He clasped his hands between his knees. That glittery dark gaze trained on him made him feel guilty and uneasy. "It's been a pretty trying year. The house we rented hasn't been ideal. Not that I'm trying to blame a *house*. Anyway, we have to move out soon because our landlady's coming back. Let's hope the next place we find will be more friendly to my muse. If I still have one."

Magda mumbled something fairly lengthy and inaudible.

"I'm sorry, Magda, I couldn't hear you," said Hugo.

She rolled her eyes at him and expelled an angry hissing sound through her parched lips. Some kind of muck had dried at their corners. "I *said* . . ." she began again slowly, as if talking to an idiot, "in . . . my study . . . the ideas are still thick. They're waiting, poor things, but their mother's never coming back."

Hugo could not think what to reply to this.

"Meanwhile," the crackly voice went on, "I've accomplished work in here . . . it hasn't been easy. With certain people thwarting and *competing* all day long . . ." The wizened face turned briefly on its pillow, alluding to poor Francis Lake at his post by the window. "Would you like to read what I've written so far?"

Surely she can't still write, thought Hugo. Ray Johnson says she can't even read anymore.

"Yes or no," pursued the voice from the bed. "Time is no joke, my friend. Yet it's the biggest joke of all. But I'll soon be in the clear. Without my life in the way, I'll understand my life. Francis?"

"Yes, Magda?" He was bending over her in a shot.

"Get my final."

"Your what, love?"

"My bloody *final*. Don't play dumber than you are. The *blue books*."

"The blue books? You mean . . . the ones I brought earlier today?"

"See how he always tries to take credit?" Magda said to Hugo. "The ones *he* brought." The eyes closed in exasperation.

"Magda's talking about some exams of hers from back in graduate school," Francis explained in a soft voice to Hugo. "I found them in her files for her this morning. She thought she needed some blue books, you see, for—"

The eyes snapped open. "Don't talk *over* me, Francis. Just do as you're told. Go get the fucking blue books."

Poor Lake looked as if he might cry. Her language had brought a rush of blood to his gray face.

"Aren't those blue books? On the bed there?" Hugo put in quickly. He had just noticed them, half-concealed in a fold of bedspread, on the other side of Magda. Her body under the spread was so much *smaller* than before. Almost like a child's. It didn't seem possible . . . that big woman.

"Oh . . . oh, of course. Oh, good. *Here* they are, Magda. Right on your bed all the time." Francis snatched up the three blue books and offered them to Magda.

"Don't give them to *me*. Give them to *him*. He's the one who's going to read them."

She waited until Francis moved quickly around the bed to present their visitor with the booklets. "Open anywhere you like and read," she croaked magnanimously to Hugo. "Anywhere you like."

Uncertain of what was expected of him, Hugo looked down at the top examination book. *Magda Danvers. 17th Cent. Brit. Lit., Professor Withers,* was penned across the bottom of the cover in a flourishing, cocky hand he recognized from the sympathy note she'd written them. A date in May 1964. "You want me to read aloud?" asked Hugo.

"Of course, read aloud," said Magda scornfully. "How can we listen, otherwise?"

Hugo opened to the first page. "'An Exegesis of Defensive Allegory,'" he began slowly, his own voice sounding rusty to him. "'Lines eighty-five to one-oh-one "The Second Anniversary," by John Donne' . . ." He certainly hadn't imagined his visit to Magda turning out anything like this. But then, as Cal might say, his father was always so intent on imagining people and outcomes *his way* that when they finally emerged on terms of their own, he felt hoodwinked or betrayed.

Magda gave a little "mmm" of satisfaction and closed her eyes. Francis retreated on tiptoe to a corner chair and sat down.

"'The poet comforts his soul by comparing Death to a groom slowly approaching with a taper.'" read Hugo. He heard Alice's footsteps coming down the hall. "'At first the soul spies the merest glimmer of light coming from the taper in an outer room, then gently the groom brings it closer into view. . . .'"

Alice entered. Francis had already risen to give her his chair. She sat down in it without any fuss, and Francis perched companionably on the windowsill beside her. Alice, with her usual quick tact, had entered at once into the spirit of the proceedings. Both she and Francis had their faces turned attentively toward Hugo.

"'The human mind associates light with reassurance,'" Hugo continued, his voice becoming more eloquent. "'Death, usually equated with darkness, is turned into a bearer of light, thereby reversing the prevalent attitude toward death. Then with a further masterful shift of equations, Donne goes on, in line eighty-nine, to make death equal heaven, in that its approach resembles the approach of Death as groom. . . .'"

Magda opened her eyes wide and mumbled something at Hugo.

"I didn't quite get that, Magda."

"Brilliant. Just what I needed. Thank you so much. Who wrote that?"

"Well, you did, Magda," said Hugo.

Magda looked confused, then gave Hugo a condescending smile, as though she'd caught him in a preposterous lie.

"No, you did, Magda. It says so on the cover here. It's your old exam book from a course in seventeenth-century lit."

"My good husband," crooned Magda, smiling weirdly at Hugo. "The only one I want."

Hugo was appalled: could she mean him? Then Francis sprang forward from his windowsill perch and hovered above his wife. "Here I am, love, what is it you want?"

Magda rolled her eyes at Francis, then looked at Hugo and laughed. Oh God, thought Hugo, who had just understood. She meant the groom in the poem, she meant Death, but the poor guy naturally thinks she means *him*.

"I'll leave them to you," Magda announced to Hugo with a regal inclination of the white head. "Frannie, make a note of it. Those blue books go to him. But, Francis . . . ?"

"Yes, Magda."

"Who *is* he?"

"Who is who, love?"

"The man who was reading, dummy."

"Why, it's Hugo, Magda."

"Hugo who?"

"Hugo Henry, love." Francis sought Hugo's indulgence in an apologetic little side glance. "Alice's husband. Alice and Hugo came together today."

"What bullshit. She's not here . . . and she's not married."

Alice rose at once from the chair on the other side of the room and came forward to stand at the foot of the bed, in Magda's line of vision. "Yes, I'm here, Magda."

"Well . . . you'd better come forward and defend yourself. Tell my buffoon you are not married."

"But, I am, Magda."

"To this man who was reading?"

"Yes," Alice assured her, but in a somewhat constricted voice, Hugo thought.

Magda expelled some word that sounded like "Bah." She blinked her eyes in annoyance, then focused more sternly on Alice at the foot of the bed. "It's not like you . . . to tease. Come over here . . . come closer so I can see your face. Stand beside *him*. I want to see you together."

Alice, a flush creeping up her neck, came slowly around the hospital bed to join Hugo. Hugo was in the act of rising from his chair to give Alice his seat, but one of Magda's yellow hands shot out and waved him down again.

"I heard a car door slam," Francis said suddenly. "I'll just go and see who it is." He hurried out of the room.

"That's Prince Humdrum for you," snorted Magda, "fleeing for his life from anything personal. Well, it's too bad, Alice . . . I thought you had more sense. Not that he isn't a nice man. He reads very well. . . ." She continued to look at them, moving her head slightly from side to side on the pillow. Then the cracked lips curled in a derisive smirk. "But I still don't believe this man is your husband."

"Nevertheless, it's true. Magda," replied Alice in a small but stalwart voice that made Hugo sad for both of them.

This day has gotten progressively worse, and it's not nearly over yet, thought Alice, standing beside the seated Hugo in this diabolic pose Magda was forcing on them, whether from scrambled brain circuitry or some witchy purpose known only to herself.

The first dark note had been struck this morning outside the butcher's, when Alice had plucked a *Catskill-Record* from the newspaper racks, as she did most mornings now, because of the real-estate ads. There on the front page—the headline, in fact—was the news that another local couple, in addition to the Bennetts, were bringing a suit against Dr. Romero. This was a couple who, despite some difficulties in the home birth of their child, had remained loyal to Romero, giving effusive testimonies on his behalf during the height of the controversy. But now it had been discovered that their boy had suffered motor and brain damage during the birth and would always live a substandard life.

She and Hugo had decided not to sue, because she found the prospect both draining and repellent, and they'd agreed that Hugo's temperament would never stand it. Hugo was much too volatile and worst-case-scenario-oriented to endure prolonged bureaucratic uncertainties. He threw a tantrum every time he got any sort of notice from the IRS, made shouting or whining phone calls to his accountant ("How can I be expected to *write* with this goddamn sword of Damocles hanging over my head?"), thudded around creating dire futures for himself of crescendos of government harassment leading to total ruin, and gave no one, least of all himself, any peace until the problem (usually a minor one, singled out by an overzealous IRS computer) was resolved. In Hugo's boyhood, there had been a farmer, an acquaintance of his father's, who had shot himself through the mouth when the IRS seized his small farm; soon after the man's death, they admitted they'd made an error. Hugo was obsessed by this story and brought it up every time there was a discrepancy in his bank statement or a dispute over a utilities bill. "That farmer in Calhoun" was Hugo's rallying cry against all the bastards hidden within officialdoms who were out to destroy all you had worked for.

But when she had read about this other couple in the *Catskill-Record* this morning, some crossed-circuitry in *her* thought process had produced a tenth of a second's false hope in her: *Perhaps we could still sue—and get the baby BACK!*

These displacements in thought struck a frightening note of familiarity. And she'd experienced two others recently: one while looking at a rental house furnished with some rustic pieces that had twiggy edges that stuck out and snagged at you as you passed by; the other in a badly built contemporary whose high-pitched staircase had no railing.

"Too dangerous for a small child," had been her first instinctive reason for rejecting both houses.

These synapse misfirings in the brain or the psyche, whichever place they emanated from, resembled too closely for comfort that solitary drive of hers back from Connecticut after settling her aunt's affairs: that time when she had talked to Andy all the way back to Princeton.

Folding the *Catskill-Record* and tucking it under her arm (she had been shaking a little), she entered the butcher's, steadying herself with a silent litany of the present realities (the baby is dead, Andy is dead, Mother is dead, Father is dead, Aunt Charlotte is dead, Magda will soon be dead. . . .) as she stood in front of the meat counter and considered the possibilities for today's menu.

She had already decided this would be a day when she would go and visit Magda and take Francis something. She couldn't go every day, of course, that would be too intrusive, but she allowed herself to go two, sometimes three days a week. She would always make the food first, *then* phone and ask if today was a good day to come: she was scrupulous about this ritual, as though she must put herself through the uncertainty in order to be allowed to come.

In these past few weeks, as she walked through the rooms of other people's houses, automatically assigning this living space to Hugo, that one to herself (though she wasn't at all clear as to *how* they were to go on living together even for one more year), the truly engaged and *comforted* part of her mind was over at Magda and Francis's house.

Strange as it might seem to anyone but herself, she was happier there than in any other place; when she was not there, she could put herself there by a simple effort of conjuring up the house she had come to feel so at home in. She could enter the sickroom with its sheer fluttering white curtains and its smell of fresh flowers and death: cross around the bed and sit down in the chair, whose faulty caster Francis warned her of every time he slid it under her.

And then sink once more into the mysterious deathwatch with Magda, a vigil that somehow remained equally important and mysterious whether Magda was snoring with her mouth open, emanating whiffs of that frightful smell, or black-eyed and snappy, regaling you with witticisms, or excluding and taunting you with her incomprehensible murmured monologues with their occasional audible flashes of wisdom and discernment. It was almost like going to a religious sanctuary, some place of high seriousness, set apart from the ordinary round of chores and cares and plans, where you could really *listen* for the first time to something that was always going on.

Today Hugo had not only intruded on her precious sanctuary, but, in just the few minutes it had taken her to put Francis's food away, had commandeered the scene for himself, though she realized how unfair she was being—he had a right to see Magda, too, even if he had left it so late, and Magda must have *asked* him to read from that old exam book. And why shouldn't Hugo come here with her; he *was*, after all, her husband, for which transgression Magda now seemed to be punishing her, forcing her to stand beside him in this disturbing tableau.

What was Magda doing to them, what was she *seeing* with those fathomless dark orbs of hers as they posed together like this, under her orders?

It was then that Francis, bless him, had broken the spell by professing to hear a car door slam, and off he went, Magda remarking how he always fled any kind of personal talk and recalling to Alice the memory of an earlier visit when Francis had rushed out of the room when Magda began to speak about the first time she'd ever seen him with his clothes off.

And then Magda had challenged her with that gruesome, knowing curl of the lips and the incredible pronouncement. "*I still don't believe this man is your husband.*"

She's either gaga or a witch, thought Alice, frozen to the spot, but what difference does it make? She has read my heart.

Nevertheless, she found it in herself to reply as loyally as she could that Hugo was indeed her husband. Curiously, despite all the animosities and strains compounding between them, Alice felt in that moment that Hugo was by far the most vulnerable of them all, and that it fell to her to protect him both from Magda *and* from her own most secret self.

A new voice, mingling with Francis's, rose to them from below. There really was someone; it hadn't been Francis just looking for an excuse to bolt.

Magda heard it, too, because her silent cross-examination of Hugo and Alice ceased as she cocked her head to catch the sound. It was a woman's voice, fast-paced and aggressively confident, coming nearer.

"Magda, love, it's Leora Harris stopped by to say hello," Francis called ahead as he and the new visitor climbed the stairs.

"Shit," said Magda, quite audibly. She sank deep into her pillows and slammed her eyes shut.

The president's pert-featured wife, crisply turned out in mint-green slacks with a matching scoop-neck tee and linen blazer, preceded Francis into the room. If she had overheard Magda's remark, she showed no sign of it. On the contrary, she gave the impression of being someone perpetually conscious of the benefits to be gained by others from her well-turned-out, exemplary appearances in their lives.

"Well, my goodness, *both* Henrys. Hello, hello. I told Francis I didn't want to *crowd* things up here, but he insisted I come up just for a minute. How nice Magda's feeling fit enough to hold court."

"Please sit down, Leora," urged Francis, pushing the chair by the window closer to the bed. "Magda seems to have dozed off, but she'll want to see you when she wakes. She often does that, takes little catnaps, then wakes up more refreshed than ever. More refreshed than I am, sometimes."

"What an understatement, Francis, when anyone with eyes can see you are absolutely exhausted," said Leora Harris. Her tone implying, however, that she was the only one with eyes. As the president's wife took her seat her hand brushed Francis's bare arm in a consolatory upward stroke. Magda had told Alice of the nickname she had given Leora Harris as well as the reason for it. "The Pastel Patter," Alice noticed, had yet to look once at the motionless figure in the bed.

While all this was going on Hugo rose quietly from his chair next to Magda, took Alice firmly by the shoulders, and pushed her gently down into his place. There was mute relieved sympathy between them: Leora's timely entrance had let them off the hook of Magda's little persecution, however deliberate or unwitting it had been. As Alice sat down they exchanged fugitive ironic glances. Both of them knew that Magda was shamming sleep. Hugo had been apprised by Alice of Magda's contempt for Leora, and also the provenance of the nickname. Alice's visits to Magda were one of their treasured "getting through time peacefully together" topics, like Cal's new life. Though recently their "safe" subject of Cal had turned volatile. The other evening at dinner, during a Cal discussion, Hugo suddenly put down his fork and snarled morosely: "So? I have a twenty-nine-year-old son who's happy in his work and happy in love. What's so damn tragic about that?" Hanging in the air had been the unspoken follow-up: *I wish I could say as much for myself.*

"Hugo, Ray Johnson tells me you're off to grace your native library with the keynote speech," piped Leora from the other side of Magda's bed. "And will you be going along, too, Alice, to share his laurels?"

"No, I'm not." The starkness of her own reply sounded rude, even to Alice, but Leora Harris's determined expeditiousness in conversation always seemed to reduce Alice to these simple, unqualified answers.

"Alice wants to stay here and find us a place to live . . . our landlady's returning at the end of June," put in Hugo. On this occasion, Alice was grateful to have Hugo answer for her, though normally this habit drove her wild.

There being only two chairs in the room, Hugo, as well as Francis, had each appropriated a windowsill to sit on, while still semistanding. Just like those medieval monks, resting their butts on those misericords in Francis's slides, Alice thought, amazed at how much this simple recollection sweetened her spirits.

She looked across at Francis in his windowsill, his lean figure angled straight-legged out into the room, his arms folded over his chest with hands tucked into the armpits, his head slightly bowed, so that the usual swatch of faded hair fell over the left brow. Hugging himself to himself, he nevertheless gave the impression of being contentedly a part of whatever transpired around him: a self-important visitor, a dying wife shamming sleep: it scarcely mattered what. On certain occasions, this attitude frustrated her: his indiscriminate acceptance of things as they unfolded day by day, his refusal to be selective or *intense*. But now she was enveloped in its peculiar, private solace. She felt she was his intimate partner in it, though they were on opposite sides of the room and he wasn't even looking her way. Today he was wearing that soft blue cotton shirt that she had come to feel possessive about, ever since she'd seen it lying damp and crumpled in the chair with his underwear and jeans, that time he'd asked her to wait in his room after Magda's mishap. Today, of course, it was freshly ironed, as his shirts always were.

Leora Harris was quizzing Hugo—she appeared to have given up on monosyllabic Alice for the time being—on their exact requirements for a house, as if she were just waiting to produce it from the crisp pocket of her mint-green jacket if only he'd be specific enough.

The president's wife was well-known for "drawing people out." Because of a crucial exercise class last fall and then, later, the baby's death, Alice and Hugo had escaped both presidential dinner parties during the past academic year. Leora Harris's faculty dinner parties had a notorious reputation: Leora would wave her conductress's baton and force each trapped seated guest in turn to perform a solo about his or her most recent favorite book or film, or one's most interesting challenge over the summer, that kind of thing.

There was a wonderfully naughty story told about Magda's performance at one of these dinners soon after she and Francis arrived at Aurelia.

Magda herself had told Alice the story at Ray Johnson's party in early December, the first time they'd really sat down and talked at length alone. The memory came back to Alice now, accompanied with a vivid image of the old Magda before her illness . . . well, before her illness was diagnosed: the Magda (of less than six months ago!) of the coiled flaming hair, attired in a bright, intricately figured caftan, billowing the largess of her presence across an entire love seat, while Alice, her own presence ample enough by then to cover the whole of an adjacent ottoman with *her* garments, turned raptly toward this lively person who, amazingly, seemed equally delighted to be talking to *her*.

Magda had been pointing out various faculty members to Alice, summing them up in wicked thumbnail epithets, when Leora Harris bobbed into view. "That's the first lady over there," said Magda, "the *coiffured* one in powder pink with the magpie features. You and Hugo missed the dinner for faculty, didn't you? Lucky you. The first—and last—time Francis and I were invited, we were fools enough to look forward to it. We'd heard she did sit-downs, and in college life one does get so tired of making a tray out of one's lap. But at that dinner we had hardly unfolded our napkins when Leora at the head of the table—*he* sits at the foot—embarked on her interrogations. Each of us had to respond like kindergartners to her little 'assignment.' The assignment that evening was to ... was to *share* . . ."—and Magda Danvers started chuckling in anticipation of her own narrative— "was to *share* with everyone around the table our most enjoyable experience of the past twenty-four hours. Oh dear, oh dear ..." Here Magda had dissolved into rollicking, shaking laughter. She gulped a sip or two of sherry. Judging from her uninhibited merriment and her flushed face, Alice gathered she was already tipsy.

"Well, let's see, Ray Johnson came first, I think, with one of his forgettable brown-nose offerings ... then, oh, yes, quirky old Sonia Wynkoop ... your *landlady* ... hers was something self-serving and obscure that gave her a chance to show off her Italian: an article she'd come across that day on some '*cinquecento*' altarpiece that had been divided up among four museums. Then, dear Tony Ramirez-Suarez, who had the old-world manners and simplicity to report to his hostess on the evening's sunset and be done with it. After that was this woman from the Psych Department, she's gone now, who got rather emotional: it seemed she had awakened that very morning and realized her parents *hadn't* loathed her, after all. And then it was my turn.

"In all honesty, Alice, until I opened my mouth that night I had no idea what was going to come tumbling out: I knew *something* would, it always does when I'm standing before a class. I mean, I *was* their most recent prized acquisition, after all: I could have described the *waffles* Francis fixed that morning, and they would have been impressed, but then my devil took over and I said, actually quite demurely for me: 'In the interests of decorum, Leora, and out of respect for my esteemed colleagues, I'd prefer not to report on my most enjoyable experience of the past twenty-four hours. And I'll take the liberty of declining on my husband's behalf as well, since I'm certain his would have been the same.'

"There were some snickers and a few subdued laughs and one or two perfunctory gasps, and then Leora pulled herself together and thanked me icily and 'called on' the next kindergartner, and the game went on—every damned one of us, except, of course, for Francis, was forced through our number, including old 'Gresh' himself—his was something expedient and obviously 'prepared': a raised accreditation for our dear Aurelia in some guide to colleges he'd 'just happened' to receive that day. When Francis's turn came, Leora said coyly, 'Well, Francis, I guess under the circumstances you'd better pass, hadn't you?' and he blushed becomingly and passed. Leora's never forgiven me, but she's had the hots for my husband ever since. She never misses the opportunity to pat and rub up against him at parties, though thank God we've been spared any more of her sit-down dinners."

As Magda had been approaching her denouement Francis Lake had come up behind his wife, carrying a plate generously heaped with hors d'oeuvres obviously meant for her. After acknowledging Alice with a friendly nod, he stood quietly beside the love seat holding the plate, his head bowed forward intently as he listened to Magda finishing her story. When Magda got to the part where she had 'declined on his behalf,' and his becoming blush, and Leora's subsequent 'hots,' he had raised his soft eyes behind the horn-rimmed glasses and smiled diffidently at Alice, like a boy being forced to endure a mother's proud narration of his exploits to a new friend. The dark suit he was wearing that night, with its out-of-date narrow lapels and skimpy jacket, had made him seem a smaller man than he was.

Such an unassuming consort for this bold personality, had been

Alice's first impression. She wondered how they had ever gotten together—this was before Hugo had heard via the campus grapevine how Magda had "stolen" Francis out of a seminary. And naturally, after the story Magda had just finished telling, Alice couldn't help wondering how they were together in bed. Probably everybody at the president's dinner table had been picturing one thing and another after Magda's infamous demurral.

Were they true, Magda's juicy intimations? Or was she putting up some kind of smoke screen? Who could tell? Who could ever tell for sure about other people's marriages?

Did they ever try to have children? Alice had gone on to wonder as Magda was winding down her tale. Of course Magda was quite a bit older, as conventional marriages went, but they seemed to have been together long ago enough for there still to have been time, if they had wanted at least one child.

Back in December, the whole world for Alice had been about people wanting and having children.

L eora Harris was describing a riverfront condo belonging to a couple she knew who were leaving the area soon. "It would be ideal for you two Henrys. Not large, but extremely well appointed. It's not even on the market yet, but I could put in a word for you. Since you're on the Aurelia faculty, they might be willing to assume the mortgage themselves. Get around the lawyers' and realtors' fees."

"We're not buying, Leora," said Hugo brusquely. "And we're going to need something sooner than your 'soon.'"

Alice knew how Hugo hated it when well-meaning people tried to organize his life, but it always put her on edge when he became abrupt.

"I'm sure we'll find something," she spoke up confidently, to deflect the president's wife. "I'm going to devote myself to looking full-time."

"Well, do let me know if you'd like to run over and *look* at the condo," continued the unstoppable Leora. "I could arrange it easily. And though you say you aren't thinking of buying, I find many people reconsider when they find something really suitable. Why throw rent money down the drain, when you can be building an investment? I'm sure you'd agree with *that*, Hugo. And it's a certainty you could always resell that condo, with its view of the river, for more than you paid for it."

Magda began to snore. Her jaw had gone slack, and were it not for the rattly, almost obscene, noise coming out of her open mouth, she could have passed for a corpse.

"My goodness," said Francis, who had been looking sideways out of the window in which he reclined. "There's a little girl down there on our lawn. She's trotting round and round in circles."

"Oh, bother," said Leora. "Is it a *fat* little girl, Francis?"

But before Francis could reply, she was already out of her chair, edging up beside him to look out and see for herself. Alice saw how Leora's shoulder took the opportunity to press against his.

"That child. I told her to stay quietly in the car and play the radio. It's only little Elberta Elmendorf; she's a sort of . . . "—Leora gave a brittle laugh—"assigned project of mine. I take her out with me at least once a week. Along to the mall for whatever shopping I have to do. Then to the Pizza Hut. That child can put it away, I'm telling you."

"Shouldn't we invite her in?" inquired Francis, who appeared oblivious of Leora's shoulder clamped to his. "I don't mean up here, that might not be wise. But maybe she'd like to have a glass of milk downstairs, with some of those cookies you brought, Leora."

"The last thing she needs is more food," said Leora. "Leave her be, she's fine as she is, gallumphing round in her circles. She plays these odd little games with herself. Don't worry, she won't pick your flowers or anything. She's really quite docile. If anything, she needs to learn to put herself forward more. When you consider she's going to inherit the Elmendorf fortune. Her grandmother, Mamie Elmendorf, recently adopted her and renamed her after her late husband, Elbert. Now Mamie's badgering us to let the child go along on the Alumni Cruise in August. Which will cause all sorts of snarls for us, one way and another, but I suppose we're going to end up saying yes." With an arch laugh, she reached up and caught hold of Francis's collar and, as if it were just the two of them alone in the room, pulled him close to her to confide: "Mamie is dangling some of her millions to help Gresh with a certain project he's got his heart set on, which I'm not at liberty to divulge at the moment."

"Oh, I see," murmured Francis politely. But he did turn his body slightly in such a way, Alice noticed, that would have made it extremely awkward for Leora to keep holding on to his shirt.

"I propose . . . that *we all go*," came Magda's slurred but electrifying voice from the bed.

Her head had risen out of the folds of her pillow, though still resting upon it, and her black eyes were scornfully fixed on the president's wife, whose hand was just then in the act of hastily removing itself from Francis's person.

"Would you like us to go, love?" Francis was immediately attentive. "I think we may have overtired her," he said to the visitors. "Why don't we all go downstairs? I'll make tea, and, Leora, we'll ask the little Elmendorf girl to join us."

"No, no, no, Mr. Literal-Mind," said Magda, rolling her head from side to side on the pillow. "I meant . . . *on the cruise*. Why don't we *all* go on the *cruise* in August?"

Nobody spoke or moved. Alice felt herself get goose bumps. Tears pricked at her eyes, yet she was equally afraid she might start giggling hysterically and be unable to stop.

"Well? What's the matter? Cat got everybody's tongue?" continued the merciless voice from the bed. "For your information, Gresh asked me *months* ago to do the lectures. I was his first choice. I declined, because I told him . . ."—Magda shook with silent laughter—"I told him I was already booked for another journey." Then she winced with pain and Alice saw her grab at herself beneath the covers.

"Magda, my darling, shouldn't we leave you to rest?" Francis, stooping over her now, was pleading. He looked about to cry, himself.

"I have all eternity to rest. But right now I want to go on this cruise."

Leora Harris regained her tongue. "The cruise is not until August, Magda," she said pertly. "Are you sure you'll feel *up* to it by then?" Her exultant glance round at each of the others seemed to be taking up a collection of praise for herself for rescuing them with her disingenuous reply.

"Oh, I'll be in perfect shape," responded Magda. "Francis will have to carry me, but he would have gone anyway if I'd been the star lecturer. Francis can lecture *for* me. He can lecture on his misericords and take people on tours to see them in the churches. He's the world's most informed person on that obscure subject. He's got hundreds of slides. They'll lap it up. People on cruises love to learn esoteric things so they can come home and impress their friends."

"Francis, this is the first I've heard of this esoteric knowledge of yours," scolded Leora, brushing against him.

Magda gave a raucous snort.

Not at all discomposed, Leora Harris plunged on in her self-appointed role as defender of the true facts from a dying woman's addled fantasy. "Hugo, you know, Magda, has agreed to be our star lecturer. Hugo's going to share his secrets of the creative process with us."

"Bully for him," said Magda.

An impacted groan escaped from Hugo.

"And Gresh and I are still hoping Alice will reconsider and go along," proceeded the indomitable Leora. "She says she needs to get them settled in their new place, but I'm sure it will be more fun for Hugo if she goes."

"Of course, Alice has to go," snapped Magda. "She will have to help Francis carry me. He'd never bear up otherwise."

"But, dear Magda," Leora said, adopting a supercilious tone of pity as she glanced around at the others once more, "the cruise is not until *August*."

"We're already on the damn cruise, Leora," Magda croaked majestically. "The future is *now*. As I tell my students, prophecy is not a thing in the world more than seeing into the heart of what people are doing now. Poetry, now that's a further matter. The poet has to re-create that vision through language. When I go with you on the cruise in August, I won't be able to talk back, that's all. I'll be in my jar. Well, some of me. I've asked Francis to scatter a good bit around the base of my favorite purple lilac ... lilacs thrive on ashes ... but the rest of me will be *honored* to accompany you out to sea. So that after Hugo the Writer spills his creative secrets and Francis mystifies the plebes with his misericords, you can all toast me with good champagne and toss me over the side...."

"Magda, please don't ... please don't tire yourself," stammered Francis, who looked close to breaking down.

"I think I am going to vomit," Magda suddenly announced formally. "Will everyone please leave? Francis, get the—"

"God Almighty, what an awful woman," said Hugo, driving them home.

They both knew he didn't mean Magda.

"She's so awful she's *fascinating*," Hugo went on, gathering steam. "Not an ounce of humor, not a scintilla of self-awareness, yet she *knows* she's God's gift to mankind. Did you see the way she tried to brush her nonexistent tits against poor old Francis? And her condescension to Magda. To *Magda*, who could have eaten her alive when she was well. Not that Magda didn't tear off a couple of stringy chunks today, but the crying shame is that the bitch wasn't even aware of it!"

"No, she wasn't," agreed Alice.

"But, you know, it's hard to pity Magda the way you do most dying people ... like my own mother, for instance. She just lay there and gave up, my mother: she'd given up years ago. Whereas Magda, even though she looks like a horror and has memory lapses, why, by damn, she's still running the show from the bed. And that thing she said about the future being now, that was good stuff, wasn't it? But it flowed right over that presumptuous harpy's hairdo."

"The Pastel Patter," Alice reminded him.

"Oh, right." Hugo laughed. "Poor old Francis, that's all he needs, is that virago rubbing up against him. Well, you never can tell what will turn some women on."

If the future *is* now, reflected Alice, does that mean Hugo and I have years ahead of us like this, driving home from places and doing a number on the people we've been with? Hugo's good at it, and he enjoys it, especially when it calls for flourishing invective. No, that's not completely fair. Hugo is perceptive: he really sees into people. He's probably even one of Magda's "poets," who can see into the heart of what people are doing now and put it into language. If only he *would* start putting something into language again. And why does he have to keep calling Francis "poor old Francis"? Why does it give him such *pleasure* to imply that there's something ridiculous about a woman being attracted to Francis?

"But you know, Magda didn't even know who I was. That surprised me a little. Or she pretended not to know. And that business about us not being married. I almost got the feeling it was her way of punishing me for not coming with you sooner. Oh, she's a subtle creature, all right, even as she lies there dwindling away. She uses her situation to the greatest advantage: shamming sleep, enjoying watching you squirm while you try to decide whether you've just heard a deep truth or some bibble-babble from a rotting mind."

"Maybe she doesn't always know the difference herself. But even when she isn't making sense, she always seems to be *working*."

"Right, right. A model for us all. I hope I do as admirably when my time comes. So fucking Gresh asked her first, did he? That lying toady Ray Johnson told me *I* was the president's first choice. Christ, I wish I could tell all these second-raters where to stuff my cushy salary and benefits. But I can't. Rosemary's little swindle wiped out my savings, and I've had my last payment on *Manigaults*. What if this artistic *stasis* is the way it's going to be for me from now on . . . what if I'm living in *my* fucking future now? Maybe that busybody Leora Harris has a point: we'd *better* buy instead of rent. I'll vegetate in style here for fifteen more years until I'm sixty-five, play psychoanalyst and foster father to adolescent scribblers while we pay off the mortgage."

Alice imagined fifteen more years at Aurelia with Hugo. When they paid off their mortgage, she would be forty-nine. Francis would be sixty-one. Would Francis marry again? The mere thought of Francis marrying somebody else made an ache start in her chest. Perhaps he would sell the house and move away after Magda's death. He didn't have any close friends here. He and Magda had been each other's best friend.

"Perhaps the trip to South Carolina will give you the stimulus you've been waiting for," she told Hugo, hearing echoes of her previous dutiful encouragements even before she finished speaking.

"That's what you said when you were sending me off to Prague," he growled back.

I will never again offer encouragement, she vowed. Let him stew away to his heart's content in the muck of his worst-case scenarios.

He reached over and laid a hand on both of hers, folded in her lap, then withdrew his touch quickly, as though he knew any more prolonged contact would not be welcome. He knows I was hating him, she thought. That's the trouble: he *does* know. He does see into people's hearts. And her heart hurt for Hugo; but in a different way than it had hurt when she imagined Francis married to somebody else.

"What did you say to that little girl—that not-so-little girl—as we were leaving?" Hugo asked, after driving in silence for a minute. "You went over and spoke to her while I was trying to extricate myself from Leora's real-estate schemes and poor old Francis's gratitude. What was wrong with that child?"

"She's probably just shell-shocked from being transported to her new environment. And from loneliness," said Alice. "I just went over and introduced myself. And then she told me her name had been Crystal Slocum before her grandmother changed it to Elberta Elmendorf. She said she missed her puppy. She and her father . . . Mr. Slocum . . . had acquired a puppy shortly before Mrs. Elmendorf descended and swept her off to her best interests."

"Did she actually say all that?"

"No, just about the name and the puppy. The rest was my own contribution."

Back to the only thing they could still do as amicably as ever in their marriage: discuss and analyze other people.

"Can you imagine changing a child's *whole name* like that? Jesus, the *arrogance*. And what a name!" Hugo laughed harshly. "No wonder 'little Elberta' eats. And after an afternoon spent in Leora Harris's enlightening company, I'd be galloping round and round in circles like a horse myself."

CHAPTER XIV

The peonies had opened. Dr. Rainiwari came again, then Dr. Zeller. For the first time since they'd known him, Dr. Zeller did not tell Magda and Francis about the latest movies he had seen.

While rubbing Magda's back when she was in pain one night, Francis discovered a bedsore. Early next morning, he called Zeller and Rainiwari and left a message, and the receptionist called back later in the day and said Francis was to order an "egg crate" mattress from the same medical-supply place that was going to be delivering the suction pump.

Francis had recognized the bedsore from the description he had read in the book on terminal care he had borrowed from the hospital library. In the same book, there was also a pain questionnaire, with a mind-boggling array of words for describing pain, and a pain measurement scale, which went from mild to excruciating. As far as he had been able to judge, Magda was at the "uncomfortable" level most of the time, even with her medicine, which Dr. Zeller said she could now take oftener if she wanted it. But then, without warning, the pain would jump to the "distressing" level. But Magda herself had better ways of describing it.

"It's like . . . *soundings* . . . coming out of my depths," Magda had told Francis in one of her clear intervals, when she was liking and trusting him and confiding in him as she used to do, not mixing him up with some other person in her life, or accusing him of obscure treacheries. "They're always there, like *warning* notes in a throbbing bass voice. Muted by my 'pain management' cocktail, but I can always feel them *thrumming* at me from below: '*Do-o-o-n't forget, M-a-a-gda . . . you belong to me-e-e.*' "

She could still be so funny, she was still such an actress, though she could only whisper and croak . . . could hardly move.

"Then a big, rolling one will *build*, like a wave, and break through, thrusting up through my fathoms until it crashes over the deck. It reverberates all the way up to the top of my skull. That's probably when you hear me scream."

She had such a unique way of putting things, even now. She made that pain measurement questionnaire, even with its impressive collection of words, seem like an elementary quiz.

The ones that thrust up through her fathoms to the top of her skull were, he guessed, the excruciating. But who was he to guess? As close as he was to her, he could not be inside her, feeling it as she felt it. "What's keeping her going now is her strong heart," Dr. Zeller had told Francis, shaking his head, as if Magda's strong heart itself had become the disease.

A foam-rubber mattress with protrusions on one side similar to the ones on the bottom of egg crates was delivered to the house along with a medium-sized cardboard box containing the suction pump.

Next morning, a supervising nurse and another nurse arrived shortly after Diane. The three of them, assisted by Francis, got the egg-crate mattress under Magda. She was lethargic today and only moaned angrily at them without opening her eyes.

Then the supervising nurse unpacked the dreaded box. "Now, Mr. Lake, I'm going to show you how to suction the patient's mouth. It's really a simple procedure."

Francis pressed himself against the wall to make room for her as she stooped to plug in the machine, a small unadorned motor with a blue plastic suction device attached to a long cord. The supervisor's wide, round bottom was accentuated by very tight, flowered pants. Just as well Magda was lethargic this morning, or she might have been moved to coin one of her unflattering epithets.

The nurse switched on the motor. It seemed unforgivably loud in a room where a person was so gravely ill. A muscle twitched in Magda's right cheek, or rather in the hollow where her fleshy cheek used to be, but her eyes stayed closed. The other nurses stationed themselves at a respectful distance from the demonstration.

Francis hung back, appalled, as the supervisor deftly inserted her fingers in Magda's mouth and effortlessly pried open the jaw. "You'll have to come closer, Mr. Lake, if you're going to watch this," she chided him above the racket of the motor. "We can't save her, there's nothing we can do for her now but keep her as comfortable as possible, but what I'm concerned about is, I don't want her to choke to death." She was a young woman, younger than Diane. A strong will and a self-regard shone out of her no-nonsense face.

"The saliva collects in the sides of the mouth. So what you have to do is just . . . whip around in the corners. . . ." In went the blue plastic vacuuming device. There was a greedy mechanical slurp, then another. Magda's eyes flew open, outraged. What are they doing to me now?

"Is that better, Mrs. Lake?"

Magda nodded solemnly, like a child, and closed her eyes again.

"That's all there is to it," said the supervising nurse to Francis, flicking off the motor. "You can do that easily, can't you?" She flashed a mouthful of healthy teeth at him.

"Yes, I think so, but . . . how often? How often should I—?"

"Whenever you hear her struggling to clear phlegm. Or if you're really conscientious about it, take a look in, whenever you can, and if you see it starting to build up . . ."

"If Mr. Lake isn't conscientious, I'd like to know who is," spoke up the loyal Diane in a rather emotional voice from the foot of the bed.

Outside, the trees, the grass, the flowers, everything aggressively growing. Inside, the smells, the breathing, the sporadic twitching of the face, the cramps in the feet, the increased dosages, helping her get a sip of water down, the swabbing of the foul stuff from the mouth, the "conscientious" checking for the phlegm, the fouled sheets, the everlasting washing of the sheets . . . the time she pulled the catheter out of herself and he cursed her (Diane, off duty, would have been cured of her admiration of him if she'd heard him *then*).

Inside Magda, there was something aggressively growing, too. Soon it would break her down completely and gobble her up—her "Gargoyle"—but meanwhile he must tend to this thin thread of spirit that connected her to that great mystery we were all in respect of, whatever religious beliefs we held, or didn't hold, or had held without ever questioning, and then, just as spontaneously, lost.

Every time he came back into the room, he would check first with his eyes for the rise and fall of her chest . . . then with his ears for the labored breathing . . . as if she were climbing a hill, wearily, but eager to get to the top.

Thoughts came to him that he would like to share with her. They seemed to him, oddly, just the kind of thoughts she would have liked for him to offer her in the past, the kind she had tried so unsuccessfully to pull out of him over the years.

Though it hadn't been the full two weeks since Dr. Rainiwari put her on the Brompton's Cocktail, the mental stimulation he'd promised she would have from it seemed to have expired prematurely. To the best of Francis's memory—which was admittedly addled from exhaustion—Magda's last brilliantly conversant interval had been that first afternoon of the cocktail, when they all came at once: first Ramirez-Suarez, bringing the new medicine from the drugstore and then staying long enough to benefit from its initial effects; then, soon after *his* departure, Hugo and Alice Henry, followed by Leora Harris.

Though by that time, Magda had become slightly confused, proposing they all go on a cruise. But then she had turned it around into sort of a double-level joke, saying she hadn't meant it in the literal sense. Even he, whom she was always accusing of being literal-minded, had followed her right along on both levels on that one. And then she had turned it around on them *again*, with that part about throwing her ashes over the side of the ship. (He would honor her wishes about sprinkling the ashes around the purple lilac; he had agreed to her cremation because she wanted it; nevertheless, he would have preferred for her to have a grave so he could go and visit it. But that was exactly what she didn't want, she had said: she could just see him, driving back and forth in traffic to some cemetery, spending all his time trimming the grass around her headstone, when he could be home fussing with his own grass and flowers.)

With Ramirez-Suarez on that last really conversant afternoon, she had joked in a similar double level way about her Final Exam.

"Something awful has occurred to me, Tony. What if, however hard you try on your exam, or however stupid or smart you are, *everybody gets the same grade* in the end?"

"Dear lady, you are truly inspired today. And of course we *do*, we all *do* get the same grade, in the sense I think you mean."

"Tony, you are one of the few who *do* know what I mean."

She had been running her thumb up and down the corpus on the crucifix Tony had given her, the one belonging to his late mother. "You know I'm not a religious person in the conventional sense, but this guy has always interested me." She held the little figure up challengingly at Tony. "What do you think he was really *like* as a person?"

"Well, he must have been a very . . . *attractive* person," Ramirez-Suarez ventured.

"Oh, no doubt about *that*"—Magda had laughed—"look at all the trouble he was able to cause."

S he saved her little remaining wit for others now. Or perhaps it was that the others, the visitors, stimulated her in ways that he couldn't, being there as he was with her around the clock, being simply her own, thoroughly known, "Prince Humdrum." But when she did speak to him, he tried to listen for all the meanings. He knew the time was soon coming when they would no longer be able to communicate in words. Therefore he took care with her every utterance, in case it turned out to be the last.

"Let's get out of this awful house," she had whispered a few nights ago, when he was rubbing her back. (The bedsore was slowly healing. How odd, he'd thought, that parts of the body could still repair themselves when the totality was breaking down.)

"What house, darling?" He knew that she might not mean, most probably did not mean, this house.

"Dreadful . . . never should have come. Why did you bring us?"

"Bring us where, love?"

"Oh, shush the love stuff. They'll hear, they heard us squish-squashing away in here last night through the thin wall. They make me feel like some randy old— Do you know what she *said* to me?"

"Who, Magda? Who said what to you?"

"Marie. Your *sister*. She said, 'Thank you for saving our little brother.' Yes, that's what she said."

So that's where they were, back in Alpena, Michigan, in the guest room of Jeannine's house. Poor Jeannie was dead now, had died of a stroke when she was a year younger than he was now. It was the first summer of their marriage, and he had wanted Magda to meet his family. What was left of them. Jeannine and her husband and children. His other sister, Marie, and her husband. Both sisters' husbands worked in the cement factory, as Francis's father had. Francis and Magda had taken the bus from Chicago. Going backward over his route of the previous November, the bus trip that Magda would always be quizzing him about, the detour that would become his life.

It hadn't been a very successful visit, in Alpena. He saw better now why, though at the time it had puzzled and disappointed him. Everybody had tried hard, but there were just too many differences, too many surprises.

Perhaps the biggest problem had been that his own family hadn't known what to make of him anymore. For most of his life, they had thought of him proudly as their future priest. "Will you come and work in the cement factory with Daddy now?" his seven-year-old niece asked him. "How can you be a priest if you got married?" his ten-year-old nephew wanted to know. When Francis explained he wasn't going to be a priest anymore, the boy had burst into heartbroken sobs, and Jeannine's husband made him leave the table without dessert because boys didn't cry. "That's too hard, Fred, when you know how Jimmy has always worshiped Francis," Jeannine had protested, almost in tears herself for her son. Then they'd begun to argue over whether Jimmy should be allowed to come back for his dessert, and Francis had realized from a hastily restrained movement of Fred's, followed by an instant humiliated flinch on Jeannine's part, that his brother-in-law was in the habit of hitting his sister when they were alone.

At first Magda had tried to be a good sport and fit in, listening to family stories, going on walks to the dock with Francis and the children, helping to peel potatoes and washing up with the other two women afterward, but she soon became demoralized, and stayed in the guest room for long hours, reading. She stole a book from the local library, just walked in and slid it from the shelves into her large satchel. He didn't find this out until they were packing to leave and he reminded her not to forget her book. That's when she told him what Marie had said to her in the kitchen. "They think it's a marriage of convenience, that this middle-aged schoolteacher took pity on their baby brother after he had a crisis of faith and left the seminary and lost his divinity status. Of course they know you lost your virginity as well, with these paper-thin walls, and that bed that clanks like a truck full of scrap metal, but I guess they're consoling themselves that it could have been worse. Marie tells me her husband's best friend just got sent home from Vietnam in a bag. No, *Lord Jim* saved my sanity on this visit, and I'm unrepentant. Marie can return it to the library, she owes me one. So the librarian will think the Lake girls' sister-in-law is a thief, but she won't be back for a while, if ever. I'm sure they're counting on us to divorce the minute the war is over. My God, they have no idea *at all* what sort of creature I am."

After they got back to Chicago, they'd gone through a very bad time. It almost seemed that the visit to Alpena had made Magda hate herself. Or at least hate herself in connection *with him*. She tormented him with her endless psychological speculations about his reasons for marrying "an old bag" like herself: he wanted a replacement for his mother, he was afraid he was queer, etc. She coined horrible epithets: Granny and Frannie. Some others he'd rather forget. It had gotten so bad that he decided she'd be better off without him; he took the bus downtown to the army recruiting office and signed up. He didn't tell them he was married. His original plan was to stay apart from her, take a room at the Y until the trip to the induction center, but he didn't have the money. All his money came from Magda. So he'd continued to share her apartment, share her bed, hoarding to himself the secret that he would soon be leaving her. During this time he became more aggressive with her in bed than he'd ever been, before or since. It was somehow connected to his plan to desert her forever, perhaps to go and get himself killed, and her being so vulnerable to this whole new secret side of him—the side that was going to hurt her so badly. As he forced himself on her, night after night, sometimes several times, his heart was wrung on her behalf: in her ignorance she had never seemed so helpless. She of course didn't have a clue he'd tried to enlist, until he returned home on the evening of the day he'd been rejected at the induction center: for poor eyesight. He'd never even known his eyes were bad.

After Magda bought him the glasses, he went around startled by the sharp outlines of people and things. In some ways, he liked the old fuzzy shapes better. "Now I guess you can see what a blowsy old bitch I really am," Magda challenged him. But she was joking again; the old confident, mocking tone had returned to her voice. The bad period had passed. They were each other's mainstay again; they were two against the world. Except for a subsequent visit to Magda's mother in Great Neck, later that summer (a visit equally uncomfortable, in a different sort of way, as the visit to Alpena), they were like orphans who had found shelter in one another. Each *was* the other's family, each was all the other needed in terms of a private life. As for work, Magda had her teaching, and his work became Magda.

Coming in during the night to check on her, he would sometimes sit down very quietly in the chair by the window so as not to disturb her sleeping, and listen to the labored, uphill breaths. She seemed to be climbing away from him, striving to get somewhere else and leave him behind. Then something, some unwilled movement on his part, a ragged intake of his own breath, would alter her breathing. Occasionally, then, an exasperated sigh would escape her. As though, just when she had almost succeeded in escaping, some awareness of his continued need for her had summoned her back again, the reluctant but obliging wife, to abide with him a little while longer until he could bear to let her go.

CHAPTER XV

Hugo, waiting his turn to descend the rickety metal steps from the plane, was broadsided by his first impact of Calhoun's flatland heat and humidity. He was certain the June air had not been this hellish when he was growing up here. However, he repressed the urge to whip out his handkerchief and mop defensively at the droplets already forming on his brow and neck. His welcoming committee might be watching from inside.

As he crossed the tarmac his reflection, laden with black leather garment bag and matching carry-on (birthday gifts from Alice—in hopes he would travel more?), trudged toward him from the terminal's long glass windows. A stocky, bulldog-faced, gray-haired man in a tan suit and open-necked dark polo, advancing under lowering eye-brows toward the awaiting duties and just desserts of his profession.

Inside, his practiced, author-being-met glance swept the greeters massed at the arrival gate. Now, where was that cluster of snooty la-dies with their classic clothes and understated daytime jewelry? ("We'll be there with bells on," Mrs. Chace McCandless had prom-ised in her last phone call, her lilting contralto drawling out the "theh-ah," assaulting you like an old treacherous melody.)

Then, for a heart-stopping moment, everything else around him vanished as he spotted his dead father in a skinny, sharp-chinned old geezer hunkering by the gate. It was his father's cheap white see-through shirt, the pink flesh and sleeveless undershirt visible be-neath; it was his father's exact posture: a sly blend of subservience and insurrection.

A lovely girl materialized in the background, standing by herself and coolly smiling as she waited for him to notice her. She displayed, at unobtrusive chest level, a hardcover copy of *A Month with the Manigaults*. Even at this distance he could see that the book, encased in protective plastic, was gratifyingly well-worn.

He sauntered over, adjusting his garment bag so he could more easily shake her hand. "Am I the one you're waiting for?" he rumbled modestly.

"You sure are, Mr. Henry. I'm Cam McCandless. Welcome to Calhoun. Or maybe I shouldn't say that, when you grew up here."

"It's always nice to be welcomed," he assured her, and stopped at that. Any added gallivanting flourish ("... by such a lovely com-mittee of one," etc.) might strike her as too forward, brand him in-stantly out of her class. Which he was, oh, wasn't he ever, but he was returning to his home turf as a Knight of Art, and whatever the origin of your knighthood, a knight didn't take liberties with la-dies. For though she was barely in her twenties, if that much, Cam McCandless was already stamped *lady*. (She was obviously the daugh-ter; her voice was not at all the mellow, lilting contralto that had en-ticed him down here over the telephone.) This girl had been bred and protected and reserved for the best. Golden privilege was evident in the disciplined swing of her simply but expensively cut blond hair, in every one of her silky gestures as she moved with him toward the exit. The proximity to this sort of girl used to rouse a sullen self-hatred in him, because he could not aspire to her.

But Cal could have. His son Cal was elegant enough to have gotten one like this. If he had been so inclined.

"Have you got all your luggage, Mr. Henry, or do we want to go along to baggage claim?" The gracious "want to," not "have to," with its implications of being put-upon. Ah, he would have to retune his ear to their perfidiously delicate codes. The writer in him rejoiced at the native treasures to be plundered on this visit; the mill hand's son quailed at the prospect of missing a step in their ornate, fronded, subtle terrains and falling flat on his face.

"Nope, this is it. My rule is, if I can't carry it, it doesn't go." If he had a hundred dollars for every trip he'd said that to some stranger meeting him at an airport, he'd be rich.

"You sound just like Mother. She travels light, even to Japan. Whereas if I go away for the *weekend*, I have to pack the kitchen sink." Her green eyes shone at him as she sang out the cliché—an old one at that—as joyously as if she'd just produced it on the spot for him. "Mother so much wanted to come to the airport, but she's had an illness, and has to stay out of the sunlight. But she's coming to the reception and speech tonight. And the dinner afterward, if she's up to it. She's been *so* excited about meeting you. You're her favorite living author. She's read every single one of your books and recognizes lots of the characters."

"Well, I'm greatly looking forward to meeting your mother, too." Christ, did he *know* Mrs. Chace McCandless? Could she have been one of those girls who had made him sullen with self-hatred? He was on the brink of asking the daughter what her mother's maiden name had been, but decided to cling to his knightly reserve. The mill hand's son would have been unable to resist asking what the illness was that made her have to stay out of the sunlight. Who was her favorite *dead* author? the jealous writer in him wondered.

As she marched ahead of him over the zebra crossing to the parking lot, he saw the heavy calves and ankles below the graceful camouflage of her swaying skirt. Not a damn thing they could do about heredity, even with all their privileges. Vindictive elation surged in his spiteful boy's heart, until the Knight reproved him for being mean and small.

After she'd raised the hatch of her snappy Japanese estate wagon and they'd stowed his luggage in its red-carpeted interior, he made a point of walking the driver to her door and opening it for her. He saw it register on the girl's face as a quaint gallantry on his part, and forgave himself somewhat for his churlish spite on the zebra crossing.

It was in going around to his side of the car that he again spotted the dead ringer for his father humbly jackknifing himself into the backseat of an old fin-tailed Pontiac already overflowing with women and children. A pie-faced young matron in bright pink sat gunning the motor, a cigarette dangling from her lips. She was frowning but looked pleased with herself, a mission accomplished, something rightfully belonging to them retrieved. They had picked up somebody, one of the women in the car, perhaps a child. There had been a woman and one child on the commuter plane with him from Columbia, but he'd had other things on his mind. Was the old man the grandfather or the great-grandfather of these children? Hard to tell. Hugo's father had looked seventy when he was forty-five. If he'd made it to seventy, he would probably have looked a hundred, but his lungs gave out at sixty-three. Smoke smoke smoke that old cigarette. Though the deadly fluff from the cotton mill alone would have done the job all by itself.

When Hugo had come down to Calhoun to bury his father, he found his first novel, *Sticks and Stones* (the only one published at the time), among his father's effects at the convalescent home. He still had it, with its cruel, smart-ass inscription: *To my progenitor, Wayne Leroy Henry.* For years, the book smelled of Lucky Strikes—or Hugo liked to believe he could detect the unregenerate brand his father had favored. He would open the novel and sniff it as he fanned through the pages, trying to imagine what his father had felt when he held this book in his hands. Knowing full well that his father never even got through the odious inscription.

Cam McCandless backed the sleek wagon out of its spot and headed for the exit, then was forced to stop and wait, engine whispering tranquilly, for the fishtail Pontiac full of Hugo's people, which had stalled halfway out of its space.

"Nice car," murmured Hugo urbanely between the angry *thruff-thruff-thruff*ings of the stalled Pontiac ahead.

"Thank you. We all drive these"—the girl laughed almost apologetically—"on account of Daddy's foundry here makes the casings for their engines. He's over in Tokyo right now on business, otherwise he would certainly be at the library gala tonight."

"I don't remember there being a foundry in Calhoun," said Hugo. "Back when I was a boy, it was mostly textiles here. Oh, yes, and I seem to remember a chemical plant, too." As if textiles and chemicals had figured with equal remoteness in his boyhood past.

"Oh, we only moved down here fourteen years ago. I was just a little girl. Our foundry used to be in West Virginia—Daddy's grandfather started it—but back in the late seventies, labor conditions there got pretty impossible, so Daddy made the decision just to pick up, lock, stock, and barrel, and move down here, where things were a lot better."

You mean a lot worse, thought Hugo. The old Pontiac's motor had finally turned over and jolted away with its human cargo. But the old progenitor—if indeed he *was* that—was squashed in a far corner, out of Hugo's sight, to make room for the rest of the dynasty. ("There you go again, Dad," Cal would be scolding now, albeit good-naturedly these days: "That old guy might be a bachelor *uncle*, for all we know.")

If the McCandlesses moved here only fourteen years ago, then how the hell could Mrs. McCandless recognize a lot of the characters in his books? And if the McCandlesses moved here only fourteen years ago, they had no way of knowing his background. Mrs. McCandless probably thought he was from one of the old families, and would take a less adoring view of his work if she found out he came from mill trash.

("Why do you always have to dwell on the *negative* implications to yourself in every situation, Hugo?" he could hear Alice saying.) Oh yes, he carried his loved ones' voices with him wherever he went. ("As long as we're saying negative things about you," Alice would probably add.)

"Now, Mr. Henry, the hotel you're going to be staying at—" the girl began brightly when they were out on the highway.

"Please, Cam, just Hugo is fine."

"Well, it's the Marriott, it's our best hotel, but they're just so impossible about some things. Their check-in time is *two*! Mother's pleading finally got them down to one, since you were such a celebrity, but, in the meantime, since it's not even noon, is there anything you'd like to do or see? I could drive you around your old haunts if you like, or, Mother said if you wouldn't think we were taking advantage, she'd love to have you come by the house for a cup of coffee."

"I think I'd prefer the cup of coffee." His old haunts. Now that would be a skit, wouldn't it: "Yes, young lady, let me take you on a slumming tour. I'll show you some really impossible conditions."

Not that he'd even be able to find his way to those old haunts, if they still existed. Everything they were passing looked totally foreign to him; she might have been driving him through the tackiness of commercial zoning anywhere in America.

"Well, that would be just great then . . . if you're sure."

He noticed she still had avoided using his first name.

The wagon's Japanese engine, sheathed in Mr. McCandless's Calhoun foundry casing, purred them through subsistence-level housing developments and their feeder malls (all new since Hugo's time), into the "better" suburbia of Malvern Valley with its spiffier shopping complexes.

"When I was a boy, this was all fields around here. Then came the golf course, and over there, where the mall is now, was the old Malvern Valley Country Club. It used to be surrounded by lovely old trees." He heard himself through Cam McCandless's ears: a nostalgic oldie. To his own ears, he sounded like what he was being at the moment: an old fake. She would assume he had *belonged* to the club.

"Oh, really? Mother and I like the Jordan Marsh at Malvern Valley for some things, like linens, but the new Cedar Hills Mall has Ralph Lauren and Gap, so we tend to go there more, even though it's way on the other side of town."

He remembered himself in a finer hour, sitting in that coffeehouse last April in Prague and seeing, via Kafka's Castle on the bluff, the only aspects of the Malvern Valley Country Club that mattered to him as an artist. That afternoon, he had felt grateful and chosen in his outsiderhood. Now here he was, insidiously misleading this rich girl.

They entered the city limits and grazed the old downtown section. The street that used to run down the middle had been sealed off to create a pedestrian boulevard, mostly for blacks, from the look of it. The two arrogant old department stores that had stood side by side competing for the best trade (the windows of the Gentile-owned establishment curtained on Sundays) were now amalgamated into one giant discount store. How the mighty are fallen.

"I took us just a tiny bit out of the way," Cam McCandless confided, "so I can run you past the new library and give you a sneak preview of where you're going to be tonight." The Japanese wagon nipped into the side street which, Hugo remembered, led to the Armory. But already he could see that the square old yellow fortress that had hulked at the end of the block was gone, and in its place rambled an evidently new, low-lying suburban building of rock and glass, generously landscaped with a variety of young trees and shrubs. Red clay was still visible through the recently planted lawn, which had been cordoned off with ropes. Balloons floated above the rock-and-timber sign: CALHOUN PUBLIC LIBRARY. Slotted into its glass-fronted announcement board was today's date, Friday, June 7, and his own name, listed as the keynote speaker, below *Gala opening and reception*, 7:00 P.M.

"Very attractive," he said.

"*Isn't* it? I don't want to brag, but Mother was instrumental in bringing this new library to fruition. They'd been dithering around down here for *years*. They'd divided themselves into two warring camps. One side wanted to renovate the old library on Main Street, which would have cost more than a brand-new *building* by the time they got rid of all the safety hazards. Those old cement stairs alone! Children were always falling down those old stairs, myself included."

Hugo remembered the steep stairs. They always smelled like someone had recently peed on them. He'd always assumed an adult vagrant pee-er, but perhaps it had only been the latest child who had fallen and lost control. He had an image of an awkward little girl, new to town, tangling with her own heavy legs on those stairs and going down with her library books in a clump of shame.

"Then the *other* faction wanted to build out near the new high school, but that would mean only people who had cars could get to the library. Mother thought it was very important that people who needed to could *walk* to the library. She told the development committee, 'Some people in this world don't *own* cars, and they need to read just as much as anyone else. Maybe more.' Mr. John Carteret, he's a good friend of ours, he's still teasing Mother about that, on account of, you know, Daddy being more or less in the car business. Mr. Carteret will be there tonight. He says you two went to school together. He hopes you'll remember him."

"Johnny Carteret, sure." *He hopes you'll remember him.* "What's he doing now?"

"Oh, still real estate. He took over his father's business. Mr. Carteret Senior passed away a few years ago, I guess you knew that."

Our old mill-village slumlord: may hell's flames be grilling his skinflint bones to crumbly charcoal.

"No, but I'm sorry to hear it," he rumbled insincerely to the girl. Had Johnny recognized his jowly sire in Hugo's portrait of Manigault, the cotton-mill owner? Probably not, even if Johnny had been able to read the damn book. He wouldn't have made the connection. Johnny, though friendlier than most of their kind, had never had much between the ears. And besides, what son remembers his father being as bad as he was? Look at me back at the airport, thought Hugo, going all sentimental over that old redneck in his see-through shirt.

"It's a very attractive place, your new library," he reiterated. "Literacy will be well served. My compliments to your mother."

The thing she'd said about people being able to *walk* to the library had hit more than one reverberating chord. It was almost uncanny, the juxtapositions here. This new building on the site of the old armory, all the rest of it. The summer Hugo was thirteen, the department of motor vehicles had been moved temporarily to the armory while they were renovating the county offices downtown, and he'd had to go along when it came time for his father to renew his driver's license. In the past, Hugo's mother had taken part in this particular conspiracy (there were quite a few of them, built around his father's secret), but she had died the previous spring.

On entering the high, echoing, dark building, his father already had his hackles up because the *layout* was going to be different. Then for a minute it had seemed the jig was up: the chairs with writing arms where you had to sit to take the exam were too close to the person on duty behind the makeshift counter where they were issuing the licenses. Over at the county offices, you got to go around a corner to do the written exam. But wily Wayne Henry had found a way to make the darkness of the armory work for him.

Hugo's father sidled up to the unsmiling woman behind the counter. "I been having some trouble with my eyes," he confided. "Would it be all right if I carry one of them chairs down to that big window at the end so I can see what I'm reading and writing on this piece of paper?"

Surprisingly she let him. Thinking perhaps she'd fail him farther down the line on the eye test.

Until his father could get settled in, Hugo, hands in pockets, did his best to create the appearance of a bored boy loitering restlessly about the big old armory on his own. Some more people came in to take the test. There was a basketball hoop at the far end, near where his father had set up shop near the big window, and Hugo loped down and shot a few phantom baskets before ambling casually over to stand behind his father's chair. Heart thudding (Could they be arrested for what they were about to do? But if they didn't do it, how would his father get to work . . . or drive *him* anywhere?), he peered over Wayne Henry's skinny shoulder and plunged into the blocks of print. For a moment he was not close enough, and he had a sickening insight into his father's disability. *This is just patterns of black marks to him. The marks don't convey any words or images.*

"Check the second box on the first one . . . then the first box . . . now the second . . . then the third . . . now the—"

"Hold your horses, son."

"No, the *third* box, Dad."

"Well, damn it to hell, you're *rushing* me. Now look what you done, I already made my mark in the second box."

"Just scribble over it, like you made a mistake, and check the third box. The next one is . . . let's see. . . ."

"Hurry *up*!"

"I'm trying to think." If two cars get to an intersection at the same time . . . "Check the first . . . no, wait a minute, the second."

"Make up your mind, son."

While they waited their turn for the dour woman to check the exam, Hugo and his father stood some distance away, pretending to examine marksmanship plaques on a wall. "The eye chart is the same one they had downtown," Hugo was relieved to be able to report.

His father snickered. "The old AZDFE?"

"That's right. Then CRSBV, DN—"

"—STZ, I know, I know," his father had scornfully completed the line from memory. "Stupid son of a bitches, never even change their chart." Then he balled up a fist and socked Hugo playfully on a biceps, and the son had cherished a rare moment of approbation from his father.

But when they were out in the sunshine again, the new license tucked securely in his father's wallet, Wayne Henry had spat on the sidewalk. "Christ, son, any fool knows that the car on your right has the right of way. She said I would of had a perfect score if it hadn't been for that." And then, as if that hadn't been enough, he'd whined resentfully at Hugo, "I always got a perfect score with your mother."

Cam McCandless negotiated them in air-conditioned comfort through a heat-shimmering grid of faintly remembered streets undergoing urban transformations of varying kinds. Then, dipping down onto an expressway, she full-throttled them past half a dozen or so exits to one marked BRIARWOOD HEIGHTS.

They ascended into the cloistered preserves of the well-to-do. "This all used to be just countryside and pinelands in my time," Hugo could only murmur as the engine, shifting into a soprano range, sang its way home up the curving, shady road into denser and denser greenery surrounding larger and larger estates. Even though the temperature in the wagon had not changed, it already seemed much cooler.

"A lot of it was in my time, too," said the girl wistfully. "We could play in the woods on all four sides of us, when we first built our house. Now, of course, there are houses all around, but Mother says you can't tear down trees and build your pile and then not expect others to want to build theirs."

We'll soon meet this paragon of democracy, thought Hugo, experiencing a first twinge of loathing for Mrs. Chace McCandless.

"You have brothers and sisters?" the gracious Knight inquired.

"Two brothers and a sister. Emily Ann's married now, she just got married last September. To a great boy. Chace Junior, my older brother, lives in Oregon with his girlfriend. They raise llamas. Willie's the baby, he's fourteen. I wish you could meet Willie, he's everybody's love, but he's in Japan with Daddy. It's his reward for making all A's and B's last year. And it was his first year away at school, too."

That's right, they all went away to prep school at fourteen or fifteen. Hugo remembered his relief in tenth grade when, at the beginning of the year, he looked around and saw his classes virtually emptied of those crewnecked, penny-loafered snots who lounged together in the hallways, drawling in casual voices about dances at the club and checking you over for sartorial flaws as you walked past—or worse, looking right through you. Their removal from the scene took a clamp of self-consciousness off him. There was more room for him to shine in. Certain girls, the ones on the cusp between impossible and available, might see him now. One did. She surprised him by asking him to the movies three Saturday afternoons in a row. She wouldn't let him lay a finger on her, but there she was beside him in the dark theater. He had treasured her remoteness: it would enhance the value of his conquest, if and when it came.

But with Thanksgiving break and the return of the preppies, his little idyll was dashed. He found out she'd been reporting her dates with him in her letters to Merriweather Stokes, off at Woodberry Forest. He overhead two of the snots discussing it on the other side of the shelter where you waited for buses downtown. "It's probably Colette's way of keeping Merry jealous," said one. "But I thought Merry has the hots for that girl at Chatham Hall now," said the other. "Well, what old Colette doesn't know won't hurt her, will it?" said the first. They had both snickered.

After that, Hugo turned down "old Colette's" invitations. He said he had work to do for his father on Saturdays. That overheard exchange at the bus shelter had completely devalued her for him. It didn't occur to Hugo until years later that the two snots, friends of Merry's, might have spotted him first and staged the whole thing for his benefit. In retrospect, too, he realized he had hurt the girl. Not that she hadn't deserved it. But the really painful lesson to be learned from all this was that the enemy *hadn't* gone away and left room for him to shine in.

And it never would, Hugo realized as Cam McCandless pulled up in front of what her mother would no doubt call "a pile." Wherever he lived, whatever he achieved, the enemy would always be in town, devaluing, snickering, cramping his space, spoiling his glories. Such as they were.

"Oh, she is going to be so delighted I've brought you," said his pretty driver, swishing silkily beside him through the dense heat along a winding brick walkway between heavily scented flowering shrubs heads taller than he was. Magnolia trees and tropical palmettos provided incongruous surroundings for the dour, new-old, gray stone Tudor looming ahead of them.

She unlatched, then thumped open with the pad of her palm, a massive door under the archway and led him into a dungeon-cold air-conditioned entrance hall. "Mother," she called out, "I've brought you some company."

He followed her around a corner into a grand manorial layout. Two vast drawing rooms, each one with the square footage of an average person's house, opened on either side of a great hallway into dim recesses of wainscoting, faded tapestries, and gargantuan sideboards. Some decorator had filled both rooms to the hilt with overstuffed couches and armchairs whose custom-faded fabrics too exactly picked up on the tapestries. The windows were mullioned, with that old wavery glass you couldn't see through. Somebody here has baronial visions of himself, thought Hugo, starting to wish he had asked Cam to drop him at the Marriott. He could have waited more comfortably in the lobby until check-in time.

Then, floating toward them down the grand hallway, her little slippered feet soundless upon the Oriental carpeting, approached the eeriest lady Hugo had ever laid eyes on. Incredibly light, both in movement and hue, she gave the effect of being translucent. She was clothed in flowing Japanese-type trousers and tunic of a silvery fabric. Her hair, gray like his, fell over one shoulder in a single thick braid.

Her eyes, a smoldering dark brown, gave the only color to her pale and startlingly moon-shaped face.

"Mr. Henry, I'm Bea McCandless. I can't tell you how I have looked forward to this." The voice, that had lured him down here with its rich contralto warmth, seemed too substantial for such an airy frame.

"Please call me Hugo," he said, surprised by the strength of her handshake. She held him eye to eye for a moment (she was a little shorter than he), keeping his hand clasped firmly in hers. He focused rigorously on those lively, burning, dark eyes, to avoid giving the impression of being appalled by her freakishly round face. Had she been born like that, or was it something to do with her illness? Well, he sure as hell wasn't about to ask.

"I will, with pleasure. Camilla, I hope you haven't left my *Manigaults* at the airport."

"Would I do a thing like that, Mother? It's in the backseat. Would you like me to go and get it?"

"If you would. I'm going to take shameless advantage of our guest and ask him to sign *all* his books. If you'd be so kind . . . Hugo."

"I'd be honored."

"Come, let's go to my part of the house. What the children call my offices."

Releasing his hand, she rustled softly ahead of him back down the grand hall. From behind, she was ethereal, diminutive perfection. What a shame about that face!

Left turn and down a wainscoted passageway, then suddenly into the very antithesis of the oppressive baronial reception rooms up front: a light bower of gracious, domestic comfort. Bea McCandless's "offices" were a state-of-the-art kitchen—the kind you saw advertised in *Architectural Digest*—combined with sitting room, library, and glassed-in porch. The glass, Hugo noticed, had a slight smoky tint that bathed everything in flatteringly muted, rather than glaring, daylight. He also noticed the stack of novels sharing the glass-topped surface of the wicker desk with a porcelain bowl overflowing with roses in many colors: his entire oeuvre (minus the one volume being retrieved at this moment by the daughter), all encased in protective plastic but bearing evidence of usage.

"Now, Hugo, what can I get you?" Her burning, straightforward look into your face. Part of her personality? Or developed as strategic defense against your looking too intently at her face?

"Coffee would be just fine." That was what he'd been invited for.

"Oh, there's always coffee. I can even fix you cappuccino, Chace is very fond of it." She laughed. "So much so, he presented me with a cappuccino machine for my birthday. But perhaps you'd prefer a whiskey ... or some wine, maybe? You must just say. Also, it's getting to be an acceptable hour for lunch, you know."

The daughter sashayed in and laid *A Month with the Manigaults* on top of the pile of his books. They made a respectable stack, when you considered he hadn't published until he was thirty-four. Eight books in sixteen years, an average of one every two years. Not bad.

But this coming fall *A Month with the Manigaults* would have been out two years.

"Will you stay and have something with us, Camilla?" the mother asked.

"No, ma'am, I think I'd better go practice."

"Take something up to your room, then. Art demands stamina." The smoldering eyes in the moon face sought his concurrence. "Doesn't it, Hugo?"

While the girl arranged a cold plate for herself out of a refrigerator that looked as if it had been stocked by a caterer an hour before, the mother boasted. "She's been accepted at Peabody for the fall. And just this past January she was solo pianist with our Philharmonic in Columbia. I was once a pretty fair musician myself, but I'm happy to say Camilla is the real thing."

They were left alone. "Let's sit over here in my favorite corner." She gestured for him to join her in an inviting enclave of sofas facing the glassed-in porch, which looked out over a stunning flower garden. Hardly had he seated himself when she sprang up again and, in her rustly silvery shimmer, transported his novels from her wicker desk to the round, glass-topped table in front of the sofas. She made two charming trips out of it. On a third trip, she brought the porcelain bowl of roses, placing it like an offering before him, next to his books.

"Now, do let me bring you something." The moon face hovered expectantly above him. "You couldn't have had anything very substantial on the plane. Why don't I make you up a little plate of snacks? And meanwhile, what may I get you to drink?"

"The snack plate sounds irresistible. But I'd like just a simple cup of black coffee, if it's not too much trouble." A tall, frosty vodka tonic set down next to his novels on this glass-topped altar to himself would have been the crowning pleasure in this idyllic setup, but experience had taught him to be wary. There were still the afternoon and long evening to get through, and he had to be up for his speech.

"No trouble at all." A silky whish, the flip of a switch. "Sometimes the simple things *are* best, aren't they?"

While she busied herself filling his plate Hugo studied an exhibition of leather-framed snapshots on the end table beside him. He recognized Cam, or Camilla, a few years younger. The siblings were uniformly light-haired and suntanned, clad in the up-to-the-minute play clothing of the rich. The skinny, balding, hawk-faced guy in the black-and-green-striped rugby shirt must be the foundry magnate who'd moved the family business to the poorer South to take advantage of "better" working conditions. And in the lovely lady with the brown eyes and the braid (a darker hair color then), he recognized his hostess. So the moon face was a recent disability; he should have known. What grandee is going to choose a woman with a deformed face to perpetuate his dynasty?

When she set down his plate, and cloth napkin beside it, he was certain she knew he had seen the strategically placed pictures. That was the class-act way to do it. If he himself had been so afflicted, he probably would have met people at the door with a disclaimer. ("Please excuse my face: a recent setback. I sure as hell wasn't born like this.")

Cold chicken, ham biscuits, carrot slices, and deviled eggs. All his favorites as a boy. "But aren't you having anything with me?" he asked, slightly discomposed by the prospect of eating alone while she watched him.

"Oh, I'll join you in some coffee." She brought a little wicker tray bearing a silver coffeepot and two cups and saucers. "I drink mine black, too." Holding his gaze with the eloquent eyes, as though confiding an intimate habit they shared.

He unfolded his napkin demurely across his knees. Shortly after they married, Rosemary had upbraided him after a dinner party for shaking out his napkin "like you were airing a *rug*, Hugo. When anybody does that, it's a sure sign they grew up with paper napkins." He had won that round by replying, "Well then, I've fooled them good and proper, haven't I? Because I didn't grow up with any napkins at all."

"These were all my favorite things as a boy," Hugo told Bea McCandless, gingerly picking up a chicken thigh with thumb and two fingers.

"I know," she said, seating herself close by on an adjacent sofa. "I've read *Blue Smoke*. That church picnic! It makes your mouth water. And also Waldo, in *One Stayed Home*, has that dream in boot camp about his mother's deviled eggs, doesn't he?" She poured their coffee, smiling to herself. "I hope my children will dream about my deviled eggs, sometimes."

"I'd forgotten all about Waldo having that dream at boot camp." What a dream of a reader she was.

"But don't you ever reread your own books?"

"Nope, never. Oh, when the thing's first published, I go through it, read passages to myself, congratulate myself that it exists, that I finished it. I love the *heft* of a finished book in my hands." He caught himself gesturing with his chicken, but Mrs. McCandless only seemed to gaze more adoringly. She had made all this food for him. What if he had decided to go straight to the hotel, or let the daughter drive him around? Would she have been crushed, insulted? Or equally cordial when she met him this evening at the library-do? Just as cordial, he decided. "But then, after that, I'm on to the next one. Or worrying about a next one. It's as if I'm not allowed to build on my past efforts. I have to start all over from scratch each time. And each time I wonder if I'll ever be able to do it again."

"That's probably why you've continued to grow. You haven't rested on your laurels." Like her daughter, who must have learned it at her knee, she could make an old cliché sparkle as though she'd minted it just for you.

"Well, I'd like to think so," he murmured between bites of chicken. "What beautiful roses . . . so many different kinds. Did you grow them yourself?" The modest Knight, deflecting praise.

"They're from my garden . . . gardening was my great passion, but someone else has to do the work now. I'm not allowed in the sun anymore. However, these were *picked* by me this morning. I went out with my basket and shears at four-thirty, before the sun was up, and cut only the very prettiest, in your honor."

"I'm glad I got a chance to see them."

"Oh, if you hadn't been able to come to the house, I would have brought them to the reception this evening. But the Marriott's inconvenient check-in time was to my advantage, wasn't it?"

"Let's say, to our advantage." He started on a deviled egg. It had the requisite chopped sweet pickle, just like his mother's. Was Bea McCandless a sweet-pickle person herself, or had she gotten that out of his books, too?

"When I was out in the rose garden at that magic hour this morning, I told myself, 'Bea Davis McCandless, you're going to risk it. The worst that can happen is he'll say no. And what a shame if he might have said yes, and you were too chicken to ask!' " She laughed and sipped her coffee. "I'd be like your man in *The Chickenhearted Lover*, who was always denying himself his heart's desires for fear of making a fool of himself."

"Oh, right, poor Dudley Trask," rumbled Hugo wryly. As if Dudley Trask, that prototype of insecurity, were miles removed from anyone like himself. Then rage at his lackadaisical agent blackened the pleasures of this present moment. He'd been after Arthur for over a year now to get the rights back on *Chickenhearted Lover*, which, along with *Sticks and Stones*, was out of print. Damn it to hell, did you have to carp and nag at your agent round the clock to protect the investment of you both? Yet if he dumped Arthur and found another agent, which he frequently fantasized doing, Arthur would still represent those eight books. Screwed every way.

An impressive barrage of piano notes pealed out from a distant part of the house: the girl was warming up with some very advanced exercises. The mother raised her dark eyes approvingly toward the sound and then smiled at Hugo. "I recognize so many of the people in your novels," she said.

"So your daughter tells me," he replied warily. "But, as I understand it, you didn't grow up in Calhoun."

"No, though I am a South Carolina girl. My people came from Sumter. But what I meant was, I recognize their types. They're *like* people I intimately knew, or was once intimidated by, or put on a pedestal and later had to take down again. Only they're . . . *clearer*, somehow, in your books. One comprehends them better. That's your art. And, though your main characters are usually men, I feel they're very much like me. They've helped me understand so much about myself! Good books can do that. That's why I'm always bending everybody's ear about literacy programs. Books can save you, I truly believe that, don't you? But first, you have to be able to *read* them." She stretched out her small hands in a beseeching gesture, appealing her cause with the eloquent dark eyes.

Hugo contemplated in midair the carrot stick he was in the act of raising to his lips. The morning's memories boiled upward, aching for utterance. Yet, had she not spoken so recently of chickenhearts, her example derived from his own work—more important, had she not set him such a brave example in her manner of communicating despite her own impediment, he couldn't have risked it. Though the desire to risk himself to Bea McCandless didn't totally account for his motive. It was more. He wanted to give this lovely lady something precious of himself in return for her faith in his work.

He returned the carrot stick to the plate, though he knew it was rude to put food back once you'd picked it up. "My own father couldn't read or write," he heard himself telling her in a voice that sounded surprisingly calm and gentle. "He was taken out of school very young, they could get away with those things back then; they needed him for the farm work. And after he and my mother married and they came to Calhoun to take jobs in the mill, he learned to fake it. While she lived, he faked it brilliantly. He wasn't a stupid man, by any means. . . ."

"Most of them aren't! They're gifted in all sorts of ways!" Her eyes were brimming at him, the pale moon face glowing passionately. This was clearly one of her Causes.

"This all came back to me this morning, because, well, first I saw a man who reminded me of my father at the airport, when your daughter was meeting me, and I was remembering the inscription I'd written to him in *Sticks and Stones*. It was the only book of mine he lived to see. He couldn't even read my inscription, except for his own name. He had learned to recognize that, and to produce a sort of scribble that passed for his signature. . . . I'm sorry, is this upsetting you?"

Bea McCandless had begun to weep. "No, please go on." She motioned him with the little hands. "It's a wonderful story. It's just that I'm so very touched . . . it's wonderful that you would see fit to tell this to *me*. Oh dear"—she patted at a pocket in the silvery tunic—"where's my tissue gone?"

"Have this." Gallantly passing his handkerchief. From above, the distant piano burst into a professional cascade of melody.

"She's showing off a little, in your honor," said Bea, dabbing at her eyes with his handkerchief. "That's the Mozart she played with the Philharmonic. She should be practicing something new, but I'd probably do the exact same thing myself if my mother were entertaining a famous writer downstairs. Please . . . Hugo . . . go on with your story. There *is* more, I hope."

"As a matter of fact, there is, but I warn you: what's coming now is the kind of thing a fiction writer would hesitate to put in his novel today . . . the coincidence is too pat. It would offend the cynical modern reader's belief in randomness."

"Oh, I'm at the other end of the scale from cynical. But, would it be wise for me to hang on to your handkerchief?" She was smiling broadly at him again.

"Better keep it available." He was so perfectly at ease with her by now, he could even joke before embarking on the story of his father and himself at the armory: "Who knows? I might need it myself."

"You know, Hugo," she said excitedly as soon as he had finished, "you have just *got* to tell this story tonight. Why, it has been practically *sent* for the occasion. A world-famous writer standing on the actual physical *spot* of such a memory as he blesses the new library."

He gave an edgy laugh. "Oh, I don't know if I'm quite up to that, Bea." He could just see himself standing up there spilling the family shame in front of Johnny Carteret, and God knew what other tormentors from his old life who would be showing up tonight. "Besides, I've already written my speech. I think you'll like it."

"Well, of course we will! We were so fortunate to get you down here at all."

She backed off at once with beautiful tact, pouring him more coffee. He munched on a ham biscuit. The daughter was playing something else now. There were pauses, then passages repeated.

He felt suddenly downcast. Though she professed to be such a devoted fan, she didn't understand him as well as she thought. For all her goodwill and good works, she didn't understand that late-comers to security like himself always had to wear a hidden truss of dignity, to keep themselves bolstered up.

"How did you and your husband happen to get together?" Resorting to his old security blanket of Asking People About Themselves. "Being as you're from down here and he's from West Virginia. You two go to college together?" Whoa, there, answering his own questions again.

"No, it was much more romantic than that. Chace was my Prince Charming. We were very plain people, my family. The reason Chace and I ever met at all was because in summers my father managed the golf shop at the Greenbrier. Halfway through the summer of sixty-three, he had to have some minor surgery, so I drove up from

Sumter and ran the cash register till he was on his feet again, and Chace came in to buy some golf balls . . . then he came in alone to buy some *more* golf balls. . . ."

"And you two fell in love." Oops, pardon me, Alice.

"Well, no, not exactly. I had other grand plans. I'd just won a music scholarship to Converse. It was very exciting for me, the idea of going off to college—we never could have afforded it, otherwise—and doing exactly what I wanted for four years. And then I had hopes, you see, of becoming a professional musician, though I see now I could never have made it. I didn't have the stamina for it. And I didn't have the . . . *self-assurance* you need to be a performer. Now, Camilla has both of those things in buckets, and her technique is a thousand times better than mine ever was. . . ."

"So did you go to Converse in the fall?" Block her from digressing into more praise for the musical daughter.

She was examining her hands thoughtfully. For their lost musical prowess, or reading the past in them? "Yes, I did. But, come spring, I'd dropped out and was planning my wedding. Chace loves a challenge, and I guess I was a challenge because I didn't want to have anything to do with him at first. But he's a superb strategist. That's why he's done so well in his business. I do wish you could have met Chace, I know you two would have hit it off. . . ."

"So, what was his strategy with you?" Block the digression into praise for the successful husband.

"Well, it *wasn't* with me. That was his pure genius. As soon as he saw I was going to be impossible, he waited until my father was back on his feet in the golf shop. After I'd gone home to Sumter, he won my father. Then my father came home and went to work on my mother. Then Chace came down to Sumter and won my younger sisters and brothers. When all of *them* ganged up against me, I knew I didn't have a chance. So I gave in gracefully . . . to my fate." The eyes sparkled at him enigmatically in the eerily round face. "Chace has been absolutely wonderful to my brothers and sisters. He put them all through college. They were right to sponsor him."

Did Hugo pick up the faintest acrid note from the lady who professed herself to be "at the other end of the scale" from cynicism?

"And what about his own family? Did he have to win them over, too?"

"Obviously there must have been *some* effort required there," the daughter of plain people remarked with a laugh, "but when Chace's parents showed up for the wedding, they were charm and kindness personified. Chace's father died soon after we married, but Chace's mother and I get along famously now. She's taught me a great many things I'm better off for knowing. And I've taught her a few things as well."

I'll bet you have, thought Hugo, believing he could imagine some of the things each woman had taught the other.

"She's not in good health herself now, but she's been so dear to me since I became ill. Why, she even joined the Lupus Foundation of America—that's what I've got, a form of lupus—and she sends me on all manner of hopeful or informative pamphlets after she's gone through and read them first and underlined them for me."

So that's the way you do it, thought Hugo. Drop it softly, a non-chalant little bomb, well insulated in the casings of McCandless family praise.

"Of course, with all the specialists I've had, I feel like I'm the world's authority on systemic lupus by now, but it's provided her with a diversion from her own less dramatic ailments. Not that you don't suffer just as much, perhaps more, from those tedious failings of age that just slowly wear you down. She's extremely brave in her way. . . ."

"Flannery O'Connor had lupus, didn't she?" Hugo put in quickly. Block the digression into the brave mother-in-law with the boring ailments.

"She did indeed!" exclaimed Bea McCandless delightedly. "I felt so honored when I read that she had it, too. Though my doctors wouldn't approve of my saying that. They like to emphasize that each case is different, you know, so you'll keep your hopes up. And she did get to go in the sun and feed her peacocks, didn't she? Hers wasn't the photosensitive kind. But she gives me hope. Look at the splendid work she was still able to do. And I have so much I still want to do, now that I've gotten over my silly vanity about the ste-roids making my face look like a loaf of Irish soda bread and overcome my great disappointment at not being able to work in my garden or go outside much in the daytime. My younger son Willie says I'm the good lady vampire now. I'm so grateful all my children were blessed with a wonderful sense of humor, it's made all the difference."

He prepared himself to block the digression into the children's wonderful sense of humor—shouldn't it be wonderful *senses* of humor?—when her attention was deflected by a black man stooping to do something outside in the garden. "Oh, there's John, regular as a clock, turning on my soaker hoses."

"Speaking of clocks," said Hugo, looking at his watch for the first time, "I should be off to my hotel soon." He was surprised to discover how long he had been there.

"Forgive me. The good lady vampire has been shameful, keeping you trapped here. But it's done me a world of good." She cocked her soda-bread face ceilingward. "As soon as Camilla comes to the end of her Brahms, which won't be long, I'll call her on her telephone, and she'll take you back to town."

"I've enjoyed this very much ... Bea," the gallant knight assured her. Truthfully. It had been a long time since he had felt himself thoroughly liked by a good woman. "It has done me a world of good, too."

"You're very kind to say so. I hope we will keep in touch. Now, John's little girl Selma is a very bright child, but she's dyslexic." She laughed. "See, here I go with my literacy crusade again. I've arranged for her to have special tutoring—I'm not qualified to do that—but she and I have started reading aloud for pleasure some afternoons. Well, I have to tell you this story, Hugo. We were just starting *The Secret Garden* the other day. I picked it, because it was one of my favorite books as a child, and so I naturally assumed Selma would take to it, too. Well, we got to the place where it says ... oh, dear, what was the little girl's name in *The Secret Garden*?"

"I can't remember at the moment either." Hugo laughed.

"Hello, senility! But I didn't forget *your* character's names, did I? Anyway it's right at the beginning, when the family's still in India and the little girl's parents have a busy social life. We got to the sentence ... oh, something like, 'Her mother was very gay,' and Selma's eyes got big as saucers and she said, 'Far out!' Of course we stopped then and talked about the old-fashioned meaning of the word versus the new meaning, and then I also had to explain what the little English girl's parents were doing out in India. I hadn't take into account that Selma might not know things like that. Well, Hugo, the whole thing taught me a valuable lesson. We must never presume that another person's reality is just naturally going to be the same as ours. Of course *you* have always known that, it comes across so profoundly in your work."

"In my work, maybe—by some unearned fluke, like perfect pitch or something—but in my life I've only just begun to get the message," Hugo confessed to his new friend sadly.

The daughter finished the Brahms and then the piano stopped for a while before she commenced to work on something else, and something else after that. It was Camilla who finally phoned downstairs to the mother, and Hugo did not arrive at his hotel until three hours past the early check-in time Bea McCandless had wangled for the visiting celebrity.

CHAPTER XVI

Alice watched Hugo's truculent figure, strapped with the luggage that had been her birthday gift, march away down the ramp of the feeding tube to his awaiting jet to Columbia. From there he would take a commuter plane into his old hometown of Calhoun, where he would be the center of attention for the day and the night and then return, the conquering hero, at this same airport late tomorrow afternoon. As his grizzled head and tense bulky shoulders disappeared from her sight, she experienced a sharp wrenching away from the overpowering Hugo-ness of him, followed by a sense of emptiness and peace.

What if the jet were to crash? What if this had been her last glimpse of him? Would she surprise herself by being inconsolable, dwelling on his lovable aspects, forgetting her animosity and all the unease between them in these recent months? For that was the puzzle of it. As soon as he was out of her sight, his too solid presence out of her force field, she could acknowledge and even appreciate his favorable aspects.

Leaving the Albany terminal, paying her short-term parking ticket at the gate, getting back on the thruway south, and for much of the return trip to Aurelia, she lived through this fantasy of the plane crash. First would come the phone call from the airlines—or some local person would hear it on a news update. Rhoda King, perhaps, yes. Being right there are at the radio station. ("Alice, I hate to be the bearer of such awful news, but have you heard about Flight 1068?") No, how would Rhoda King, whom she hadn't seen in weeks, know Hugo happened to be on Flight 1068 this morning? It would have to be the airlines. ("Is this Mrs. Hugo Henry? We are sorry to report . . .") Or would they hedge and evade as the state trooper had done, seventeen years ago, standing on the porch in Connecticut in the rain, murmuring about visibility being practically zero and then not looking at her?

She would have to break it to Cal. No, the right thing would be to call Rosemary, and let Cal's mother break it to him. On her own behalf, there were no family members left with whom to share the news of her husband's death.

The college would have to know. One call to Ray Johnson would guarantee everyone's hearing about it within the hour. He would call the president, the president would call Leora, Leora would no doubt hop in her car and drive over to Magda and Francis's, to convey the sad news in person—and take advantage of any opportunity to rub against Francis if she could.

Would Alice have to fly off somewhere to identify the body? What sympathetic soul would insist on driving her back to the airport, seeing her off on her grim mission?

At this point she realized that, except for Magda, and possibly Francis—neither of whom could come to her assistance at the moment—she had made no friends in Aurelia. So rather than endure the bossy intrusions of Leora Harris, or Ray Johnsons's smarmy wife,

Alice chooses to drive herself back to the airport, in the evening light of early summer on the first day of her widowhood. On the thruway north, she keeps her attention steady on the road ahead. She drives competently toward strangers and emptiness. Her eyes are dry, but prickled with a wide-open, burning sensation. Her whole being feels weightless, alert . . . and unattached. A sensation she's had some experience with in the past. But this time, there is going to be a difference, she feels it. Only, she doesn't yet know what the difference is to be.

An airport official in a red jacket is on hand to meet her and escort her to her gate. Solemn and deferential as the occasion requires, he matches his footsteps to hers and sticks to the language of mechanical failure, avoiding all references to human loss.

It seems that the plane which will carry her off on her grim mission will be leaving from the same gate that Flight 1068 left this morning. Alice stands, reserved and quiet in her new circumstances, besides the red-jacketed official, who hands over her ticket—first class, compliments of the airline that has killed her husband this morning—to be stamped by the person behind the counter. Discreet phrases between the two employees convey the pathos of Alice's journey without alarming any of the other passengers. Though she does overhear two women discussing the crash. ". . . no survivors," says one. "I guess I'm crazy to fly out on the same day, on the same airline, but I figure when my time's up . . ." "I feel the same," agrees the other. "Besides, the odds of two crashes on the same day are highly unlikely."

Just before the flight begins to board, the official, still carrying Alice's overnight bag and ticket, as though fearing to trust them to her, unlocks the door leading to the feeding tube and escorts her alone down the carpeted ramp she watched Hugo descending this morning, the burly set of his shoulders bearing not only his new luggage but the greater burden of his uncertain, contentious personality.

That personality. The sheer *mass* of it, in all its energy-draining paradoxes. The quick, grasping intelligence so ill matched with the chronic self-hatred. That fine-tuned sensitivity, vigorous and subtle enough to imagine its way into obscure human corners for art's sake, yet so blunted in its everyday exchanges by belligerence and impatience. Yet weren't we all just such burdens of contradictions to ourselves and everybody else? For God's sake, who was perfect?

That's when it overwhelms her, the Hugo-ness that is gone out of the world forever. It's no longer there for anybody to depend upon or occasionally delight in or bump against or withdraw from.

It's no longer there for her. The extinguishing for Hugo has removed the last barrier between herself and free-fall. At the end of the feeding tube is not a waiting jet to carry her to her husband's blackened remains, but the alluring space she has been courting for years. With Hugo gone, she is at last free to tumble into its vast emptiness. Head over heels like a floppy doll, with straw for a heart, and burning, wide-open eyes. On and on forever, belonging to no one, unattached to anything, able only to observe and register her empyrean aloneness. No wonder the red-jacketed official is holding on to her ticket and overnight bag. They are possessions still of some worth to the human community. The ticket can be cashed in, the clothing worn, the luggage used. Where she is headed she will need nothing human.

But at the last moment she panics and refuses to go any farther down the ramp. She presses her body, yes, she still has a strong, resistant body, against the flimsy wall of the tube and digs her heels into the cheap carpeting and screams: "No, no, no . . ."

Or is she screaming, "Hugo, Hugo, Hugo . . ."?

People grab her arms on either side. To comfort her and pull her back into the terminal, put her out of harm's way? Or to push her out into the emptiness she has been seeking? She is screaming and sinking. From grief or from madness? With her history, who can tell? Is there a difference anymore?

"Now this is too much," she said aloud to herself in the car. Heading home from the airport on the morning of June 7, still married to a live Hugo (as far as she knew), although unhappily. She drove for several miles more, still under the shadow of her powerful fantasy, then was contrite, then rather disgusted with herself. This was the first time that she had let herself go so far as to imagine her husband dead, though she knew from reading novels that other wives had done it. But that didn't make it admirable, any more than adultery was made admirable by the fact that other wives did it, in and out of novels.

Funny, she had let herself fantasize widowhood before she would let herself fantasize adultery.

Then she blamed Hugo. So, you've finally infected me with your favorite self-torment of spinning negative fantasies for yourself, complete with supporting cast, dialogue between minor characters, and a seismogram of the protagonist's internal agitations throughout the ordeal. God, Hugo, I have enough *real* problems, including you.

Here she was talking aloud by herself in a car again. Was it a precursor to another breakdown, like the other time, driving home after her aunt's burial, when she had kept up that nonstop monologue to her dead brother?

No, let's keep calm here. Hugo wasn't dead, therefore she wasn't driving by herself and talking to a dead person. It was not like the other time. Nobody new was dead. She didn't *want* anyone else dead. Many wives and husbands must mutter angrily at spouses when they were out of range of hearing. No, it was not like the other time. She didn't feel weightless and removed as she had that other time, or as she had in the fantasy she'd just dreamed up for herself. She felt solidly here in the car, driving back to Aurelia, wondering where she and Hugo were going to live next and how she was going to continue living with Hugo. That wasn't madness. That was just everyday life for many people.

The free day opened ahead of her, the fine June day. A precious Hugo-less day. And guilt-free, because Hugo was still safely in the world, gone off to strut his feathers and be admired: she hadn't killed him off or even wounded him. Well, not physically, at least. He was probably just as relieved as she, whether he admitted it to himself or not, to be flying out of *her* force field, her chilly force field.

How long would it take him to seek solace in adultery again? When his last marriage was on the skids, he had told her, he and Rosemary had considered it almost a point of honor to betray each other whenever they could. His confession had shocked her, though she hadn't let on at the time. She had felt he might think her prudish—or worse, "judgmental": that most incorrect of modern stances. Well, maybe she was a little of both, but she had always admired people who were discriminating in their choices rather than promiscuous. She had been scrupulous as far back as she could remember, whether from temperament or because she was afraid to be anything else, she couldn't say.

It was times like now when she really missed her brother Andy. This was something they could have discussed, something they *had* often discussed: why they seemed to be different from their friends, more like "old-fashioned" children.

Tears came now, genuine watery tears, the kind she hadn't managed even in her fantasy of Hugo's plane crash. She delighted in them, she was proud she could still produce them for Andy. It honored him. If he had survived her, she would hope he could honor her memory as highly for seventeen years.

Yes, they had discussed it often, from early adolescence right up to Andy's death: how they had come by the traits that set them apart from their classmates: their reticence and restraint; their way of not putting themselves forward, or demanding the things from adults that their friends considered the inalienable rights of children. Not that they were spurned by their peers. They were attractive, intelligent children, admired and liked, invited to all the parties, elected to class offices, but their reserve and formality kept their friends from taking the same liberties with Andy and Alice that they did with one another. Other parents were always saying how wonderful the Questrom children were, so polite and giving so little trouble!

But *why* were they like that? Was it because their mother, older than the mothers of their friends and one of the few mothers who worked full-time outside the home, was more exacting of them and not usually in a good temper? Was it because their father was "foreign," Norwegian-born (he had immigrated to the United States as an adult, sponsored by the pharmaceutical company for which he did research), and had drummed into them his homesick litany of Norwegian virtues? Norwegians were industrious, frugal, clean living, reserved. Norwegians were honest and always kept their word. They were courageous, but never boasted. You could trust a Norwegian with your life. Norwegians weren't wasteful or extravagant, they didn't whine. A Norwegian's most valued treasure was his untarnished self-respect. According to their father, Norwegians didn't even swear, not even Norwegian sailors.

"When we're older," Andy promised Alice, "you and I will go to Norway. First we'll look up our father's relatives in Trondheim, then we'll fan out into the remotest corners of that small country. We'll conduct a thorough inspection into the recesses of the Norwegian character. Just the two of us will go so we'll be able to decide for ourselves whether these folk who make up half our blood are the paragons Father says they are."

"And we'll be perfectly honest about it to each other, won't we?"

Laughing, he hooked his elbow round her neck. "I don't see how we can be anything else. Aren't Norwegians always perfectly honest?"

That's what she still missed: his personal blend of mental quickness, humor, and intimacy when it was just the two of them. She'd never again experienced the confidential rapport they'd shared, the easy belonging to each other, the never-wearying pastime of poking and probing into what you were *in the company of someone who was actually part of you.* (Or who, at the time, you had believed to be actually a part of you.) With others of their own age he'd given much less, even with his girlfriends. What might have become of their rapport when he became really serious about some girl, Alice would never know; he didn't live long enough for it to happen. In fact, she was almost sure Andy had died a virgin, unless there had been someone during those first two months of college.

At the beginning of her senior year in high school, when Andy had gone off to Yale, the high school proudly acquired its first guidance counselor, an officious, head-waggling little man with a presumptuous, knowing smile. He administered a battery of psychological tests to the entire student body, and then set up appointments with individual students for "one-on-ones," as he called the private conferences. As soon as she sat down in his office for her "one-on-one," the counselor waggled his head at her and smiled the knowing smile. "Alice Questrom is a person who likes to do well on tests, am I right?" was his opener.

She admitted it to be so.

"Well, you've done *very* well on these tests, Alice. You answers present the profile of nothing less than a saint."

In the meaningful pause he left for this to sink in, Alice knew enough not to say thank you. The counselor didn't approve of her, though she had still to figure out why. Adults had always approved of her.

"That is," he went on after a moment, "unless you checked the answers you did because you felt those were the *right* ones, the ones I would *expect* you to check. Did you do that, Alice?"

"No, I just checked the ones that were the truth."

"Ah, the truth," he said, putting a mysterious spin on the word. "I'm going to level with you, Alice. There are no truths on these kinds of tests. Anymore than there are right or wrong answers. What we're trying to get at here is a lot more important."

Alice inclined her head politely, though she hoped not enough to indicate she agreed with this unpleasant man. What could be more important than truth, or the difference between a right and a wrong answer?

"We're trying to get at what you, Alice Questrom, *really feel*." He brought this out triumphantly, as if he were offering her nothing less than the keys to paradise. "So, now that I've leveled with you, Alice, I hope you'll feel free to level with me."

"I thought—I thought the answers I put down were the—the true ones." She was alarmed at her own backing down into "I thought's"; and, even more, at her craven compromise of the single essential word she wanted, for a plural approximation of it he would find less offensive.

"I hear what you're saying," the counselor said, in a tone imply- ing he heard her but didn't believe her. "Look, why don't we take a look at a specific question and I'll show you what I'm getting at."

The question was, "Have you ever stolen anything?" Alice had checked the box marked "no," without hesitation.

"Almost everyone, at some time in their lives, has taken some- thing that wasn't theirs . . . some *little* thing . . . maybe just someone else's pencil. Something that hardly seems worth remembering." He waggled his head at her in friendly, puppylike appeal. If you remember something you stole, no matter how small, we can get along, was the clear message.

"No, I'm sorry, but I haven't. I'm sure I would remember it if I had. It would bother me." She kept her eyes focused on her feet so she wouldn't have to register his increased disapproval of her. Also to hide her disdain for him. She knew he was going to write unfavorable things in her file, but no point adding to them.

When she got home from school that day, she wrote a long letter to Andy. "It was bad enough that he made me feel untruthful, unclean. But what's worse was that he had the power to make me back down. I ended up *apologizing* for not having stolen anything."

Her brother phoned her on the evening of the day he got the letter. "What a creep. But what you've got to remember, Alice, is that integrity is a threat to people who don't have it. And there are a lot of them around; there are a lot of them here at *Yale*. They feel better when they can convince themselves the world is full of squalid creepy-crawlies like themselves. You were right to stand your ground, and you were also smart not to show your disdain for him. That's the big trick, I'm finding. You have to hold on to your standards, but you can't get smug or show contempt. Otherwise, you give them just what they're looking for, the *right* to despise you. So hang in there, little Norwegian."

Her brother's final advice to her, in the last conversation she was ever to have with him.

How would he have taken it if he'd lived to learn he wasn't part Norwegian? Would he have turned bitter and rebelled against those values his father—no longer his father—had proudly promoted as "Norwegian" ones? Or would they still have gone to Norway for her sake? She believed Andy might have been noble-hearted enough for it, but it would have been too sad for her.

Here she was, back at Aurelia. Having killed off and resurrected her husband, visited with her dead brother and buried him again, and it was still only a little past ten in the morning. How would she spend the rest of her Hugo-less day? Get the paper and go check out some rentals first, then perhaps call Francis, to see if she might stop by and sit with Magda for a while.

As she entered the house the phone was ringing, just as in her fantasy. But her sanguine certainty that it was not the plane-crash call she welcomed as a positive sign of mental health.

It was Ray Johnson, with some truly unimaginable news. Their landlady, the art-history professor, was getting married to an Italian restaurant owner and staying in Italy. "Sonia phoned Gresh at home early this morning . . . afternoon, her time in Rome. She's asking for a second year off without pay, and then she wants to negotiate some deal with the college where she can go back and forth, commute between her job and the hubby and pasta in Italy as it suits her. Gresh said she was being very unprofessional about the whole thing, but when Cupid's arrow strikes, you have to allow some leeway, he said, especially when the person in question publishes as much as Sonia Wynkoop. And also, who knows"—Ray Johnson gave his insinuating chuckle—"after a year she may have gotten considerably less addicted to pasta. But the reason I'm calling posthaste, Alice, is because Leora herself phoned me and said you ought to be informed at once so you could stop beating the bushes for a new domicile. The house is yours for another year, same exact terms, if you want it."

"May I let you know tomorrow, Ray? I'd like to consult Hugo. I just saw him off to South Carolina, but he's back tomorrow evening."

"No problem at all. That's right, Hugo's off to wow the homefolks, isn't he? Oh, wait till you hear the name of Sonia's intended. Remigio *Medici*. Isn't that superb? Gresh said that if he knew Sonia, she was as much swayed by the prospect of becoming Mrs. Medici as by any of Remigio's other conceivable attractions. Though conceivable isn't a very apropos word in this case. Our Sonia's over fifty."

After Ray's call, Alice walked slowly through the house, going into each of the rooms (except an extra upstairs room where Sonia Wynkoop had locked up her things) and withstanding the memories of their life here over the last ten months. It certainly had not been a happy house; the best that could be said was that some rooms had witnessed fewer painful scenes than others. The kitchen, very small, but organized and well lit, was the mildest culprit. She had prepared their meals, while Hugo stood in the doorway and talked to her, or sat sideways in the narrow breakfast booth and drank a cup of coffee. There'd been a few unfriendly exchanges in the kitchen, but no major animosities. They'd never eaten in the booth. It was always too constricted for Hugo, and by November Alice couldn't have squeezed herself into the narrow passage between the seat and table. Sonia Wynkoop must be a very skinny lady. Would Signor Medici, the restaurant owner, be able to fit into the narrow, maidenly booth? Perhaps after another year of pasta, Sonia wouldn't be able to squeeze in, either. Ray Johnson had realized his faux pas about his "conceivable" remark. Alice had picked it up in his uneasy laugh and his subsequent hurry to get off the phone. The good part was that she hadn't winced from it as much as she would have a short time ago.

For Next Least Painful, the dining room and living room probably tied for second place. The dining table had witnessed major animosities, but there had been many enjoyable meals as well, especially in the months when there was the baby to look forward to. Whereas there had been no animosities at all in the living room, but only because they found it so unwelcoming they hardly ever sat there.

Hugo's workroom and present sleeping quarters, the downstairs bedroom where their landlady had decreed the home birth must take place, was not as unequivocally painful as might be imagined. On that bed, the midwife, arriving before the doctor, had spread a plastic sheet—to protect Sonia Wynkoop's mattress. On top of that went Alice's favorite sheets: small blue flowers on a white background.

"Oh, these are pretty," said the midwife, a woman not much older than Alice, who herself had given birth to two children at home.

"I'm going to save them for my child," Alice told her, between contractions. "I'll tell him, 'You were born on these.' "

"What a nice idea," said the midwife. On top of the sheet with the blue flowers went an underpad. "Like a large Pamper," commented the midwife good-humoredly as she adjusted it under Alice.

"Did you use cloth or disposable diapers with your two?" Alice asked her.

"Oh, I'm old-fashioned"—the midwife laughed—"I used Pampers, same as my mother."

"That's what I plan, too," said Alice, feeling very close to the other woman. "Oh . . . oh . . . OWWWWW."

"That was a big one," said the midwife encouragingly. "I think that's Doctor's car outside, now. He has as many holes in his muffler as a colander, but no time to get it replaced. All these babies coming at the same time."

Upstairs was the master bedroom, where Alice now slept by herself, with its large connecting bath of pink tile, wall-to-wall shag carpeting, marble vanity countertop, and separate tub and shower stall. Hugo had pointed out the place where the old wall had been knocked out of another room to enlarge this one. "Looks like old Sonia's a *bathroom* sybarite, at least," he'd remarked. Across the hall was the room in which their landlady had locked her things, and next door to that, a drafty spare room where Hugo and Alice stored their boxes and hid away from their sight the few pieces of art—a convoluted wrought-iron sculpture of some animals either fighting or mating, a set of toothy brown tribal masks, an oppressive icon with a murky Madonna and Child, and a frayed, moth-eaten tapestry—the art-history professor had deemed safe enough to be left out for her tenants' enjoyment.

Alice had never gotten around to unpacking her thirty-two boxes of books.

They had given away the few things they had purchased in advance for the baby—a Moses basket, a package of newborn disposable diapers, a soft white cotton blanket, some little white kimonos. Alice, being superstitious, had followed the example of her roommate Anna, who told her Jewish mothers-to-be always waited until the baby was born before bringing elaborate layettes into the house.

She crossed back over the threshold of the master bedroom and lay down on top of her satin comforter. Her gaze swept back and forth across the ceiling. She knew every buckle and crack in the white plaster. This room, where she had spent major portions of her time since the baby's death, the room most permeated with her grief, was the room with the most pain. Would it one day oppress Signor and Signora Medici as they lay side by side in this bed? ("I don't understand it, Remigio, I made them have the baby downstairs, the one that died, but somebody's left a load of negative vibes in this room. Don't you feel them?" "I feel only you, *carissima*.") Had Sonia Wynkoop fallen in love, whatever that mysterious phrase was supposed to mean? What made an independent, scholarly spinster over fifty suddenly decide to marry an Italian restaurant owner? Did he make her feel beloved and secure? Or maybe he saw *her* as a special being, this finicky, selfish American *professoressa*, so unlike the women he was used to. "Quirky old Sonia Wynkoop," Magda had called her. Maybe Signor Medici was also getting on in years, and needed a little extra security himself: Sonia's pension, Aurelia's excellent health benefits. Maybe he was the kind of man who needed the comfort of having a woman to take care of, even if she could perfectly well take care of herself.

Marriage, whatever it was, was certainly a mixed bag of motives. Love, whatever *it* was, was a complete mystery.

The phone rang beside her bed.

"Alice? I hope I'm not calling at a bad time." It was Francis Lake. An uncanny feeling went over her, for as soon as she heard his voice she realized he had been hovering right on the edge of her thoughts. It was as if she had summoned him. This was the first time he had ever called their house.

"Not at all. I was going to call *you* very soon. How is Magda?"

"Well, last night I thought I'd lost her. She didn't seem to hear me anymore. When I talked to her, she would twitch occasionally, but it didn't seem related to anything I was saying. Only, once, when I was crying, she squeezed my hand. Oh, Alice, that squeeze was such a relief! I spent the night in the room with her, she passed a quiet night. This morning, she grumbled at Diane and me when we were changing the bed. She called me an idiot. I was never so glad to hear myself called an idiot. Just like her old self, but so very, very weak. What I was wondering . . . if you were planning to stop by today . . . you know she always *rouses* herself for you, and I thought maybe . . ." He sounded on the brink of breaking down.

"I'll come now," said Alice, swinging her feet off the bed.

"Well, that would be . . . I don't want to take advantage of your kindness. . . ."

"I'm on my way."

He was watering the flowers in the urns when she drove in. He turned off the hose and hurried down the walk to meet her, wiping his hands on his jeans. He came toward her so trustingly, squinting and smiling into the sunshine. He wore a clean beige polo shirt with the ironing creases still sharp in the sleeves, but his floppy hair looked lifeless and unkempt today.

"The nurse ordered me outside to wait for you. She said our lobelias were drooping, but I think it was just an excuse to get me outdoors. Diane's such a nice person, but she worries about me far too much. How is Hugo?"

"I saw him off at the airport earlier this morning." She was annoyed with herself for being disappointed that the nurse was here. Why shouldn't the nurse be here on a weekday morning?

"Oh yes, I forgot. His speech in South Carolina. I forget everything these days, Alice." He held her lightly by the elbow as they went up the walk together.

"Well, it's little wonder." She had a strong desire to reach for his hand, link her fingers with his, under the acceptable guise of spontaneous sympathy. Then instantly recoiled from the urge: it was so exactly the kind of advantage Leora Harris might have taken.

"Diane says Magda's deteriorated a good deal since yesterday," he said as they entered the house. "But I thought she was more her old self again this morning. When Diane and I were changing the bed earlier, she called me an idiot. Or did I already tell you that on the phone?"

As she started up the stairs ahead of Francis, Alice heard a high-pitched mechanical sound start up.

"That's just the suction pump, don't be alarmed," he said. "Diane always does it when she's here. It clears the saliva buildup from Magda's mouth. I do it when I'm alone, but I'm sure I don't do it as effectively as it ought to be done. I find it upsetting, I'm not sure why."

"Should I wait until she's finished?"

"Oh, no, it only takes a minute. See, it's stopped now. I told Magda you were on your way over. She seemed quite pleased. We gave her another swig of her Cocktail. The doctors say she can have it as often as she likes now."

They went in. The nurse, a strapping young woman in a bright green smock and white trousers, was wiping Magda's face and mouth with a moist towelette. The tray table beside the hospital bed was overflowing with implements and medical supplies.

"Well, Diane," said Francis, "I've brought Magda's visitor. This is Alice Henry, who's been so good to us."

"Hi, Alice," said the nurse, barely looking up. "We're almost ready to receive company. Just getting freshened up some here. Magda, can you make an 'O' with your mouth so I can swab out these corners? That's a good girl."

The yellow face uttered something unintelligible. Magda's head looked so small and frail, almost like a shrunken skull, cradled in the firm, healthy grip of the large hand.

"What's that, Magda?" said the nurse. "You'll have to speak louder."

". . . *not* . . ." An angry gurgling sound.

"Oh, sorry, Magda. You're not a girl. Spunky, all of a sudden, isn't she, Mr. Lake?" The nurse laughingly appealed to Francis.

"That's just what I was saying to Alice," he replied happily. "Magda's always animated when Alice comes. Alice stimulates her mind."

"Let me just clear away this stuff. . . ." The nurse swooped up an armful of equipment and used towelettes. "I want to sterilize this nozzle and have it clean for you for the weekend. Did you remember to get us another bottle of alcohol?"

"Oh, dear, no, sorry, Diane, I completely forgot. But I could put on the kettle . . . wouldn't boiling water be as good?"

"It'll have to, won't it?" She took a bossy, intimate tone with him, Alice noticed, and looked at him with what could only be described as possessive adoration. "I hope you didn't forget to water our lobelias. They were on their last leg when I came in this morning, and it's going to be a hot weekend, and I won't be here to remind you."

"No, I remembered to do that. Oh, wait, Alice, let me move your chair closer for you. You have to be careful, or that caster falls off. And then, if you'll excuse me, I'll go down and start the kettle for Diane and see what else she needs."

"See you on Monday, Magda, nice to meet you, Alice," said the flushed Diane over the top of her armload, departing the sickroom cheerfully with Francis in tow.

Our lobelias . . . did you get *us* another bottle of alcohol . . . Well, well, thought Alice, sitting down in her accustomed chair with the caster Francis never failed to warn her about: so Leora Harris and I must make way for a third member in the Francis Lake fan club. Or "Mr. Lake," as Diane addresses her idol.

Magda was scrutinizing her in a puzzled, weary way. Was it possible she no longer even recognized her? She looked worse than ever today. How many more degrees of worse were there before she let go? And poor Francis called this "animated." How much he must want to hang on to her.

"Hello, Magda, it's Alice."

The lips parted. The sick woman croaked something.

"I'm sorry, I didn't hear you."

"*Wa*–ter."

"You'd like a drink of water, Magda?"

Magda nodded wearily and closed her eyes. Her mouth made little sucking motions.

Alice's first impulse was to go and fetch Francis. Then she saw there was a plastic glass on the tray table, with a straw sticking up through its lid. When she picked it up, it sloshed softly with melting crushed ice. Was there enough liquid to satisfy Magda, or should she quickly refill the glass from a bathroom tap? But Magda's mouth was making those pitiful little sucking motions.

Alice stood up and leaned forward so she could better angle her body to the task. Lifting and supporting Magda's head with her left hand, she nudged the straw between the purplish lips, which clamped down on it at once. The invalid began to suck lustily, drawing the water up through the ice with grotesque slurping sounds. Magda's cropped white head felt soft and damp against Alice's palm. When her hand began to tire, she slipped her arm behind the head and supported it in the crook of her elbow. Such a small, soft burden, Magda's body; it hardly weighed anything. Yet it still had life in it, and a will of its own. The lusty, grateful slurping went on and on. Alice was profoundly moved, but willed herself to stay in control. Any tears that fell would drop directly onto Magda's head. She could hear Francis and Diane downstairs in the kitchen, not their words but their voice patterns. Francis's diffident, engaging drone punctuated by the nurse's pert, bossy thrusts. Francis was so undiscerning he probably didn't even suspect he'd made a conquest.

"Thank you," said Magda, feebly pushing away the straw. The dark eyes brooded intently upon Alice. *I wish I knew what she sees,* thought Alice, releasing the downy head to its pillows.

"You're welcome, Magda. Is there anything else I can do for you?"

"I'd like to go back to my room, now." The slurred words were a polite, childlike petition to someone in authority.

Alice wasn't sure what to answer. It might be cruel to say, you're *in* your room. Who knew what room in her life she wanted to go back to? "Let's wait for Francis to come back," Alice stalled.

Magda nodded, but her eyes darted about the room, troubled. "I want you to . . ."

"What do you need, Magda?"

"Have my books . . ."

Could she mean those blue examination books? The ones she'd made Hugo read from last week? "You mean the blue books, Magda?"

"What the hell do the *colors* matter? It's what's inside. You're as bad as him. The two of you should get together. Ha, I know . . . I'll leave him to you . . . in my will. Get me a . . ."

Alice, thoroughly discomposed, was relieved to hear Francis's light step on the stairs. "Here comes Francis," she said, "he'll know what you want."

"Don't bet on it."

Francis came in. "Magda's asking for some books. . . ." Alice told him.

"What books, love?" Francis leaned over Magda from the opposite side of the bed. He was pale and flustered.

"Not books." The cadaverlike face grinned up at him mischievously. "I have a bequest . . . come here."

When he bent closer, her emaciated, yellow hand shot out and grabbed a hunk of his hair and pulled him down to her. For a horrible moment Alice thought the dying woman was going to kiss him on the mouth, but it appeared she only wanted to whisper something in his ear.

"You're not making sense, Magda," he said, blushing as he listened.

She pushed him away from her in disgust. "You're on your own," she slurred wearily. Then she closed her eyes and, with that unnerving adroitness of hers, simply vacated her being, leaving behind a slack-mouthed, unresponsive, hardly breathing visage on the pillow.

"She lies here and thinks of things she wants to leave to people," Francis explained to Alice, raking back his floppy hair in a distraught manner, not meeting her eyes. "I try to keep track . . . I always write them down, even if they aren't practical, because they're her wishes . . . like, you remember, she wanted Hugo to have those old examination books. And I have to remember to give Tony Ramirez-Suarez back his mother's crucifix. But sometimes the things she wants to leave her friends are just not rational."

Alice nodded. She was pretty sure she knew exactly what unrational wish Magda had been conveying to Francis—the gift of himself to her, no less—but felt she must protect him from knowing she knew. She was in such agitation at the moment that surely the safest thing she could do for all concerned would be to get out of here as fast as possible. Go home to Sonia Wynkoop's cold house, where pain had been sorted and relegated to appropriate areas, and crawl under the satin comforter and quarantine her distress and confusion to the room already permeated with them.

"She wants to rest now," said Alice. "I'd better run along."

"I'll walk you down," offered Francis obligingly.

It makes no difference to him whether I come or go, she thought, going ahead of him out of the room. He accompanies us all up and down the stairs, Diane the nurse, Leora Harris, Ramirez-Suarez, Ray Johnson. We're all the same to him. We're valued for the life we bring her. I was wanted today because he thought I might "rouse" her. Well, I was the one who got roused by her, but he doesn't know that. I'm glad he doesn't. I'm thankful for his obtuseness. At least I have kept my troublesome and inappropriate feelings to myself.

"She was so animated before you came," Francis was apologizing as he accompanied her out to the car. "Diane may have exhausted her with all that tidying up. Diane always gives her a sponge bath and runs the suction machine just before she leaves so I won't have so much on me later, but it seems to have put Magda over the edge. It's a pity. She was looking forward to your visit, her eyes lit up when I told her you were on your way. I disturbed your morning for nothing. I'm not quite myself, or I wouldn't have taken advantage of your kindness like that. . . ."

"But I liked it . . . I was glad that you felt you *could* call. . . ."

They were standing beside her car now. In a minute she must get in and drive away, when the only place she wanted to be was here.

"And you didn't disturb my morning," she added. "I had nothing important to do. In fact, I may not even have to house-hunt anymore, if Hugo doesn't mind staying where we are. Ray Johnson phoned just before you did, to say we could have Sonia Wynkoop's house for another year. She's getting married to an Italian and staying on in Rome for a while. . . ."

"Sonia Wynkoop getting married? How very strange. Magda will get a kick out of *that*. Did you tell her?"

"Well no, I—" Did he really believe Magda in her present state would "get a kick" out of it? Would she even remember who Sonia Wynkoop was?

"You know, Alice," Francis suddenly confessed in a ravaged voice, "I'm not sure I'm going to make it."

"You mean, through—through this?" she stammered, surprised. He nodded sheepishly, his lips stretching wider and wider into what first looked to be a sinister parody of a grin. Then his chest heaved and crumpled, and arms dangling helplessly at his sides, he began to cry. I mustn't touch him, was Alice's first reaction, because I want to so much. But immediately after, she disregarded her feelings along with the scruples, and simply took the exhausted man in her arms.

"Tell me what I can do," she asked, holding him as she would have held any friend or brother in distress. "My day is free. Please take it. What can I do to help you get through it?"

"I'm sorry . . . I'm so sorry . . . I'm just not myself—" His arms were around her now, clinging to her, but more like a lost child. So she believed he would have clung to anyone who offered comfort at this moment.

"Tell me what I can do," she murmured against his wet face. "What can I do to help you? Should I go get that alcohol?"

"Maybe that would be good. I remembered the other things when I was out this morning, but completely forgot Diane said we were out of alcohol."

"Just ordinary rubbing alcohol?"

"Well, Diane likes this certain brand . . . I think it's called Swan. They have it at the drugstore."

"Swan," she repeated, her mouth actually moving on his skin. Because she had savored it too much, she made herself step back and release him. She didn't want to take physical advantage of the situation, as Leora Harris would have done. But then she was obliged to grab him again to steady him, until he repositioned his feet so he could balance himself.

"I'd go myself," he said in a broken voice, making an effort to get control of himself, "but I don't like to leave her alone. . . ." He took off his glasses and wiped them on a handkerchief. "She hasn't much longer. She *can't* have. I love her so dearly, how could I even wish it?" He beseeched Alice with his reddened eyes. "Yet I do . . . I do sometimes wish it. Last night, when she didn't seem to hear me anymore, I felt so lost."

He slipped the glasses back on, adjusting them behind the ears, then took a deep shuddering breath. "I know I can't be with her every single minute, but I'd like to be with her when she dies."

"I would feel exactly the same about someone I loved," Alice assured him. "Do you have any food in the house?"

"I'm not sure what I have and don't have in the house anymore."

"I'll pick up a few simple things."

"That might be wise. If it's not keeping you from something else you have to do."

"I told you," said Alice, "my day is yours."

CHAPTER XVII

Magda was reading aloud to a class of high-school students about to graduate. She was in acute pain, but it was their last class and she thought she could brazen it out. She heard her voice intoning competently, but somewhere along the way she had stopped understanding the meaning of the words. It was as if she were reading aloud to them in a foreign language. She seemed to be getting away with it, only the vitality had gone out of her voice and they were showing signs of restlessness and inattention. A boy looked out the window and yawned, another checked his watch; a round-faced girl with black ringlets took out a puce-colored leather manicure kit, exactly like the one Magda's mother kept by her bed until she expired, selected a tool, and began pushing back her cuticles.

Magda put the book face down on the desk and began to stroll back and forth in front of them. She was in such *pain*, but this was their last class and she was determined to make it memorable. She began making up a story to reclaim their attention.

"There was this woman, she was dying," Magda said.

They perked up at once. The yawning jaws snapped smartly shut, windows and wristwatches lost their allure, the cuticle stick hovered, arrested, above a forgotten nail.

"Yes, dying," said Magda, pleased. "Irrevocably, unquestionably dying. She was done for and they all knew it. She lay there rotting away, because that was her destined mode of expiration. Some of us will be snuffed out quickly and painlessly, but with no time to reconnoiter the mysterious route by which we have arrived at where we are. Others of us are charted for a slower, more agonizing exit, but with the consolation prize of being allowed to take stock of our lives as we lie there and disintegrate."

What they didn't know was that her own guts were rotting away, even as she spoke, beneath the substantial flowing garment she wore. A clever combination of old-fashioned nun's habit and billowing maternity gown, it successfully camouflaged the gaping hole at her center and the unraveling entrails spilling forth. Prowling up and down in front of them, the heavy skirts dragging impressively behind her, she felt glamorous and secure. In pain, but she had been in pain so long now it had become like an added organ in her body. So long as she did not start to smell.

"The dying woman had many visitors at first, then she got too ugly and didn't make sense, at least not in the way she had in the past, and so they stopped coming, all except a few loyal souls, and one or two persons who had hidden agendas of their own. They would congregate around her bed dutifully, even though they thought she was gaga, and she could see right through them."

"You mean she could read their minds?" cried a boy eagerly.

"Not the way they do in the movies, no, but she could see what was in their hearts. The reason she could see was because *she didn't want anything from any of them anymore.* Once you get yourself out of the way, you can see everything the way it is. Your self isn't blocking the world from you, once you have sidestepped its shadow."

Some of them frowned or looked threatened. Well, it's natural at their age, thought Magda, turning on her heel and trailing her garment majestically back in the other direction. Some of her entrails had slipped out of the hole and were hanging down like a rope of sausages beneath the capacious robes, but no one seemed to notice the bulge. When I was their age, thought Magda, I had no intention of getting myself out of the way either.

"Anyway," she went on, "that's the situation the dying woman found herself in: she could see things and people in their right relations. She could see what they wanted and were scheming to get, and what they were afraid they wouldn't get, and whom they loved and didn't love. She could see even those things they didn't know about themselves. She saw what would be good for them and what would be bad for them. Only she was no longer able to communicate any of this and save them time . . . or save them from their mistakes. And besides, who listens, anyway, when someone tries to tell you what's good or bad for you?"

Understanding laughter. All of them thinking of their parents.

"And frankly, as the days passed and she grew weaker and weaker, it mattered less and less to her. They would sort things out for themselves, as she had had to sort them out for herself. All she wanted now was to be left in peace, allowed to get on with the interesting job of her death. She had taken her Final Examination, and was satisfied with the results, and now, with herself out of the way, wanted to be very still and wait for what came into the place *she had cleared out.* But there they were, still coming and going, still needing things from her: talking at her, pulling and turning her this way and that, wiping and sponging and vacuuming the spit from her mouth, dosing her with drugstore firewater to disguise the pain and make her declaim like a precocious vegetable. . . ."

The round-faced girl with the inky curls was waving her cuticle stick in the air, trying to flag Magda down. My God, realized Magda, it's my mother. My mother as a young girl, come back to sit in my class, with her everlasting manicure kit.

"Yes, Mother," she said with a sigh.

"Sorry for interrupting," said the girl, who didn't look at all sorry, "but didn't this woman have a husband?"

If there had been any doubt who the girl was, there was none now. It was exactly the question Magda's mother would have asked, at any age. "Marsha, how did you do it?" her mother had exclaimed, truly impressed for the first time by an achievement of her daughter's, when Magda had brought Francis home.

"Yes, she had a husband," she told her mother along with the rest of the class, stepping over the sausages that were now dragging on the floor, wrenching forth from her with startling pain beneath the camouflage of her arrogant robes. "I should have mentioned him sooner. He was a good husband, as husbands go. . . ."

"Magda, love, can you lift up so Diane can change your pad?"
Oh, the pulling, the wrenching . . . stop it . . . where was I, this is *important*! I want to finish this story. Leave me alone, damn it, while I am at the top of my form. This is a story they need to hear before my guts spill out. And you. You of all people, whom I was just about to praise, you interrupt my *last class* in order to wipe my ass.

"Damn nurse. Dumb cow."

"Please, Magda, don't fight us. . . ."

"Oh, oh, ugh! Stop it, Francis. Oh you idiot. You hopeless fucking *idiot*."

"She spoke to us, Diane! Did you hear?"

"I heard, all right."

"I thought I'd lost her during the night. I was afraid I'd never hear her voice again. But she still knows me, did you hear her say Francis? Oh, Diane, I've never been so glad to hear myself called an idiot."

"Magda love, guess who's coming over? Alice."

Now, who was Alice?

"I took the chance of phoning, just to see if she might be coming today, and she's on her way over now. I'm so glad. You enjoy talking with her, she stimulates your mind. Do you want a little sip of your tonic?"

Why not? It was clearly what *he* wanted.

Arrrrgh-arrrgh-arrrrgh. She was at the dentist's. No, in bed, having her putrid mouth suctioned out by the nurse with the strong arms and those hard piggy eyes. The nurse was in love with Francis, and had it all planned out how she was going to move in with him. Didn't the nurse have a child, and a mother, too? Probably had their room already picked out in this house. Child next door in that little narrow room where Francis sleeps now. The mother down the hall in my study. They'll pack up my books and give them to a library. The mother will set out her knickknacks on the bare shelves. And randy Big-butt herself already has her strong arms and haunches wrapped around Francis in our old bed. And Mr. Unconscious doesn't even suspect. His unconsciousness is his big drawing card. They can put whatever fantasies they like inside him, and he can carry them, because he never bothered to claim the space for himself.

"Hello, Magda, it's Alice."

Lovely, clean girl. If only I could remember *what she was to me.* Like a daughter, only I didn't have daughters. But she likes me. I like *her*, only I can't remember just why. Something bad happened to her, she's unhappy. I wish I could remember. That damn nurse has suctioned all the wetness from my mouth. Water . . .

"You'd like a drink of water, Magda?"

Bless her simple attention. Most people are so wrapped up in themselves they can't see someone dying of thirst in front of their face.

I'd like to give her something. My Blake pictures? Some books? I seem to remember we liked some of the same books. We could go back to my study and select them together. Or the room that was my study before the nurse's mother moved in. No, wait, she didn't move in yet. Was that only my fantasy?

"I'd like to go back to my room, now," I tell Alice.

"Let's wait for Francis to come back." She's nervous. Lost faith in me, too, thinks I'm gaga.

"I want you to . . ."

"What do you need, Magda?"

". . . have my books. . . ." Surely that's lucid enough. Though the surprise element will be lost now.

She asks me if I mean the "blue" books. What the hell do the *colors* matter? It's what's inside the books, I tell her. You're as bad as him. The two of you should get together.

Now, that's an inspired idea. Save him from the nurse and that other magpie predator with the thousand pastel outfits and the insatiable curiosity about other people's sex lives. I shall pick this clean, serious girl as my successor. *He* won't mind, he'll be glad to have it settled for him.

"I know what I'll do," I tell kind Alice, whoever she may be. "I'll leave him to you in my will. Get me a . . ."

She looks shocked and found out. Ah, boys and girls, what did I tell you? The dying woman in my story could see things in people they didn't know about themselves yet.

And I thought the match was my bright idea.

"Here comes Francis." She pretends she hasn't understood me. "He'll know what you want."

Don't bet on it.

She tells him I've been asking for "some books," and he's leaning down asking what-books-love.

Not books, I say. I have a bequest . . . come here. His hair needs washing, he's letting himself go; oh, I've got to get out of here, I've tarried long enough, my rotting carcass is serving no purpose now that I've taught my last class.

"Have Alice," I croak my instructions against the warm whorl of his ear, "she'll suit you. I'd like you to have her after I'm gone."

"You're not making sense, Magda," he says, resistent as a stone wall. Unlike her, he hasn't entertained a single thought of any attachment, not even unconsciously. I can feel it through his skin: his pure unreceptivity. Yes, boys and girls, the husband of the dying woman, a good husband, as husbands go, was completely faithful right to the end. Amazing, isn't it, in these wanton times? Are the obtuse more easily virtuous? A possible exam question, though I may think up more beguiling ones.

"You're on your own," I say, pushing him away. I feel the counterthrust of his sweet release. Go, good-bye, go.

CHAPTER XVIII

Francis waited until he saw Alice reverse her car safely out of the driveway, then went back into the house. This morning's load of sheets awaited their transfer to the dryer in the basement, but he would run upstairs and look in on Magda first. Whenever he'd been away from her, even for a few minutes, he felt the urge to check back, just to be sure she hadn't given him the slip.

Alice said she would feel exactly the same about someone she loved.

Imagine his breaking down like that in front of Alice. Though she had taken it with such lovely calmness. Such a dependable, kind person, Alice. But poor Magda, in her present state, could certainly come up with some irrational ideas!

Health-insurance paperwork covered the dining-room table. Hardly any mahogany surface showed between the closely stacked piles. He had worked out a system, but if anything happened to him, nobody would be able to figure it out. There was still stuff coming in from Magda's very first tests. Some of the bills were duplicates of earlier ones which had been paid long ago. Much of the correspondence seemed to be in direct contradiction to earlier correspondence. This is not a bill. This is a bill. This bill has been paid by us. This bill has not been paid and we won't pay it. It made a person feel so lost, as though there was no one at the center of things. At the beginning, before Magda took up almost every minute of his day, he had followed up on every discrepancy, letting himself be shuttled mercilessly back and forth between unyielding—sometimes downright hostile—telephone voices, each of which made him plead his case in a different way until he became confused. He had always been a person who liked to pay a bill as soon as it came into the house, but his heart had finally hardened. Now if there was a question, and there usually was, the bill went into one of his many "postponement piles." Let them wait, there would be plenty of time to sort things out later.

As he went up, he noticed how frayed the stair carpeting had become. The floral pattern was completely worn off in large patches. His constant running up and down these past six months must have helped things along considerably.

"What hideous carpeting," Magda had remarked to the real-estate lady, the first time they climbed these stairs five years ago. "No flowers like this ever existed, or could exist. My parents had a silk-flower factory, and *they* were scrupulously faithful to nature in producing their fakes. Every pistil and stamen had to look authentic." She had stopped on the stair to catch her breath and Francis, right behind her, realized how out of shape she had become. I have failed her, he thought, by allowing her to eat carelessly. But what can I do when she's away all day teaching? She forgets to eat lunch and then gets ravenous at three in the afternoon and stuffs herself with junk food from those vending machines. Then she picks at her well-balanced supper and later eats chocolate bars on the sly while grading papers into the night. After we get settled in at Aurelia and organized in our house, I'll insist on packing wholesome lunches for her.

"And if it looks this bad *faded*," Magda had continued playfully, regaining her stamina, "just imagine what it must have looked like *new*. Oh my, and look, it's all over the upstairs hall as well. Now, what kind of people, do you wonder, would have gone into a store and actually *picked out* such carpeting? Why did this particular florid eyesore call their names? What did it connect them to in their past, do you think?"

The real-estate lady got very defensive, not realizing Magda was by this time simply amusing herself by elaborating on one of her favorite themes of why people did things. She pointed out to Magda and Francis somewhat frostily that they could easily rip up this carpeting and replace it with something more to their taste.

They inspected the upstairs rooms. "Oh, look, Frannie, a small fireplace! I always wanted a fireplace in my study. Pity there are no shelves in here."

The real-estate lady pointed out that they could easily build shelves. "Your husband could perhaps do it," she suggested, having warmed toward them since Magda's enthusiasm over the fireplace.

"My husband's domestic prowess has pleasured our home life on many fronts," Magda told the other woman, laughing huskily and rolling her eyes in that suggestive way that embarrassed him, "but carpentry is not among his many gifts."

Well, he'd managed, after some frustration, to install the shelves, although the catalog had deceived them into thinking they would arrive looking like shelves. Getting Magda's study ready had taken priority. Next, the kitchen—"his" kitchen, as she called it— had to be made ready. All the surfaces, the windowsills, even the ceilings, had been covered with a fine layer of grease. It had taken him a week and a half to scrub down every inch, using up several containers of Murphy's oil soap and at least a dozen of those plastic scouring pads.

"I've never seen anybody look so happy scrubbing a dingy ceiling," Magda had remarked on her way to school one morning as she collected her prescribed lunch bag from the refrigerator. (A regime he'd finally agreed to abandon after a few months, because she neglected to eat it and continued her practice of snacking from the vending machines.)

"I am happy," he told her simply.

"The first time I ever saw you, you were up on a stepladder, scrubbing that fanlight over the entrance to your seminary. You looked happy then, too, I remember. What were you thinking about that day, to make you look so happy? Or is it just that you're a person made happy by stepladders and scrubbing? That's all right, don't tell me, keep me guessing. I've still got all my retirement years to batter you into some retrospective insight." She opened the lunch bag and frowned in at the foil-wrapped shapes. "Am I the healthy recipient of carrot sticks or celery sticks today? Now, you *would* tell me that, but don't. Let me be surprised."

It *had* been one of the happiest times of his life, scrubbing that kitchen, getting it organized, laying down shelf paper, arranging their dishes. Knowing they were at last living in a house they could call their home. Magda had just turned fifty-three. She would stay on at Aurelia until retirement: that had been her agreement with President Harris. Until then, they would plant trees and shrubs and perennials, and await the day when she would bring home the rest of her books from her college office. If she hadn't done so by then, she would settle down and complete the long-awaited sequel to *The Book of Hell*. And he would keep the fire going in the little fireplace in her study, and try to stay abreast of her scribbled output on his word processor. In summers they would travel.

That had been the plan for the rest of their lives. And here she was dying, and they hadn't even gotten around to ripping out the hideous carpeting.

When he entered the room, she was lying very still. He couldn't hear any breathing. Rushing to the bed and putting his face close to hers, he heard nothing except the pounding of his own heart. Then the skin between her brows suddenly crinkled, as it habit-

. ually did when she was in deep concentration or pain. Surely her face couldn't move like that if she had stopped breathing!

No, here came a faint, rattling exhalation. Had she been holding her breath all that time? Or simply forgotten to breathe?

Leaning over her, he gently touched her forehead. It was warm. He began massaging the crinkles between her brows in the soothing, circular motion he'd always used when she had a headache. Her wasted body rose and fell with each labored set of breaths. The breathing became shallower and uneven, as it had been last night, when he thought she'd gone beyond him. But last night he had talked to her, wept, implored her to give him a sign of some kind, whereas now he could not bring himself to speak. He was afraid to interfere with that solemn concentration so manifest on her forehead, though he felt it was not an intrusion simply to smooth the crinkles gently with his fingertips as he had done so often in the past.

He kept on massaging, his fingers moving on her puckered skin in the familiar old circular pattern that had always soothed her. So many thoughts she had carried to completion in that active brain of hers! Though he hadn't been able to share in the more analytical and audacious ones to the extent that she would have liked, maybe he'd at least provided a soothing background for her to have them in.

His nails, rotating on her dry, parchment-colored skin, looked disgustingly healthy and pink. Sometimes when he had rubbed her back, she used to tell him the world was divided into two kinds of people, the ones who would rub your back as long as you wanted, and the ones who got tired after a few minutes and said, "Okay, now it's your turn to rub mine." "Lucky for me," she would murmur, with a sensuous wriggle, "you're one of the tireless ones."

He supposed this was an accurate description of him, though his back was beginning to ache from stooping over her. Yet he was reluctant to stop, even for as long as it would take to pull over the chair for himself. It seemed to him, in his almost hypnotic fatigue, that they were working together somehow, he making the circles so that she could continue to breathe until she had come to the completion of that awful concentration.

Then she took a sharp, startled breath. Francis held his own breath, waiting for her to exhale. A car passed on the road in front of their house, a swatch of rock music blaring from its open windows. Then utter green quiet surrounded them outside the motionless white curtains. When an exhalation finally came, it took him a moment to realize it was only his own. His fingers had ceased to move, but remained upon Magda's forehead, which had gone completely smooth and relaxed. Her whole face was suddenly relaxed and free of tension. How strange. It was the same emaciated, yellow face he had come to accept as hers in these last months, but the expression on it was remarkably young, younger even than when he had first known her. Through his fingertips he could actually feel the warmth leaving her body. So soon! Where was she now? With his thumb, he couldn't help signing that smooth forehead with a cross. A shudder went over him. The last time he had done this was on his mother's forehead, when she had been lying in her open casket in the parlor at home. Too late, he had thought, a rage rising in him as his thumb blessed and sealed that cold, embalmed flesh. Why wasn't I here when she could feel it and know? What's the use of going on with any of this, when she won't feel it or know?

If only he could tell Magda this. It was exactly the sort of thing that she was always trying to pull out of him: the way he'd stood over his mother's casket and felt the terrible but exhilarating abyss of freedom opening around him.

But it was too late for that, also.

Francis lowered the hospital bed until it lay flat. Gently he lifted aside the sheet and freed her body of the catheter she'd hated. The bag, recently changed by the nurse, had very little in it. He contemplated it for a moment, this last vestige of Magda's recent aliveness, before disposing of it in the bathroom.

He returned and straightened the bedclothes, neatly turning back the top sheet and laying Magda's hands, already losing their resilience, on top of the monogram. ("Since you're taking care of the domestic side, Frannie, it's only fair we should use your surname on the sheets. Especially when mine's invented! We'll snuggle together beneath our MLF, and the hell with Emily Post.")

Then, knowing Alice would soon return from her errands and be there to see him through the inevitable next chores, he pulled up the chair and sat alone with his wife for the last time.

PART TWO

Go and find the miseries, my love.
—MAGDA DANVERS

CHAPTER XIX

To Faculty and Trustees of Aurelia College

Dear Friends,

I write to bring you the sad news that Magda Danvers died on Friday, June 7. I am told by her husband that she was alert and relatively comfortable to the end.

A memorial service will be held at Aurelia College. I will pass on detailed information as soon as I can.

Yours sincerely,
Gresham P. Harris
President

■ ■ ■

"Two weeks sooner would have made all the difference," said the president to his wife. "I'm going to have a hell of a time scraping together a decent memorial service. Half the faculty have already left town for the summer. As if I didn't have enough to worry about, with this damn cruise only half-filled. I don't understand it. Back in April, the reservations were pouring in. Then things dribbled to a complete standstill. What is Mamie Elmendorf going to think of a college that can't even fill a pleasure ship with loyal alumni?"

"She'll be having such a lovely time that she won't think about it at all. Small cruises are more intimate. People get to know one another better. Besides, Gresh, it's not as if only ten people signed up. You've got fifty-six firm commitments ... with *deposits* ... from alumni and spouses ... or 'companions,' and you said the travel agency would break even with just forty-two. Then on top of that, there's *us* ... and Mamie Elmendorf and Elberta ... and some of our faculty members and spouses ... and the speakers and *their* partners. If the Henrys take Sonia's house for a second year, Alice will have no excuse to stay behind, and Stanforth from Columbia is bringing his daughter. . . ."

"His unhappy, druggie daughter. That's typical Stanforth, he tells you *all* the bad news when it's too late to do anything about it. . . ."

"Well, there is a ship's doctor. And maybe she'll have a shipboard romance and come home happy and cured."

"Who's she going to have a shipboard romance with, if there are no available extra men?"

"I thought we might invite Francis Lake," said Leora.

"Francis *Lake*?" The president looked utterly nonplussed.

"Why not? He's an available extra man, isn't he? Quite personable, in his way. The right age, too. He'll be beside himself with loneliness now."

"That may be, Leora, but I don't see us appropriately inviting him on a cruise before we've even scheduled his wife's memorial service."

"Oh, I meant after it's scheduled, naturally," said Leora. "Besides, Magda herself suggested it, the last time I was over there, so it's already been put into his head."

"Suggested *what*?"

"That Francis go along on the cruise. He's an expert on misericords, and she suggested he might lead expeditions into churches. People on cruises love to learn rarefied things so they can come home and impress their friends. That's what she said." Leora didn't feel it expedient to her present purpose to add that Magda had also said to bring along her ashes in a jar.

"What exactly are misericords?" asked the president, gloomily rubbing his chin. He was remembering that afternoon in March when he had taken tea with Francis Lake. The man was personable enough, in his diffident, aging-choirboy way, but if they asked him to lead expeditions, wouldn't they be expected to pay his expenses?

"Oh, they're these fascinating little carvings under the choir seats. I was asking him about them later, I told him he'd been holding out on us, hiding his esoteric knowledge. He showed Elberta and me some of his photographs . . . Elberta loved one with some snails making goo-goo eyes at each other. He's got slides, too, if we wanted to do a slide show. . . ."

"You took Elberta over there?"

"Not up to see Magda, of course. She waited outside. But Francis saw her playing on the lawn and wouldn't be satisfied until he'd offered her a glass of milk and a cookie. *Quite a few* cookies, as it turned out. Alice and Hugo were there, too, but they left, and Elberta and I stayed on awhile. You could tell he was lonely and wanted company. That's when I asked about the misericords. Don't worry, there was nothing morbid about my taking her over there. She and Francis got on famously. He talked to her in that simple, modest way he has with everybody and brought her out of herself a little. She could do with some bringing out."

"Well, let's not bring her out too much until after the cruise. The more she blends into the landscape, the better for our alumni, who have left their brats at home. So she and Lake got on, hmmm? Maybe we should take him along as Elberta's governess."

"Oh, Gresh, don't be cruel."

"I'm perfectly serious. I don't mean tell *him* that. We'd just ask him to conduct a few tours around churches. But he'd be there to keep the child company, and then in the evening after she went to bed, he could change his hat and manifest himself in the cocktail lounge as an available man. I wonder if he can dance."

"If not, I could probably coach him in a simple fox-trot between now and August."

"Well, you can't go fox-trotting yet. We can't do *anything* with Magda's widower until we decide something about the memorial service. If only we could have it in the fall. I could combine it with an announcement of the completed fund drive for the Magda Danvers Chair. And all the faculty would be here and could wear their regalia. I've got Archibald Drayton coming for the year as the Owen G. Lax Distinguished Visiting Professor, and Archie'd have his crimson gown and little velvet tam from Oxford."

"Why not have it in the fall, then? We've been to memorial services that were held months after the person died. We can make a real occasion out of it in the fall."

"On the other hand, it's fresher in everyone's mind now. The sentiment level is higher. Tony Ramirez-Suarez was in tears when I saw him in the post office this morning—I was thinking Tony could do the keynote tribute to Magda, in his Yale blue regalia, whether we decide to do it now or in the fall. But Lake might feel we're slighting his wife, if we put it off till fall."

"Not if it's explained to him that we want to make it extra-special, befitting *her* extra-specialness; he would feel he owed it to her memory. And if you're going to be announcing the completed fund drive for her chair, the occasion would be a celebration of her continued presence among us rather than just your ordinary memorial service."

"That's certainly true—that's well put, Leora. If *he* could be made to see it that way."

"Why not leave him to me? After all, you assigned me Elberta and I haven't let you down there, have I? I think I might be trusted to handle Francis Lake about the memorial service *and* the cruise."

■ ■ ■

Tony Ramirez-Suarez had just finished reading aloud to his wife the note they had received that day from Francis Lake, accompanying the little package containing the crucifix which had belonged to Ramirez-Suarez's mother.

"I liked that about the sacramental power of objects," said Ramirez-Suarez. "If they are given and received in the right spirit."

"It was kind of him to include me in the note," said Lydia Ramirez-Suarez. "When I never managed to get over to see her."

"They knew you have a full-time job." Mrs. Ramirez-Suarez was a medical receptionist at the local family-practice center.

"I wonder what he'll do now. He's still young, he could marry again."

"Somehow I don't think so. Perhaps I'm an incurable romantic, but he always struck me as the type of man destined to love only one woman—if he could find her. And he did find her and was totally devoted. They were devoted to each other, in their different ways."

"I've seen her get pretty sharp with him on occasion."

"It was not a typical union by any means. In their case, one could almost reverse Milton's much-out-of-favor dictum for an ideal marriage—'He for God, and she for God in him'—and say, with Magda and Francis, it was 'She for God, and he for God in her.' "

"I don't see how you can bring God into it, Tony, when he didn't even have a religious service for her."

"Those were her wishes. Immediate cremation, no funeral. Magda hated orthodox trappings, but she loved the living fire behind them. That fire was her passion. Believe me, Lydia, I know of what I speak. That's what drove her, that's what came out of her and attracted others. My humble theory has always been that he recognized it in her, probably unknowingly, he is not at all a self-reflective person, and it was more compelling to him than those moribund practices in the seminaries that were killing off young vocations by the thousands back in the sixties."

"But he didn't actually run away with her from that seminary, you said."

"No, no, that is only salacious tattle. He found her again later. She was about to tell me the whole story once, when we were having lunch at the college, but someone joined us. Ray Johnson, I think."

"You know, Tony, I've just thought of something useful I might be able to do. Didn't you say his table is piled high with medical bills and insurance paperwork? I could take care of those for him. I do it all the time anyway for patients who come into the office. It would make me feel better about not getting over to see Magda."

"That would be a very kind thing, Lydia. Oh, they're scheduling Magda's memorial services for the fall. President Harris phoned to ask if I would give the main tribute."

"Such a long time away! It still seems wrong, Tony, no burial service. I know if you're cremated, there's not much to be buried, but still. *I* certainly don't want to be cremated, remember that."

"I will honor your wishes, *querida*, in the unlikely event you precede me. And Francis must honor hers. She did want him to sprinkle her ashes around an old lilac at their house, he said. If that's done in the proper spirit, I'm sure it will have sacramental power."

Dear Alice and Hugo,

I really don't know what I would have done without all your kindnesses while Magda was dying. As you know, Alice, Magda loved nothing better than a stimulating conversation, and she always looked forward to seeing you. And I myself will always be grateful for your generosity in bringing food, and especially for your support on the day of her death. I can't think of anyone else who could have assisted me in such a calm, understanding manner as you did.

Hugo, you may remember how, after you had read aloud to her from one of these examination books, Magda saying she wanted you to have them. I know you will be able to appreciate the symbolic gesture behind it. Magda looked upon the last months of her life as her "final examination." But toward the end, she sometimes confused the symbol with the reality. When she asked you to read from them that day, she thought you were reading from something that existed only in her head. Of course they were only three blue books from her graduate-school days, but you somehow picked the perfect reading and it settled her heart. It was the very thing she wanted to hear.

Please know how I treasure the friendship and kindness of you both.

Yours ever,
Francis Lake

Hugo, in his bedroom/study at Sonia Wynkoop's—or was their landlady Sonia Medici by now?—paged at random through Magda's old exams, penned in the bold, black, cocky script by a hand that was now reduced to ashes. But there in the blue books remained her personality, her thoughts, her young determination. He glanced at the 17th Cent. Brit. Lit. one, from which he had read that day. Francis was right, it had been a damn good choice. Downright providential. *The poet comforts his soul by comparing Death to a groom slowly approaching with a taper.* Well, now she'd met him face-to-face, her Groom. "The only one I want," she'd croaked, weirdly smiling, diminished by then to a hardly human residue in the bed. And poor Francis had thought she meant him.

Well, it's going to happen to all of us, mused Hugo. The thought of his own guaranteed mortality cheered him up. Recently, the whole idea of diminishment down to bare essentials had the power to lift his spirits: divesting, stripping bare: he was all for it. Take away all you'd thought you needed and see what you couldn't live without. He was glad they were keeping this house for another year, glad it was bare and barren. If they stumbled over anything, it would at least be only their own familiar losses and lacks, their own familiar, unhappy history, and not some strangers' clutter.

He picked up another of the blue books. His little inheritance. *Magda Danvers, Yeats Seminar, Professor Crampton. December 1962.* 1962 was the year Cal was born.

Hugo turned to the first page of the Yeats exam. "I shall trace the evolution of personal emotion into poetic resolution in the early Yeats poem 'Words.'" "Personal emotion" and "poetic resolution" were underscored with fierce inky slashes. Her intention to impress you sizzled up from the yellowed page.

> When Yeats was in Paris visiting Maud Gonne in 1909—he was forty-four—he wrote in his journal that he had just realized Maud "never really understands my plans, or nature, or ideas."
>
> Never really understands my plans! Or my nature! Or my ideas! Now, that's a lot for somebody you have been in love with for twenty years not to understand about you.
>
> Could you stay in love with someone for twenty years, when that person does not, or cannot, understand your plans, your nature, or your ideas?
>
> Of course you could. Particularly if you happened to be a poet.

No wonder her students loved her, thought Hugo. What irresistible narrative drive. In 1962, she would have been what? Twenty-nine. Same age as Cal now. Cal and Laurence were due to stop off on their way back from Wellfleet. For a terrible moment, on the phone with Cal yesterday, Hugo had thought his son and his lover planned to stop off *for the night*. Who would sleep where? There were only two bedrooms, with a double bed in each. In the agonizing hiatus before Hugo understood Cal was only proposing stopping off for *lunch*, Hugo realized he had been more humiliated at the prospect of Cal and Laurence learning that Hugo and Alice no longer shared the same bedroom than at the thought of tucking Cal and Laurence away into the same bed.

> For, what does our unhappy lover do next? Lie down and weep? Go out and get drunk? Go bang on Maud's door and demand: 'Why can't you understand my nature, damn you?' If so, it is not recorded. What IS recorded is the first draft of the poem "Words":

> I had this thought a while ago
> 'My darling cannot understand
> What I have done, or what would do
> In this blind bitter land.'

A poem which concludes that:

> . . . had she done so who can say
> What would have shaken from the sieve?
> I might have thrown poor words away
> And been content to live.

Here we have an excellent example of the unhappy lover subsumed by the poet. The poet in Yeats has taken the lover's woe and used it to fashion a poem. A poem, furthermore, capable of convincing himself and us that we build specifically on the materials of our unsatisfied longings and even our woes.

True, thought Hugo, nodding. True, true. The consolation of art for the writer as well as his readers. (Bea McCandless saying his books had helped her understand so much about herself.)

Since there is some time left over, I would like to conclude by commenting on Yeats's religious imagery in this poem, though it goes beyond the scope of the assigned question. "We have no common religion but we have not stopped being religious," John Crowe Ransom says in his seminal essay on Yeats and his symbols. Yeats was a tireless improviser of religious imagery, and the freshness and aliveness of this imagery contributes to his greatness as a poet. The first draft of "Words" contained a direct allusion to God:

> And had she done so He can say
> Who shook me from his sieve

If I'd have thrown poor words away
And been content to live.

In the final draft, God actively shaking us through a sieve
is changed to our *being shaken* through a sieve. But we get
shaken and strained whether we believe in a Shaker-and-
Strainer or not. It's that inspired use of the concept of sieve, the
invisible God as kitchen utensil, the powerful symbol of fate,
whether personal or predicate, that changes the raw materials of
us into what we become, that makes Yeats the master *he* became.

S mart girl, thought Hugo. Why didn't you write more books on
this kind of stuff if you could do that at twenty-nine?

But the professor had given her only an A-minus. "Some quite
striking thoughts in evidence here," he had written in a tiny, grudging, red-ink chicken scrawl, "though I found your colloquial, and at
times sensationalist, style of presentation off-putting."

Old fart, thought Hugo. No doubt his way of getting his own
back for her impolitic little addendum about there being "some time
left over," and for announcing her intention to go "beyond the scope
of the assigned question." No, Magda dear, thought Hugo, swinging
his feet up on the windowsill and smiling to himself at her young arrogance, that was not very diplomatic of you. He felt paternal and
sympathetic to the early Magda, so fiercely determined to shine.

As she had, briefly, with that *Book of Hell* (which Hugo had often seen, in plentiful stacks, in the college bookstore; in print longer
than any of *his* books, its new edition had a spiffy black-and-white
cover, diagonally slashed by a red flame; he kept meaning to buy a
copy and read it). But after its publication, what had happened to all
that ambition and drive?

Maybe if she'd been married to an impossible beast like me, he
thought, she would have done more. Or if she'd stayed a spinster
through her productive years, like old Sonia Wynkoop, who was an-

nouncing a new publication in almost every *Aurelia News & Notes*.
Maybe Magda's husband had made her too comfortable.

> I might have thrown poor words away
> And been content to live.

Could that be it? That Francis Lake, with all his fussing and
caretaking, had made her content to "just live"?

Well, in my present domestic circumstances, thought Hugo
dryly, at least I'm in no danger of that happening.

Since their brief but horrific fight when Alice was driving him
back from the airport after the South Carolina trip and she had
unsportingly withheld the news of Magda's death until he had related
his triumphs so she could then accuse him of being self-centered, and
then he had retaliated with a pretty unforgivable remark himself,
they had entered into an even more rarefied state of their . . . of their
what? You couldn't call it marriage anymore. "Marriage," with the
irony of quotes, maybe.

A state of shared isolation? No, shared was too sharing a word.
Polite apartness. Assiduously polite. As if they were in *competition*
to see who could be the politest, without yielding a millimeter of precious apartness. He'd never danced such a frosty minuet with anyone
in his life. No, minuet was the wrong dance. People still touched in
minuets. There was no touching in the dance they were doing. It was
closer in style to the solipsistic gyrations the young performed now,
waggling themselves vigorously to deafening rock music in little
spotlights of isolation. Only instead of gyrations, his and Alice's
dance was stiff and dignified in movement, performed without much
vigor to the silent music of private thoughts. They still talked, of
course. That was another rule of the contest (though who in God's
name was judging it?): to keep a decent minimum of dialogue going,
without bringing up any of the million and one subjects which might
detonate into a fight.

Why didn't Alice leave him? She was still young, she had mar-
ketable skills. She'd had several job offers since they'd been married.
Or she could go back to school. She had enough of Aunt Charlotte's

money left to see her through several years. At least he hadn't sponged on that. (He'd never felt right, living in Alice's apartment even for that short time, he wasn't that sort of man.) Alice was still a lovely woman, if she'd come out of her trance. Though some men might be turned on by her recent Sleeping Beauty passivity. But such men were almost always brutes or psychopaths. (Here Hugo experienced a twinge of protectiveness on her behalf.)

Was she staying out of a sense of *honor*? That was a big mainstay of hers, honor. Or had the remoteness that had grown more marked in her since the death of the baby deteriorated into downright pathology?

That's how the fight had started, on the thruway coming home. He'd suggested, in what he thought was a calm, friendly manner, that it might be time for Alice to get some professional help. After all, she had had one serious breakdown. Wasn't there that nice lady therapist in New York? Why not give her a call, arrange a refresher course?

He'd been mulling it over on the plane coming back from South Carolina, inspired by his unexpected new friendship with warm, brave, munificent Bea McCandless, and revitalized after his overwhelming reception at the library the night before—people in tears, women *and* men hugging him afterward (he had taken the leap and given the unwritten speech about his father). He had felt generous and blessed with that impartial clear-mindedness into the problems of others that sometimes comes after having had your own emotional needs thoroughly satisfied.

And so, having given Alice a few highlights from the extremely gratifying return to his hometown as they walked together to short-term parking, and having noticed she listened with scrupulous politeness but made only the most comatose of responses, he determined to speak to her on this subject of therapy as soon as they got on the thruway.

But when he began to do so, citing her comatose response, she tore into him. Abandoning all her usual ladylike restraints, she called him a monster of self-promotion, interested only in his career and public image. Then she turned from the wheel long enough to beam on him a look of cold, pure hatred.

"Just because I can't effuse over your triumphs to the degree you think you deserve doesn't mean I need therapy. How dare you bring *therapy* into this! God, Hugo, how can you be so unremittingly self-centered? You're fifty years old and you still believe you're the center of the universe. I'm glad for you that you recovered some of your flagging self-esteem down in South Carolina, you're much easier to live with when you're not moping around denigrating yourself and expecting sympathy, but why couldn't it occur to you that I've lived through some experiences of my own, during our thirty-six hours apart?"

Then she dropped on him *her* big news: Magda had died the day before. Alice had been with Francis when the undertaker came to remove the body, she had stayed with him most of the afternoon. There was a mean-spirited triumph, he thought, in the way she sprang this on him. If we were going to be talking of triumphs.

Hey, dirty poker, had been his first reaction. It wasn't sporting of her to sit on this news while I blabbered on about my speech and gracious Bea McCandless with her funny face, and Johnny Carteret coming up and embracing me afterward. It wasn't fair or kind. By withholding it, she *turned* me into a monster of self-promotion.

He wished now he'd said that. Oh, that would have gained him points. What he *had* said, unfortunately, he hadn't been able to prevent it from spewing venomously out of his mouth, was: "Forgive me, who can compete with a *death*? We all know how you get off on death."

A more emotional woman would have wrecked the car. Alice simply drove on, more efficient than ever, though he saw her hands whiten as she gripped the steering wheel. After a moment she'd replied in a remote, dispassionate voice, the voice of a weary adult who has given up on a very bad child—a fifty-year-old child: "Everything isn't a competition, you know, Hugo."

Oh, wasn't it? he'd wanted to retort. The whole damn fulcrum of marriage, as he had experienced it, was weighted on the principle of competition. Though there were many forms and styles of vying for power, some more subtle than others, some more healthy and beneficial, what it all came down to was that marriage was a constant seesawing for ascendancy. Surely she must know that she was riding high on the seesaw at this moment. And it was he who had put her there: his own base retort had catapulted her to the pinnacle of justified self-righteousness.

But because she had "won" and he had "lost" (for the one currently in ascendancy was the one currently in control), he must forfeit the rest of his ammunition for this round. (He would have liked to follow up on that unfair bit about his "expecting sympathy." It seemed to him that in these last six months, *he* had been, by far, the prime bestower of sympathy in their sad household.)

"Poor old Francis, how's he taking it?" He forced himself to play the Knight. Monster of self-promotion that he was, he could still play the Knight.

"He's taking it," she had replied, after a brief but considered silence, "the way you would expect someone to take it when the person they love most in the world has died."

Behind those relatively innocent words a harsh wind blew for Hugo. She doesn't love *me* most in the world, was the message he distinctly got. Bracing himself, he had waited for the subsequent feeling of chill forlornness.

But other thoughts, surprisingly, had come instead. Magda, the last time he ever saw her, confiding to him through parched lips with that muck at their corners, ". . . in . . . my study . . . the ideas are still thick. They're waiting, poor things, but their mother's never coming back."

And Bea McCandless, herself doomed somewhere down the line, despite all the expensive doctors trying to shield her from it, valiant little Bea tipping her soda-bread face up to him on the sofa and confiding joyfully, "I have so much I still want to do. . . ."

And, though borne along in the same vehicle with this pale-knuckled, silent wife, who harbored so much against him, Hugo had experienced the survivor's irrepressible quickening of spirits when he compared his lot with those other two: *he* was still alive, and *could* return to his progeny of ideas; he, too, could say, along with Bea McCandless, "I have so much I still want to do," but with the advantage that *he* wasn't fighting a shifty disease with a very iffy prognosis.

He liked that image of Magda's: your own little cluster of incomplete inspirations and ideas awaiting you like dependent children: your mental progeny, languishing for Mother or Father to return to the study and help them grow up into something substantial.

A nd here he was, in late June, feet propped up on the windowsill of his study-cum-bedroom, for another year, it looked like. A child of his flesh had died in this room, but there were a few mental progeny milling about at loose ends. He had brought them into the world; now it was up to him to nurture and organize them into something.

Though Hugo hardly dared admit it to himself, things were beginning to mesh again in the old exciting way that had the power to make him feel moments of intense hope and happiness, regardless of whatever shit might be raining down on him at the time in his personal life.

It had begun down in South Carolina. After Hugo's speech, some old blueblood acquaintance of Johnny Carteret's had sauntered over in his rumpled seersucker suit and, after pumping Hugo's hand warmly and thanking him for his affecting talk, had proceeded to relate "a little story that comes out of my *own* family." About a slave going off to college with his young master, to light his fires in the morning and lay out his clothes and cook his meals. Many sons of plantation owners took a slave off to the university with them. But this slave, who was apparently very bright, had learned to read and write on the sly. Kept it a secret, of course, because it was against the law for them to read. But years later, after all concerned parties were dead, the slave's letters to his mother had been found. The mother, who couldn't read, had been the personal maid to the plantation owner's wife, and the fact that the letters had been found among the papers of the plantation owner's wife led people to surmise that she herself had read the letters aloud to her maid.

As the man in seersucker had been urbanely recounting his "little family story," an acrid resentment had somewhat occluded what Hugo was in the process of hearing. It wasn't until later, after the smoke from his hurt pride had been burned off in the ensuing blaze of vigorous hugs and praises, that Hugo could sniff the marvelous aroma of the inspiration he'd been handed on a platter by this relative stranger.

His resentment had come from the gratuitous put-down (or what Hugo's chronic touchiness sensed as gratuitous put-down) implicit in the man's story: *We once had this slave who learned to read, whereas your own father never did.*

But the aroma was one he had gone a long time without sniffing. Too damn long. From the story of the slave and his young master and the contraband letters rose the unmistakable scent of something which, if pursued to its lair, Hugo knew could address important longings and woes of his own. And, as the young Magda had said in her exam, didn't the writer have to build specifically on those very things?

A historical novel (hell, all that damn research!) would be new for him. But for the first time it attracted him, the possibilities. Hide behind history and tell some unbearable all-time truths.

Emanations of other involved persons in the story, trailing their own hidden attachments and motives, began proliferating in his imagination almost faster than thought as he sat here with his feet up on the flaking white paint of Sonia Wynkoop/Medici's windowsill. He didn't even have to close his eyes against the contemporary view of a neighbor's yellow sprinkler whirling in an adjoining lawn, summer of 1991, to see, with a potent and vivid clarity, a lovely woman incarcerated in her grand plantation house by a mysterious illness. She's looking out on a June day in 1855 on the gardens she's not allowed to tend anymore, thinking of her children, particularly of her son, who's going off to the university in the autumn. There's a knock, a familiar figure enters her bedroom . . . a black woman, a slave. The two women share many things, some known by everyone, others known only to themselves.

Hugo heard Alice leaving the house, starting the car. Going to shop. To walk by herself at the reservoir, something she'd taken to doing lately. Perhaps to drop by and see Francis Lake. Whatever, he'd hear a scrupulous report of her day at dinner. She still fixed a meal every night. He lit the candles and set the table and then she brought in the food and they chewed their mouthfuls and, in between, conversed on nonvolatile topics. Then she excused herself and went up to bed while he cleared the table and loaded the dishwasher.

Sometimes lately he caught himself feeling interested, in a novelist's disinterested way, in how long they would stay together.

Yet, as the car drove away, there was no doubt about it: he felt lighter, as if a load had been removed. The ballast of marriage dropping off for a few hours.

> I might have thrown poor words away
> And been content to live.

Nope, that was never a possibility for me, thought Hugo, and I'll bet it wasn't for Yeats, either. I always knew words were my ticket out, even before I knew where they were going to take me. And I've kept my belief in them, even when I've lost faith in everything else around me. Why, hell, look at me over there on Riverside Drive, in an ecstasy of wrapping up my *Manigaults*, while Rosemary was simultaneously downtown at her lawyer's, stealing every rug and chair out from under me as I composed those last chapters.

And I'll bet Yeats was the same. He knew where his life's blood lay at forty-four. By forty-four any true writer knows cotton-picking well what he can and can't live without. Why, if recalcitrant old Maud had come knocking on Yeats's door while he was in the fervor of drafting that poem, he'd have probably sent her away so he could keep on writing about how she might have changed his whole life if she'd come knocking on his door.

The truth is, anybody can live without anybody. Even Francis Lake is going to have to live without Magda, however good their marriage was. No marriage, whether it's good or awful, lasts beyond the grave.

But, now, books do, thought Hugo, exultantly flexing his shoulders against the back of his typing chair and gazing over the tops of his crossed sneakers at the whirling spray from the yellow sprinkler next door.

He hadn't told Alice about his new idea. Withholding it from her at their evening table talks seemed like his first infidelity in the marriage. No, that wasn't the right comparison: the thing was too pure, there was nothing tawdry about it. If he'd been a woman, he might have said it was like suspecting you were pregnant, but holding yourself very very secretly and carefully, until you were sure, because you wanted this baby so much.

That was what it felt like, whatever sex he was. And the way everyone was mixing up the sexes these days, why the hell shouldn't he appropriate a woman's figure of speech?

The lovely, doomed woman in his head began to speak in a warm, animated, contralto voice as the black woman stood behind her, undoing her long braid. Picking up a silver-backed brush and whisking it through her mistress's crisp graying hair until it crackled, the black woman responded in elliptical murmurs. They were speaking, in their long-accustomed private rhythm of discourse, about their two sons going off together, this coming autumn, to the university.

Dear Father Birkenshaw,

I wonder if you will remember me. I was at Regina from 1963–66. I left in November of '66, after my novitiate year at North Lake House.

When my wife, Magda Danvers, died last month, I got out my old breviary, to say the office of the dead for her, and in the weeks since then, many memories of Regina have come back. Though it may sound strange, coming from one who "dropped out," most of the memories were happy ones. I found myself wondering what had happened to some of my classmates and, of course, how you were, and Father Floris and Father Rolf. (Though if Father Rolf is still alive, he would be very old now, wouldn't he?)

I don't know if you'll remember this, but I met my wife when she came to give a lecture in October of '66 at Regina. Magda had a wonderful career as a teacher, right up until this past December, when her cancer was diagnosed. She was in pain, but alert to the very end. One might say she worked to the very end, because it was important to her to understand the meaning of everything, even her own death. I know she has influenced many lives for the better. She certainly influenced mine. She was much beloved by many others as well as by me, and I'm still wondering how I'm going to get on without her. But I'm so grateful to have shared a life with her for what would have been twenty-five years this coming November.

Well, Father, I hope this letter reaches you. Having been out of touch for so long, I have no right to expect that it will, but you have been in my thoughts (you yourself were an important influence) and I wanted to say hello.

Faithfully yours,
Francis Lake

P.S. It might please you to know that over the summers, while accompanying my wife on her research trips abroad, I took up the pastime of photographing misericords. I first heard about them from you, in your slide lectures on church architecture and iconography. I have collected over five hundred slides of my own, and quite a few more black-and-white prints (many prints just don't transpose well to slides) and arranged them into categories. Recently, I have been going through them in some detail, because the president of Aurelia College, where Magda taught (there will be an endowed chair of Visionary Studies in her name), has invited me to give some informal slide lectures and perhaps lead a few small tours to churches and cathedrals in England and Ireland. This is in connection with an Alumni Cruise around the British Isles in August, sponsored by the college. To tell the truth, I don't feel like going anywhere at all, but the president's wife reminds me that it was my wife's own suggestion, in the week preceding her death, that I go along on the cruise, in her place, and do these misericords lectures.

Francis sealed the letter and addressed it to the old address. He had to look up the zip code in his zip-code directory, which was itself nineteen years old. For all he knew, Father Birkenshaw was dead. There might not even be a Regina Seminary anymore, though his sister Marie in Alpena would surely have mentioned its closing, if she had known of it. Marie, who had never forgiven him for leaving the Church, always informed him in her annual Christmas note of the demise of yet another Catholic school or college—as if he himself must carry a share of the blame.

But Father Birkenshaw had been on his mind a lot lately and so he wrote. Strange, how recent those old days suddenly seemed. Was it because Magda's absence left such a gaping space between then and now?

He looked out at the lawn. Still brown. No rain in the forecast. Would it be like two summers ago, when people were told to stop watering their lawns and gardens? He wanted to wait until the lawn was green before sprinkling Magda's ashes. Ideally, it should be just before a rain so that the ashes would soak into the roots of that deep purple lilac. That's how she had imagined it when they had discussed it. He wanted to do things the way she'd imagined them, whenever possible, because hadn't she said that would be her way of haunting him?

Lately some things had occurred to him that he wished he could discuss with Magda. What he was going to do with himself for the rest of his life, for instance. The other night he had been loading the dishwasher when there suddenly flashed on him a semi-instinct for something he might like to do next. But that was all it was, a semi-instinct. No pictures or people were attached to it. But, Magda will know what I mean, he had thought, and he had actually started out of the kitchen with the intention of going upstairs to Magda in her study, to see if she could pull it out of him. Then the ludicrousness of it struck him: he was going in search of Magda to ask her what to do with himself now that she was dead. And furthermore, he had been headed for her study, which she had not entered for at least three months before her death.

Magda's ashes weighed five pounds, six ounces. They had come from the funeral home by United Parcel. As soon as the truck pulled out of the driveway, he opened the box and took out the container. He carried it upstairs, removed the sealed plastic bag inside, and placed it on the bathroom scales. Five pounds, six ounces. Maybe a little less. Magda often complained these scales weighed on the heavy side.

Since then, he'd kept the container with the ashes on the huntboard in the bedroom, with a vase of fresh flowers next to it, and his old breviary from Regina in front of it, guarding it, you might say, until the grass got greener and he could carry out the sprinkling the way she'd wanted. He had moved back into their bedroom. It hadn't been as painful as he'd expected, sleeping alone in their bed, but then of course he'd been sleeping alone since January, so he'd had plenty of time to get used to it.

Last night he'd had such an odd dream. He'd been undressing Magda. Only it was more like you would unwrap a large parcel. He was reaching his arms around her—she seemed to be very large— taking off these sort of shroud wrappings to get down to her naked body, because she was sick and he had to put her to bed. Like that first time he'd put her to bed in Chicago, when she'd been slick with sweat and raving out of her head. In the dream he'd felt sure he could take care of her and make her better, just as he had felt sure of it in Chicago. A great warm feeling of his own power surged through him; the closer he came to unwrapping her, the more his whole body throbbed with the desire to love and heal and be of service to what he found inside. At last he got to the end of the wrappings and there was just a small, plain wooden box. But the odd thing was, he wasn't disappointed. He felt the same reverence and desire to serve this box that he had felt toward the living Magda.

What would Magda have made of such an odd dream? he wondered, rifling through his cellophane envelope of postage stamps in search of a suitable one for Father Birkenshaw. And then, as he often did now, he "heard" Magda say exactly the kind of thing she *would* have said under the circumstances. "Isn't that just like you, Frannie, bringing me all your mental nibbles and dreams after I'm safely out of the way from making you face them."

All he had left in the envelope were a few Love stamps and the American flag over the stone faces at Mt. Rushmore.

Definitely the stone faces for Father Birkenshaw.

As he was licking the stamp an awkward, squarish little girl in cartoon-patterned pink shorts loped into view on the dry lawn, carrying a picnic basket. Leora Harris, in crisp yellow slacks and sleeveless top, followed briskly behind, a faded patchwork quilt draped over one arm. My goodness, was it midday already?

Francis hurried outside to greet them, blinking from his sudden entry into the dazzling sunshine. Over the course of the last several weeks, Leora had been extremely mindful of his welfare, stopping by regularly with her baked goods, keeping him up-to-the-minute with information about that cruise and, of course, the latest developments for Magda's memorial service in the fall (an important Blake scholar had been invited to say a few words, and there was to be a string quintet, with harp). Though he found Leora a bit bossy at times, he was grateful for her many kindnesses, and he admired her energy. She had so many projects going, so many people's welfare at heart. Look at the time she spent with Mrs. Elmendorf's lonely little granddaughter. The picnic they were having today had been Elberta's idea, Leora said, when she phoned this morning; Elberta was preparing everything herself. "With the help of Mamie Elmendorf's cook, of course," Leora had added with a laugh. "Elberta adores you," Leora told Francis. "She *worries* about you; she said you were pale from staying inside writing all those letters and we were going to entice you outside for an old-fashioned picnic."

Francis was sure that Leora exaggerated Elberta's esteem for him, as well as Elberta's loquaciousness. In his presence, at least, the child was very reticent and awkward. But Leora was one for putting her own ideas in people's heads, it was part of her take-charge nature. Nevertheless, he thought it generous of her to take such time and trouble over such lonely waifs as himself and Elberta.

"Hello, hello," Leora called in her chipper voice as he ambled toward them across the dry lawn. "Elberta and I are deciding where to set up for our picnic. Weren't we, Elberta?"

Elberta responded with a jerky exaggerated little shrug, which would have been read as rudeness in a child more sure of herself. When Francis greeted her, she uttered an abrupt "Hi!" which sounded more like a bark of pain or outrage and stared fiercely down at her round-toed white play shoes. She was the most ill-at-ease child Francis had ever met. But he felt a protective sympathy for her. Leora

had told him Elberta, whose name used to be something else—
"something not at all suitable for a future heiress," said Leora—had
been virtually bought by her grandmother. What would it be like, at
eleven, to be suddenly removed from everyone and everything you
were used to and have your complete name changed? Though Francis
had never missed being a parent, he didn't understand how a father
could accept money for his child. He must have been pretty desperate. But there were many desperate people in the world. Mrs. Elmendorf's daughter, Elberta's mother, had died from an overdose of drugs,
Leora had told him.

"We could go over there, under the old sycamore," Francis suggested. "That way, we'll have its shade and the shade of the house,
this time of day. I'm sorry the grass is so brown. . . ."

"Well, it's hardly *your* fault," Leora chided him, linking her arm
through his and giving it a playful squeeze as she led them briskly
over to the tree. "Come, Elberta, we're setting up under the sycamore." Leora seemed unusually cheerful and energetic today. "Oh,
and Francis, I brought you some copies of the addendum Gresh is
sending out to our passengers, about your joining the cruise. It's not
in color but it's quite impressive. We've listed you as our 'ecclesiastical specialist.' Remind me to give them to you. They're in the car."

"Oh dear, I wish you hadn't listed me that way, Leora. I'm not
a specialist of anything. I just did it as a pastime while Magda was off
in her libraries."

Francis still wasn't totally sure how it had come about that a little more than two months after his wife's death, he would be leaving
on a trip. Yet, commit himself to Leora and President Harris he certainly had done. Of course he was glad to render what small service
he could to the college that was going to perpetuate Magda's name
with an endowed chair, but nevertheless it felt very strange to be going on this cruise.

"My dear modest man, Magda herself said you were the world's
most informed person on that subject. If you don't remember these
things, *I* do." Leora gave him another familiar squeeze before removing the arm linked through his to spread the patchwork quilt under
the tree.

"I do remember," said Francis, his spirits suddenly sinking. He could still forget for whole minutes that Magda was not here anymore, and then when it hit him afresh, it was like falling into a hole. "But Magda often meant things in a mischievous sense."

"Mmm . . . oh, and we have to discuss musical selections for the memorial service. Now, between Tony's tribute and Professor Genrette—he's the Blake scholar from SUNY who'll be coming over to say a few words about Magda's contribution to Blake studies—the chamber group says they can do either Saint-Saëns 'Swan,' with cello and harp, or Debussy's 'Sacred Dance,' with just solo harp. What is your preference, Francis?"

"Well, maybe . . . the 'Sacred Dance'?" said Francis, going down on his knees to help the other two smooth the quilt over the dry grass. Not knowing one piece from the other, he chose the title he thought would appeal most to Magda. Neither he nor Magda had been very sophisticated about music, though Magda had sometimes liked to play tapes of Gregorian chants or early church music when she was working on her visionary articles.

"Elberta, dear child," said Leora, "don't you think you could wait until we set out all our things before you start eating?"

Caught in the act of furtively stuffing a cookie in her mouth, Elberta tried to swallow it down and choked. Her plump, square hands flew to her mouth, but not before a spray of chocolate crumbs hit Francis's arm. Snatching up a paper napkin, Leora made rather a production out of wiping away the offensive splatter. Elberta turned very pale and looked away.

"I think mourning doves live in this tree we're sitting under," Francis said, sensing the girl was mortified. "I hear them in the early morning, and at night. You know, when we bought this place and I told Magda we had an old sycamore tree next to the house, she laughed and said, 'So that's what one looks like.' But on the other hand she was able to tell me that in ancient times people believed that birds who lived in sycamore trees were souls of the departed. My wife was full of wonderful information like that. She said she didn't know one tree from the other, to look at, but that was my department, the mundane things. When I met Magda, she didn't know the different times that flowers bloomed. Her parents had owned a factory in New York which made silk flowers, and she used to say until she met me she thought all flowers were like silk flowers and bloomed at the same time."

Elberta snorted with amusement. "That's pretty dumb, isn't it?"

"And *that's* rude, dear," admonished Leora, sending Francis a look of comradely exasperation over this trying child as she passed around paper plates and cups.

"Well, Magda meant it partly as a joke, of course," Francis said. "Magda often said things you had to take on several levels at once."

Elberta clasped her hands together and put them to her mouth. After a few unsuccessful tries, she made a sad foghorn-y sound issue forth.

"Well, my goodness," said Francis. "That's exactly the way my mourning doves sound."

"I know," said Elberta.

"That's clever, dear," said Leora. "Where did you learn it?"

"From my dad," said Elberta, not bothering to look at her patroness. "I can teach you to do it, if you want," she told Francis. "It's not too hard. You just have to remember to keep your fingers together."

A lice walked fast along the old brick causeway across the reservoir. The water table was low due to the present drought and because of the lack of snow last winter, but the rampartlike causeway, high above the lapping dark blue waters, at eye level with the mountain peaks in the distance, exactly met her needs. With its miles of unpeopled space all around her and the impersonal sun burning overhead, the landscape was large and uncluttered enough to contain all her feelings and the desire for solitude that went with them.

Other people came here to walk, of course, even Rhoda King did her workouts here—it was Rhoda, in fact, who had told Alice how to get to the reservoir—but during the week, around midday, Alice had never found it crowded. The serious walkers, with jobs, like Rhoda, came in the early morning; the families, on weekends.

To walk both ways took approximately an hour. A mile and a half in length, with only two slight curves in it, the causeway afforded long views of other souls approaching. Alice thought of them as souls, because that's how they appeared at first: all you could discern about them was that they were other human beings. Then, as the space diminished between you, they went through gradual transformations and became men or women, old or young, outgoing or in-turned. Yet even then the causeway, starkly elevated in the midst of the sweeping landscape, gave metaphysical properties to the persons who passed. An old woman with a wavering but determined gait and a frosty blue glitter in her eye was all old women with their knowledge of many winters. A girl with a panting puppy on a leash, her blond ponytail bouncing in rhythm to her springy, aerobic step, was all young girls with their expectations panting ahead of them.

There were mothers with their babies and small children, in carriages or strollers, others just at the point of being able to lurch and toddle forward on their bandy legs. Her child would have sat like a small god in his stroller, being bumped pleasantly over the bricks by a tall, benign presence he took for granted, but was beginning to realize was a separate being (though still very receptive to his wishes). His bottom bounced on sudden soft rises of grassy mounds between the bricks. His cheeks, brushed by little tickle-feathers of breezes, glowed warmly. The bright thing above his head made his eyes blink if he tried to look directly at it.

Eyes the color of those dark blue waters lapping below.

After the midwife had cleaned him up, Alice had held his perfectly made body in her arms, trying to memorize as much of him as she could for the rest of her life: the dark brown hair; the flat rounded ears with the slightest elf-points at the top; the wide, full mouth with its sensuous puffy pad in the middle of the upper lip; the manly little shoulders; the tiny mushroom penis; the sturdy arms and legs. But the eyes, with their wet lashes, were closed.

"I'd like to see the color of his eyes," she told the midwife, "do you think we could open them?" The other woman had complied immediately without a word, stroking back the lids so that Alice could look into the eyes that would never gaze back on her, reflecting her love.

"What an unusual dark blue," said Alice, "I wonder if they would have gone darker later?" She was already feeling groggy from the sedative the doctor had given her. Hugo came back into the room to report that the ambulance was on its way. There was some hemorrhaging, the midwife explained; also, possibly some placenta remaining inside her. It would be better to go to the hospital and have a D&C, to avoid complications later. The midwife then asked Hugo if he would like to hold the baby for a moment.

"No, let him stay with his mother until the ambulance gets here," Hugo replied gruffly. But he stationed himself just above them, brooding down on them with a face that seemed suddenly old and battle-scarred. Gently he zigzagged a forefinger along the baby's forehead. "Look at that," he said to Alice in soft surprise. "He's got your widow's peak exactly. Amazing . . ."

Just before they were transferring her to the stretcher, the midwife brought the small blue blanket Alice had ready for the baby and capably swaddled him while he still lay in his mother's arms. Then she bent close to Alice, her eyes above the gauze mask as trustworthy as those of a kind parent tucking you in for the night. "Will you let me take care of him for you now?" she asked. And, knowing this other mother would handle him sorrowfully and tenderly, thinking of her own children, Alice gave over her boy.

Having reached the south end of the causeway, which ended abruptly in pinewood trails and old access road, Alice doubled back. The return walk faced the spectacular, remoter vista: craggier, more austere mountains, the sky a closer presence than any land or water.

If an approaching walker on the causeway took on a male shape, as one was in the process of doing now, there would sometimes be a short interval in which Alice liked to imagine it turning into Francis Lake. Lanky legs in long pants, an absent, swaying style of walk, could lend itself to moments of vivid fantasizing of how it would look and feel if Francis, having decided to walk at the reservoir, should be coming toward her.

But there was hardly a split second of false hope in this approaching figure. His pumping legs were already too thick and muscular, his walk too fast and furious, his head too dark and shaggy . . . his orange pants out of the question.

Francis knew she liked to walk here at this time of day, she had mentioned it several times when she'd dropped by his house afterward. Ever since spending the day of Magda's death with him, she felt she could allow herself a friend's intimacy of dropping by, without phoning first, and Francis always seemed glad to have her company.

When she'd returned that day, June 7, with groceries and the rubbing alcohol, she'd entered the house, calling out to him, and then following his faint answer upstairs to Magda's room. Francis was sitting by the bed, in the chair he always placed for visitors, and when she saw the book lying open in front of him on the edge of the bed, she first thought he'd been reading something to Magda. But a quick glance at Magda, and then back at him, told her Magda was beyond words.

"Yes, it's over," he said. He looked dazed. "I just read a collect for her out of my old breviary from seminary. 'Now that she is dead to this world, may she live united to You. . . .' She knows what that means now, even if we can't."

"Yes," agreed Alice, standing motionless on the other side of the bed. Francis made no move to rise from the chair where she herself had so often sat, the one with the faulty caster. There was something so *dead* about the body that lay between them. Where, then, was the sucking, thirsty Magda whose downy head Alice had cradled so recently in the crook of her arm like a helpless infant's, or the Magda who just afterward had croaked at her witchily, "The two of you should get together . . . I'll leave him to you in my will . . ."? How could there be such a difference between the body of an hour ago and the yellow husk lying there now? What a powerful contribution Magda's spirit, even in its last hours, must have made to that weak, rotting body!

"I was with her," Francis said. "I was rubbing her head the way I do when she has one of her headaches. She didn't say anything, but she was still there. And then, she took a breath . . ."—his voice expressed a quiet awe—"and just wasn't, anymore."

"I'm glad you were with her," said Alice. "I know that was important. I never knew—" Abruptly she stopped herself from speaking the rest of her thought. I never knew my child when he was "there." The husk I saw was beautiful, but I never got to see his living spirit. It was already dead to this world when they pulled him out of me.

("Shoulders too wide," said Romero. "Boy, does this little guy have football shoulders. Push, Alice, keep pushing. . . ." She pushed, kept pushing. She was soaking wet. The neck and armpits of Romero's green gown were soaked from his own sweat. "Hell's bells, looks like we got a double whammy here," he said to the midwife. "Wide shoulders *and* a cord . . . did you get a reading on the monitor yet?" "He's in distress," said the midwife quietly. "Okay, let's go for the Woods maneuver. I'll rotate the shoulders . . . see if you can get an arm out . . . can you get an arm?" "It's not coming, Doctor." "Alice, I have to do a quick episiotomy on you to facilitate delivery." A cut, a warm gush. "Okay, let's go in there pronto and pull the little guy out. . . . just relax, Alice, we've got him, we're pulling him out now . . . I've got the shoulders, you hold on to the head. Okay, here we go . . . here now, here . . . he's coming . . . here he is . . . get that blasted cord off. . . ." A sudden emptiness, snipping and hearty smacking sounds . . . then a silence . . . then more smacking and slapping . . . then someone's defeated sigh, followed by Romero's low, angry "Shit . . .")

But for Francis's needs, that Friday afternoon, it was those perfectly chosen words of the midwife, as she asked permission to take charge of the lifeless bundle in the blue blanket, that Alice took for her inspiration: *Will you let me take care of him for you now?*

"Will you let me help you take care of her now?" Alice had asked the man sitting beside his dead wife.

Thus she had wakened him gently from his long vigil and stood by him while he phoned the undertaker, who arrived soon after with an assistant. Francis went up with them, but Alice waited downstairs. Presently they descended bearing a zipped navy-blue bag on a stretcher, which they transferred to a gurney and then rolled outside to an unmarked van. Francis stood in the driveway and watched the van out of sight. Then, with that absentminded raking motion of his hair, he returned to the house and stepped, dazed, across the threshold.

He looked at Alice. "What do you suppose we ought to do now?"

"Well, perhaps phone the college?" she suggested.

"Yes, of course, the college has to know. But who, I wonder?"

"Why not Ray Johnson? He'll be quicker than anyone else to see that word gets around."

"That's just what she would have said," replied Francis with a bleak laugh. He made the call, his voice breaking for the first time, and then they went up together and stripped Magda's bed. While Francis loaded the washing machine Alice heated some canned soup and made cheese-and-lettuce sandwiches. It was going on three in the afternoon by the time they sat down to lunch. As they slowly ate, Francis told her a story about Magda coming to lecture at his seminary in 1966, and how, due to an outbreak of diarrhea from some wrong spice in the dessert, he, who had given his dessert to a fellow seminarian, had been the only one fit to drive her to the airport next morning. Then Ramirez-Suarez arrived, and Alice reluctantly left Francis in the charge of his tenderhearted friend.

... And I myself will always be grateful for your generosity in bringing food, and especially for your support on the day of her death. I can't think of anyone else who could have assisted me in such a calm, understanding manner as you did.

Though she had tried to read all she could into those words in Francis's letter to Hugo and herself, there was only so much she could squeeze out of them. *I can't think of anyone else....* Might he not have written the same to anyone who'd happened to be with him during those hours?

And couldn't you feel all the gratitude and admiration in the world for someone's *calm and understanding manner* without feeling a single iota of love or attraction for them?

Alice nodded to the dark, shaggy man in the orange sweatpants as he panted past her on the lonely causeway. He dipped his head and flashed her a wolfish side smile without breaking his fierce momentum. A quick glance was enough to reveal him to be a man as totally conscious of himself and his effects as Francis was unconscious of his. Wasn't it mysterious, this thing they called attraction? Objectively, he was a virile, attractive, alive-looking man, about her own age. Some woman was probably fantasizing right now about being married to him. Several women, perhaps, if he weren't already married. Or even if he were. Yet all Alice felt toward him was a slight resentment that he wasn't Francis Lake.

At least now she had proved Hugo wrong, though he didn't know it. "You prefer the company of the dead to the living," he had bitterly observed back in the spring when she wouldn't emerge from her grief and apathy. "You're more in love with death than me," he had accused before he went off to Prague.

Well, all that had changed now. And in some ways it was worse. When you loved no one alive, there was nothing more to lose or get hurt by. And now there was everything again.

There was no reason Francis *shouldn't* someday show up at the reservoir, one of the most beautiful spots in the area, except she knew he wouldn't on his own. It simply wouldn't occur to him. He was very much a creature of habit and established routines, she had discovered. He did his housework in the morning and wrote letters, then made himself lunch, then stumbled out into the sunshine to tend his flowers and plants.

If she *asked* him to meet her at the reservoir and walk with her, he undoubtedly would. He acquiesced willingly to the wishes of others, she had discovered that, too. She had been rather surprised that he had let Leora Harris talk him into going on the cruise.

But hadn't the idea been put in Leora's head by Magda herself, that day when she was taking such pleasure in bedeviling everyone gathered around her bed? That day, all of them had come in for a portion of Magda's sibylline (or demented) flak, when she had pretended not to know who Hugo was, insisted that Alice defend herself against the accusation of being married to him, called Francis "Prince Humdrum," and baited Leora by proposing that they *all* go on the cruise, and that Francis take Magda's place as lecturer.

And now, isn't it strange? marveled Alice. They are all going to do exactly as Magda ordered and go on the cruise.

Except for me.

But hadn't Magda included Alice herself in the bedeviling deathbed injunction? *Of course Alice has to go. She will have to help Francis carry me. He'd never bear up otherwise.*

But that's not possible, I can't go, thought Alice, slowing her pace on the old pink bricks as she approached the starting point, and thus the end, of her round-trip walk on the causeway. Under the present circumstances, the last thing in the world I could decently and honorably do would be to accompany Hugo on this cruise.

Even though Leora had been making a pest of herself, badgering Hugo over the phone as recently as yesterday to convince Alice to change her mind.

"Holy Hannah, that harpy sure can harp," said Hugo, putting down the phone. He went into his silly-woman voice to "do" Leora: " 'Now, Hugo, you must use your influence to change Alice's mind, there's no excuse for her to stay behind anymore, since you two don't have to move. Oh, we're all going to have *such* fun on this cruise, *everyone's* getting on board.' What's really bugging the first lady and her spouse is that everyone *isn't* getting on board, and old Gresh is afraid he'll lose face with his big donors. The cruise is nowhere near full. I had it from bigmouth Ray Johnson himself. He told me I could have an extra single cabin for myself to use for my *writing*, since I'd sacrificed the deluxe cabin. Can you beat these people? Does he really think I can just hop into my 'writing cabin' and tap out a few pages of deathless prose after lunch every day . . . on a *cruise*? But I defended you valiantly to Leora, I told her you'd been looking forward to some quiet time to yourself. You heard me, I told her you still had some healing to do."

"That was nice of you, Hugo. He would have been six months old in two weeks."

"I know. I was thinking about that this morning."

"It's pointless, but I sometimes go back and try to change things so that other things wouldn't have had to happen."

"How do you mean?" Hugo's interest was roused. This was more like their old way of talking.

"Well, say if my brother had died instantly, and there hadn't been all that frustration at the hospital, when they wouldn't let me stay with him . . . I wonder if I might have had a different outlook on hospitals, and then later when . . ."

"Don't do that to yourself, honey. I know what you're going to say next, only if I say it, you'll accuse me of completing your sentences. Don't torture yourself. Romero was a very impressive guy. I mean, it wasn't like he was some quack in a butcher's smock. He had references from satisfied mothers a mile long, he had personal appeal. . . ."

"*You* had doubts at first. . . ."

"I did, I admit, but mainly because it was something new to me. It wasn't my generation's style of doing things. Rosemary went to the hospital and had a spinal block. In those days, the fathers waited outside until it was all over and then were ushered ceremoniously in and presented with the fait accompli of mother and child nestling together on the pillow. Except in Rosemary's case, she'd fallen asleep and the nurse was holding poor little Cal, who was crying his eyes out. But Romero won me over quickly, so it was my decision as much as yours. He was very convincing about it, especially in the case of young, healthy, independent-minded women like yourself who distrusted rigid routine and preferred to remain in control."

"Oh, yes, in control," Alice bitterly remarked. "You ought to hate me. It was your son, too."

"I don't hate you, Alice. Far from it. I wish I could stop you from hating *yourself*, blaming yourself so much. I wish I could help you more, but I don't seem to be able to, at least not at this time. I wish you could find someone who *could* help you, but I'm not about to make any more suggestions on *that* topic. But please remember, whatever you think of me personally, I'm on your side. Anyway, I got Leora off our backs, though she did threaten to keep trying, in hopes you'd have a last-minute change of heart. I told her she'd better not keep her fingers crossed."

Hugo sounded almost cheerful that she was not going. And who could blame him? He'd had thirty-six happy hours without her on his South Carolina trip, hadn't he? Met that rich patroness of the arts with lupus who'd since been sending him devoted notes (which Hugo assiduously shared with Alice) clipped to flattering reports of his speech in the local newspapers and a gushing account of the event written by the lady herself for the library bulletin. Just think what eleven fruitful days alone, on a cruise ship full of admirers (or half-full), might do for Hugo's spirits.

Though his spirits were good lately. He'd retrenched for a while into a bearish mope after their ugly exchange coming home from the airport (as much her fault as his: they'd just lived intensely through important separate experiences). But he'd recently become friendly again, in a benevolent but cheerfully absent and undemanding manner that gave her ample room to live her secret life.

She and Hugo seemed, in fact, to be coexisting well in their separate secret lives at the moment. She suspected his secret life came from the energizing impulse toward a new book, judging from his frequent retreats to his study-cum-bedroom, and the rapt, smug fullness in his face when he emerged. She had never seen that look before in their marriage: the look of someone hoarding a vital private resource, the look of someone newly and secretly in love. But then, Hugo had never been writing a book during their life together.

Many comfortable marriages in the world undoubtedly rested on each partner's willingness to accept that he or she was not the dearest private resource of the other. Not the most vital love. And then together they made a friendly, undemanding place in which the separate passion of each could be intensely lived. Perhaps, if things had turned out differently last January 10, they could be making such a marriage now. Hugo falling raptly in love with his next novel, Alice fueled by the central passion of her child.

But not now, not now, not now.

Of course Alice has to go. She will have to help Francis carry me. He'd never bear up otherwise.

Of course I *cannot* go, Magda. He'll bear up. Others will console him.

To share a cabin with Hugo, while pining for Francis Lake, would be an atrocity against the sensibilities of all three. And before she and Hugo could even think about sharing a cabin, they would have to resume their bed life. She would have to initiate it, have to pretend. Have to convince him she wanted him back again . . . wanted even maybe to try for another child.

She couldn't do it. It went against every impulse, physical and moral. She might not have been in love with Hugo when she married him, but one thing was sure: she hadn't been in love with anyone else.

She hadn't, when she said yes to Hugo, been in the least aware she had it in her nature to care as intensely about anyone as she cared for Francis Lake.

It wouldn't be decent, it wouldn't be honorable, I would lose respect for myself, thought Alice. I'd be like those scheming, dishonest adulteresses in and out of novels.

Even if Hugo and I were to stay in separate cabins . . . I might sleep in that "writing cabin" Ray Johnson offered . . . no, that's getting murky. I'd still be going on false pretenses. I'd be going as Hugo's wife, but pining for someone else. I'd be mutating into what Andy called the squalid creepy-crawlies of the world, the undiscriminating people with no integrity.

But I *will* drop by and see Francis on the way home. It's not sacrificing my integrity to allow myself the pleasure of being with him for a little while. When I'm with him, something goes out from me to him that revives some vital thing I thought was dead and buried.

Surely I can subsist on that, on being able to feel so much, even though it's hopeless. Surely it's not wrong to feel more alive than you have in years because someone exists in the same world with you that you can dearly love. How many people have that much?

So long as I can face myself, Alice thought, surely I should be able to sustain myself on *that*.

In Hugo's opinion, the lunch with Cal and Laurence was going surprisingly well. They'd arrived punctually from Wellfleet at the designated time, had drinks outside on the new lawn chairs Hugo had bought at Sears for the occasion, and then Alice served them a delicious lunch of cold salmon with fresh vegetables and fruit salad. Everybody seemed relaxed and easy, and even abstemious Cal had put away a beer first ("I get so thirsty when I've been driving") and his share of the wine with lunch. Hugo had never seen Cal looking better, as a matter of fact. He'd always had to be careful of his fair skin, but two weeks on the beach, even with maximal sunscreens, had given him a lovely rosy-gold color. While all of them had been re-marking on Cal's color, Hugo had undergone a moment of nervousness (was this an appropriate topic of conversation in front of Laurence?) but almost immediately realized nobody else seemed the least bit aware of any problem. It was only some time blip from his own Southern past.

The confounding part of it all was that Laurence really could be considered an ideal partner for Cal. He brought out the best in Cal, a vigor and assurance Cal had heretofore lacked. He brought out—if it didn't sound too paradoxical—a new manliness in Cal. Except for Hugo's brief blip, the race thing had worn off. Three quarters of the world was Laurence's color, anyway, or some shade of it. When you looked at it from a numbers point of view, it was *Hugo* who was the minority, only he'd never thought of it this way until now. Nevertheless, Hugo gave himself credit for his readaptation on that score. He was, after all, Wayne Henry's son.

Though Laurence seemed another species from the subservient shadowy blacks who haunted the perimeters of Hugo's childhood.

Laurence seemed another species from Hugo's own father.

On the other matter, Hugo had more evolving to do. He still couldn't feel comfortable about—nope, even though Laurence was such an admirable and likable man.

"I really think you ought to go," Cal was saying to Alice as he helped her clear the plates. They were on the subject of the cruise again. Hugo realized he wasn't sorry to hear Alice's cheerful but firm reply in the negative as she went ahead of Cal into the kitchen. God, the two of them were so similar in build, in their styles of beauty. The two of *them* would have made a lovely couple, if someone else in the destiny department had been put in charge of the matchmaking.

He became aware that Laurence was watching their retreat with the same admiration, and perhaps even with similar accompanying thoughts. This man and I could be friends, he suddenly thought. Then, immediately after, had to resist a choking backlash of disgust as he conjured up an image of this man in bed with his son.

"Hey, Laurence," he said, getting up from the table, "why don't we take this second bottle of wine and go outside?" He was relieved to hear himself speaking in the genial tones of the Knight as Host. "The youngsters can do the clearing up and join us."

As they were crossing the lawn together, Hugo carrying the bottle and his own glass and Laurence the other glasses, the man's lilting, thoughtful voice broke the silence in a way that made Hugo wonder if Laurence had read his mind inside the house. "Well, so here we are, Hugo. Under this flawless sky after a superb lunch. Getting to know each other better in a situation new to both of us."

Hugo laughed gruffly. Was Laurence implying that he'd never been taken home to meet a lover's parents before? Yet he felt impelled to respond in the same forthright spirit of . . . ground breaking. "New situations make new demands on the imagination. But you strike me as being a man of imagination. And I hope I am . . . hell, I'd better be, in my line of business."

"That's the truth." Laurence laughed appreciatively.

They had reached the new lawn furniture.

"I had the chaise last time," said Laurence, smiling. His front teeth overlapped slightly. "It's your turn."

"No, please, you take it, I prefer a straight chair." Oh, *shit*, shouldn't have said that.

"In that case, I will, thank you." Laurence, settling his elegant body in its rumpled chinos and faded polo shirt onto the chaise, either didn't register Hugo's accidental double entendre, or else was being a gent about it. He crossed his ankles, and seemed to contemplate his out-of-date sneakers. "This is very comfortable indeed. I'm a lazy man by nature."

Hugo filled Laurence's glass and then his own and sat down in the chair he wished he'd called straight-*backed*. "You certainly don't give that impression. All those projects you were telling us about at lunch. The new shelter, that big-brother program you're organizing for fatherless boys, the food canteen for the homeless near the bus station. You never seem to stop."

"That's because I know if I do stop, I might find myself a comfortable redwood chaise like this and lounge in it happily for the rest of my life, with a nice glass of pouilly-fumé like the one I'm drinking now. Oh, I'm a born voluptuary, all right. But now, Cal, he's a born worker. That's the difference between us. I want to stop, but know I'd relax too well if I ever did. He never wants to stop, and couldn't relax if he did. I often have to make him stop to eat. At Wellfleet, he had the dining table covered with his lists and charts the whole time we were on vacation. We had to take our food outside and eat on the deck. And those chaises weren't nearly as comfortable as yours."

"Cal a born worker? Surely we're not talking about the Cal I know."

"One and the same," Laurence assured him.

"He must have matured."

"We all do some of that eventually, praise the Lord." As Laurence bent his head to take a sip of wine, Hugo noted the grizzled hair and the deep gray pouches under the man's eyes and reminded himself afresh that Cal's partner was close to sixty.

"He gets the nonrelaxing part from me," Hugo ruefully conceded.

"Well, if he did, he also got your creativity. He has your enviable ability to conceptualize in great detail. You should see the scale drawing he's made for the kids' quarters."

"The kids?" repeated Hugo uneasily. Jesus, was Laurence breaking it to him that they were planning to go the whole route and adopt children?

"I mentioned at lunch we're expanding the shelter in the building I own to include a twelve-bed dormitory. It's going to be for twelve youngsters. Twelve's not a lot when New York seems to have become the city of homeless kids, but at least that will be twelve more off the streets."

Questions crowded to Hugo's tongue, but he was afraid of sounding sheltered and naive. He'd certainly bumped into his share of homeless people in New York, but it outraged him to hear that there were great numbers of homeless kids roaming around. How had this happened? When he'd thought about it at all, he'd always assumed they were being taken care of by the welfare agencies.

"How did you get into this kind of thing?" he asked Laurence instead. "I mean, it's a hunk to take on, what you're doing."

"Oh, it's not even a teaspoon of relief out of an ocean of need. I despair about it all the time, Cal will tell you. I'm endeavoring mightily not to become like the man who went to India for the first time and saw the beggars. You know, the first day he leaves his hotel and goes for a walk and gives away all his spare rupees to beggars. The next day, he cashes more traveler's checks and goes out into the streets again and gives a rupee to every beggar he meets. This goes on for several days, until he realizes he's never going to cover all the beggars, and he just gives up and closes down. For the rest of his time in India, he averts his eyes until he stops seeing beggars. He behaves like a normal tourist. I've been close to that a number of times ... I think, hell, man, I'm not a billionaire, I can't save the world, I'm not even a very big millionaire. Why don't I just let it all go and be content to collect my antiques and read medieval history—that was my major—and behave like a normal tourist in the world. But then I come across this eleven-year-old boy and his eight-year-old half sister we found living in a burned-out car on Riverside Drive, which is what stimulated us to get moving with our new shelter. Two great kids. Maybe we can save them from drowning. Maybe we can't; maybe after what they've been through it's too late. But I still have my belief that it makes a difference to care. Especially in this era when self-righteous noncaring has reached such endemic proportions. But you know, Hugo, I was close to losing that belief when I met Cal at a lecture at the Metropolitan. I was in one of my low periods when I was tempted to return to my hotel and keep my rupees to myself. That's what my dad did. He made his pile in Cleveland real estate and then sat back and drank good whiskey and watched the world go by on TV until he bought the big one. But Cal gave me a transfusion of his young idealism and so here we are instead, moving in beds on Monday for our kids' shelter."

Cal's idealism? When had *that* surfaced? Had something in Laurence fished it up in him? Cal at a lecture at the Met? What was the lecture on? Hugo wondered. How did the two of them first make contact? How did this "transfusion" take place?

But he couldn't bring himself to ask. With his "enviable ability to conceptualize in great detail," he didn't want to imagine more than he could handle. And there was obviously going to be plenty of time for him to learn to handle it in. Twelve beds, twenty beds, fifty beds, a hundred beds. With so much of the world left to shelter, and as long as Cal's youthful idealism and Laurence's money held out, their partnership might well outlast Alice's and his.

"But what about you?" asked Laurence. "Are you at work on a new book?"

"Well, a book is finally starting to work on *me*, I'm relieved to say. But it's all very recent. I got the idea while I was down in South Carolina. I haven't even told Alice much yet." Hugo hadn't told her anything, but he owed her that degree of loyalty.

"Ah, well, I don't mean to pry. It's just that I find the whole phenomenon so fascinating. There you are, this man walking around like the rest of us, but there's this whole other world you make. It comes out of you, but it exists on its own. I can go live in it without ever knowing you, and be enlarged by it. Who was it said that novels help to convince us that other people exist?"

"I don't know, but I like it."

"So do I, so do I," said Laurence happily. "I've been on a boat about twice in my life, I'm a terrible sailor, but I completely understand the seagoing mentality because of Conrad. *And*"—he laughed—"I know exactly how it feels to be poor and a governess . . . from *Jane Eyre*. Nineteenth-century stories, granted, but on the important levels of experience, the centuries don't matter much, do they?"

"I hope not, because I'm about to venture into another century."

"Now, that's interesting. Are you going to venture forward, or backward, in time?" He was scrupulously casual, but a telltale twinkle in his intelligent eyes betrayed that he was flattered by Hugo's sudden overture of trust.

"It begins in 1855, on a plantation in South Carolina. In the opening scene there are these two women in an upstairs bedroom. One's the mistress of the plantation—she has a mysterious illness, we'd recognize it as lupus today—and the other is her servant, but they're a lot more than that. They grew up together, the servant came with the mistress to her marriage. And there's another, powerful link, but we won't find that out till later. In this first scene, they're discussing their respective sons, who are going off to college together.

That is, the mistress's son is going to attend college; the maid's son is going to take care of him while he's at college."

"Of course," said Laurence.

Hugo was proud of himself for narrating this much without ever once using the color word. But for clarity's sake, he felt he needed to add, "Apparently that was a common practice in that milieu. Young men took a servant . . . well, in that world they were slaves."

"Slaves, yes," affably murmured the reclining Laurence, putting down his glass on Sonia Wynkoop's scruffy lawn and making a graceful steeple with his long fingers upon his chest.

"I want to use a historical setting to tell some all-time truths," continued Hugo. "And also, there's something about this story that . . ." He cast about for a way to express himself, then seized on Magda's idea from the old exam book, about Yeats making a poem out of his despair over Maud Gonne. "Something about it addresses longings and woes of my own."

He was surprised at how easily the story, with all sorts of ramifications, poured out. He knew more about it than he had *known* he knew. It took shape as he elaborated on it to Laurence, who, with his relaxed but keen attentiveness, seemed to draw it out of him.

"It sounds like a story tailor-made for you," said Laurence, when Hugo had finished. "Your new novel sounds like the natural successor to *A Month with the Manigaults*."

"How so?"

"Well, many of the concerns are similar, aren't they? Your young slave who goes off to college with his master and secretly learns to read and write is a kind of counterpart to Woody in *Manigaults*, isn't he?"

"Hey, you may be right." Hugo was elated by Laurence's casual phrase "your new novel," as if he took it for granted it already existed.

"Yes, it's the same theme, really, isn't it?" the reclining Laurence mused on, tapping his fingertips softly together above his chest. "We can't grow up, we can't escape our tormentors, we can't be *free*, until we can express ourselves well enough to be heard by others, can we? Only then can we tell our story. And only by convincingly telling our story can each of us do our bit to help the world grow up."

Then he laughed softly, a stealthy, worldly-wise laugh. "Little wonder they outlawed reading and writing for slaves, right, Hugo?"

It's understandable why Cal should enjoy the company of this man, Hugo was thinking just as his son came out of the house with Alice.

"Hey, guess what, Dad, I've managed to talk some sense into Alice," Cal called ahead robustly, linking his fingers through Alice's as they crossed the lawn.

If I were suffering from a short-term amnesia which blocked out the past two-and-a-half years, thought Hugo ruefully as the lovely young pair approached, and then I suddenly came to myself here in this moment, I would believe myself to be in a happy moment: my son Cal, whom I recognize from before the amnesia, has brought home the right girl, anyone can see that, just the sort of girl I would have picked for myself if I could have found her. And now he's calling across to me and this man—who must be a distinguished colleague I met during my amnesia, perhaps a visiting writer from another country, perhaps we're over at his house—that he's at last talked her into marrying him.

Look at him, my formerly sullen, critical son, how his whole countenance glows! His deep-set aquamarine eyes, the exact eyes of my mother, are shining and clear and focused on a happiness in reach. It's like getting to see how my mother's eyes would have looked with happiness in them.

And the girl's downcast blush, as if she's a little ashamed to have been talked into what she wanted to do anyway, that's exactly right for the occasion, too.

That's what I would think, if I unfortunately didn't know what the real occasions were.

CHAPTER XX

"Gresh Harris phones me and says—this at the eleventh hour, mind you, Hugo—he says: 'Listen, Jack, would it put you to great inconvenience if I asked you to lecture on Jane Austen instead of Thomas Hardy on the cruise? If you'd be willing to substitute her house in Chawton for Hardy's Dorchester, then Francis Lake would be able to lead a tour to nearby Winchester Cathedral.' As it so happens, I'm perfectly willing. She's the far greater writer. I prefer her breezy sanity any day of the week to Hardy's belabored pessimism. I have enough pessimism in my own disposition. I told Gresh I was equally conversant with Hardy or Jane. I'd be a poor representative of my trade if I couldn't ramble on equally well about any and all of them. The fact is, we'll be better off with Jane for the purposes of this jaunt. Even these people have heard of *Pride and Prejudice*. Heard of, I said, not read. Jane Austen is a recognizable brand name to them. But maybe you'll be able to tell me, Hugo, why was this important last-minute change made to accommodate the widower? He seems personable enough, but why is he signed on as an 'ecclesiastical specialist'? What are his credentials? What has he done? What does he do for a *job*?"

"Well, he did spend some time in a seminary when he was young," Hugo told Stanforth, "but since then, he's been a house husband. You know, like those wives who stayed at home that men used to have."

"Yes, I vaguely remember that historical era," said Stanforth, smiling under his droopy mustache at Hugo across the middle bulkhead seat Alice had temporarily vacated.

"Magda's specialty bordered on the religious stuff. Francis probably picked up a lot of his knowledge from her."

Stanforth quietly belched. "Yes, I'm acquainted with her *morceau* on the popular visionaries. Hysterical, but who wouldn't envy its reprintings."

"Well, but you called Lawrence hysterical back in the departure lounge, so she's in good company, isn't she?" Hugo cheerfully goaded his companion.

"But Lawrence had flashes of genius. *Flashes*. I conceded that back in the lounge."

"True, you did." Hugo stretched out his legs in the roomy bulkhead. He was feeling quite comfortable with Stanford, after their initial set-to, really more like two male dogs sniffing each other out, in the departure lounge at Kennedy. There was something morosely appealing about his co-lecturer, with his elongated, scarecrow proportions (which had secured for them these bulkhead seats), his droopy walrus mustache and matching reddish-brown curly hair, both obviously dyed, because the shaggy eyebrows were white. The juxtaposition was rather startling. From a distance, especially from behind, he could pass for a man in his fifties. Then you got close and saw those Father Time eyebrows and the bloodshot, world-weary eyes regarding you gloomily. Stanforth was sixty-seven, Hugo had looked him up in a dictionary of American scholars before the trip. He'd been at Iwo Jima. But he wasn't in the big *Who's Who*, which assuaged Hugo's ego. It more than compensated for the overseas war credentials and the dramatic height difference between them. (Stanforth's daughter, a sort of aging Peter Pan with cropped greeny-yellow hair and a viper's tongue, had taken one look at them standing together and labeled them Mutt and Jeff.)

"And who, exactly, is that stout adolescent girl my daughter is seated next to—when my daughter is seated. Is the girl also some concession to the widower?"

"No, no, that's Mamie Elmendorf's granddaughter," Hugo told him. "Mamie is what Gresh calls a PBD. Potential Big Donor. She's been making serious noises about forking over some millions for his cultural center in Aurelia."

"Ah. The overdressed lady he's up in first with."

"That's right."

"But why is the granddaughter not up in first?"

"She gets on the grandmother's nerves. Not turning out according to Mamie's blueprint, they tell me. Mamie bought her from her father. The mother, Mamie's daughter, is dead. Mamie bought her and brought her home and changed the child's name to Elberta—"

"Elberta? No. Like the peaches?"

"I'm afraid so. Mamie's late husband's name was Elbert. Gresh's cultural center, if he gets it, will have to be called the Elbert Elmendorf Cultural Center. . . ."

Stanforth, looking down the vast length of his legs at his huge red-brown Wallabees planted side by side against the bulkhead wall, stroked his walrus mustache and chuckled soundlessly. He seemed to be enjoying Hugo's misanthropic rundown of Aurelia's dramatis personae. Hugo was glad Alice was not there at the moment to modulate his bitchiness. After the movie, which none of them had watched, she had moved back to visit with Francis and Elberta until such time as Jill Stanforth, still strolling lethally about the aircraft in her pink socks and accosting strangers, should decide to reclaim her seat.

"The reason Leora seated Francis Lake next to Elberta," Hugo went on to explain, "is because she's very shy and awkward, very easily threatened. But she seems to get on well with Francis."

"Who certainly doesn't give the impression of threatening anyone," mused Stanforth.

"I have all this from my wife," said Hugo. "Alice got very attached to Magda when she was dying. She still goes over to see Francis a lot."

"Your wife is lovely," brooded Stanforth, still stroking his mustache. "A lady, too. Imagine that, in this day and time. How old did you say she was?"

"I didn't," said Hugo testily, "but she's thirty-four." He waited defensively for some December-May charge, the Joel Mark kind of thing about riding off into the sunset with his young prize.

"Jill's thirty-nine," said Stanforth. "Though with all the wear and tear, I expect she looks older. Maybe they'll become friends on the trip, maybe your wife will have some influence on her." He laughed drearily. "But highly unlikely, I suppose. Jill puts people off. Yet she was an adorable child."

The sudden, uncharacteristic wistfulness in his tone touched Hugo. "What seems to be the problem?" he felt he could ask, one father to another.

"The problem? I suppose *at bottom* it's bound to be me and her mother. That's the politically correct answer, right? Her fourth husband, the one she met in the drug rehab center last year, is a member of a religious sect that strongly believes in devils incarnate and waging serious war against them, and he just kicked her out because he says she's definitely one. If I were to venture a humble answer myself, I'd say she's mad as hell because she can't find work to suit the needs of her temperament or a husband worthy of her wit. But of course I'm her father and fathers are susceptible to partiality."

"Is she an only child?"

"No, she has two older brothers. Fine enough specimens, each in his way. They both got through school, though not brilliantly, like Jill, and now they have good jobs, in the banking and computer industries respectively, and pretty, educated wives and some rather nice children, though of course grandfathers are also known to be partial. But Jill has always been our smartest and most interesting offspring, even at her worst." Stanforth crossed his long legs, and sighed. "Wish

I could smoke my pipe, but that's no longer politically correct, either. But now tell me about your offspring."

"Well, I have just one son, twenty-nine, from my former marriage. He's gone through his periods of rebellion, but he got through college with fairly good grades, majored in history, and now he's working for a charitable organization in New York City and seems very happy and fulfilled."

"Sounds like an admirable young man," said Stanforth. "Married?"

"No, he—he has a friend."

"Someone you like?"

"Yes, I do, a lot. I had some qualms at first, not what I expected and all that, but I can genuinely say I like and admire Cal's friend."

"Does she have a profession?"

Ah, here it comes, thought Hugo. Here it comes, for the rest of my life. But, I can't, I just can't yet, not even with Stanforth's daughter's drugs and four husbands. "They're both in social work," he said. "Actually, they both work for the same network of charities." Sorry, Cal, but I just couldn't yet. Sorry, Laurence. I know Rosemary's all but sent out engraved announcements about Cal's orientation, but I guess I need a little more time.

"How commendable of them," remarked Stanforth, with just the tiniest edge of irony. "They sound like the perfect pair. Shades of *Little Dorrit*, after she and Clenham marry and are venturing forth into the morning to help others. How does that wonderful ending go? 'Went down into a modest life of usefulness and happiness . . . went quietly down into the roaring streets, inseparable and blessed.' I'm leaving out a lot, but it'll pass for the nonce. It'll certainly pass with *this* group when we have our London literary walk. Wonderful, smarmy ending, isn't it? Dickens was a genius through and through, that's why he could get away with as much smarm as he liked. Not that your son and his friend necessarily have to marry, please don't think I was implying that. With the world in its present state, I think most young people would do better to hold off making promises that they can't keep. I wish my daughter had simply gone and lived with those men, each more impossible than the last, rather than committing herself to matrimony each time. Ah, here's the lovely Alice back."

Alice, smiling, slipped into the seat between them and fastened her belt.

"So how are Elberta and Uncle Francis?" asked Hugo.

"Oh, they're very sweet together. We talked a little, then Jill came back."

Alice did look lovely, Hugo was proud to be seen publicly as her consort, though he continued to be vexed by the mystery of how their going on this trip as a couple had come about. Why had she suddenly reversed herself about coming on the cruise?

"So how did Cal manage to sell you on it?" he had asked her as soon as his son and Laurence had driven away, the day of the lunch. "Whatever he said to you in the kitchen must have been very persuasive."

"He wasn't trying to *sell* me on anything, Hugo. I guess I was just ready to change my mind, and exploring it aloud with someone helped. I've been thinking about it for several days, actually. When I was over at Francis's the other afternoon, I met Leora there and she was urging me. All the outside double cabins on the lido and promenade decks are already taken, but she said there was still a block of nice outside singles. She assured me you wouldn't have to give up that extra single they promised you for your writing . . . I could just have one of the others nearby, she said. And she made me promise I'd think about it, so I promised, just to get her off the subject. You know how persistent she can be. But then when I was telling Cal that I'd been giving it some thought, he was so encouraging that I just . . . well, I just decided, Why not? That is, if you don't *mind* my going, Hugo."

Her face was suddenly suffused with that maidenly blush again, exactly as it had been when she came out of the house hand in hand with Cal. The blush of a girl who has been "talked into" doing what she secretly desired.

Did you tell Cal there were no double accommodations left? Hugo wanted to ask, but didn't. He was pretty sure he knew the answer anyhow: she hadn't. She would protect Hugo's pride. That much equivocation was admirable in a wife, however honest, and she wouldn't shrink from it. Yet, for the first time, Hugo had sensed some *further* equivocation in Alice. What was it? He hadn't been able to figure out why she would want to endure his company for two weeks when she didn't have to, and he still couldn't.

"Why should I mind?" he'd forced himself to reply gallantly.

"I know I haven't been the easiest person to get along with, Hugo. And I know we've been keeping, well, separate. And it's probably a good idea for us to continue those arrangements at present . . . I mean without making a public announcement about it." Here she had looked distinctly uncomfortable. "But Cal said it would be good for me, and I've come around to believing it would be, too."

"Well, in that case, we'd better phone Leora and make her happy."

"Only if you're sure, Hugo. I mean, I don't want to—intrude on your space or anything."

"Why shouldn't I be sure?" he had snapped back rather shortly, having realized during the course of their exchange how much he'd been looking forward to being alone for those two weeks, away from his failed year and the baby's death and their strained marriage, able to give his best mental energies to the one partnership that had never let him down yet: the partnership between himself and the book he was writing, or *knew he was going to write.*

"I feel like dozing," Stanforth announced to them, letting back his seat and rearranging his long legs. "They turn down the oxygen in these jumbo jets, after they've fed you. A friend told me that. You think it's your digestion going to work and making you sleepy, but they do it to save money."

"I think I could sleep, too," said Alice, rising and elegantly stepping over Stanforth's legs to open their overhead bin. "Anyone else want a pillow? Hugo?"

"Yeah, thanks, honey."

"Blanket, too?"

She was such a combination of loveliness and young wifely concern, standing above him like that in her dark red silk blouse and well-cut, flowing trousers that he forgot himself for a minute and responded in his old way. "Sure. I'll take one of everything you're offering."

Stanforth chuckled indulgently like an approving senior satyr, but Alice looked annoyed as she handed him down his sleeping rations, and then proceeded to do the same for Stanforth. Well, shit, excuse me for living, thought Hugo. Old Stanforth, basking in her services, probably hadn't noticed. And if he had, he would have interpreted it as her ladylike modesty kicking in. What he doesn't know won't hurt him, thought Hugo, covering himself with the blanket and stuffing his pillow into the wedge between the seat and the window. He turned away from them, curling his body as far away from Alice's seat as he could.

Let old scarecrow-walrus rest in his mistaken illusions about my marriage with this lovely young lady he hopes will befriend his unlovely daughter, thought Hugo. Let him rest in his equally mistaken illusions about my commendable son setting forth arm in arm into the needy streets with his selfless girlfriend. The window felt cold against his cheek, but Hugo stubbornly reveled in his separateness and his discomfort. The whole plane load of them could go to hell, as long as he had a book to write again.

"When is she going to come back?" Elberta asked.

"Who?" The sudden question startled Francis, who had been so deep into a reverie about the different times he and Magda had flown transatlantic that for a moment he almost thought the child beside him was referring to Magda.

"Jill. Why doesn't she stop walking around and come back and sit down in her seat?"

"She's just restless," said Francis.

"She doesn't like us, probably," pronounced Elberta, in her flat, glum way.

"Oh, no, I don't think that's the case. She's just a little restless and wants to roam."

"But she's sitting down in seats, talking to *other* people," Elberta pursued with her fatalistic glumness.

"Well . . . I'm sure she'll be back soon." It was after the movie, the lights had been turned on, and Jill had still not returned to her aisle seat. He was pretty sure he knew the source of her restlessness. He saw in her behavior the signs he had learned to recognize the hard way from that time he and Magda accompanied the junior girls from Merrivale on their semester abroad. A few of those girls, though quite a bit younger, of course, had acted like Jill over the course of the trip. That same quality of keyed-up-ness, the flushed, sweaty faces, the pinpointy pupils and the no-appetite, the frequent trips to the toilet and constant moving about—the promiscuous jabber with strangers.

But he didn't think it would be wise to discuss it with Elberta, whose own mother, Leora had said, had died from a drug overdose, or mixing drugs, they were never sure which.

During the dead of night, on that flight to Rome with the Merrivale juniors, Francis had opened the door to what he thought was a vacant toilet only to find one of his and Magda's charges hunched over the sink. At first he thought she was crying. He was backing out when she jerked up and pulled him into the tiny cubicle with her. It had all happened so fast. He thought she must be sick and required his help. But then she gave him a lurid smile and danced her pinpointy pupils at him and said, "Oh, Mr. Lake, want to score?" He'd been relatively innocent then—it was the beginning of the trip!—and thought she meant score in the romantic sense; some of the girls occasionally developed crushes on him, he'd been younger then. "Now, you behave yourself, Kimberly," he said, backing out of the cubicle. "You straighten up right now, or Magda and I will send you home so fast your head will spin." The uncharacteristic stern-ness had been to cover up his embarrassment, but had, surprisingly, effected a change of behavior in that one girl. She had given them no trouble for the rest of the trip, though others surely did. Though maybe, Francis thought, looking back on it now, it was just that her supplies had run out sooner than those of the other girls.

But this Jill was an adult, she had the means and the freedom to provide herself with an unlimited stash, and Francis certainly couldn't follow her to the toilet and threaten to send her home. She would laugh at him with those sawed-off little teeth and treat him to another sampling of her foul language.

What was it she had said about her father, Professor Stanforth? They'd been talking—across Elberta, who was seated between them— about teaching. He was starting to tell her what a magnetic teacher Magda had been, when she bared those short little teeth at him and uttered a neighing laugh. "Oh, Jack's like that," she said with a jerky shrug. She called her father Jack. "Jack has that stage presence that can sucker whole rooms full of students into believing he's God, even when he doesn't know dick about shit." Elberta laughed out loud and sent Jill an adoring look. She'd been pining for her ever since dinner came and Jill, barely glancing at her tray, said, "Excuse me, folks, this is where I came in." "You're not going to eat your *dinner*?" Elberta called after her as she pranced up the aisle in her tight jeans and spangly blouse and pink socks. "I never eat airline food," Jill shot back, "you eat mine for me." The child had done just that. Had started with Jill's tray and religiously devoured every morsel, then started again with her own, leaving only the salad on the second tray. Francis wondered if Jill reminded Elberta of her lost mother. It was probably not the wisest thing to put the two of them together, but Francis was sure that Leora had acted in good faith. Leora couldn't have known what Jill was going to be like. She had probably assumed that three lonely people like themselves would compose a little family of sorts.

Leora, who was being sort of an ambassador-at-large on the flight, had been by a couple of times to check on them, sitting down on Jill's abandoned aisle seat, bringing news about the others. Apparently, Hugo Henry and Professor Stanforth, who'd had some literary argument in the passenger's lounge, were getting on quite well now. That was probably Alice's calming influence, Francis thought. He was so glad Alice had decided to come: it made the trip more real, somehow, like a continuation of the life he knew rather than a sudden jolt into strangeness. Leora was sitting with Sue-Ann, their liaison from the travel agency, and the retired physician from New Jersey who was going to be the ship's doctor. They were at the moment engaged in making seating plans for all the dinners aboard the ship, Leora told him, so everybody would have a chance to get to know everyone. That was the sort of thing Leora managed so well.

Suddenly Francis was hit by a wave of incomprehension. Why am I sitting here beside this peculiar child I hardly know, he asked himself, and feeling responsible for her welfare and worrying that Jill, whom I met only a few hours ago, is going to be a bad influence? Why did I agree to go on this trip, to let them put my name in the program as a *specialist*? I'm no specialist at anything. The only specialty I ever had was Magda, and she's gone. Is this what the rest of my life will be like without her? Going places I don't really want to go, finding my responsibilities in people I have no abiding attachment to?

His hand automatically went to his left inside jacket pocket and made contact with the folded Ziploc bag he carried next to his heart. Remembering Magda's dictum on her last lucid visitors' afternoon, when they were gathered around her bed, and she was playfully proposing that she "join them" on the cruise, he had saved out a small portion of the ashes from those he had sprinkled around the lilac on the late-July afternoon when it finally rained. At some appropriate moment aboard the ship, he would fulfil her wish. Playful or not, it was something she had imagined, had pictured, while she was alive. If I carry through what she pictured, I will in some sense be carrying *her*, Francis thought, finding a sort of peace in resting his fingers against the plastic bag.

"I wish they'd show another movie," Elberta said grumpily.

"We ought to be getting some rest," Francis told her. "It's the wee hours of the morning on our old time. It won't be long until we'll be landing at Shannon, and you don't want to be sleepy and miss your first sights of Ireland."

"No, first they have to serve us breakfast."

"Well . . . better get some rest until they come with breakfast, then." He tried to sound convincingly authoritative. He himself was not at all sleepy, but children were supposed to require more rest.

He wondered what it would have been like if he and Magda had had a child. Would he have felt less desolate now? As far as he knew, it would have been possible, but they'd never seriously considered it. That child would be in its twenties now. But he couldn't get his mind any farther around the concept of this child of his and Magda's. He didn't really want to. Even the idea of it somehow created a distance between them. No, we were all right, exactly as we were, thought Francis.

How he dreaded giving his slide lecture on misericords. Leading some few interested persons around a cathedral, pointing out things, that he could comfortably do. But a scheduled evening lecture in the ship's lounge, in front of a roomful of people: how could he possibly hope to hold their interest? Magda could have; she could have shown the slides upside down and held their interest. But he could see himself fumbling with some unfamiliar slide projector in front of an unfriendly audience, while Jill, pacing back and forth in the outer darkness, would whisper to whoever was next to her: "He doesn't know dick about shit and has no stage presence either." How had he gotten himself into this?

He reached down and unzipped his carrier bag and pulled out the two letters he'd received from Father Birkenshaw. He must have read them twenty or thirty times apiece by now, and still hadn't been able to deal fully with their contents.

Dear Francis,

As you see, your letter reached me. Same address, same edifice, but radically different place. Regina as college and seminary graduated its last class (of eight men) in May of 1985. The event coincided with my seventy-fifth birthday, and also with a radical change in my own edifice. More in due time about that.

I remember you, of course, as do I remember the circumstances of your leaving us. Before Father Floris died, we sometimes discussed you and the role played by his cultural forum in your departure. (Since you asked, Father Rolf has also gone to join the Church Triumphant. Of your classmates, only Philip became a priest and stayed one.) I assumed you had married the lady in question, because the pastor of that church in north Chicago whom you asked to perform the marriage telephoned me to verify your story that you had been with us up until that time. Wanted to make sure you hadn't committed matrimony before, as I recall. Seems he'd had some trouble in the recent past with hasty young men wanting to tie knots when they already were knotted to someone else (I'm speaking sacramentally, not legally) before rushing off to Vietnam, or Canada, or whatever apocalypse was in the offing—there were so many of them to choose from.

My condolences on the loss of your wife. It must be a consolation to you that she led the useful and influential life you describe. You neglected to mention what line of work you eventually took up.

The structure you knew as Regina Seminary remains exactly the same on the outside—H. H. Richardson built his edifices to last. But inside, all is much changed. We are now a thriving retreat center, catering to a spectrum of groups: Freedom in Sobriety, Pre Cana, Women's Recovery, and of course America's fastest-growing age group (fifty-five and over). We administer personality tests, teach bread baking, a capella singing, birdcalls, arts and crafts, beginners' yoga, you name it. There are three resident priests on the staff, of whom I am one (half-a-one, to be more precise, since I can no longer celebrate the Eucharist in chapel, but do manage the occasional preached retreat). North Lake House, where you served your novitiate year, was condemned by the fire department in 1976 and demolished the following year. We are shortly to break ground for a one-story Catholic nursing home up there, to which I will ere long be shunted off when my emphysema (a recent development) renders me too short-winded for public appearances.

In June of 1985, shortly after the last class of Regina seminarians graduated and at the onset of my seventy-sixth year, I walked into the hospital to undergo surgery for a tumor in the spine, and never walked out again. The tumor turned out to be benign, but I have been a paraplegic ever since. It has been an interesting experience, looking up at the world from my wheelchair, rather than down at it from my former height, and having to depend on others for my most personal needs, but I can't say it's improved my character. In fact, Father Floris (whom I greatly miss fighting with) claimed it made me more of a flinty old cuss (his words) than before.

Well, thank you for writing to me. If you do so again, I will probably answer from either this place or our new nursing home up the road, unless I am too far disintegrated or have gone to join my brothers in the Church Triumphant.

Yours in Xist, (I am presuming, since you mentioned you still used your breviary)

R. Birkenshaw, OSR

And the second letter, sent the following day:

Dear Francis,

Like a typical lonely old man, I got so carried away in answering your letter as soon as I got it, that I neglected to respond to your postscript concerning your proposed lecture tour in England and Ireland. As you didn't specify *where* in England, I had our copy center run off these pages from Remnant's *Catalogue of Misericords in Great Britain* (I have made check marks by the ones not to be neglected if you are within feasible distance from the location in question). Also enclosed is Bond's (*Wood Carvings in English Churches*)* listing of misericord collections by chronology. Exeter has the most extensive oldest collection (thirteenth cent.) and definitely should not be pretermitted. In Ireland, only a single set remains, at St. Mary's Cathedral, Limerick. You would do better to concentrate on the extensive offerings in England, in my opinion.

Yours in Xist,

R. Birkenshaw, OSR

*Though we no longer have seminarians burning the midnight oil at those long oak tables in the library, we are fortunate to have kept our extensive collection intact, many of whose volumes I myself ordered in the bygone days of sufficient library budgets.

4:30 P.M.: I have imposed further on our copy center and had them run off a copy of Bond's excellent chapter on the historical purpose of misericords, as you might want to incorporate some of the interesting bits of background into your lectures. Since I wrote the above this morning, I had leisure to read the chapter, about our stalwart ancient brothers who were expected to stand for the eight offices per day (plus psalms, canticles, and hymns) as well as the High Mass and the additional daily private Mass required of every priest. The first break in the old posture system came when some damaged relics like me were granted "*reclinatoria*," or leaning staffs, i.e. crutches. However, you had to put your crutch aside during the reading of the Gospel. The crutch was disallowed altogether by true conservators of ancient usage, including St. Benedict. (I myself, I reflected with some irony, in my prewheelchair days, would have fought adamantly against this letting down of discipline!) But once it gets its foot in the door, progress will have its way, and next came the little "mercy" ledges on which the aged and infirm could sit while appearing to stand. And so on and so on, down through the dispensations until we reach birdcalls and beginners' yoga in abandoned seminaries. The exercise provided me with an interesting hour of reflection on the progress of mercy, and of progress in the guise of mercy, and mercy in the guise of progress, and so on. I'm still pondering on it.

But I'll get this packet off, before I grow tiresome.

> In Xist,
>
> RB, OSR

What got to Francis most, each time he reread the letters, was the beginning of that second letter. Father Birkenshaw referring to himself as "a typical lonely old man"!

While Alice was waiting for a free toilet at the rear of the airplane, Professor Stanforth's weird daughter, Jill, materialized next to her out of the stale darkness. Balancing herself on one pink-socked foot and crossing her arms, she lolled her boyishly cropped head against the vinyl partition.

"I guess you missed the great movie, sitting up there in the forward bulkhead with my father. But I'm sure Jack provided you with superior entertainment."

"Oh, was it . . . was it great?" stammered Alice, who had been torn out of her own thoughts and caught off guard by the other woman's goading, familiar manner.

"How should I know? I never watch airline movies, but my assigned traveling companions watched it *avidly*. I found more interesting things to do."

She gave a sharp whinny-laugh. Alice could imagine those nubby, strong-looking little teeth tearing open packets of junk food, perhaps biting someone who offended her. Alice had seen Jill prowling the aisles, dropping down into empty seats beside this person or that one; she was very much aware that Jill had spent much of their time in the air *not* sitting in the seat next to her "assigned traveling companions," a seat Alice herself would have been happy to sit in and stay in *avidly*, if circumstances had only permitted.

The door to a toilet opened and an elderly man, smelling strongly of after-shave, came out. It was the retired doctor who was going to serve as their shipboard physician on the cruise.

"Old Romeo, gussying himself up on the freebies in the middle of the night," commented Jill with a snicker. "He's been cruising the aisles, scoping out the single women. I've watched him."

"Will you . . . go first?" Alice asked her.

"With that freckled old brontosaurus? Do I look that hard up?"

"Oh no, I meant the toilet."

"The *toilet*?" Jill repeated with a mystified blink. "Oh! No, I just stopped to be chummy. I'm making my rounds, seeing what I can see. Now I'm going to make some more rounds. We owe it to ourselves to make the rounds, don't you agree?"

She was gone, down the dim passageway, before Alice could have replied, even if she'd had a reply.

Making her way back to her seat between Hugo and the professor, Alice's practiced eye scanned the rows until she located Francis's head. Many surrounding passengers had turned off their reading lights, so he was all the more noticeable as he bowed over a long letter, its folds and single-spaced typing spotlit by the little beam of light. Elberta hulked disconsolately forward in the middle seat next to him. Jill's empty seat gaped.

Alice, outwardly composed, passed on up the aisle, enduring her secret ache. Who was the long, closely typed letter from? Why was he reading it so intently? Was it some special condolence letter that said good things about Magda, or was it from someone in his past who wanted to claim him again? The sight of his familiar floppy hair, cut shorter than usual for the trip, intensified her ache. Everything about him that was different from the way he was during Magda's illness seemed a potential threat. Even the healthy color in his face from all his summer yard work had the power to hurt her. How she missed the peace of the death vigil they had shared. Oddly, she had felt he was more safely hers while Magda still lived. Now she must share him with all the others, and risk losing him as well. So his presence in the same airspace with herself was both joy and torment, the prospect of having him in her physical vicinity for twelve consecutive days equally wrenching and glorious.

("Oh, Alice, it would be great if you would go. I mean, it would be especially nice for me. It would make this whole venture seem less ... well, strange.")

His actual words, said that day under the sycamore tree, when she had dropped by after her walk at the reservoir and interrupted him and Leora and Elberta at the tail end of their picnic. Leora had begun at once to badger her about changing her mind and "coming on board" the cruise, and that was when Francis had suddenly uttered his amazing words.

"Well, I like that," Leora had archly teased, "*we're* strange, but Alice isn't?" He had been all over himself apologizing, but Leora was already leaping on ahead—sensing some new opening in Alice's resistance?—and itemizing the good cabins still available as fluently as if she carried a diagram of the ship's plan inside her head.

There were no outside *double* cabins anymore, not on the good decks where you had a view, that was a pity—two schoolteachers had just booked the last outside double accommodation on the lido deck, but there was still a block of singles with portholes on the lido deck ... Alice could be guaranteed a porthole if she signed up now ... she could still be only a door or two away from Hugo. ...

No double cabins left.

Oh, Alice, it would be great if you would go. I mean, it would be especially nice for me.... He had said that: she hadn't imagined it, because here was Leora, teasing him some more about their being strange, but Alice not.

Let me think about it, she'd told Leora.

Yet one of their twelve precious consecutive days together was already gone. They were now into their second day of the trip. I could at least sit with him for a few minutes, decided Alice, suddenly exalted by her own boldness. Remind him there's someone closer than the person in that letter. Make him feel less strange. I'm a fool if I don't take advantage of a gaping empty seat. I'm a fool if I don't *use* my eleven days.

"Please, Jack, don't get up," she said before Stanforth, talking to Hugo across her empty seat, could rise to let her through. "Listen, Hugo, I'm going back to visit with Francis and Elberta a few minutes while Jill is up and about."

"That's nice," said Hugo approvingly, as if she had announced her intention to perform a tedious good deed on behalf of them both.

"My daughter's still perambulating, is she?" remarked Stanforth with a roll of his rheumy eyes. Then animatedly resumed whatever he had been telling Hugo.

How easy it was to deceive, she marveled, with an uneasy mixture of compunction and guilty elation, as she made her way back toward Jill's (miraculously, still empty!) seat. All the easier when you had been an honorable person all your life.

Francis was tucking his letter back into its envelope—no, there were *two* letters—and Elberta was still hunched glumly forward when Alice dropped down into the aisle seat beside them.

"Oh, Alice, how nice—I was just—"

"I thought I'd visit you two for a minute—"

She had interrupted him out of sheer nervousness. Now she would never know whether he might have been going to say *thinking of you*. He looked as pleased by her unscheduled appearance as

Elberta looked put out. Now, why was that? On the few occasions she had met Mrs. Elmendorf's granddaughter, she had always gone out of her way to be friendly. In her guilt, Alice wondered if perhaps Elberta, considering Francis her own property, had somehow sensed Alice's secret. How could that be? Was it suddenly closer to the surface? If Elberta could pick up on it, what about others?

"Were you able to catch the movie?" Francis asked, leaning forward to speak across Elberta, who had not made any adjustment to facilitate their conversation. "Jill said something about people in those forward bulkheads having to move to other seats if they wanted the movie."

"No, we just talked. Professor Stanforth is an entertainment in himself."

"That's what Jill says. Elberta and I watched it, we liked it pretty well, didn't we, Elberta?"

Elberta shrugged.

"I talked with Jill a little, just now," said Alice, mainly for something to say, as she and Francis uncomfortably strained forward around their impediment. "She said she was making her rounds."

"Where?" demanded Elberta, showing her first sign of interest in the conversation.

"Well, she didn't specify."

"No," said the girl impatiently, "I mean where did you *talk* to her?"

"Oh, back at the toilets."

Francis looked at his watch. "We should be touching down in Ireland in a couple of hours."

"No, they have to serve us our breakfast first," Elberta corrected him. With a long-suffering sigh, she thrust herself up from her seat. "Excuse me, I'm going back to the toilets."

Alice stood up to let her out, and sat down again next to Francis in Elberta's empty seat. Why not, since she had gone this far?

"Elberta doesn't seem too glad to see me," she told him.

"She's just grumpy," said Francis. "She thinks Jill doesn't like her because she hasn't spent much time sitting with us. I explained to her Jill was restless. What do you make of Jill?"

As he asked this he tipped his head toward her so that it was practically touching hers. He gazed at her trustingly over the tops of his glasses. She could smell his clean hair.

"A little weird." She giggled, out of sheer nervous elation at their proximity. "But probably not harmful."

"That's what *I'm* hoping. Because Elberta seems to have taken to her." His right hand with the letters reached over to touch her for emphasis, and only when the envelopes crackled against her arm did he seem to recall he was holding them. "Oh! I was just rereading these. They're from my old rector at the seminary I attended back in Michigan. He's a very impressive man. I guess he was a great influence on me." He held up the letters so that Alice could see the craggy, though somewhat shaky, script marching evenly across the top envelope. "You know, Alice, it's funny how those old seminary experiences seem suddenly much closer since Magda died."

"Closer in time?"

"Yes, well, that . . . and in the other sense, too."

"You mean you still have an affinity for them?" In the act of clarifying his meaning, a disquieting realization surfaced in her that Francis might be in danger of being claimed by a far more formidable rival than any she had heretofore imagined.

"Yes, an affinity, that's a good way of putting it. I guess there were many aspects of the life that suited me. Though at the time there was so much else going on." He laughed apologetically. "I mean both inside and outside myself. But then, of course, Magda appeared and kind of pulled everything together for me like a magnet."

"Are you perhaps considering . . . going back to the seminary?" she asked bravely, just as she might have asked with the same fatalistic desire to know the worst and get it over with: is there another woman?

"You mean, be a priest? Oh no, oh no, that's not for me. It's what my mother wanted for me, she wanted it so much all during my growing up that I *thought* I was the one wanting it. But there were other aspects . . . other aspects of the life that suited me."

"Such as?"

"Oh, well . . . I don't know . . . washing windows, or . . ." He looked suddenly flustered, as if she'd put him on the spot. "Just doing whatever there was to be done at the time and having that be enough." He craned his neck to look back over the top of his seat. "I wonder if Elberta has been waiting all this time for a toilet."

"Maybe she's gone to look for Jill," offered Alice, realizing she'd had her ration of introspective talk from Francis for that night.

"Isn't it funny, the way Elberta has suddenly taken to Jill?" Francis mused wonderingly.

"It happens," said Alice, forcing herself to overcome her reserve and look at him straight on as she spoke. "People *do* just . . . suddenly take to someone . . . and that's their person."

Francis's gentle eyes suddenly sparkled at her behind the glasses. She felt he might be seeing her in this light for the first time, until he said happily: "That's so true, Alice. That's exactly what happened when I met Magda. Of course, I didn't completely know it was happening at the time, but something in me must have known because I acted on it. Poor Magda was always after me to account for . . . for why she was my person . . . but I never could explain it to her satisfaction. It makes me sad now that I was unable to account for it. Nevertheless, that didn't make it any less true, did it?"

"No," Alice assured him, "it didn't make it a bit less true."

"After Elbert's grandfather lost his shirt in the collar-stud business—that's funny, isn't it? 'Lost his shirt in the collar-stud business'—Elbert's father made up his mind *he* was going to make *his* fortune in something that didn't go out of style. . . ."

The president of Aurelia College, his face arranged to look fascinated, was in first class next to his quarry, Mamie Elmendorf, who Never Traveled Any Other Way. The rest of the tour, numbering a disappointing sixty-two out of a possible one hundred and thirty—there had been some last-minute cancellations—were back in tourist, including his own wife and Mamie's granddaughter. They'd had their first-class dinner and watched their movie (he'd heard from Leora that the one in tourist was better), and now, in addition to all the complimentary wines, Mamie continued to quaff one free glass of champagne after another, growing more oratorical and less likable by the glass, but unfortunately no more sleepy.

First he had been treated to a self-congratulatory How I Did It testimonial of the snaring of Mr. Elmendorf. A child of the Depression, the young, hungry Mamie from Troy, New York, had chosen to be practical-minded and Build Up the Ego of the shy, skinny classmate who was heir to the Elmendorf Commercial Laundry fortune, even though she had Given Her Heart (and other things as well, the meaningful batting of her eyes conveyed) to the handsome captain of the football team Without a Red Cent. Why is she telling me this cold little tale of flattery and deceptions? wondered Gresh Harris. Would she be telling it to anyone sitting next to her in her present bubbly condition, or has she recognized in me a fellow flatterer and deceiver, out to get what I can of someone else's bucks? No, he decided, she's too wrapped up in herself to see into anyone else.

Now he was captive listener to the saga of the second Elmendorf fortune, which, with his specialty in American history, he found more interesting, despite Mamie's self-serving style of narration. ("Elbert's father used to say to me—Elbert's father, I'm afraid, had quite a fancy for me—'Mamie, fashions are fickle, though no one wears them better than you, but the reason I got where I am today is because I bet my money on something basic in the American character. Americans, come hell or high water, war or depression, are always going to insist on being *sanitary*.' ")

It would have been interesting to write a book on American cultural patterns, the president thought. There would be a chapter on how things going in and out of fashion (collar studs axed by attached shirt collars, canals made obsolete by railroads, etc.) could ruin whole industries and influence wide segments of the population. What am I doing here? he asked himself, becoming suddenly depressed. What difference will it make to *me*, ultimately, if I do wangle bucks out of this tiresome selfish woman and construct an Elbert Elmendorf Cultural Center at Aurelia College? Why am I a president of a second-rate college with a reputation for fund-raising and not a scholar whose insightful comments on the society in which I lived might have outlasted me, as Magda Danvers's one book on the visionary poets has outlasted her? Red wine always depressed him, he reminded himself, but you couldn't order white wine with filet mignon. He was also apprehensive about the cruise. Only fifty-three real (paying alumni) passengers, when you subtracted himself and Leora, Mamie and Elberta, Stanforth and his malcontent daughter, Jill (who was already showing promise of being a noxious influence), Hugo and Alice Henry (whom Leora had convinced to join them at the last minute), and Francis Lake. All, except Mamie, traveling at the college's expense. Mamie was paying full fare for her deluxe suite, and her own first-class fare, but in a dirty maneuver typical of the rich, she had socked him for a separate (free) cabin for Elberta, although the initial agreement was that they would be sharing the suite. Mamie's initial enthusiasm for her granddaughter's company had worn off: Elberta got on her nerves something awful, she had told him. Besides which, the aggrieved grandmother added, the child simply refused to take constructive criticism about her personality and figure.

Although the travel agency had assured him they'd break even with forty-two paying passengers, it was still a sad, sad comedown from his expectations. He was trying hard not to read personal parallels into his diminished hopes for this first-ever Alumni Cruise.

And there were all the minor compromises and brewing fuck-ups which could add up to one big bad image. The standard tour bus held forty. So the first-ever Aurelia alumni tour would be caravanning along the highways and byways with a full bus followed by a half-empty one. There had to be a guide per bus, and the guide who got assigned to the half-empty one was bound to feel slighted, and would probably give a lackluster or resentful performance, and then the alumni on that bus would go home feeling slighted. Though, on the whole, the alumni who'd signed up for this cruise seemed an unimpressive lot. Older yuppies, with the right luggage and leisure shoes, but no significant achievers or—more was the pity— substantial fortunes among them. (Here the president bolstered his sagging spirits by going over the names of the most likely PBDs . . . no, except for Mamie, there were no potential big donors among this bunch, he'd have to coin a new hardship acronym for the cruise . . . SPGs, perhaps. Smaller Possible Givers. Anyway, he'd keep tabs on the Tobiases, the Fantinis, the Mercks, and the Gormleys—though the Gormleys weren't married. Make sure they were having a good time.)

Oh: that half-empty bus. Smiling and nodding at Mamie's nonstop recitation, the president eased the little black book from his inside pocket and scribbled a note to himself: *Tell Sue-Ann to rotate guides on buses every day so no one feels slighted.* Sue-Ann was the agency liaison traveling with the tour. There would be another liaison, Brad, awaiting them on board the *Galatea*.

His two prima donnas, Hugo Henry and Jack Stanforth, had already had a confrontation in the passenger lounge at Kennedy before they even got off the ground. (Something to do with D. H. Lawrence, Leora had reported.) Now one could only hope that the two of them, who had been seated next to each other for purposes of becoming better acquainted and coordinating their lecturing schedule, would not come to blows during the course of the flight.

And Stanforth's daughter, Jill, probably high on something, had unbelted herself from her seat next to Francis Lake and Elberta as soon as the sign went off, had refused dinner, and had been prowling restlessly up and down the aisles of tourist class in her stocking feet, or stationing herself outside the toilets, saying peculiar things to people. This he'd learned from Leora's first note to him from tourist.

Mamie's granddaughter was at least doing well. Having eaten both her own dinner and Jill Stanforth's, Leora had reported in her most recent note, the young heiress was being attended by Francis Lake and Alice Henry, who had temporarily filled in for Jill.

Surprisingly, Francis had turned out to be a third prima donna, in his low-key, modest way, over those damned misericords. He'd been in correspondence with some old priest in Michigan, also the world's greatest expert on the subject, who'd sent Francis a daunting list of key sites, with "not to be pretermitted" written beside most of the cathedrals which were too far inland to do by bus in one day, if you were going to do any other substantial sight-seeing. Francis had passed on a photocopy of this "not to be pretermitted" list via Leora, with the (too many) cathedrals checked off that Francis wanted to include on his misericord tour.

After some touchy negotiating between the travel agency, Stanforth, and their "ecclesiastical specialist" (Leora adamantly taking Francis's side throughout), a compromise was arranged: the tour would disembark at dawn from Avonmouth in order to get to Bath an

hour and a half earlier so that Francis could lead an optional afternoon tour to "not to be pretermitted" Wells Cathedral some twenty
miles away. This meant having breakfast on the ship at an ungodly
hour (which the staff would resent) and rescheduling the hotel lunch
at Bath for an hour earlier (for which Aurelia had to fork over an extra
fee to compensate the hotel for the inconvenience).

However, in return for this, when the ship docked at Wey-
mouth, Francis would relinquish his claim on out-of-the-way Exeter,
whose misericords, according to this Father Bracken-something, were
the oldest of all. But in *compensation* for this, Francis would get
Winchester Cathedral, if Stanforth would be willing to substitute
Jane Austen's Chawton for Thomas Hardy's Dochester so everyone
could go in the same direction.

Stanforth had curtly agreed, pronouncing himself equally conversant with either novelist, but confessing he was utterly mystified
as to why this obscure person, without even a B.A. in anything,
should be so deferred to at the last minute.

Well, thank goodness Ireland, where they would spend their first
four days before sailing for England, was free of the misericord problem. There was only one set left, according to old Father Brickabrack,
and that set pronounced negligible.

Mamie was telling him about the time Elbert's father, "who admired me a bit too much, if you know what I mean," had taken her
on a tour of one of the Elmendorfs' many laundry works, where she
got a flick of Clorox on her jade-green silk blouse and he'd insisted on
writing her a check for a thousand dollars, right on the spot, so she
could purchase a whole new wardrobe.

Stanforth had told him that the University of Chicago was doing
a cruise that exactly followed Ulysses's voyage in the *Odyssey*
(". . . except for the Cyclops and the Sirens and so forth, of course").
Now that was a class-act cruise. And here he had been congratulating
himself on his conventional literary cruise around the British Isles:
ragbag snippets of Yeats and Joyce and Wordsworth and Austen and
Dickens. And with Francis Lake's misericords tagged on.

"I don't know about you, but I'm ready to wet my whistle with
a little more champagne," said Mamie Elmendorf with flirtatious pet-

ulance, which seemed to be her staple tone. "If we can find our girl, that is. Now where is our girl? Don't you find people who are paid to serve you are never around when you want them?"

The president raised a discreet finger at the svelte blond attendant who, having been in easy earshot of Mamie's plaint, was already moving toward them with a faultless, if somewhat disdainful, smile. He certainly hoped she didn't think Mamie was a relative of his.

What wrong turning did I take, he wondered, that landed me here beside this vulgar woman, not even a class-act PBD? Who knows how much time I have left, I could drop dead from a heart attack on this trip, I could be dead from cancer in six months, like Magda, who at least left a book behind her. How has it happened that I am spending the majority of my time, in the last of my peak years, sucking up to people I don't even respect?

CHAPTER XXI

Hugo had chosen to pass up the full-day excursion to the Lake District and stay behind on the ship and lick his wounds. The tour buses had departed from the dock less than an hour ago, carrying away Alice and the others to the splendors of Wordsworth country. He had the sun deck of the *Galatea* all to himself on this sparkling morning in a place that might as well be anywhere in the world, for the use he was planning to make of it. All he wanted of Heysham, England, on Saturday, August 24, 1991, was for the waters of its port to keep this cruise ship calmly afloat so he could sit here alone for six or seven hours, assess the damage, and pull himself together.

His lecture the evening before had been humiliatingly bad. When he considered his South Carolina triumph only three months ago! Why, even the speech in Prague last April, about which he'd entertained some serious last-minute doubts, had been a downright crowd pleaser compared with last night's fiasco. Had he miscalculated his material or his audience, or both? Okay, he'd tried to cover too much material in the hour ("English Influences on My Work"), but when he'd realized his overload halfway through, why hadn't he been able to winnow out the highlights, mercilessly discard the lengthy or lesser quotes, and then shift into emergency gear and finesse the wrap-up by the force of his personality alone? He'd done it often before, when speakers ahead of him at book-and-author breakfasts had gone on too long, and in the insufficient time left, he'd had to compress his material to the essential remarks that would zap them with a lasting impression. He'd always been able to count on resources in himself to get him through such crises.

But last night, the resources hadn't been there, he'd flopped. It was like finding himself impotent for the first time when always before he'd been able to summon a passable hard-on, for pride's sake if nothing else, in uninspiring circumstances. Standing before his audience in the ship's lounge last night, he'd suddenly lost faith in himself, lost his bearings. What was he doing here, swaying behind a lectern on a moving ship, being transported backward (his lectern faced the stern) down the coast of England, plying these sated people (who were being served drinks and canapes by waiters even while he spoke!) with too-long, out-of-context quotes from English novels they would probably never read? All he really desired was to be alone in his little bedroom office in Sonia Wynkoop-Medici's house, finding his way through his own novel, now that he had one again.

Alice had told him later last night, when he'd gone to her cabin and asked for an assessment, that his lecture had been going well enough until "you looked at your watch and then completely altered your tone."

"How do you mean, altered it?"

"Well, you went off your audience. Or at least it appeared that way to me."

"How did it show?"

She'd sighed. "Hugo, it wasn't all *that* bad. You're making too much of it. I'm not saying it was your *best* lecture. But you'll do a great second lecture and that'll be the one they'll remember."

"Not if you don't tell me what I did wrong in the first one."

A long-suffering sigh. She laced her hands together in front of her stomach, as if to build a little wall between herself and him. She sat fully dressed on the edge of her bunk bed in her single cabin two doors down from his. He had knocked humbly at her door, a petitioner eager to hear the worst about his performance from one who had always told him the truth when she loved him and would certainly not withhold it now. "Well, you started rattling off all those quotes as if you couldn't wait to be done with them and had a sort of contempt for them. Whenever you did lift your eyes from your notes, you shot disgusted looks at people. And during the question-and-answer period, you showed impatience when anyone dared to ask you anything. You were very curt to Jack Stanforth when he asked the first question. I thought you two were good friends."

"That's exactly the point. It was condescending of him. *He* never has such problems, with all his decades of teaching. His lecture on Yeats that first evening in Galway began on the dot of eight, held them captive for fifty minutes, and then on the dot of nine he magnanimously accepts 'one more question.' When he jumped in so quickly with his opening question after my lecture, it gave the impression he was afraid no one else was going to ask anything and he, my shipboard pal, the champion lecturer, was determined to help me save face."

She had uttered an exasperated little cry. "Ah, Hugo, when it comes to putting the worst interpretation on things, *you're* the *world's* champion." Then she closed her eyes and, shaking her head from side to side, raised her palms at him in a warding-off gesture. No more of these obsessings. No more of *you*. If she had wanted to impress upon him the wrongness of his being there in her chaste single cabin, she couldn't have done a better job. He'd had no choice but to heave himself out of the armless little pouf that passed for a chair, thank her for telling him the truth, and back clumsily out of her presence like a lout taking leave of a princess.

Lying on his bunk in his own cabin afterward, taking consolatory sips from his old monogrammed silver flask (a present from Rosemary upon one of their early anniversaries, when they were still in love), Hugo was painfully struck by the incongruity of his present circumstances. That unsympathetic young woman sitting fully dressed on the edge of her bunk in a cabin two doors down from his was his *wife*. Yet nothing in the cabin, neat as a schoolgirl's awaiting inspection, spoke of their life together. It had further discomposed him to see Magda's book lying on the end table: that black-and-white paperback edition with the slash of flame he'd seen in the college bookstore and had been meaning to buy and read himself ever since Francis Lake had sent him Magda's old blue books. When had Alice bought it? How was she finding it? In the old days he and Alice had shopped for their books together, discussed them as they read them, and often read parts aloud to each other. It seemed a portentous blow to Hugo that the book his wife was reading should come as a surprise to him. It was almost more intimate than suddenly realizing she loved someone else. That morning an odd little scene had taken place, which hadn't been lost on Hugo. When Alice entered the dining room late, a waiter had been about to lead her to the table where Francis sat with Elberta and Jill, whereupon the maître d' had admonishingly snapped his fingers and pointed to Hugo at another table: She goes with *that* one. The waiter instantly corrected his mistake, but in passing gave his superior the merest shrug: How should I know, she spends her time with both of them.

If waiters were wondering, others must be, too.

What a consummate mess it all was. But the fact that *he* was a mess must be his paramount concern right now. Had to be. If he didn't salvage himself, who the hell else would care enough to do it? As he sat all alone on the sun deck, after the others had departed for the Lake District, he registered with disgust that even his most reliably comfortable khakis had let him down. Their waistband cut painfully into his bulging flesh from all the force-feeding of the last week. You didn't need or even want a full, cooked breakfast with eggs and bacon and *fish*, for God's sake, and two kinds of sausage, and fried mushrooms and tomatoes, but then you thought: Why not? Everybody else is having it. Same with the seven-course dinners: what else was there to do here while everyone around you gorged themselves?

Last night at dinner, after his failed lecture, that awful Mamie Elmendorf, who had been cramming her face with crab mousse, had actually invited him and the others at table to watch while she put down her fork and demurely let out her belt two notches. Then she proceeded to describe to Hugo, with frank admiration, a "girlfriend" of hers who regularly took two cruises a year, gained thirty pounds per cruise, and spent the intervening months at fat farms. "And Marva gets it off, too! Every single ounce!"

The image of some worthless rich bitch annually dedicating thousands to balloon her guts, knowing she has thousands more to spend in the worthy cause of flattening them again, had been kerosene dashed on the perpetual embers of his poor boy's wrath. It was unreal, this whole damn experience, he should be back in Aurelia, bad as it was, writing his book. He'd been just drunk enough to let rip with a lively screed, admittedly heavy on the scatology but, frankly, he thought, a hell of a lot more inspired than his dead lecture on "English Influences."

When Mamie predictably took refuge in maidenly umbrage, you should have seen those two suck-ups, Gresh and the ship's doctor (whose opportunistic freckly old hand had been roaming Mamie's skirt under the tablecloth), rush in to repair the damage. Gresh hadn't looked Hugo's way again for the remainder of the meal, not even when he was delivering his ominous put-down as he and Dr. Leech helped gorged, giggly Mamie out of her chair: "Well, Hugo," said the president with frosty urbanity, making eye contact with someone at another table as he spoke, "we'll be looking forward to some revelations in that next lecture of yours."

Implying that there had been no revelations in this one.

Implying that there'd damn well better be some in the next one. Enough to make up for his first flop, *and* for his ill-considered attack on Gresh's great white hope for his culture center.

So his final lecture, which he must completely redraft today in these precious hours alone on board, had to be a goddamn knockout. Hugo tensed in his chair on the sun deck. He'd brought out his legal pad, several black pens, and a red pen for rubrics and underlining. Now he dragged over another chair and put his feet up, then was forced, by the increased pressure on his gut, to reach furtively beneath his T-shirt and unhook the waistband of his khakis.

On the lido deck, directly below him, came the intermittent scream of the blowtorch as the crew resoldered a broken guardrail. When the *Galatea* docked at Heysham earlier this morning, some wrong maneuver between tug and tide had rammed her stern against the cement berth. When Hugo was seeing Alice and the others down the gangplank to the waiting buses on the dock, the captain had suddenly appeared and beckoned Brad, the tour liaison, aside and said something quietly but apparently scathing. How Hugo wished he could have heard the soundtrack behind the satisfying picture of complacent, towering, bossy Brad, who resembled a giant, fleshy, pink child in those perennial white shorts and basketball shoes, withering under the dignified assault of the small, compact Greek captain in his black uniform.

But why the fuck should I care? thought Hugo, still obsessing over last night. Maybe the best thing that could happen to me at this point in my life is if I do something *worse* between now and next Friday when we fly home, something that would give Gresh no choice but to cancel my contract. Hugo tipped his face up to the sun, sketching fantasies of being banished from kneejerk Aurelia College. The nature of the unpardonable, yet-undone deed that would cause Gresh to deal him the coup de grace interested him not at all. It was its result that brought gleefulness of heart. He'd be released from the present deadlock of his life, he'd be *set free to start over*. He could snatch up his lovely new characters and leave, the way he used to snatch up his old typewriter and plunk it in the passenger seat of the car and drive off with it like a mistress into the promising dark, after he and Rosemary had one of their killer fights. Only this time he'd keep driving, he wouldn't stay overnight in some Howard Johnson's and return haggard and unshaven next morning, having remembered his duties to little Cal.

Who wasn't little anymore, who would soon be thirty. Who had survived his parents' stormy union and was actually happy in a union of his own. Hugo kept seeing Cal, as he had looked coming out of the house with Alice on the day of the lunch, his fingers linked with hers, Cal's beautiful eyes, the eyes of the grandmother he never knew, alive and shining with the happiness she'd never known. Rosemary also was happy, in her fashion. She had money and a man she could run.

Perhaps the happiest thing he could do for Alice was rid her of his burdensome presence. Walk out and let her get on with the rest of her life. She was too scrupulous to do him the favor. Scrupulous, hell. Let's call it by its exact name. Too passive.

That she had chosen to accompany him on this cruise still perplexed him. Though she did seem to be enjoying herself. She talked to all sorts of boring people, she listened to them, she hadn't been the least bit seasick that he knew of, she was devotion itself to Francis Lake and that poor Elmendorf kid. She got along with Stanforth's peculiar daughter. She took care with her clothes and hair and was a credit to him when she joined him for cocktails in the lounge or sat beside him at meals (unless it was one of those dinners like last night where influential passengers were assigned by Leora to the Author's Table). Up until that waiter's mix-up at breakfast yesterday morning, instantly corrected by the maître d', Hugo had taken it for granted that everybody on the ship assumed that Alice was indisputably his. Nobody thought anything about the separate cabins because Leora, ever promoting herself in the role of Den Mother to the World, had made it widely known on board—he'd heard this from Stanforth— that Alice, still healing from the tragedy, had only been persuaded by the force of Leora's resolute proddings to join the cruise after all the double cabins had been filled.

But it was one thing to do their stately married dance step in public for two weeks on a cruise with people he didn't care if he ever saw again, and another to continue in their private hell of the last six months. Frankly, he didn't think he had the stamina for another year of it. Of course, he and Rosemary had coexisted in open warfare for years, but he'd been younger, with more energy to squander, and there'd been Cal to consider. Besides, they'd both let off steam in their affairs. He wasn't interested in affairs now; he wasn't even that interested in sex, frankly. He was interested in writing his book. Oh sure, he had pangs when he remembered the sweet times with Alice;

he still loved her, he guessed. He certainly didn't love anyone else. But if it came down to a *choice* of where he was going to put what energy he had left, he'd choose his book. Sorry, Alice.

He felt the thrum of footsteps ascending the metal stairs; shit, someone was joining him on the sun deck. He was relieved when the captain's curly gray head and neat black shoulders rose into view. He'd halfway been dreading that Gormley woman, who'd stayed behind in their deluxe suite with her twisted ankle from the James Joyce tower in Dublin. Only her name wasn't Gormley, she was just Gormley's ladyfriend.

"Having a quiet day?" asked the captain pleasantly.

"I passed up the Lake District tour," said Hugo. "I've got some work to catch up on."

"And so have I," replied the other. "Thanks to our Brad." His lyrical Greek accent stopped just short of the tour manager's name, isolating it in an oafish-sounding flatness.

"Sounds like your crew is getting things on the mend, though," said Hugo.

"Oh, yes, we'll have her primed and repainted by sailing time this evening. It could have been worse. Sorry if the noise is disturbing you."

"No, no. The noise of something being fixed is always a hopeful sound."

The captain mused on this remark. "That's true," he said, giving Hugo an appreciative nod before passing on to the railing of the sun deck, where he stood looking down on the crew at work below.

Hugo felt the urge to go over and join him, and did. The two of them leaned over the railing companionably, engrossed in the repair work going on below. The air was burned with the odor of blow-torched metal. The resoldered guardrail lay detached on a large sheet of plastic on the deck below. A bare-chested man with a bandanna tied round his head was painting the patched stern with a harsh-smelling orange primer.

The captain took several sniffs of the caustic fumes rising from the deck below. "And is the *odor* of something being fixed also hopeful?" he asked Hugo, smiling.

"Hell, yes, just so something's getting fixed," said Hugo. The captain laughed. Hugo felt understood.

"But it need not have happened," the captain said tersely, "and it won't happen again. We'll have ship's tenders waiting at Tresco. The passengers on this cruise are not handicapped old people, they're capable of stepping in and out of a tender boat. We'll have to go all the way into Avonmouth tomorrow because it's such a long harbor, but they have an excellent harbormaster. He'll take her in like a lady, none of this bashing and bumping. But for Tresco, it's disembarkation by ship's tender. If he opens his mouth to me again, they find themselves a new master of the *Galatea* or a new Brad."

"I expect it would be a lot harder to find themselves a new master," said Hugo, liking the captain. He was what was known in the old days—when you were still permitted to make such identifications—as a man's man.

"I expect so," the captain echoed, then returned to his grievance. "For him it's all prancing around, and public relations with the passengers. This ship is *real*, I told him. And I am sorry to inform you that you need a real ship if you are going to have a cruise. We are not playing games of toy boats out here. We'll see how much your agency likes it when they see the bill for the tug I've hired to keep her fresh paint from scraping the dock for the next five hours."

Here the captain of the *Galatea* paused to converse briefly in Greek to the crew below as they fitted the guardrail back into place. Then he switched back into a more tranquil, philosophical English. "This ship is not play for me, she's my life," he explained to Hugo. "I won't break her for a *tour*."

"I agree completely," said Hugo. The captain had given voice to his own exact mood, on this morning of assessing damages and reasserting priorities.

" 'It was a clear sky, a heavenly morning. I sowed the flowers, William helped me. We then went and sat in the orchard till dinner time. It was very hot. William wrote the Celandine. . . .' "

Professor Stanforth, mike in one hand, an open paperback volume in the other, his gangly figure swaying wildly as the bus took the sharp curves of the road into Grasmere, was skillfully excising passages from Dorothy Wordsworth's journals and her brother's poems to highlight his own remarks and get the travelers aboard this half-empty bus in the right mood for the splendors of the day ahead.

Alice was already in the right mood, because at the last minute she had been able to sit beside Francis. At first Elberta, clinging to him as always when she couldn't have Jill, had glumly plunked down beside him. Alice, taking the seat behind, was joined by Stanforth. But then when it turned out that the guide for their bus had failed to show up and Stanforth had told Leora he would pinch-hit, hurrying back to the ship to fetch his Wordsworth volumes, Jill, in an uncharacteristic reversal, abandoned her antisocial sprawl across the long backseat of the bus and moved to the front in order to dole out the books to her father as he would need them in the course of his commentary. "I can grab my shut-eye later," she informed Alice, swaggering barefoot up the aisle, multicolored sandals dangling from her hand. "Every sorcerer needs his apprentice." Elberta, ever alert for a chance to be close to her heroine, had instantly abandoned Francis and hurried forward to claim the empty seat beside Jill. That left the field free for Alice, though she'd almost lost out through a moment's hesitation. Leora, sitting up front with Sue-Ann, the agency liaison, had been quick to note Elberta's abdication and had already risen from her seat to collect her jacket from the rack above. When she saw Alice moving forward, however, she concealed her pique with an insincere little wave of approval. Meant to convey, Alice guessed, "That's right, just so *one* of us keeps the poor man company."

But the best thing of all had been Francis's look of surprised pleasure when she asked if she could join him. "Oh, Alice, how nice. I was just thinking about you, isn't that strange?"

"What were you thinking?"

"Well, there was something I've been meaning to ask you, only I forgot what it was." He gave his diffident laugh. "It seemed fairly important, but maybe it wasn't."

"Maybe it will come back to you."

"Magda used to get so impatient with me. She said I intentionally forgot certain things."

"What kind of things?" she felt she could dare to ask. With Francis you had to creep up so gently. The merest rustle of your intentions to know him and he was startled and gone.

"Oh, I don't know." He raked at his hair, and that baffled look she was becoming so familiar with glazed his soft gray eyes. "Magda had this theory that I wasn't facing up to things in myself."

She was wondering whether she might risk pursuing this interesting topic when Francis cut off the option by adding, "Though this wasn't anything about myself. It was something to do with Magda, that much I remember."

"Well, if it comes back to you, I'll be around." Saying even that much had seemed a little dangerous, but still, she'd wanted to risk it.

" 'Oh the overwhelming beauty of the vale below—greener than green,'" Stanforth intoned over the mike, still quoting from Dorothy's journal. With the backs of his elbows, he steadied himself as the bus took another sharp bend into a vista that could have been the one the poet's sister was describing. " 'Two ravens flew high in the sky and the sun shone upon their bellies and their wings long after there was none of his light to be seen but a little space on the top of Loughrigg Fell. . . .'"

The professor paused to survey his straggly audience on the half-empty bus. The bus for the second-class citizens, Hugo belligerently called it, after the cheery memorandum from Leora had gone around to staff members and accompanying companions, asking for their team spirit in leaving the "Number One Bus" for alumni and "other paying passengers" since the best guide would naturally be assigned to the full bus. Stanforth's spooky white eyebrows rose till they touched his oddly tinted reddish curls; his gloomy eyes darted back and forth, ready to pounce on the somnolent or inattentive. He does resemble a sorcerer, thought Alice. "Now isn't that a *great* image?" he demanded of them, as if he himself owned a share in it. "Those soaring, sleek bird-bellies, way up high, reflecting the last light of the sun? Wordsworth frequently availed himself of his sister's picturesque images. So did their good friend Coleridge, and no wonder! I mean, what smart poet wouldn't, if you had such a useful sister or friend?" He succeeded in getting a round of warm laughter. "Now Jill, girl, if you'll hand over the poems, I'll read these good pilgrims Dorothy's description of the daffodils and then we can see how her brother incorporated her vision into what many consider his most famous poem. . . ."

Alice was glad Hugo was not here for his sake as well as her own. He would just be made jealous and contentious by the way Stanforth, with no preparation, had them all in the palm of his hand. Even on a moving bus, with the panoramas that dazzled the Romantic poets competing on both sides. And Stanforth was *enjoying* himself so much.

Francis suddenly leaned close to speak to her. The intimate naturalness of his gesture, and the sensation set off in her by the movement of his lips upon her hair, caused her heart to lurch.

"You know, Alice," Francis confided happily in her ear, "Professor Stanforth reminds me a little of Magda. Magda had that same way of getting people's attention. She could say exactly the thing that would make them feel she was going to tell them something important about their lives."

"I wish I had been able to sit in on some of her classes."

"Oh, you would have been mesmerized. Everyone was."

"Did you, ever?"

"Sit in on her classes? Well, no. Except of course for that one lecture she gave at my seminary, and . . ."—laughing, he rested his hand on Alice's arm for emphasis—"you know the result of *that*."

Whenever Francis touched her—and Alice could still count all the times—it was as if she became aware of a layer of extra-fine sensitivity to pleasure that she had never known she possessed. And yet, at this moment her pleasure was equally matched by the painful certainty that she was doing Hugo a wrong. By any strict accounting of herself, she should not, as Hugo's wife, be greedily hoarding up the times Francis had laid his mouth against her cheek or hair or put his hand on her arm in conversation. By any strict accounting of herself, she should not have come on this cruise as Hugo Henry's wife— whatever the cabin arrangements—when she was in love with Francis Lake. It was false of her, she had deceived poor Cal in the kitchen, letting him think he was "talking sense into her" on his father's be-half, letting him believe that he was being the instrument of their conjugal restoration after the difficult spring following the baby's death. She knew, even as she was admitting to Cal that she had been thinking of changing her mind, that she was being perfidious and that if Cal had been able to read her mind he would have disapproved.

But what should she have done instead, if she *had* been aiming for the one-hundred-percent rate of accountability? Stayed behind in Aurelia and tried to domesticate their rented house by putting in spice shelves and unpacking her books? Wasn't that equally false when she could not truly declare to herself that she looked forward to another year of married life with Hugo—or even another hour?

What, then? Where *was* her place, if she were determined to be strictly accountable for her feelings? Was her only rightful place at the moment outer darkness?

Other than outer darkness, the only place in the world she could call up as her rightful one—that is, a physical place where she could be her true self without hurting anybody else—was Magda's sick-room. All summer long, Alice had found her mental refuge in mem-ories of the death vigil she had been privileged to share with Francis.

But that place was gone. Magda's sickroom no longer existed as Magda's sickroom. It was Francis's bedroom again—he had moved back in, he had told her; and had been surprised at how well he slept in the room where Magda had died, but of course it had been the room they had shared before her illness.

Alice could hardly admit that the only place left in the world where she could feel her true self was the bedroom where Francis slept peacefully within the honorable embrace of his long and happy marriage. And even if she did admit it, she certainly couldn't feel it was her *rightful* place, not even in fantasy, while she was still mar-ried to Hugo.

The Aurelia group was obliged to wait outside Dove Cottage until the preceding tour group had passed through.

"That's because the rooms are so small, and they have very low ceilings," Francis explained to Alice and Elberta, who had rejoined them reluctantly when Jill had deftly vanished on some itinerary of her own. "Magda and I went through Dove Cottage once. It was, let's see, the summer of eighty-seven. No, it couldn't have been eighty-seven, because we stayed home that summer, it was our first summer in our house at Aurelia. It must have been eighty-eight. Yes, I'm sure it was eighty-eight, when she was doing research at the Bodleian for her Drama of the Soul's Choice chapter, which she never completed. We took a train from Oxford. The connections were very complicated, and when we finally arrived, we splurged and hired a taxi because Magda was tired and she was never much of a walker anyway. Well! Guess what his name was?"

"Whose name are we talking about?" demanded Elberta irritably, looking up and down the street for Jill.

"Oh, sorry, our driver's," Francis clarified himself with good humor, "the driver of our taxi. His name was Bill Wordsworth. It made Magda's day. And he claimed to be a direct descendant of the poet."

"Well, he would, wouldn't he?" snorted Elberta, looking up at Francis as though he were a simpleminded child. "I'd tell people my name was Bill Wordsworth, too, if I had people in my taxi stupid enough to believe it."

The soft summer sky of the Romantic poets was shattered by a frightening roar. Elberta covered her head with her hands and ducked. Francis grabbed Alice's arm. Mamie Elmendorf, standing in a cluster of ladies nearby, screamed.

"It's okay, everybody," rasped the indolent voice of Dr. Leech, coming up beside Mamie. "It's only two combat jets, having a little game of chicken. There's an air-force training base near here." He slipped his arm protectively around Mamie. "You okay?" he asked possessively.

"I thought we were being *bombed*," Mamie fluttered up at him. "I almost had a heart attack."

"Oh, come now, you've got a very good heart," the doctor assured her in his lazy, raspy voice, squeezing her shoulder with his freckled fingers. "It will last you a long while yet."

"Gross old toad," muttered Elberta, skewering her grandmother and the doctor with a disgusted look. "It would serve her right if she found him on her pillow."

Francis and Alice exchanged a tolerant, amused glance. Since Elberta had glommed onto sharp-tongued Jill, she certainly had become more outspoken, perhaps more observant of others as well. Just now she had skirted the borders of wit. But her humorless, heavy-handed malice was still a long way from Jill's spritely gremlin thrusts.

Elberta could be ours, we could easily have an eleven-year-old daughter, mused Alice as Francis let his hand slip from her arm as absently as he had grabbed it when the combat jets flew over. Alice found hope in the ease with which he increasingly took her presence for granted. As a man so long used to being part of a couple, Francis would perhaps find it very natural to transfer his old habits—reaching for a hand or an arm, whispering confidences into an ear—from Magda to her. It also gave Alice a peculiar thrill to think that any stranger, noticing the three of them standing together on the sidewalk in Grasmere, would assume she and Francis were an American couple on vacation, exchanging tolerant, amused glances over their grumpy pre-adolescent daughter.

The first people in the Aurelia group had begun to inch forward through the low door of Dove Cottage. "How long is this tour going to take?" Elberta demanded.

"Oh, maybe a half hour," said Francis pleasantly. "Or no, I'm not sure. When Magda and I were here, it was late in the day and there were only a few people in our group. This may take longer because there are so many more of us to go through the rooms."

Elberta groaned. "And *then* we're going to have lunch, I hope?"

"Well, no," Francis explained patiently. "After Grasmere, we go on to Rydal Mount. Don't you remember? It was all written up in the little itinerary they slipped under our cabin doors this morning. Then after Rydal Mount, we drive on to Windemere and have lunch in a nice old hotel there. But Rydal Mount ought to be very nice, it was the place Wordsworth lived after he was famous. There are supposed to be beautiful hillside gardens he put in himself. I'm sorry Magda and I never got to Rydal Mount, but it was too late in the day and we—"

"I can't *believe* that they're going to make us go to another whole *town* in between before they let us have our lunch," protested Elberta, outraged.

"Rydal's not a town, it's just a beautiful spot, hardly three miles from here," contributed Alice, happy to share any task with Francis. "When Wordsworth and his sister lived in this cottage, they walked over to Rydal most evenings after supper."

"Well, but they'd had their supper, hadn't they?" retorted Elberta.

Soon it was their turn to leave the sunshine and crowd with their group into a dark, brownish room. The guide, a pasty-faced young man with strong BO, rattled off the story of the Wordsworths in a high-pitched singsong. He had a disturbing mannerism of keeping his eyes tightly shut except when taking breaths.

While they were still crammed around the walls in the first room of the tour, a depressing little parlor, Elberta mumbled something to Francis, who, for the second time that morning, poked his mouth into Alice's hair to whisper something. "Elberta is feeling woozy," he announced. "I'm going to take her outside, I don't mind."

"I'll come with you," replied Alice.

Released to the fine day again, in the small, rather overgrown little garden behind the cottage, Elberta plunked down on the nearest stone wall and put her hands over her face.

"Do you feel faint?" inquired Francis, hovering beside her.

"I felt *weak* because I was tired of standing up, and I was *hot* and *hungry* and also there was a disgusting smell in there. You two didn't have to come with me, if you didn't want to. I'm not a child."

"I'm not sorry to be out here, myself," said Francis, taking off his glasses and cleaning them with his handkerchief. "It was starting to make me sad in there, remembering when Magda and I were in that same room. I could *hear* her, those Magda-type remarks she was always muttering to me under her breath, about people and things. Though our guide that day was a very pleasant, informed, older lady. Our guide today could have used a bath. Why did he keep his eyes shut like that, Alice?"

"Maybe he was bored, from having to say the same thing over and over again." Alice suddenly felt tired herself. Is it possible to be jealous of the dead? she wondered. "And it *was* awfully *pungent* in there, with everybody pressed so close. I'd just as soon remember it from Dorothy's journals. I did a paper on her in college. I got very caught up in the details of her life in the cottage with her brother. William didn't marry until relatively late, and Dorothy always remained special to him. I suppose I was trying to imagine what it would have been like if my brother had lived. He'd been killed two years before and we had been extremely close."

"How was he killed?" asked Elberta, interested.

"Alice lost her whole family in a car accident," put in Francis quickly, as if wanting to protect her from having to answer. "When she wasn't much older than you."

"How much older?" Elberta wanted to know.

"I was seventeen," said Alice.

"And how many of them were killed?"

"My father and mother and Andy, my brother."

Elberta slumped frowning on the stone wall. "That's two more than me," she calculated slowly, "because I didn't *have* a brother, and my father's not dead yet. But, it's about the same, because I'll probably never see him again. Did you have a grandmother to go and live with?"

"No, but I had an aunt. I lived with her until I went off to college," said Alice.

On her wall, Elberta slumped further down, if that was possible, and pondered. "I may not make it to college," she announced with ominous significance.

"Of course you will if you want to, if you study hard," Francis chided her cheerfully. Alice couldn't tell whether he had missed Elberta's morose inflections or whether he simply thought it was wiser not to encourage her in them. Either way, his reply was pure Francis, in that you couldn't be sure.

"I've always regretted that I didn't finish college," Francis said, holding his newly polished glasses up to inspect them. The sun picked up the golds and reds left in his hair and made him look shining and young for a moment, until he replaced the glasses. "If I had,

I might have been a better companion for Magda," he went on. "Though, if I *had* finished at the seminary, I wouldn't have had Magda. My life would have been altogether different."

"What's a seminary?" asked Elberta.

"Well, it's like a college, only when you graduate you go on to be a priest."

"You a priest?" Elberta cocked her head at Francis and snickered.

"Don't laugh," said Francis, with what Alice considered remarkable good nature in the face of Elberta's rudeness. "My whole family expected it of me. My mother used to say the only reason she went on living was to see me ordained a priest. My surviving sister hasn't forgiven me to this day. I think she blames me for everything that's gone wrong in the Church since."

"So what did your mother do when you didn't become a priest?" asked Elberta.

"Oh, she died, you see. She died at the beginning of my fourth year in seminary. I hadn't even known she was ill."

"You mean she didn't *tell* you she was sick, or what?" Elberta doggedly pursued.

"Well, she told my sisters—I didn't find this out until afterward—that she didn't want me to come home to see her, because then I wouldn't be able to come for the funeral. And she thought my being at the funeral was more important for the family. My mother was like that, always thinking of what would be best for the whole family rather than for just herself. But you see, she didn't know the rules had changed. In the old days, seminarians *did* have to choose between making a deathbed visit to a parent or going to the parent's funeral. In fact, my uncle, who was a priest, used to tell the story of how he'd sneaked out of seminary and walked past his dying grandfather's house, in order to see him while he was still alive. The family had the old man propped up in the front window and my uncle—his name was Francis, too—walked past the house and he waved at his grandfather and the old man waved back. That way my uncle got to go to the funeral as well. But, you see, neither my mother or my sisters knew the rules had been changed, and that I could have gone to the sickbed *and* the funeral. Or at least that's what my sisters told me at the funeral." Raking his fingers backward through his hair, Francis caused several wisps to stand straight up. He did this whenever he seemed beset by something, Alice had observed. Magda must have amassed a whole collection of such small physical guides to Francis's obscure inner states.

"How *stupid*," said Elberta.

"Yes, well, it was all very sad and strange. I think I must have been very upset. But it was all so long ago. Magda used to get impatient with me for not remembering more of what I felt at the time."

Elberta's glum attention was suddenly transferred to the figure emerging from the rear of the cottage. "Where *were* you?" she demanded, her round, heavy face lighting up, as greeny-haired Jill, looking like a sinister sprite in her tights and sleeveless tunic, stepped lightly into the garden.

"On the tour, where else?" Perching on the wall beside Elberta, Jill favored Francis and Alice with a knowing, glitter-eyed grin.

"But I didn't see you in there."

"That's because I was standing in my illustrious father's shadow."

"But I didn't see him in the room either," Elberta accused.

"Ah, *that's* because we went on ahead. Jack *is* one of the world's authorities on Wordsworth. We didn't require the memorized spiel of that malodorous hippie."

Elberta snickered, gazing raptly on her idol.

"Did you and your father notice how he kept his eyes closed," Francis asked Jill.

"Did we 'notice'?" Jill shot Francis a sarcastic look. "Well, it wasn't exactly a *subtle* thing, now was it? Basket case was my simple diagnosis, but Jack says he knows perfectly sane professors with similar fixations. They have to stare at the ceiling, or a blank wall, or sometimes at just one person, whom they aren't even seeing, before they can lecture. It's like they can't process their thoughts and see anything at the same time. Speaking of seeing, did you see that narrow, lumpy little bed upstairs? Can't you just imagine William boffing Mary on it while poor banished Dorothy lay on her sofa downstairs with her hands over her ears, recalling the dear old bachelor days at Tintern Abbey?"

"We didn't go upstairs," Alice said. "Elberta was feeling a little weak."

"But nothing that a fifteen-course lunch won't cure, eh, *ma petite*?" Jill taunted. She reached over and roughed up her worshiper's smooth brown hair rather sadistically. Elberta closed her eyes in ecstasy.

"Poor old Dorothy." Jill giggled, her glittery eyes bright with malice and perhaps something else as well. "Cooking and ironing and planting the garden and copying out dear William's poems in the evening. What a life! Though, when I was a teenager, I must confess I used to have this little daydream that my mother would die and then I'd get to be Jack's little mainstay and fix his dinners and type his manuscripts. Ah, well, can't have everything, can we?"

"Well, I don't know, it sounds like a good life to me," said Francis, characteristically bridging the awkward silence that followed. "Dorothy's life, I mean. Cooking and ironing and planting the garden and copying out the poems. Why, actually"—he laughed, looking around at each of them in amazement—"it sounds a lot like my life with Magda."

All of us in this garden are in love with people we can't have, thought Alice.

The *Galatea*, assisted by the tug that had steamed in place for several previous hours to hold her repainted stern away from the berth as the tide went out, had sailed from Heysham at six. In the darkened card room on the lido deck, the ship beginning to rock gently as it left Morecambe Bay and reentered the Irish Sea, Francis Lake was nearing the end of his slide lecture on misericords.

Things were going much better than he expected. Now he couldn't remember exactly what he had been so afraid of, but whatever it was, it hadn't come to pass. The group was small, only about fifteen people. At the last minute the president had thoughtfully moved the lecture from the cocktail lounge, where, he had pointed out to Francis, you could always hear the rattle and clinking of glasses and bottles. The card room would be more intimate, President Harris suggested, and also it would be easier to darken.

Perhaps it was the card room which was contributing to the friendly mood of the people who sat attentively in front of him, murmuring surprise or pleasure over almost every slide. Some of the French and German misericords, which Francis had decided to include even though his lecture was listed as "English Misericords," had been very popular, especially the ones depicting scenes from domestic life, and particularly the lovers. "There seem to be more lovers on the Continent," he had remarked aloud absently as he clicked a personal favorite onto the screen. It hadn't been in his notes, but the spontaneous observation earned him a round of warm, indulgent laughter. He could pick out Alice's low, appreciative laugh among them. It had been that one of the circumspect lovers, from the cathedral in Cologne. Alice had liked that slide, too, the night he had shown her some of them after supper, when Magda had still been alive upstairs. Alice had said she liked their formal restraint.

Now he was bringing things to a close with his misericord slides from the choir at Wells Cathedral, where they would be going on Monday. Whoever chose to go along with him on Monday, that was. Probably many people would prefer to stay in Bath for shopping. Francis had just explained to the little group in the card room that in Wells they wouldn't have enough time to examine all sixty-four of the carvings—agreed upon by misericord experts to be the most beautiful set in England, according to Father Birkenshaw—but Brad had been in touch by phone with the verger at Wells, who had generously offered to remove the embroidered cushions and have the seats lifted ahead of time on the ones Francis specified. "And we'll take a brief tour around the cathedral itself," Francis told them. "Wells is full of treasures you shouldn't miss. My wife, Magda Danvers, was particulary fond of a stone carving in the chantry of a man with a toothache. One of her specialties was seeing what you could learn about human beings from the art they made. Though I'm vastly oversimplifying, as usual."

As the projector clicked his Wells slides onto the screen, Francis began to experience unusually vivid recollections of himself lying or squatting between the stalls on the morning he'd photographed these misericords. Each image on the screen brought with it a startlingly clear and visceral memory of what he'd gone through to get it.

There was the one of the man riding and whipping a lion, and Francis not only recalled but *physically felt* the difficulties he'd had that day in finding the best position for his shot. The fourteenth-century carver had presented the scene as if viewed by someone floating a few feet above, like a guardian angel perhaps, and Francis had wanted to be true to the carver's unusual perspective. As Francis now regarded the top of the man's curly head on the screen, he felt the dust and grit from the choir floor as he had crawled about that morning in Wells, searching for the best angle.

And when, presently, his exquisitely photographed little dragon flashed on the screen, he found himself telling the group how he had stroked its head for a while before starting to photograph it. "Now, this little sleeping dragon was especially nice. One of the pleasures of misericord carvings is that they're so agreeable to *touch*. Sometimes, as you run your hands over them, you can get more of a feeling for the carver's intention. I remember wondering if perhaps the carver of this small dragon had some household pet in mind. Because, as you can see, it's not a fierce or ugly dragon. It's a sweet, small dragon, innocently asleep with its fledgling wings outstretched. Its face is really shaped more like a small dog's, isn't it?"

As he spoke to them of this slide he was especially proud of, a painful ache began to grow inside Francis until it branched into troubling memories. That morning in Wells, he had almost despaired of capturing the little dragon on film: it was nearing noon, and he was due to meet Magda in the north transept just before the famous clock went through its noon performance with the quarter-jack and the jousting knights. I won't be able to do him justice, he had thought, aiming the insufficient flashlight beam this way and that on the dragon, tensing as it grew more urgent to him, then losing hope. No, impossible, it was too overcast today, there was hardly any light coming through the upper windows of the cathedral.

And then he had been overcome by a bitter, childish anger toward Magda. A totally irrational anger. They had *agreed* to meet under the clock just before noon, he himself had suggested it, she had even asked him at breakfast if that would give him enough time to do his misericords—they were staying at an old inn, the Swan, near the cathedral, it was that summer she was doing her Soul's Choice research at Oxford and they traveled around the country on weekends, the summer of '88 that he'd been telling Elberta and Alice about earlier today in Grasmere.

But all the same, he'd had no power over his anger. It was almost like *hatred*. It was as though he'd suddenly heaped on Magda all the resentment from some old, old grievance that had been lying for years, perhaps all his remembered life, at the bottom of his heart. *I'll never belong to myself*, he had raged inwardly as he played the inadequate circle of light up and down the flanks of the little dragon. When am I ever going to get to do what *I* want?

Nevertheless, he was preparing to shoot a few pictures anyway, accept whatever he got in the gloomy light. Might as well have *some* record of the appealing little creature. And that was when a shaft of brilliant sunlight unexpectedly burst in from a high south window above the choir and solved his problem.

When he'd met Magda under the clock and told her about the sudden lucky burst of sunlight at the last minute ("It saved the morning. I don't know why, but that little dragon was very important to me"), she had laughingly slipped her arm around his waist and remarked in that knowing way of hers that always seemed to mean several things at once: "Well, good for the light, if it stroked your little beastie out of its shadows, eh?"

And then the quarter-jack on the famous clock hit the bell with his little hammer and the four knights came out of the castle above the dial and clashed, and one was killed. When the big bell in the cathedral's main tower finished striking twelve, a priest's cultivated voice came over a loudspeaker. He reminded all visitors that this site had been a place of worship for the past twelve hundred and eighty-six years and requested they stop whatever they were doing and pause for one minute of prayer. Francis had closed his eyes and said the Our Father along with the priest, and Magda had removed her arm from his waist and kept silence. Magda had always been extremely respectful of what she liked to call his religious life, not that there'd been any to speak of in their years together.

Then they had walked slowly back to the Swan, exchanging their experiences of the morning, enjoyed a prolonged and hearty lunch (steak-and-kidney pie, a bottle of claret between them, finishing off with a trifle) and afterward gone drowsily up to their room for a nap. He hadn't mentioned anything about his spell of anger, of course. Hadn't even remembered it again until now, in the darkened card room of the cruise ship, after Magda was dead.

How strange, he thought, I must have looked at the slide of this little sleeping dragon dozens of times, with and without Magda. We both thought it was one of my most successful efforts. But the powerful surge of hatred that had been a part of its making had been completely buried until now.

"Are there any questions?"

The lights in the card room had been turned on, and Francis stood nervously in front of his small audience, wondering if anyone would ask anything.

He was so relieved and grateful when Hugo Henry spoke up immediately. "I always thought a 'misericord' was a dagger you used for putting your wounded enemy quickly out of his misery. You know: dealing him the coup de grace. Is there any element of coup de grace in your church-seat kind of misericords?"

Francis blanked, the way he often did in school when the teacher would hit him with a question from an angle he hadn't foreseen. But recalling Father Birkenshaw's last letter, he was able to explain to Hugo and the others how church misericords had evolved out of *reclinatoria*: those leaning sticks that had been forerunners to the hidden "mercy ledges."

"So there *is* a relation, you might say," Francis found himself inspired enough to conclude. "Because, well, all those things that took pity on someone's weakness, from your coup de grace daggers to the hidden seats, they all had to do with the progress of mercy, didn't they? The word 'misericord' itself comes from the Latin words 'pity' and 'heart.' "

Alice, sitting next to Hugo, sent Francis a look of delighted regard. She probably thought "the progress of mercy" was his own idea and was impressed. He felt slightly guilty at deceiving her, but not much. However, he would be sure to tell Father Birkenshaw, when he wrote to report on the slide lecture, how Father's wonderful phrase, "the progress of mercy," had come to his rescue. The idea of the tall, proud rector referring to himself as "a lonely old man," and confined to a wheelchair for the rest of his days, smote Francis's heart every time he thought of it. Before Magda came along, he suddenly realized, it had been Father Birkenshaw whom he most admired in the world.

Afterward, people were very flattering and kind. Leora swooped down upon him in his chair at dinner and kissed him with surprising force and told him he'd won all their hearts. President Harris clapped him on the back and said he thought the whole thing had gone very well and he hoped Francis hadn't minded being moved to the card room. During dinner, Mrs. Fantini, who sat next to him, encouraged him to talk about his travels with Magda. After dinner, Hugo and Alice and Professor Stanforth insisted on buying him a brandy in the lounge and he accepted, though he'd never liked brandy. When the dancing started, Jill kicked off her shoes and dragged him out on the floor despite his protests that he wasn't much of a dancer. After a few minutes of pushing and pulling him around, she threw her urchin head back and uttered her neighing laugh. "You're right," she said, "you're not much of a dancer. But you know what you've got? A certain *Bambi*-ish appeal. I find myself quite taken with it." She was suggesting they just stand with their bodies touching and hold on to each other and sway with the music when, fortunately for Francis, her father broke in and whirled her off in an elegant two-step.

Other couples had risen from their tables and were slowly circling the floor. President Harris and Leora comported themselves like proficient graduates of a ballroom-dance course. The Fantinis flung their plump bodies into enthusiastic twirls and flourishes. Tall Alice's wan face, looking distant and suddenly sad, drooped like a weary flower above Hugo's aggressively churning shoulders. Mamie Elmendorf, safely enfolded by Dr. Leech (neither had appeared for the slide lecture), danced with her eyes closed. On a corner sofa by a window, Elberta sat by herself, eating the cherry off the top of a frothy pink drink.

Francis went out into the clear night and walked slowly around the lido deck. The stars were bright and close, round as saucers, but there was no moon. A couple had neglected to draw the curtains on their porthole, and he could look in and see their two sets of feet in companionable proximity at the end of adjacent bunks. Just the feet. The man's in black socks, aligned neatly side by side, the woman's crossed at the ankles and bare, with painted, wiggling toes. The two owners of the feet could have been sharing their impressions of the day, or each could have been simply lying on his or her respective bunk, reading. Francis turned his eyes away and continued his walk, feeling he had no right to spy on such intimacy.

He was alone now. As he climbed the steps to the sun deck on the bridge, he tested the words softly, under cover of the breeze: *I am alone now.* Balancing himself against the rocking of the ship, he gingerly crossed the deck threading his way between chaises and tables and deck chairs. When their tour had returned from the Lake District late this afternoon, there had been Hugo sitting all by himself on this sun deck, his feet up on a chair, writing fast in a notebook. People had laughed and waved at him as they descended from the buses on the pier. He looked so funny down there, because the ship was about twenty feet lower in the water; the tide had gone out during the hours they'd been away. "You've sunk!" Alice had called down to him. "Yeah, don't I know it, but now I'm planning to rise again," he'd shouted back at her rather menacingly. But it was Hugo's nature to be gruff. Beneath the gruffness there was a good, kind man. Magda had been fond of Hugo. Though, on Hugo's last visit to the house, there was that moment of embarrassing confusion when Magda started insisting in front of everybody that Hugo wasn't Alice's husband.

Francis leaned over the rail of the stern. The spray wet his face refreshingly. He gave himself over to the hypnotic constancy of the wake. There was something both sad and exulting about the spumy V-shaped tracks cutting through the black water, on and on and on: always pointing toward you, yet leading you away from where you had been. He'd never been on a ship before: it was different from how he'd imagined. Less romantic, but also less threatening. He remembered Magda trying to describe her pain to him: "Then a big, rolling one will *build*, like a wave, and break through; thrusting up through my fathoms until it crashes over the deck." That had been closer to his image of how it would be: big waves and spray and heaving and creaking of timbers: and maybe some men out of an old boyhood sea story crying excitedly, "All hands on deck!"

But of course they weren't out in the big, open sea, this was only the Irish Sea. Also, it was a calm night. And, of course, he was alone, so how could it be romantic?

Yes, now I am alone, thought Francis, staring down into the wake. It occurred to him that this would be a suitable moment to reach into the left breast pocket of his jacket and take out the Ziploc bag, and offer Magda's remaining ashes to the V-shaped spume.

But hadn't she said they should all be present—Alice, Hugo, Leora, and himself? The same group that had been gathered around her bed that afternoon—her last good afternoon—when she'd been playfully ordering them to take her with them on the cruise. "I've asked Francis to scatter a good bit around the base of my favorite purple lilac," she'd said, "but the rest of me will be honored to accompany you out to sea. So that after Hugo the Writer spills his creative secrets and Francis mystifies the plebes with his misericords, you can all toast me with good champagne and toss me over the side."

Well, Hugo had given his talk, or at least one of them, and he had done his misericord lecture, though he'd be happier to think no one had come away mystified. But, to fulfil Magda's complete order, he still needed the champagne ... and the others. That was how she'd imagined it, and hadn't she said that her imagining what happened later would be her way of haunting him? And he had told her he hoped she did haunt him. And had meant it with all his heart.

The trouble was, even when he was trying to carry out her expectations, unexpected things kept creeping in, things she couldn't have imagined and might not have been happy to imagine.

For example, during his misericord lecture this evening, it surely wouldn't have made her happy to know that while he was showing them that slide of that little dragon, it had come back to him how intensely he had once, briefly, hated her. If it gave him such pain to recall such a moment, wouldn't it give her more pain? It would, he was sure, but then she would want to discuss it. That's what she had wanted all along: for him to bring her clues to his hidden "beastie" so she could stroke it into the light with her analytic words.

Yes, this had been the thing she'd wanted from him when she was alive, but what good would it do to offer it to her now?

Francis removed the Ziploc packet from the inside pocket over his heart. "This is what I want to do now, my love," he said, plucking apart the closure of the plastic.

Leaning far out over the stern, which smelled of new paint, he slowly upended the bag and committed its powdery contents to the Irish Sea.

"Eternal rest grant unto her, O Lord. And let perpetual light shine upon her." He prayed with his eyes open so he could keep watch over the V-shaped spume as it carried her away.

Sometime later, he went down to his cabin and wrote a long letter to Father Birkenshaw.

CHAPTER XXII

Aurelia College Alumni Cruise
Today's Events

Sunday, August 25 * Port of Avonmouth

06:30–08:00 Breakfast is served in the Ship's Dining Room.

08:00 DISEMBARKATION (please be prompt) for:

Full-day excursion to Stratford-upon-Avon, birthplace of William Shakespeare. We visit his childhood home, with its museum depicting his life, times, and work; continue to Hall's Croft, the fine Tudor town house where his daughter Susanna lived with her doctor husband; see the garden that marks the site of the playwright's great house. After lunch visit 13th Cent. Holy Trinity Church, where Shakespeare was baptized and buried. Mr. Francis Lake will point out the misericord carvings at Holy Trinity. End the tour at Anne Hathaway's picturesque thatched-roof cottage.

17:30 Estimated return to GALATEA.

18:00 Cocktail Hour begins in the Lounge.

18:30 LECTURE: author Hugo Henry presents his second of two lectures, "Beginnings, Middles, and Ends," in the Lounge.

20:00 Dinner is served in the Ship's Dining Room. (Attire informal.)

Following dinner, come and enjoy Ricardo playing your favorite tunes in the Lounge.

"I'm a believer in the fateful beginning," Hugo told his audience. "If you get the beginning of your story right, it already contains the seed of its own ending. And if the ending's right, it succeeds in making the beginning inevitable. The Greek playwrights knew all about this. Oh, boy, did they! That's why it doesn't matter what order you see their plays in. Sophocles didn't even *write* his Theban plays in chronological order. Most experts agree that he wrote *Antigone* first—in other words, the story of Oedipus's daughter, and *her* problems, after Oedipus was dead. Then he wrote his two Oedipus plays. The audience didn't care. They were fully acquainted with these old stories, just as the stories Shakespeare reworked were known to many in his audiences. But in Greek drama, the audience's knowledge of past and future within the play was considered on the same level with the gods'. They didn't go to the theater to see what happened, they already *knew* what happened. Their entertainment lay in the godlike pastime of watching how the characters would act out their ambitions and passions against the larger pattern of their destiny, which they couldn't escape.

"But I don't plan to give you a lecture on Greek drama this evening, I'm going to tell you a few things I have learned the hard way about beginnings, middles, and ends."

Hugo was galvanized. There was an electric current running through him. Alice, sitting in the front row to the right of the lectern, could almost feel him pulsating with his own streamlined power. She knew that this was going to be a good lecture. There would be no self-hating Hugo knocking on her cabin door later, to ask her to enumerate all the ways he had failed.

"We all thrive on familiar images, and so, for the purposes of my lecture this evening, I'm going to compare the stages of writing a novel to the stages of a marriage. Most of us have some familiarity with *that*."

A variety of knowing laughters erupted from the audience. People wriggled deeper into their armchairs and sofas, those who'd come early enough to snare them. The imbibers rattled their ice and took anticipatory gulps of their cocktails. Alice could see Hugo's audience in the act of committing itself to him palpably. And she could see *him* seeing it, and was happy for him.

"Now, let's think about beginnings. Beginnings of stories and novels we've liked. Beginnings of memorable relationships that maybe later turned into marriages . . . or maybe didn't.

"Beginnings are *attractions*, in one form or another, which may lead to something wonderful, or something terrible, or just fizzle out into nothing much at all. But you recognize a beginning, whether in a story you want to start writing or a relationship you want to pursue, from its quality of *summons*. There's an immediate flash. A signal, a visceral signal, is received right in the center of your solar plexus. Now, in my most recent novel, *A Month with the Manigaults*, the visceral signal for me—to be honest with you—was a cluster of humiliating memories from my boyhood. Does that sound odd to you, that I could be *attracted* to a cluster of memories in which I was humiliated? Well, I was. So attracted I wanted to go back and live through them once more, wallow in all their colors and sounds and smells, elaborate on all their aspects. I wanted to *get to the bottom of them*. And as I began to write, the funny thing was that I was as avidly intent on getting inside the heads of those old enemies as a newly stricken lover is obsessed with imagining the inner life of his beloved. You might almost say I had *fallen in love* with my enemies.

"Hey, wait a minute, you say, is he standing up there and telling us that we can be attracted to something painful, be *in love* with the kind of characters who have caused us, or will cause us, pain? Well, I'll leave elaborations on that topic to the psychiatrists and psychotherapists. I'm only saying that when a writer, or a lover, feels the summons of the flash, feels the visceral tug with his name on it, he's bound to follow it, come hell or high water."

What kind of flash or summons had Hugo felt with her that first day at Lutèce? Alice asked herself. Was it the percipient flash of a wonderful prospective partnership, or was it the self-hater's attraction to the rejection he sensed she had the power to bestow on him?

And yet, standing up there, gripping the sides of the lectern, exhilarated by his own message, Hugo exuded none of the self-hater's aspect tonight. Hugo looked different; she was trying to locate what it was. He customarily wore a dark polo shirt with his navy blazer; tonight he wore a yellow one, which made him look fresher, more innocent. But it couldn't simply be the color of his shirt. He was Hugo, as much Hugo as ever, the Hugo of the rumply, pugnacious face and the quick, restless eyes and the tense body, but the Hugo-ness was somehow smoother and filled in. The usual detracting amalgams weren't in evidence: all those marblings of misgivings and resentments and furies. He was like an efficiently running machine tonight, purged of poisonous emissions, purveying only the essential force needed for the journey. He was Hugo the Writer, robustly delivering a streamlined lecture with gravity and humor and care.

Looking at him now, Alice appreciated him fully for his gifts. She saw why he was special and admirable and dear. Only, through no fault of his and no fault of hers, she didn't love him the way she loved the man sitting next to her. Who didn't even know she loved him.

". . . now, we come to middles. Whether they're middles of novels or marriages, you know you're in the middle when you feel set on your course. If it's a book, this can come as early as the second chapter. The middle of your book begins when you know pretty much the kind of thing you've committed yourself to. You've gotten into the rhythm of a certain tone, you know who's going to be in the book and who doesn't belong in it. You know what kind of book it's *not* going to be, as well as what you hope it still can be. Same with the middle of a marriage, which begins when the honeymoon is over. Now, some people will swear to you they're still on their honeymoon after twenty years, and more power to them. Other people's honeymoons never get off the ground, but they don't usually go around telling you about it. . . ."

An ambivalent ripple of laughter.

"But for our purposes, the middle of a novel has arrived when the novelist's initial euphoria over his idea has faded and he soberly faces the limitations and difficulties of the chosen work ahead. 'Chosen' is the key word here. Middles arrive in a *marriage* when each of you has, perhaps sadly, put away the illusions you had about the other, and settled down to the realities of life with this *chosen* person. Each of you has seen the other's difficult and unattractive sides: he snores, she has this nervous little sniff, he tells off-color stories at parties, she flirts with other men in the kitchen, he always forgets to put in a clean liner when he takes out the garbage, she drives on an empty gas tank—you fill in your own blanks—but nevertheless, you're still committed to your choice, you still believe you can make something out of it.

"And whether it's a marriage or a book you're committed to, the middle time is also bound to be second-thought time. You say to yourself, why in *hell* did I choose to do this book in first person, I could have stretched myself more with the omniscient point of view, but no, this is still better for my purposes. Or you say, how could I have chosen a partner for life who will never give me the kind of sympathy when I am sick that my mother did, but on the other hand she can be more fun than my mother when I stay well. . . ."

Uproarious laughter.

I don't drive on empty, thought Alice, but do I have a nervous little sniff I'm not aware of? I never flirted with any men at parties, but it's probably worse to be a sneak, to go on a cruise with your husband because you're in love with someone else who's going. But she was really more interested in what Francis's thoughts might be as he sat forward in the seat next to her, arms folded across his chest, his mouth slightly open, apparently concentrating on Hugo's every word: what disappointing faults and flaws in Magda was he remembering, if any? Or was he regretting all the ways in which he had failed her? From what Alice knew about Francis, it would probably be the latter.

"But the important thing to remember about this middle period, which may last for a long, long time, is that it's still *your* middle as long as you feel it as something alive unfolding, as long as you can answer yes when you ask yourself the question 'Is this book making a space in which I can find out what I want to say?' It's still the right middle for you as long as you can answer yes when you ask yourself, 'Is this marriage creating a place in which I can unfold and be what I have to be. . . .' "'

Oh God, thought Alice.

"Or is there a feeling of sapped energy? Of being stalemated, or even thwarted? If this is the case, we may have to face a sad truth. That our book has died on us in the middle—as books will do. It happens. I've had a couple die on me. In the case of each of these books, one day I just reached the point where I knew the book and I had to part company. It wasn't connected to anything alive or unfolding in me anymore. It just wasn't where I wanted to be."

Hugo's voice had dropped to a hushed, gravelly tone. Alice focused on her tightly folded hands in her lap. She dreaded what was coming: the obvious follow-up, Hugo's description of the way a marriage could die in the middle. It would be like a public accusation.

But the public accusation didn't come. He veered off into a story of one of his two abandoned novels, "a clever little tale of adultery in which a critic who'd given me a bad review was going to get his comeuppance. I was going to give my villain, this spiteful but oafish sort of cuckholder, who gets horribly cuckholded in his turn, the *exact name of my critic. . . .*"

He had them laughing again. Even Francis beside her had come out of his earnest listening mode and was laughing like a delighted boy. It was vintage Hugo-humor, in which Hugo made a funny story out of one of his own mistakes.

She knew Hugo had spared her, either from gallantry or from his own reluctance, when he moved swiftly—too swiftly?—from the anecdote about the junked adultery novel into his discussion of endings. Whether it had been a last-minute decision, or purposely left out of his notes from the start, Hugo, who was a stickler for symmetry, had sacrificed an important symmetry in his lecture. She was profoundly touched and grateful enough to be able to lift her eyes and see whether he was aware of her relief. The way he studiously avoided looking her way told her all she needed to know.

"Remember I said earlier that if the ending's right, it succeeds in making the beginning inevitable? Now, I always tended to rush the endings of my books. I wasn't aware of this failing of mine until several years ago when my new editor informed me that in my ending some expectation hadn't been fulfilled. Well, after a bout of furious sulking, I saw that she was right, and will always be grateful to her, as I told her at the time, for bringing out the best in me and Woody, my protagonist. . . ."

Alice bowed her head.

"Now, about endings. I've given this a lot of thought lately, and I think there are two kinds of equally valid endings. There's the *closed* ending, it's the more conventional kind that we're used to in the great nineteenth-century novels—and most people would say the more satisfying kind. In the closed ending, the attraction and impetus that drove us forward at the beginning has weathered all its middle parts of familiarity and faults, and has at last achieved its goal. In this kind of ending—let's call it the 'happy marriage' kind of ending, to keep faith with my simile of novels being like marriages—in this kind of ending, things have developed and changed, but they still remain within the initial embrace of the story. We get what we hoped for, or some version of what we hoped for, for the characters in the story—or for ourselves if we're talking about real life. Our lovers stay married and grow to love each other in larger ways, but they're the same lovers who started off together in the beginning.

"Now, in the other kind of ending, the open ending, we get something different from what we anticipated at the beginning. What's happened is that, somewhere during the middle of things, we've recognized that the realities of our story—or our marriage, to keep faith with our simile—just can't make a match with our anticipations. We see the necessity for the story to go off in a new direction. But there's a validity about the new direction, there's a feeling of rightness, however bittersweet. Now, this is not your satisfying, wrappy-uppy brand of outcome, it's a *going separate ways* kind of outcome. But it's *okay* if you can trace how the characters in the situation have been true to their natures.

"And I believe *both kinds* of endings give a new authority to the beginning if they succeed in making that beginning inevitable. So, say, if we're talking about a love story, and it's a closed ending and your two people get together as expected—or *stay* together, after some difficulties—you say, 'Yes! The telltale arrows were there all along.' You can go back and trace all the little clues to this inevitable outcome.

"Whereas, if we're talking about a love story with an open ending, the two people don't get together as expected. Or they find they can't stay together. They go their separate ways. But some implicit wisdom deeper than consciousness has guided their fates all along. If we're talking about a novel, the wise author has performed this service for them. If he has been a good creator, you can say, yes, that's okay, they're going their separate ways, but it's the way it has to be for these particular people. You can even say, if it's a truly wise and cared-for outcome: yes, they have suffered within the confines of their story so far, but I can see that out of it may come more wonderful prospects later, *in a future story*. In this case, the attraction of each of them going their separate ways, *but having somewhere else to go that is right for them*, is more powerful to the reader than the old satisfaction of seeing them safely at home in each other's arms."

He knows it's over, too, thought Alice. But when did he know, and how much more does he guess?

The curtains were drawn over the portholes of the president's cabin. It was late in the evening, after Hugo Henry's second lecture, followed by dinner and dancing. Neither of the Harrises was sleepy, and Gresh, wearing his undershirt and boxers, lay stretched out on his back while Leora gave him a pedicure.

"Five more days to go," he said. "Let's hope nothing much more happens. If we can just get home with the pluses and minuses we've got so far, I'll be happy."

"What are the minuses? I know you like to start with those."

"Well, that shitty hotel on the outskirts of Galway when they promised us luxury accommodations and a central location—I intend to negotiate with the travel agency for a refund on that one—and then the deplorable lack of PBDs aboard, and of course Mrs. Gormley, who isn't really Mrs. Gormley, twisting her ankle in the James Joyce Tower in Dublin. But Leech entered it into his records that nothing was broken, so I don't think we'll have any fallout later. Speaking of fallout, our good doctor told me a humdinger today in Stratford. An older man died on one of the cruises Leech was on and the wife said she knew her husband had always wanted to be buried at sea. So they did it. The doc signed the death certificate and the captain read a service, and over he went. Only, when they got back to port the guy's real wife was waiting, mad as hell because she'd found out he'd gone off with his secretary."

"Did she sue?"

"Damn right she did. That was the point of the story. We'd been talking about Gormley's ladyfriend—whether she might cause any complications later."

"But that other couple, the man who died, you'd think the purser or somebody would have noticed that the names were different on their passports."

"That's my Leora, looking into all the corners. Leech didn't say, actually. But *somebody* caught hell."

"Is there a present Mrs. Gormley?"

"He tells everybody he's twice-divorced. But who can tell for sure? Divorce decrees aren't required on cruises, just passports."

"Well, let's hope Mr. Gormley doesn't croak aboard the *Galatea*," said Leora, penciling cuticle softener around the healthy, almond-shaped pink nail of her husband's left big toe. The first time she had ever seen Gresh's bare feet, she had been shocked by their beauty, especially in comparison with her own bruised, knobbly pair, mutilated beyond redemption by the fashionable pointy toes of her girlhood.

"But if he should, we certainly won't bury him at sea."

Leora giggled. Gresh's superior male feet, as perfectly formed and unblemished as a marble statue's, still had the power to turn her on. Whenever she felt their sex life needed a transfusion, Leora humbly got out her tools and offered her worshipful little service of foreplay. "Are those all the minuses?"

"Oh, and I guess Don Tobias getting the bee sting in Shakespeare's garden today. Boy, did he make a fuss!"

"Well, he is a dentist. They have to be so careful of their hands."

"True, but Leech was right on the spot and took care of it admirably. Actually, we could count Don Tobias's bee sting as a plus, because it was the overture to our *big* plus."

"You mean Mamie committing herself?"

"Yes, because it got Leech out of the way long enough for Mamie and me to have our tête-à-tête. Leech had been hanging on her *like* a leech all morning. I saw him cupping her bottom when we were touring Shakespeare's son-in-law's dispensary, when he was showing off his knowledge of all those Tudor surgical instruments."

"And so tell me again what she actually said, when you two were alone."

"She said, 'Oh, Gresh, let's go ahead with it.' "

"And you're sure she meant the cultural center."

"In context, yes. Because earlier, when we were looking at the Shakespeare-family relics, she'd asked if we might have a little room at the cultural center where Elmendorf family memorabilia could be displayed in handsome, custom-built cases. That was the preamble."

"So her exact words were, 'Oh, Gresh, let's go ahead with it.' "

"Her exact words. Oh, and she squeezed my hand. I'd rather she had signed her name to a check, of course, but I think we can assume we have her version of a gentleman's handshake."

"Except she's no gentleman."

"And no lady, either."

They both laughed. "The *food* has certainly been first-rate," Gresh went on, "and Hugo Henry's lecture tonight was a distinct improvement over that last belligerent hodgepodge of his."

"Yes, people were very enthusiastic. I was sitting on that side sofa where I could see reactions on faces. And everyone was talking about it at dinner."

"He said some intriguing things about marriage," mused the

president, admiring the big toenail that Leora had just finished buffing to an alabaster sheen. "Didn't you think?"

"Mmm-hmm." It had been during Hugo's lecture that Leora, weighing the assets of their marriage against the familiarities and the faults, had decided it was time to give her spouse another pedicure.

"*They* have a cool sort of marriage, don't they? Watching them dance tonight, I got the feeling their single-cabin arrangement suits them both. Is there trouble there, Leora? You usually see things I don't."

"Oh, I don't think there's any *big* trouble. She's got a huge crush on Francis Lake, but—"

"On Francis *Lake*?"

"You should have seen her break her neck to grab the seat beside him on the bus to Grasmere yesterday."

"He must have hidden assets, then."

"According to Magda, he did. Remember our dinner party, when she made that outrageous boast?"

"It's always been my understanding that people who talk about things don't necessarily do them. Speaking of which, what do you say we have a little less talk in here? Can't we send the pedicurist home?"

"**B**ut she's not going to leave him," said Leora against her husband's cool chest, a short while later, in the dark of the cabin.

"Who's not going to leave whom?" muttered the president.

"Alice Henry. All of us are prone to our little crushes, but she's not going to leave her successful husband for a nobody. No sensible woman would."

"Ah, well, maybe the shipboard dalliance will do her good, then. I don't envy anyone tethered to that combative little man. If only I could persuade her to name it something else."

"Name *what*? Gresh, what on earth are you talking about?"

"I mean if we could call it, simply, the Cultural Center, then we could still have an Elmendorf Memorabilia Room with all the fancy custom-made cases she wanted."

■ ■ ■

Mrs. Chace McCandless
1 Briarwood Heights
Calhoun, S.C., USA

August 26, 1991, 2:10 A.M.

Well, Bea, it's the wee hours in the morning of a brand-new day, and I'm comfortably ensconced in the library on the lido deck of the *Galatea*, all by my lonely. No one's astir, even the bartender has closed up shop and retired to his quarters, after delivering me a final round of cognac. The captain himself has probably turned in, since we're anchored in the harbor of Avonmouth tonight. Yet despite the day's exertions, an all-day bus jaunt to Stratford-on-Avon, followed by my second evening lecture aboard ship (I called this one "Beginnings, Middles, and Ends," comparing the writing of a novel to the unfolding of a marriage; it was right well received, if I do say so myself), I feel full of starch and zing and much inclined to fill up a few sheets of this smart cruise stationery (X marks the spot of the library, just below the ship's funnel) with musings to you.

I hope that the "small setback" you referred to in your last letter (I received it the day before we left) has been taken care of by now with the new medications your doctor prescribed. And I sincerely hope it *was* a small setback. I did get to know you a bit during our memorable time together in your kitchen last June, and my feeling is that you tend to minimize your complaints. Unlike the majority of folk! Hell, this guy in our group got stung on his hand by a bee in Shakespeare's garden today, and you should have heard the commotion he made.

I'll probably stay behind tomorrow morning, I mean this morning, when the buses take our happy campers off to Bath and Wells. I remained on board Saturday when the rest of them went off to the Lake District, and had a very productive day by myself, plus an interesting chat with the captain. Not that I have anything against Bath or Wells or the Lake District (Alice particularly enjoyed the Lake District), I'd like to see them some other time, but right now my enthusiasms aren't on this side of the Atlantic; they're not even in the present century.

At last, dear Bea, I'm into my next book and beginning to feel like myself again. Though the story is set in a bygone world, the world of our great-great-grandfathers, it will be built out of the materials of my own pressing concerns. Already I'm picking up the scent of things I burn to understand. What more can a writer ask? I've sketched out the first chapter, and hear the way they speak and the under-rumblings of their motives and desires. I've spotted the mysterious rustle of their important memories, and can intuit pretty much what's going to be in their closets and cupboards. There's research to be done, of course; tons of it. I'll have to come south for it, but I'm always glad to have an excuse to come south.

You were my good fairy, Bea. What a propitious hour it was for me when your daughter Cam delivered me into your kingdom for "a cup of coffee." What an elixir that "cup of coffee" turned out to be! It was compounded of your generous, vivid presence, your careful reading and understanding of my work, and, perhaps most of all, the way in which you conveyed your passionate belief that reading and writing can actually *save* somebody. Before I left your house, I had been recharged, both in the battery-sense, and as a knight receives the charge for his next mission.

But your effects didn't end there. You encouraged me to talk about my father, to stand up in front of all those people and deliver a speech I hadn't prepared, and because I made bold to do so, a man came up to me afterward, that friend of Johnny Carteret's from Sumter, and told me a family story in answer to my family story. So out of the events of that one day, Bea, came my present undertaking. My novel is about what happens when one person, one single solitary person, learns to read and write— that's the bare bones of this tale. A young Southern gentleman takes his slave off to college to housekeep for him, and the slave secretly learns to read and write, and because of this everything is changed for everybody involved in the story. Literacy literally

becomes destiny. As a close friend of my son's, a very educated and generous philanthropist—actually, he's my son's companion—recently said to me: We can't be free until we can tell
our story, and only by telling it convincingly can we each do our
bit to help the world grow up.

Well, I've bent your ear enough now. Thanks for listening. I picture you sitting in your cool glass enclave, looking out at your
flowers and thinking up ways you can help the world grow up.
You're a rare flower yourself, Bea. Take care, and I hope we'll
continue to keep in touch. Warm regards to Cam.

Your friend,
HH

Hugo folded the three sheets of paper, written on back and front,
and fitted them in the long, creamy envelope with the *Galatea* crest.
Then, an inveterate habit of his, he removed the letter from the envelope and "became" the person who was receiving it, reading it
through from that person's point of view. He felt Bea appreciating the
parts he particularly liked, and was fully confident that she would reread and treasure such a letter.

He could have used another cognac, a final nightcap on the previous ones, but perhaps it was just as well he couldn't have it.

The lecture had been a success, even he couldn't fault it. The
compliments afterward had been nice. Gresh said it was first-rate and
had given him a lot to chew on. Hugo could tell by the lingering
clamp of the president's hand on his back that he had been forgiven
his previous mediocre performance and pardoned as well for his rudeness to Mamie Elmendorf. Mrs. Fantini said it made her fall in love
with Mr. Fantini all over again and also made her want to read Hugo's
books, she was going to get them out of the library as soon as they got
back to Yonkers. Alice had told him it was superb and that she had actually *seen* the audience commit itself to him. Later, when they were
dancing, she had said, "It was really fine, Hugo. I'm so proud for you."

Coupled with what he had seen on Alice's face in Stratford, it
was that "for you" (rather than "of you"—Alice always chose her
words with care) that made Hugo just as glad the bartender was no
longer around to bring him refills on his nightcap.

This was definitely a night of reckoning, and it was better to see it through with some degree of sobriety. If he had been given the means to drink himself into a stupor, it would only have postponed the reckoning. And tonight at least he had the recent glow from his victorious lecture as balm, he had the consolation prize of knowing he could still get it up for an audience when he absolutely had to. He would give many more public performances in his life, he was sure of that again. He would go on being a sought-after man of letters, whoever was or wasn't there with him as his partner to tell him how well he had done afterward.

I'm so proud for you, she had said, quietly and sincerely.

A woman who still considered herself part of your life would have said, I'm so proud of you.

Today—or rather yesterday, now—in that church in Stratford, when Francis Lake had been droning on to the group about some murky carving under a seat, Hugo had, for the second time in less than five months, witnessed an unmistakable look on the face of someone important to him that he would have preferred never to have seen. The first time was on his visit last April to his son's "warehouse" in New York, when Hugo saw Cal look at Laurence. Today Hugo had seen Alice look at Francis. Francis hadn't been aware of it, he'd been bumbling along about a misericord of a virgin capturing a unicorn, but Hugo, hanging back from sheer boredom in the shadows, had seen and understood at last.

What could a man salvage from such an intercepted look, beamed from his wife toward someone else, the kind of look he had never received from her himself? Certainly not his marriage. The only use to be made of it, perhaps, was as a writer. During some clenched moment of composition in a remote future, Hugo might possibly be glad *as a craftsman* to have had it. In this far-distant future time, he would be looking for words to convey exactly how love's surrender makes itself eloquent on a woman's face, and he would recall Alice's face and once again feel the stab of utter disbelief. But then, as his fingers began to gather speed over the keyboard, perhaps he would ruefully value the experience for what it was now bringing to his art.

CHAPTER XXIII

Alice had been hoping against hope to sit beside Francis on the hour-and-a-half drive into Bath, but as they were waiting to get on their bus, the ebullient Mrs. Fantini, less reticent and with nothing at stake, simply *asked* Francis for the "privilege," and it was granted, with his typical modest demurral about it being no privilege to sit next to him. "That's right, dear, you sit next to him and bask in his knowledge, and I'll sit across the aisle and bask in your beauty," endorsed the bouncy Mr. Fantini—evoking laughs all round, followed by another typical disclaimer from Francis of having "any knowledge to speak of"—and so it was settled.

He'd be equally content sitting next to a duchess or a bag lady, whoever claimed him first, Alice brooded sourly as she boarded the bus. She hated his indiscriminacy, the diffidence he wore like a shield; she resented, and at the same time mightily envied, his seeming immunity to any overpowering wishes of his own. He would sit for one hour and a half beside round little Mrs. Fantini and be perfectly content with his lot.

As contented as he would have been sitting beside me.

She chose a window seat far in the back, immediately fished out her book, and scrunched down low. She had brought along Magda's *Book of Hell*, thinking she might employ it as an oblique tool to fish more personal stories out of Francis. But now she would continue reading it, or pretend to be reading it (who could read, in the state she was in?) in order to discourage anyone from sitting next to her.

So this was love, this humiliating state of abject dependency on little accidents and whims of fate. "Hoping against hope" (not a phrase she would ordinarily even *think*) that fortune would be kind enough to secure your bottom a place beside his on a *bus* seat.

But, oh, the lost opportunities of that hour and a half which the happily married Mrs. Fantini had robbed her of! Who knew what valuable crumbs of self-revelation Francis might have unwittingly dropped behind him as he wandered in his absent, circuitous way down chance footpaths of association, occasionally stumbling upon some sudden back road leading straight home to his past?

Also forfeited were who knew how many outer stimuli, which would have caused him to thrust his nose close to her ear and whisper companionably, "Doesn't that remind you of—?" (though it would undoubtedly be something to do with Magda) or grab her arm, as he had instinctively done when the fighter jets flew over Wordsworth's cottage.

Perhaps most regrettably lost were all the future memories *for themselves* they might have been building together during that precious gift of time Mrs. Fantini had so carelessly snatched away.

So this was being in love. "She's wasting her whole *year*," Alice remembered having once deplored to Andy about a calm, sensible, studious girl in her sophomore class who'd gone completely nuts over a senior boy. "She plots the movements of her whole day around him. She devotes her entire *mind* to figuring out which staircase she's most likely to meet him on!" Amanda Fritchie, that had been the girl's name.

I'm no different from Amanda Fritchie, thought Alice, staring straight through a passage she had check-marked in Magda's book last night, planning to use it to draw out Francis on the bus if Hugo decided not to come. And Hugo *had* decided not to come, he said he wanted to sit on the ship's deck and percolate his new book, but she hadn't reckoned on Mrs. Fantini.

All those years I secretly felt superior because I never made a fool of myself in love. That's because I was never *in* love, but I had to fall in love before I could understand I'd never been in love before. And now I'm no different from Amanda Fritchie, only she was fifteen at the time and I'll be thirty-five my next birthday.

Surely you'd expect, though, if you'd been cool and controlled enough as an adolescent to sit on the sidelines of the jerky, mortifying dance of young love, that when you came up against middle-aged love, it would be conducted by your emotions in patient, dignified middle-aged fashion.

But it didn't work that way. Apparently you had to go through the beginner's mess at whatever age you began. You didn't earn any interest or exemptions just because you'd managed not to lose your heart till you were almost thirty-five. If I'd waited to learn to *read* until I was almost thirty-five, thought Alice, dejected by her own analogy, I would have had to start where every first grader starts: sounding out the letters with my mouth, despairing yet aching toward the glimpsed embrace of total meaning.

"I'm not sure whether I've been sent to save you from that book, or whether you've been sent to convert me to it," announced Jack Stanforth's friendly sarcastic voice as he folded his long limbs into the space next to her. "Your husband praises it."

"He must have been praising her," said Alice, summoning manners to help her gracefully accept an hour and a half of someone other than Francis in the seat beside her. "Hugo admired Magda, but he hasn't read her book. Though he's tried to make off with my copy several times already on this trip." As she spoke of Hugo she was surprised and saddened by how easy it was to convey the deception that they were a compatible couple.

"But *you're* enthralled?" The professor's undyed white eyebrows lifted in skeptical challenge. He clearly had reservations about the book.

"With what I've read so far, yes. We became friends when she was dying last spring. She was very sick by then, but she was still such a powerful personality. Her mind was so bold, she had this way of pouncing on you. She would say things, ask you things ..." Alice paused, wanting to express exactly what she meant. "So for me, reading this book ... she wrote it when she was younger than I am ... is like getting to meet her when she was well and just starting out, finding her voice and her material. That's fascinating to me."

"That's certainly an incentive for you to read it, then," said Stanforth, adding significantly, "But, you see, I never had the privilege of knowing the lady."

"I take it you don't like her book."

"It's frankly not my style. Scholarship it is not. It's more of a popularized compilation. Dante, Blake, and a handful of the hippier saints, including Jesus, packaged to suit the times. Or what the times *were* in the sixties, when this was published."

"Well, but here we are in the nineties, and it's still in print. This is a brand-new edition." Alice held up the smartly designed paperback, as if physical proof were being demanded of her. Stanforth reminded her of certain English professors she'd had, men who wouldn't have approved of Magda's style, either. That was probably the reason she had never heard about *The Book of Hell: An Introduction to the Visionary Mode* when she was at Princeton.

"Oh, I'm not saying popularized compilations don't stay in print." Stanforth wiggled off the hook. "I'm saying it's not scholarship, that's all. As I remember from my brief perusal of it, it had an appealing energy and bravado—though she waxed a little hysterical at times. But as your husband may have told you, I think Lawrence was frequently hysterical."

"Well, but what about this?" Opening to one of the places she had checked with her pencil, Alice passed the book over to Stanforth, who read the passage aloud in a noncommittal voice, though with much up-and-downing of the eyebrows:

We live within a dense tissue of correspondences. They connect all the levels of our existence, whether we recognize the fact or not. The difference between your Miss or Mr. Literal-mind and the Prophet/Poet is simply this: To Miss Literal-mind, a seed is a seed. She shakes it out of its Burpee packet, covers it with dirt, waters it faithfully, and achieves her petunia. That's all she aspired to: a petunia. And when Mr. Literal-mind lowers his face into the lush heart of a rose, he sees and smells what he expected to see and smell: a rose. If by chance he spies a *worm* nestled in its innermost folds, he dusts it with pest powder and that's that, his job is done.

But when our Prophet considers the lowly mustard seed, what *he* sees is the growth process of the human spirit: how a tiny, insignificant beginning can grow into a luxuriant shrub capable of sheltering others. And when our Poet contemplates the Sick Rose, he sees beyond mere plant pathology: for him the rose's enfolding of the battening intruder is a powerful image of human sexual love with its inevitable fate of decay and death.

"Do you consider that a hysterical passage?" Alice asked after Stanforth, waggling his shaggy white eyebrows a final time, had handed the book back to her without comment.

"Not that one, no. I can see how it would be very attractive to undergraduates. Especially Blake's sexual rose. I'll bet *that* generated lots of class discussion. And you picked a good passage. But you're a gifted editor, Hugo's told me. You know what to look for. I could undoubtedly flip through and find examples to prove *my* point, but I think I'd rather talk. Speaking of love and decay and death and all that, Hugo's lecture last night knocked that crowd's socks off, didn't it? His first was too pedantic and I told him so, novelists should beware of impersonating professors, it's not what their public wants from them. But his idea of comparing a novel-in-progress to a marriage—even the ways it can go wrong and perhaps die on you suddenly—was brilliant. Didn't you think so?"

"Oh, I thought so."

"And you could have heard the proverbial feather drop when he was telling how you knew when your book was dying on you. Implying also your marriage. That was very discerning."

"It was," agreed Alice.

She slipped *The Book of Hell* back into her purse. The passage Stanforth had read aloud was one of several she had been thinking of trying out on Francis, had she been granted her "hope against hope" of sitting beside him from Avonmouth to Bath. Of course, there was still the afternoon bus trip from Bath to Wells, and the trip back to Bath from Wells, and the return trip from Bath to the ship. Surely even by the law of averages she might yet strike it lucky.

Hope springs eternal in adolescent, undergraduate hearts.

"Mr. Lake, do you mind if I ask a stupid question?"

"Please call me Francis, Mrs. Fantini."

"Well, then, Francis, you have to call me Dottie. And my husband Al. Now may I ask my stupid question?"

"My wife Magda used to tell her students there were no stupid questions. The only stupid thing, she said, is *not* asking the question you want to ask."

(". . . because that way, you *stay* stupid," had been Magda's complete thought, but Francis decided to leave that part out.)

"Oh, I *love* that. What an encouraging thing to say. From the way you speak of her, your wife comes across as such a wonderful person."

"Oh, she was. She was altogether a wonder."

"Now this cathedral in Wells you're taking us off to after lunch, it isn't Roman Catholic, is it?"

"No, it's Church of England. All English cathedrals are."

"Well, you see that's what I don't understand. All the cathedrals Al and I went to in France and Italy were Roman Catholic. Wasn't it *once* Catholic, or am I just trying to claim everything for us? Al and I are Catholics, though I have to admit we've lapsed."

Francis explained about Henry VIII and the Act of Supremacy the best he could. "But my history is very rusty," he concluded, hoping there wouldn't be complicated historical questions from the group this afternoon. "I did have a Survey of Church History course at my seminary, but of course it was *our* history, Roman Catholic I mean, and so naturally . . ."

"You went to a Roman Catholic seminary?" Mrs. Fantini's eyes lit up excitedly. "Al, Al." She reached across the aisle of the bus and tugged her husband. "Mr. Lake, I mean *Francis*, went to a Catholic seminary."

"You ever a priest?" Al asked, perking up.

"Oh, no, no," said Francis hastily, "I dropped out before I got very far. And then I married Magda." He was fudging the true sequence of things, but he certainly didn't want to go into all that on the bus, not even with the friendly Fantinis.

"Oh, well, it's understandable," said Al Fantini with a shrug. "The Church is not what it used to be. In my opinion, it hasn't been the same since they took away the Latin. Dottie and I are lapsed, or maybe she's already told you?"

"I'm pretty lapsed myself," admitted Francis.

"Yeah, well, it's understandable, it's just not the same, is it?" repeated Mr. Fantini with a listless wave of his hand. Less interested in the Francis who was never a priest, simply a lapsed married person like themselves, he settled back in his seat again.

They rode in silence for a while, then Dottie Fantini touched Francis's arm shyly. "I asked my *stupid* question, Francis. Now I want to ask what I hope you don't think is a *rude* question."

"You don't seem like a person who would ever be rude intentionally," Francis assured her, wondering what was coming. He had been hoping he and Alice would sit together, since Hugo had decided not to go today. Early this morning, just as he was waking, Francis had remembered what it was he wanted to ask Alice. Of course, she might not be able to answer him. But if she couldn't, nobody else in the world could; he'd just have to let it go. But then Mrs. Fantini had come up and asked him.

"I was just wondering—how long did you say your wife has been gone?"

"It'll soon be three months," Francis told her. "Magda died on the seventh of June." The question he wanted to ask Alice was about

June 7. Alice had been alone in the room with Magda, when he'd gone down with the nurse, and he wanted to ask if she remembered what Magda's last words to her had been. He couldn't remember Magda's last words to himself. Perhaps there hadn't been any, to speak of. But if Alice remembered the ones for herself, that would be something to cherish.

"Oh, poor man, I had no idea it was *that* recent, though Leora Harris did say it hasn't been very long."

"Sometimes it seems much longer. Then at other times it's as if she's just gone out of the room for a minute. And, you know, I can still hear her voice. Saying exactly the sort of things she *would* say."

"What will you do with yourself now?" asked Dottie Fantini. "That's my rude question. But I only ask it because I'm interested, you're such a nice man. I've often wondered what Al would do without me. One thing I know, he'd lose weight, because he can't even boil an egg."

"Oh, I always did all our cooking. Magda was our wage earner. I guess you could say we had an unconventional marriage. Or a very up-to-date marriage. Depending on your point of view."

"How very interesting. Well, my goodness, that *is* lucky, about the cooking, I mean. But what will you do with yourself to keep from being lonely? Though I suppose you have friends."

"Yes, our friends have been very good to me. I'm not too worried about being lonely, though I suppose I will be. Fortunately, Magda left me in a position where I don't have to work. But I would like to make myself useful in some way. I've been giving it a lot of thought lately. It's always given me satisfaction to serve other people's needs."

"You mean get a job in one of the service industries?"

"Something like that," Francis said.

After a morning of sight-seeing in Bath, followed by the hotel lunch, Francis departed with his small group on their optional expedition to Wells Cathedral.

When President Harris had first learned from Francis after lunch that there were only nine people waiting outside on the bus which was to take them to Wells, he had seemed put out, suggesting to Francis they might want to reconsider the stay in Bath for an afternoon of shopping, as the majority had chosen to do. But then he had asked Francis exactly who was on the bus and, when Francis reported back with the names, frowned and said, "You'd better go ahead." When Francis, puzzled at the president's reversal, had mentioned it to Leora, who sat beside him on the trip to Wells, she grabbed a hunk of his hair and pulled his head down to hers and confided that there were some SPGs on the bus. "That's Gresh's secret code for small possible givers; they can't all be PBDs like Mamie, can they?" she said, playfully tweaking his ear before she released him again.

Despite the fact that the bus driver had taken a wrong turn as they left Bath and thus delayed their arrival in Wells by a good half hour, Francis thought his tour of the cathedral had gone pretty well so far. It had to be abridged somewhat, in order to leave enough time for the misericords, but the group was friendly and in a receptive mood. Don Tobias, the dentist who got stung by a bee in Stratford, had been delighted with the toothache carvings on the capitals. You would have thought Francis had produced those stone carvings especially for Don Tobias. "Now, which was your *wife's* favorite toothache carving?" Mrs. Fantini wanted to know. And when they came to it, Francis related to them what the guide had told Magda and him when they'd been in the cathedral in '88: that with a flashlight and stepladder a person could actually look inside the man's mouth and see his tongue pressed against his tooth. Super-tall Professor Stanforth had then sauntered up to the pillar, goggled into the stone man's mouth, and assured them that not only could he see the tongue pressed against the offending tooth, but he could even smell the gin on the fellow's breath. How everyone laughed.

Sid Merck, a contractor who specialized in office buildings and industrial plants, took a proprietary interest in the massive intersecting strainer-arches crossing the nave, and proved a welcome help to Francis in explaining to the others why this configuration of arches had been exactly the right thing to put in when it was discovered in 1338 that the cathedral foundations had sunk and the tower had cracked.

Tobias and Side Merck had left their wives in Bath for the afternoon of shopping. Jill also had stayed behind in Bath, declaring her intention to "flit about a bit, *solo*, for a change." But at the last minute she had given in to Elberta's pitiful wheedling to be allowed to join her. ("On three conditions, my albatross. One, that you'll move your tushie fast and not *dawdle*; two, that you stop whining right now; and three, that you'll swear you won't even *think* the word 'snack' the whole time we're together.") Elberta, who had just put away her four-course lunch, including both her own and Jill's gateau à la mode, had sworn. Francis hoped the child was okay, but after all, Mamie was her guardian, not he, and Mamie, eager to be off on an antique expedition with Dr. Leech and the president, had given her permission.

He recalled what Alice had told him on the plane coming over when they had been discussing the way Elberta had suddenly taken to Jill. Alice had said, "People *do* just suddenly take to someone, and that's their person." Alice was so astute: that's exactly how it had happened with Magda, he had known she was *his person* even when he was seeing her off at the Marquette airport, not expecting ever to meet her again. But that was a once-in-a-lifetime thing; it also probably had had a lot to do with being twenty-one rather than forty-six. He didn't think he had it in him now to take to someone as completely and certainly as he had done with Magda. He didn't even *want* to go out of himself, be impelled by such intense devotion, again. He'd had his great devotion, his great love. But that didn't mean he couldn't perhaps honor and serve some other long-standing devotion. Lately he'd been thinking a lot about this. It was another thing he had been hoping to discuss with Alice, if they could ever manage to sit together on the bus.

It's not so difficult doing this, thought Francis, leading his little group through the door under the organ into the choir of the great cathedral which was all aburst with color from the stained glass of the eastern windows and the bright needlework of the stalls. Of course he was not a spellbinding teacher like Magda, but it was satisfying how much people appreciated it when you simply shared things you had found out only a short time ago yourself.

So far nobody had asked him anything he couldn't answer. Sid

Merck had been so helpful about the strainer-arches, and now the two lady schoolteachers traveling together, who had been shy and reticent up until now, suddenly spoke up with authority and informed the others that they were passionate needleworkers and had come here today especially to see these cushions and banners in the choir. Francis had read up on the embroideries in his and Magda's guidebook, but the teachers told it more enthusiastically than he could have. Interrupting each other excitedly, they told about the small group of ladies who had carried this unique scheme to completion during World War II, and explained to Francis's group just why needleworkers came from all over the world to admire these cushions and hangings.

As promised by the verger, who had greeted them on arrival, the seats of the misericords Francis had specified by phone had been tipped up. Francis had only to unfasten the ropes and conduct them through the choir stalls. As the rows were narrow, the group would have to view the misericords single file.

Now, what was the best way to do this? Francis positioned himself in the aisle and read off the names of the carvings in each row as the group filed past them. They stooped and knelt, laughing disparagingly at their cracking joints; they commented and quipped and touched. Sunshine poured steadily through the windows, unlike the last time Francis was here. There were bottlenecks whenever one person paused too long to examine a particular misericord.

"I can't wait to pat your little dragon," Leora intimately murmured, patting Francis on the hip as she brushed past him into a row of stalls. *"The Pastel Patter strikes again."* Francis heard Magda's derisive snort as clearly as if she had been standing right beside him.

It was not the same as being alone in the choir, lifting off each cushion for yourself, placing it carefully against the stall in front, and then gingerly raising back the ancient wooden seat and seeing what hidden marvel awaited you beneath. Occasionally you felt the spirit of the nameless carver—a man who had had a life once, as achingly real to him as yours was to you now. You felt him close by, thinking his thoughts, worrying his worries, cutting windows into his fantasies through the deft shaping of a private face or a soft remembered paw or a jagged mythical wing.

Francis was almost sorry he had instigated this part of the tour. The sociable activity of filing in a group past preselected misericords obscured the very purpose of the carved projections themselves, which had, after all, been created as hidden ledges to sustain tired bodies at prayer. It was probably the *hiddenness* of the misericords that had drawn him to them in the first place. His "beasties in the shadows," as Magda called them. His hobby of seeking them out, sitting or reclining quietly in front of them for long periods of time, getting to know them by touch and angle and finally through the lens of his camera, had perhaps been for him an odd form of prayer.

Alice was down on her knees, examining a misericord at the end of a row the others had finished with. She was always a reserved person, a quality he found both attractive and restful, but today she seemed unusually subdued, even for Alice. She seemed sad. Earlier, in Bath, he had seen her throw a coin into the Roman baths, when their guide said they could make a wish to the goddess. Noting her grave wistfulness as she performed the act, Francis had wondered if she were wishing for another child.

He had to hurry the group along in order to get them to the Wells clock on the west wall for the quarter hour. They made it just in time to see the little wooden quarter-jack striking the bells with his heels.

"It would have been nice if we could have waited for the full hour and seen the whole thing," he told Alice, who was standing beside him. "But our driver taking that wrong turn out of Bath set us back and there's not enough time left. When Magda and I were here, we saw it strike the noon hour. I'd spent the morning with the misericords, and she was up in the cathedral library looking at a book belonging to Erasmus. She'd written ahead from Oxford to get permission. Not that she needed it for her research or anything, but she said she wanted to see with her own eyes Erasmus's handwritten notes in the margins of his book."

"I don't blame her," said Alice.

"Of course they were in Greek, but Magda read Greek. Then we met here just before noon and caught the whole performance. The quarter-jack hits that bell with his hammer, and rotating horsemen come out of those little doors and have a tournament. The same knight gets killed over and over again at every rotation."

"Poor same knight," said Alice, smiling sadly.

"Oh, do you remember I said I had something important to ask you about Magda, only I'd forgotten what it was?"

"I remember," said Alice.

"Well, I remembered it again. I was hoping we'd get a chance to talk today. And also there's something else I want to discuss with you. Not about Magda, just something I was thinking of doing with myself now that Magda's gone. I would value your opinion. Would it be possible for us to sit together on the trip back to Bath, do you think?"

"I don't see why not," said Alice, smiling.

I am beside him, thought Alice. Leora, Professor Stanforth, the Fantinis, all the rest of their small group, were relegated to oblivion. For Alice, the entire cruise—with the possible exception of Hugo, hoarding his hours alone on the anchored ship and testily awaiting their return—was relegated to outer space.

He sought me out at the clock and asked me to sit beside him. He has something to discuss with me. Oh God, what? Am I a part of it?

Francis had insisted she take the window seat, but now, as the bus pulled away, he strained toward her window for a last look at the cathedral. His arm hairs brushed against hers.

"We were lucky the bus could wait for us here," he said, his face all but laid against hers as he gazed past her, the proximity recalling that other time, when her mouth had been against his cheek and she had actually tasted his tears. "That gives everyone a chance to see the Great West Front again. It means more, after you know some of its history."

"It was a good tour," she told him, though she had suffered through most of it, not knowing whether she would have him to herself afterward.

"Oh, I'm glad you thought so, Alice. I thought it went pretty well. Except I realized it's probably not a good idea to show misericords to groups. They're too inaccessible and somehow, well, private. It's best to come upon them by yourself, the way I did when Magda and I were traveling. Of course, if our rector hadn't told us about them in seminary, I would never have known to look for them."

"Is that the priest you've been corresponding with?"

"Father Birkenshaw, yes. He was such a help when I was putting together my notes for the lecture. Oh, Alice, all of this is so strange to me."

"What do you mean?"

"Well, *all* of it. My giving a slide lecture on misericords, leading strangers—I mean, except for you, of course—through an English cathedral. Being on this cruise is like a dream, it has no connection with my life. But you know, it's funny, a few weeks before Magda died I did have this dream— Oh, too bad. If the bus had been able to go down that street, I could have shown you the Swan Hotel where Magda and I stayed . . ."

"You were saying about your dream."

"Oh. It wasn't much, I've forgotten most of it. But I was in a cathedral in some foreign city and there was a group gathered around a misericord. But isn't that a strange coincidence? Only, in my dream the misericord turned out to be this tiny television set and they were all watching . . . well, they were watching Magda's funeral on it. I woke up feeling so sad. But why am I boring you with this, what was the point?"

"Because it reminds you of the dreamlike quality of this trip. Because it was a sort of foreshadowing."

"A foreshadowing, that's true!" He smiled at her, the agent of his enlightenment.

"And you're not boring me," she added, emboldened by the smile. "When someone is important to you, you want to know their dreams."

He was looking at her intently, as though awaiting further wisdom.

"And you're very important to me, Francis," she risked adding. "Surely you know that."

A confusion swam over his face. She had gone too far, she had startled him.

"And Magda was important to me," she quickly backtracked, like a coward.

He seized on this with disheartening relief. "And you were important to *her*. She always perked up when I told her you were on your way over. It was good of you to come to see her as often as you did."

"But I wasn't just being good, I needed those visits, too. I needed to be there. It brought me back to life, coming to your house. And"— she must take the plunge, she must regain the ground she had lost through her cowardice, even if she startled him completely underground—"I wasn't just coming to see Magda, I was coming to see—both of you." Ah, coward, *coward*. Why couldn't she finish her sentence the way she had planned, with the simple and truthful "you"?

"Well, both of us were lucky to have you, Alice. Speaking just for myself, I don't know what I would have done without your support."

He could have been reading aloud from the letter he wrote to Hugo and her after Magda died, thanking them for their kindnesses and support.

"My love and support are there for you, Francis, anytime you need them." There, she had said it. Though diluted by the innocuous support. She clasped her hands neatly upon her lap and looked out the window at the blur of passing scenery. The bus seemed to be rushing them back to Bath with malefic directness, compared with its errant, meandering trip out.

Then she felt something she had not thought to hope for: Francis's outspread hand, covering her folded ones. "I know that," he was saying softly, his hand fast over hers. "I know I can count on you, Alice. I count on you more than anyone now. I hope this won't sound burdensome to you, but you're so calm and receptive and wise about things, I've come to rely on your judgment."

Calm!

"That's why I've wanted to ask you—well, I have this idea about something I might do—you know, I mentioned in the cathedral that I wanted to discuss it with you?"

"Yes."

"Mrs. Fantini—I mean Dottie—I sat with her on the bus coming here—"

I know.

"She was asking me what I was going to do with myself now that Magda's gone, and something that has been forming in my mind lately, ever since we were on the plane coming over, suddenly became clear. I didn't tell *her*, but I suddenly knew it was what I wanted. I mean, if *I'm* wanted. It involves others, not just myself."

Other(s)? She did not dare to speak.

"I was thinking of going back to a place where I might be needed and at the same time paying off an old debt. You know my seminary up in Michigan? It's not a seminary anymore, but I once had a full scholarship there. My uncle, who knew the rector before Father Birkenshaw, was able to manage it for me, I certainly couldn't have gotten it on my own. And then I dropped out in my fourth year—just when they were about to realize their investment, so to speak. I've always felt bad about that. But since I've been back in correspondence with Father Birkenshaw, this idea has been growing in me that I might be of use to them as a lay person. It's a retreat center now, but there are so many things I could do. I could garden and do landscape work, I could help in the kitchen. And they're building a nursing home on the grounds. I could help with that, and with my experience of taking care of Magda, I might be of some use in that capacity as well. When Mrs. Fantini asked me—it was funny, it was actually *while* she was asking me—I thought: I'm going to write to Father Birkenshaw tonight and propose the idea to him. I'd work without pay, of course. With Magda's pension and social security and our investments, I don't need pay, just room and board. I don't really need that, I could contribute to it as well. And then I thought of you—" His hand, still encompassing her clasped ones, tightened upon them. "I immediately thought, I want to discuss this with Alice. Is it just a foolish dream, trying to go back like that? Or will it make sense to her? *Does* it make sense, Alice?"

It was only then that she could bring herself to look at him. She took in Francis in all his particulars: the skin with its former death-watch pallor restored to healthful summer ruddiness, the faded hair with its faint streakings of youthful reds and golds, the soft gray eyes beseeching her behind the glasses, (beseeching her to tell him it "made sense" to leave her!), the neck which was starting to slacken and wrinkle just above the collarbone, giving her a preview of the way he would look as an old man, when she wouldn't be with him. And of course he had to be wearing that blue cotton shirt—the one she had seen damply flung across the chair the day he'd asked her to wait in the little room while he took Magda's sheets to the basement. She took in the whole living sight of the man she was losing, the way he sat inclined toward her, his useful sun-browned hand with its net-work of veins suppliantly covering her maidenly clasped pair be-neath. She saw how their very physical turning toward each other in this moment could have represented a far happier outcome, if his fi-nal question ("*Does* it make sense, Alice?") had been preceded by dif-ferent words. It was like that other protracted moment, when she had held the baby: an *almost there* moment, in which the ghost of all that could have been still visibly hovered.

"Well, if you want it . . ." she heard her "calm, receptive, wise" voice saying from a long way off. "And you said it was what you wanted. But why do you worry that it's foolish?"

"Because maybe it's foolish to think you can go back and finish . . . something you never finished with. That's what I mean. It may be too late. I was so much younger. Maybe it's too late. I'm not even completely sure what I mean by it . . . what I'm not finished with. I've told you how Magda always used to scold me for not keeping track of myself along the way. She said if I had, I would have seen the significant bridges between the chapters of my life and it would all make sense now. She told me I'd suffer for it yet, and maybe she was right, maybe this is what she meant. But since I've lost her, I realize I do want to be in connection with my life."

"Then it makes sense," Alice told him, releasing her hands and covering his with hers. She felt free to do that, now that she was just going to be his wise, sensible friend. "To want to finish something you've never finished with? To want to be in connection with your life? I think that makes very much sense."

Francis took her in his arms and kissed her resoundingly on the lips. But it was not a lingering kiss, just a grateful, enthusiastic friend's kiss. "Oh, Alice, thank you," he said, releasing her.

"You're welcome."

"Oh, but, I almost forgot *again* . . . the other thing I wanted to ask you."

"About Magda?"

"Yes. I've gone over and over it, Alice, and I can't seem to recall the last thing she said to me. I was wondering if you remembered her last words to you. I mean, they won't be the same, of course, but it would be something to treasure."

"Did she speak to you after I left—you know, when I went off to buy those things you needed?"

"No, she never did. That I *am* sure of. When I went back upstairs, she was already beyond that."

Then the last words she spoke to me and what she whispered in your ear *were* the same, thought Alice, but how can I tell you that now? How can I, after what you've just told me, about wanting to go away to refind your life? It would seem that I was trying to use it—a dying wife's bequest—to hold you back, to keep you for myself.

"Magda asked me for some water," said Alice, "and I lifted her up and she took a little melted ice through a straw. And then afterward she said she wanted to go back to her room—"

"Oh, poor darling, when she was *in* it. . . ."

"And then she said something about wanting books. I wasn't sure which books she meant, so I asked her if she meant those blue examination books. She scolded me—she said the colors didn't matter. It's what's inside them, she said."

"That sounds just like her! Yes, I remember now, about the books. When I came back into the room, after seeing Diane off, you *said* she'd been asking for books—"

"And then—" Mightn't she prompt his memory *just* a little, and still shelter under the umbrella of honor? "And then she called you over and pulled you down and whispered something in your ear."

"Called me over and whispered something in my ear . . ." he repeated, puzzled, shaking his head. "No, I don't remember that at all. I wonder what it could have been. It must not have been important or I'm sure I would remember."

"Then it probably wasn't important to you," was all she felt she could add.

"But of course if it's the last thing she ever said, it *is* important. For that alone."

"Well, maybe it will come back to you, then. In time."

"Yes, in time . . . *that's* true." And he gave his agent of enlightenment—his wise, calm, receptive friend—another broad smile of gratitude.

If he'd asked me the Magda question first, Alice wondered, would I have told him the rest? Would I have been able to muster just the right tone of humor and unthreatening warmth and say without driving him totally into the underbrush: "And *then* she said she was going to will you to me, and I think she may have repeated the same thing in your ear, because you blushed and said, 'You aren't making sense, Magda,' and after that you explained to me she sometimes wanted to leave things to her friends that just weren't rational."

Would this journey have had another outcome if Francis had asked me about Magda's last words first? Or would it have made any difference at all? Perhaps the only difference would have been that I would now be returning to Bath without hope or pride. Whereas, here we are, soon to be entering that city, and all—(all!)—I have lost is hope.

They remained together for the last leg of the return journey, from Bath to Avonmouth. On the second bus ride, Francis became uncharacteristically voluble with her, calling up old memories of his seminary. At least three times he stopped in the middle of a story to remark, "You know, Alice, I haven't thought of that incident in years." He talked a great deal about Father Birkenshaw, his old rector. "I admired him so much. I don't mean he was my role model or anything." He raked back his hair and laughed. "At least *I* certainly never aspired to be like him, I knew my limitations. Some people felt he was too cold and unbending, and he could be terribly sharp . . . he could wither you with one of his looks. But that was his nature, he was a perfectionist and he expected everybody to be able to live by his rigorous standards. We always got along, he used to call me Brother Placidus—you know, for placid, and also a sort of play on Lake, I guess. He was like Magda in that he always meant several things at once. And he was such an imposing man to look at. It hurts me to think of him in that wheelchair, but I'll bet anything he's still an impressive figure."

"You'll soon be able to see for yourself," said Alice.

"That's right, I will. I mean, if they want me. They might not want me."

"I can't imagine them not wanting you. You're a very useful person and you're nice to be around."

"That's very kind of you, thank you, Alice. But what am I going to do about our house? I don't want to sell it. Magda and I were happy there. And yet I don't like the thought of renting to strangers. I could close it up, but that's not ideal, either."

"I might be interested in living there."

"You and Hugo! That would be perfect! I wouldn't charge you rent. It would be a relief to know good friends were there to look after things."

"No, actually I meant just myself."

"Just yourself?" He looked at her blankly.

"Hugo and I are probably going to separate, Francis."

"Oh. Oh, dear. I had no idea. And here I've been rattling on about my plans and my old seminary days and everything else under the sun, while you—I really had no idea—I'm so sorry, Alice."

His arm had slipped spontaneously around her, in a comradely gesture of comfort and sympathy. She resisted the all but overpowering temptation to lay her head against his breast and imprint her tears upon the favorite blue shirt. What good would it accomplish?

"Please don't be. Don't be sorry. It's going to be okay. It really is." She took a deep breath and composed her hands on her lap in her customary fashion, but allowed herself to linger in the curve of his beloved arm. "It's going to be like . . . well . . . like that ending Hugo described in his lecture, the ending where two people go their separate ways? But out of it may come more wonderful prospects later."

Her voice was scarcely above a whisper, but it carried such a low, soothing, steady assurance that she might have been comforting *him*.

D ancing in the lounge was delayed that evening because everyone crowded onto the bow of the lido deck to watch the *Galatea* leave Avonmouth Harbor through the lock. Most of the passengers had never seen such a spectacle before. Dr. Leech was one of the few who had, he was an old veteran of locks from his previous cruises. What they were seeing tonight, Hugo had overheard him telling Mamie Elmendorf and the ever-in-attendance Harrises, was small potatoes compared with going through a lock in the Panama Canal.

But Hugo, despite some somber ruminations during his day alone on board, was elated by the drama taking place in the falling dusk. It had the concentrated sense of purpose that he loved: the tugboat at sunset nuzzling them from the quay into the lay-by, sending up its workmanlike fumes of unrefined fuel; the crew here on deck swiftly letting down ropes with attached boards to protect the ship from being bumped against the concrete wall of the lock chamber. More men, hired locals, were stationed along the wall of the lay-by, dangling additional ropes and boards that looked homemade. The captain wasn't taking any more chances with his freshly mended lady.

The captain stood on the bridge above them, barking orders in Greek to his crew, then switching to English to communicate with the harbormaster in the wheelhouse. The harbormaster had a megaphone, through which his plummy English voice alternated with the captain's. Several times Hugo, looking up, had caught the captain looking down at him. He knows I understand what he's feeling, thought Hugo. This was what he's made for, his mind is meshing with his work. He's tense and invigorated and wholly engaged. He may have some wife or girlfriend back in Greece who's giving him grief, but tonight, at this moment, he's a happy man.

Passengers flocked alternately to opposite railings as the drama intensified. Someone on port side would cry, "Look, look what they're doing now!" and everyone from starboard would stampede over, afraid of missing some part of the spectacle. The forwardmost part of the bow, where the crew were working, had been roped off, to keep the passengers from getting in their way. At any moment now, the word went round, the water would be released.

Alice, beside him, had been extraordinarily quiet and reserved, even for Alice, ever since she and Francis returned from their excursion. Hugo, keeping company once more on the sun deck with his flock of fermenting thoughts after a deep afternoon nap, had watched them get off the bus together and cross the gangplank with the others. Alice, going dreamily ahead of Francis, had suddenly turned her head and spotted Hugo watching them from the deck and had given him a listless wave. Francis, who had seemed unusually *focused* on Alice, Hugo noticed, had looked startled and then slightly guilty when he saw Hugo.

Something had happened between them today, but Hugo wasn't about to ask Alice. I'll wait and let her surprise me, he told himself bitterly.

At that moment the waters burst from the sluices, and a roar of delight went up from the passengers.

"Isn't it thrilling?" Leora Harris cried out to everyone, as though she herself had arranged this spectacle for them.

"Wordsworth could have done the sound of these mighty waters nicely," called Jack Stanforth to Hugo as he strolled by with his weird daughter on his arm. "Wonder if he was ever here?"

"Well, if *you* don't know, Daddy, how do you expect Wordsworth to remember?" came Jill's tart answer, muted by the roar of the rushing waters.

Beside Hugo, Alice began to cry quietly.

"Hey," he said, automatically slipping his arm around her as he would have in the old days when his touch was still welcome. "You okay?"

"I will be, if you give me a minute." Usually when he forgot and pulled her to him unthinkingly, she went stiff. Now she didn't resist, though neither did she respond. She slumped within his embrace. But he could feel her shoulders tense as she gripped the rail, struggling to control her sobs.

She soon gained control of herself, and stood tall again, taller than he. Clasping her hands composedly upon the rail in her old Alice-way, she murmured something inaudible against the cataract-roar of the waters being released.

"Sorry, I couldn't hear you," he said.

"I said I think we should separate, Hugo."

Here it was at last. He was aware of checking himself over, to see how he was taking it. Nothing new seemed to be hurting. On the contrary, he was surprised at the relief he felt.

"We shouldn't stay together any longer," she went on, as if he might not have understood her meaning the first time.

"I heard you," he told her. He felt the charge laid on him to go softly and chivalrously. Not agree with her too quickly, which would be ungallant, nor to try to talk her out of it, which would be dishonest and more painful for each of them. Now that she had roused herself from her long siege of sorrow and torpor and bravely taken the initiative in dealing the coup de grace to their dying marriage, he was determined to do all that he could to make it gentle and easy for them both. Or, for the three of them, he revised himself, fighting down the spurt of acrimonious bile that rose in his throat every time he incredulously contemplated his unlikely supplanter. No, not supplanter. A supplanter was someone who took what had formerly been yours. What Alice was incredibly able to give this mild widower had never been Hugo's to lose.

Knowing himself to be an impetuous man, Hugo ordered himself to count to a full twenty before saying a word more. Knowing himself to be not always a tactful man, he selected his words with great delicacy while he counted. "I think you're probably right," he said, almost making it to the count of fifteen, "I think we ought to talk about it."

His voice sounded suddenly too loud, and then he realized he was no longer competing against the roar of the water. The sluices had been shut off and the forward gates of the lock were now swinging open, releasing them to their new level and next destination.

Having finished their embarkation duties on deck, the crew of the *Galatea* removed the rope that had marked off business from pleasure. Alice and Hugo, along with other passengers, drifted forward to the prow.

"Will you go back to New York, do you think?" asked Hugo as he and Alice, keeping apart from the others, leaned over the railing together and felt their hair and clothes increasingly wind-whipped as the ship progressed out of the Bristol Channel and reentered the sea.

"I'd like to work again, yes. And Francis has said I could stay at his house, when I need."

"You're going to live with Francis, then?" He struggled to keep his tone manly, even benevolent, though somehow he had not thought her capable of dragging him through this kind of humiliation so soon.

"Francis is going away, Hugo. He's going back to Michigan, to his old seminary. Only it's a retreat center now. He's hoping they'll find a use for him, and if they do, which of course they will, he'll go and live there. It's what he wants, more than anything, he told me today. He asked me if I thought it made sense, and I told him—well, I told him—" Her voice faltered. "I told him it was the right thing . . . if that was what he wanted most."

"Oh, my poor girl," said Hugo, quick to understand. His pride so swiftly restored to him undamaged, he was free to expend a huge anger on her behalf: when were her fates going to stop laying it on her? Hadn't she sustained enough losses to satisfy their greedy, melodramatic appetites?

For a second time he put his arm around her and pulled her to him. For a second time she let herself be held. It was dark now, but to some others on deck whose eyes were adjusted to the darkness, the sight of Hugo Henry cordoning off his wife within a protective, loving embrace was not lost.

Even after Ricardo's nimble piano fingers, caressing the timeworn opening bars of "Smoke Gets in Your Eyes," had summoned the others into the lounge, the Henrys remained on deck, a memorable and perhaps enviable couple to some who had left them out there in the darkness, a couple already forgotten by others racing to follow the alluring, colored gleams of their own dearest fantasies.

Dr. Leech was in a good mood, with his left hand curled around his drink on the table, his right hand fondling Mamie's thigh beneath it. And President Harris was in an excellent mood as Mamie triumphantly inventoried all the purchases she had made that day in Bath, some—like the Victorian turkey-stuffing spoon and the three Regency snuffboxes—already squirreled away in her suitcases, the rest—the Georgian tea set, the Tompion clock, and the Venetian lacquered credenza with its interior cartouched landscapes and romancing personages—already in the process of being crated and shipped to her back in Aurelia.

"I probably paid far too much for that credenza," she crowed, "but it will go perfectly in the far corner of the Elmendorf Memorabilia Room, won't it, Gresh? I want people to see it looming at them when they come in the door . . ."—she laughed hilariously—"this great old monstrosity that has been in Elbert's family since the seventeenth century. Now, the Tompion clock I'm going to keep for myself, it's so pretty, so completely my taste, but you can have it for the memorabilia room after I'm dead."

"You're not going to die for a long time," the doctor assured her. "You have a good heart."

"How would you know, Percy?" challenged Mamie. "You've never had your hands on *it*. Elbert used to say to me, 'Mamie, you were born with a hole in your head and no heart, but you're my heart's desire.' He actually used to cry sometimes, Elbert did, I would devil him so."

"The fate of many men in your life, I fear," said Leech, his right arm sinking deeper out of sight beneath the tablecloth.

"Poor dear Elbert. Yes, after I go, Gresh, you can have the clock for the center. I mean for the memorabilia room, of course."

"Of course," the president urbanely assured her.

"But I think we'll have *it* come from *my* family. My family should get a little recognition, too. The Mamie Willis Elmendorf Clock, Which She Brought to Her Marriage: that's how we'll label it. By the way, isn't that sweet of them, they're going to send a man all the way across the Atlantic, to install it in my living room and make sure it's running right? Of course, it was probably included in the price I paid, but still, it's such a nice *Englishy* gesture. I hope the man they send is cute."

"I'm sure that is included in the price, too," said Dr. Leech.

Mamie's granddaughter, at the far end of the table, whispered something urgently in Francis's ear.

"What's that, Elberta?"

"I *said*," she hissed, "that if you don't take me somewhere else *this second*, I am going to upchuck all over these people."

Francis immediately pushed back his chair and stood up. "Elberta's not feeling well," he told the others. "We're going to go out and get a little air."

Though Gresh and Leora and the doctor and Mamie made the proper noises, Francis had the feeling neither Elberta nor himself would be missed in the least. Squiring Elberta around the edge of the dance floor to an exit (the Fantinis were dancing cheek to cheek, Jill Stanforth and her father were talking animatedly as *they* danced), Francis realized he was greatly relieved to have something to do and somebody to do it for. He had not been enjoying the conversation, or the sweet Mai Tai Leora had insisted on foisting upon him, and he was aware that he had been feeling unaccountably sad ever since the ship had sailed.

"I couldn't stand it another *second*!" Elberta burst out at him accusingly, as soon as they were outside. "It's disgusting! And this is going to be the rest of my life, until I get up the nerve to kill myself."

"It won't be the rest of your life, and you mustn't talk that way, Elberta."

"Why not? What have I got to lose? Why are you shoving me to the back of the boat? I want to go up front."

"No, let's not go there. Hugo and Alice are still up there."

"So what? It's not their private boat."

"Well, I think they might want their privacy, so let's—" Francis tried to tug her toward the stern.

"Oh, *screw them*!" she screeched at him. "Screw-goddamn-pissfucking everybody!"

Francis slapped her. Both of them were shocked. All they could do was face each other in stunned disbelief.

Elberta was the first to recover. "You *hit* me," she said, a strange elation rising in her voice. "You hit me on my face."

"I know I did," said Francis, when he could speak, "and I'm very, very sorry. I can't remember ever hitting anybody on the face in my life—except my sisters—"

"I could have you sued now, if I want to."

"Well, I hope you won't want to, but I couldn't stand that foulness pouring out of your young mouth."

"Everybody else says and does foul things." She had begun to cry.

"But you're still a *little girl*, Elberta. Do you want to grow up and be as disgusting as everybody else, when you have it in you to be a fine and splendid person?" He was glad that, except for the glow from the lounge windows and the prickle of cold stars above, it was relatively dark out here. He was inexplicably close to tears himself.

"Only four more days of this trip, then I'll never see her again."

"Who?"

"Who do you *think*?"

"Oh, you mean Jill?"

"Yes, *Jill*, you old stupid!"

"But maybe you will see her. And you can always write to her."

"No, I already asked. . . ." A choking sob. "She said she wouldn't answer. She said I was a nice kid but she never answered letters."

"Well, but people sometimes say things and then change their minds."

Look at Alice, he thought. Why, only this afternoon she had confided in him that she and Hugo were separating. But they certainly hadn't looked like a couple separating when they stood there together like that at the rail, when the ship was sailing.

"I'll tell you what, Elberta. This may not be much of a consolation to you now, but if you write to me, I will always be very glad to hear from you and I promise you I will answer."

"Why should I write to you, silly, when we live in the same place?"

"I may be going to another place soon, to live and work." If they want me, he stopped himself from adding. "I can't imagine them not wanting you," Alice had said earlier today. "You're a very useful person and you're nice to be around."

"Oh great," snuffled Elberta. "How do you expect me to grow up into a fine-decent-splendid person when everyone decent is abandoning me?"

"There'll still be Leora, she likes you a lot. . . ." He wished he could bring himself to add, "and your grandmother," but in good faith he could not; he didn't want to insult the child's intelligence, either. "And there's Alice Henry. Alice likes you, and she's certainly decent. She's one of the finest people I've ever known."

"Yes, but she has her own life. She has Hugo—"

"Yes . . . she has Hugo . . . but that doesn't mean she can't have good friends as well. Come for a walk now. I want to take you back to the stern. We'll climb up on the bridge deck and I'll show you exactly the spot where I stood when I threw Magda's ashes over."

EPILOGUE

Early Saturday afternoon it began to snow, and Alice carried up two loads of logs to Magda's study. Before he had left for Michigan a year and a half ago, Francis apparently had been determined to stack enough firewood in the garage to last her for years.

After she got a nice steady flame going in the small grate, she arranged her pillows and blanket—a colorful mohair afghan of Magda's—and set up her weekend workroom around the old leather sofa. She had two manuscripts to read and some jacket copy and memos to draft. But first she wanted to do Hugo's letter justice. It had arrived in yesterday's office mail, shortly before a staff meeting, and she'd only had time to skim it after the meeting before dashing for her train to "your country house," as her new colleagues persisted in calling it. Despite her hasty reading of the letter, certain parts of it had lingered, accompanying her on her journey all the way up the Hudson. Scenes and figures evoked by it swirled about her in the dim interior of the Amtrak car, their presences dominating her mind with the same swarming vividness with which the pantheon of silvery wraiths besieged Queen Catherine of Aragon dreaming on her couch, in Magda's Blake reproduction that hung above the sofa.

January 10, 1993
Dear Alice,

It is an understatement to say I "appreciated" your response to the ms. of *Truebloods*. It is frankly the most encouraging response to my writing, in writing, that I've ever had the pleasure of reading. Immediately after I read your letter, I became depressed, however, for I realized that no *reviewer* will understand my intentions half so well. Not to mention the crap I'm going to take for being presumptuous enough to write from Henry's point of view and Henry's *mother's* point of view for the entire second half of the novel ("What does *he* know about being a black man? What does this white Southerner know about how it felt to be a slave? What does this arrogant white male think *he* has to tell us about the inner life of a black *woman* in slavery? And isn't it a bit cute, not to mention presumptious, for Hugo Henry to give his black protagonist the name *Henry*? Etc., etc. etc.")

Okay, I'm done. I just heard you thinking, "Hugo, you're still the world's champion at creating negative scenarios." (You see I have managed to self-edit some of the things about myself I learned from you.) Laurence also says I'm overreacting—I asked him to read it when he and Cal were down here visiting me at the beach cottage, and his response was very gratifying, though he says, for him, Tom's dying mother is the central figure and he wanted her to go on living until the very last page so she could glimpse all of the changes her kindness had wrought in the world that so passionately concerned her. I think he was a little *too* smitten with my lovely doomed plantation chatelaine, but of course I didn't tell him so. Glad you saw how Isabel Trueblood's dying was inwrought into the organic form of *Truebloods* from page one. If she hadn't been dying and confined to her room, that unlikely configuration of others would never have gathered there, she would never have had a chance to get to know and love Henry and thus contrive for him to go off to "housekeep" for Tom at the university. Her hour is over, but because she existed, a whole passel of unlikely things can now be given *their* hour. I loved what you said about "the strong one having to be taken away so that the others, missing her, will have to teach themselves to be what they miss in her." Exactly! God bless you.

I'm very glad you're working again, and I'm proud of you for holding out until you got precisely the terms you wanted from those bastards. Being a gifted editor in a mainline publishing house today is a little like my Henry at the university, covertly serving his passion for the Word while ostensibly functioning as Tom's efficient servant. And, yep, you got it right about my splitting myself into the two characters: arrogant, contentious Tom, heir to the sins of his father, and his secret brother Henry, who will literally save him through words—as I am briefly saved each time I find my way through a novel. You always were my best reader, Alice.

I've gotten to the place where I can think of it this way, and I hope you can, too: how lucky each of us was—despite our respective emotional wrenchings—to have been requited by a custom-made angel for our hours of need: Francis leaving you a house to live in so you could hold out for the right job; and Bea not only providing me with the inception of this tale but then canvassing her network of friends till she found me the ideal place to write it in.

The only one who was inconvenienced was old Gresh, having to find a replacement for me at the last minute, but at least I was able to put him in touch with Joel Mark. Glad *that's* worked out, though if Gresh has offered him a chair of writing and he has accepted it, they must both be pretty hard up. Did you catch

Joel's self-serving piece on the devastation of Yugoslavia in the *Times Magazine*? Passing himself off as a concerned political animal in order to tout his Serbo-Croatian-translated novels was quintessential Joel. Sorry to hear about Gresh's heart attack, but glad he's rallying and that the culture center is limping along in its plans despite Mamie's intervening tantrums and whims.

This oceanfront cottage beats anything that I could ever have invented for the fortunate, snotty Manigaults, and yet I often think of them fondly as I inhabit its rooms. I made them, I guess I ought to be fond of them.

Bea's still hanging in there, remarkable woman, but not for much longer, I fear. It's gone to the kidneys. I was up at their house in Calhoun last weekend, reviewing the architect's plans for the reading center, which, with her damnable modesty, she wants to name after her husband, Chace, but he and I have an understanding between us on *that* score. I'm to be the titular head of the place—my salaried job being to park the "prestige" of my "nationally known" body in Calhoun for a certain number of months per year, mainly doing what I do anyway, but appearing at a number of functions around town. (Beats faculty meetings with their endless hee-hawing and seesawing.) The plans call for an inviting upstairs office suite for me to write in (that is, if I ever get an idea for another book), while down below in formidably well-equipped and equally inviting surroundings, the literacy volunteers will be plying *their* trade.

I don't deserve all this good fortune, but will try to live up to it. Oh, by the way, Dornfeld loves the new book, I sent him an early ms., and he's made a handsome offer—for England. He's not at all worried about its American historical background; he says the Truebloods' family story transcends time and place in the same way Chekhov's and Mann's family stories do. How about *that*? Though Elizabeth Dornfeld teases that I still owe her a love story.

My best to Francis, when you next write or talk to him. It must be both poignant and strange for you, living in their house, sleeping in that bedroom where she died, working in her study when you're not in New York. (Glad Cal and Laurence were able to find you a nice pied-à-terre in the city.) By strange, I mean *potently* strange: inhabiting other people's lives. Which is what I've been doing, in my way, with *Truebloods*, and what I hope to do again before too long, before I sink into one of my between-book despairs and make myself unbearable to everyone concerned. Not that there is anyone around to *be* concerned, but, as you said about yourself in your last letter, I continue to hold out hope for the prospect of intimacy with someone eventually.

I do not forget what day it is, and never will forget, on January 10. He would have been two today. It didn't come to pass, the flowering of his life, or that life we might have had, but other good things will. I truly believe that, Alice, and I also believe there is no one who deserves those good things more than you. Thank you again, more than I can say, for your response to *Truebloods*. I'll keep you posted on developments. I'm more hopeful about this book than any previous one, though I'm superstitious about saying more.

As ever,
Hugo

A lice refolded the word-processed pages with their perfect justified margins that drove editors in search of word counts mad. Replacing the letter in its envelope, she found herself smiling. In Hugo's files, she knew, lay a duplicate of this very letter, awaiting its hour of simplifying the task of his future biographers. She could smile about so many of Hugo's habits, now that she was no longer married to him, now that he was just Hugo Henry again, a fine man and a fine writer, safely behind the fence of his prose.

She got up and put another log on the fire and went to the window and looked out. It was snowing softly but steadily. Magda's favorite lilac was draped completely in white. *Inhabiting other people's lives*: yes, that was, of course, a way Hugo might see it. But this was very much *her* life. The past year and a half had been lived with an intensity and clarity that brought its own form of solitary happiness. "I am ordering my loves," the dying Magda had explained to her. And that was what Alice seemed to have been doing, living in this place where she wanted to be—even if she couldn't be with whom she wanted—and putting in order the ideas and things and people she knew would always be part of her. And if she couldn't share a life with the person she loved, at least she had the pride of knowing who he was, and being true to that knowledge in her heart. There was a great deal of energy and contentment to be gotten simply from not living a lie.

She wondered if it was snowing up in northern Michigan. In his last letter Francis said the nursing home was nearing completion— they were working evenings and weekends. That meant he probably wouldn't call today. About twice a month he would phone the house, usually on Saturday afternoons, but she tried not to anticipate these occasions. If she did let herself hope, it made her too melancholy when the afternoon had passed and the phone had remained silent. "You were once kind enough to tell me I was useful," he had written in his last letter. "Well, now I am even more useful, having learned to plaster and put down wood floors and lay ceramic tiles."

Alice rationed her letters to Francis. She never wrote until he had answered her last letter, and she tried always to have a reason for writing. Should she renew the service contract on the appliances? The washing machine seemed to be on its last leg. The deer had killed one of the young birches at the edge of the woods with their antlers, did he want her to call Brian the tree man and arrange for a replacement in the spring? And then there were those queries from Mira Dooley, a young professor who had done her dissertation on Magda's work and was hoping to get it accepted in revised form for publication; these queries needed to be sent on to Francis, who then liked to consult with Alice before he answered Mira Dooley.

Around the hour of dusk, as Alice, under Magda's cozy afghan, was regretfully giving up on the first manuscript, which had started out so promisingly, the phone rang. It wasn't Francis, but it turned out to be news of him.

"*I* got a letter today," announced the voice, disdaining, as always, any salutation.

"Oh, Elberta. How are you?"

"If you really want to know, if you aren't just being *ladylike*, I'm terrible. If she won't let me go away to boarding school, I'm going to join the Hemlock Society."

"I thought you already had joined." Alice and Francis had agreed that a loving, offhand humor was the best way to respond to Elberta's suicide threats.

"No, that was my friend Trudy, before her parents said she could go to Emma Willard next fall. But I was just using it as a figure of speech anyway. I've read the magazine they sent Trudy. There's not one recipe in it for killing yourself. But I know the pill to get now, if I need. You're supposed to take fifteen of them and then put a plastic bag over your head."

"What did Francis say in his letter?"

"He said you didn't write him as often as I did and you never said much about yourself."

"Did he say that?"

"You can read the whole letter if you like. I could come over, if someone will bring me. She's got one of her awful men here, that disgusting red-faced old lawyer. He could probably run me over in his stupid little Corvette. We could make that cheese-and-crabmeat dish again. I could bring some, out of her freezer. I'll bring some butter-pecan ice cream, too."

"I'll be glad to come and pick you up."

"In the *snow*? I thought you didn't drive in poor weather conditions. On account of your family tragedy."

"I have good tires. It's not snowing that hard."

"It might, later. I might have to spend the night."

"Well, I'll make up a bed in the little room you slept in last time."

"Oh good. I can commune with the spirits of the dead in your sycamore tree."

"What spirits of the dead?"

"He said that *she* said that the tree was filled with them. Only they manifest themselves as mourning doves."

"Francis told you that?"

"Well, who else, dummy?"

Sunday, April 18, 1993

Dear Francis,

I came up from the city Friday midafternoon, intending to get my
laundry started in the new machine and then write you a country
news bulletin—the daffodils and narcissi are all over the place
(but I'm afraid the deer ate all your red tulips again this year!),
the cardinals and phoebes are back, and I've put up the bluebird
house, but there are no takers yet—but on the way to the house
I stopped off at the P.O. box and there was another Priority Mail
envelope from Mira Dooley, this time requesting Magda's last unfinished essay, "The Drama of the Soul's Choice in Visionary
Art," which she says you mentioned in a letter to her in May
1991, and which Mira's publisher now wants to consider including in the book on Magda. So up to Magda's study I went immediately, to search through the files for the essay so I could make
a copy first thing Saturday morning at Pronto Printer and get it
off to you. I located the essay without too much difficulty. I am
learning there's a method to Magda's filing, even a fairly consistent method. It's simply like nobody else's method, that's all! It
follows her associations rather than alphabet or general topics.

Then I decided to sit down on the sofa and read through the essay myself, give you the benefit of my editorial judgment, since
you asked me to. As you'll see, there are vintage Magda-isms
scattered throughout and my suggestion would be to excise
those gems and send them to Mira Dooley. The essay itself is in
pretty rough form, as Magda herself says in the attached note,
dated March 1, 1991, which I also enclose.

About the note, I owe you an apology, Francis. I didn't realize it
was to you until I was halfway through it. At that point I should
have stopped, but didn't. Sorry. Yet, for myself, I'm glad to have
read it. I have always had rather a cautious, fearful nature
(sometimes operating to my detriment) and the note, even
though it was meant for you, had a rousing, tonic effect on me.
It was like receiving an injection of Magda's personality.

Then, in Saturday morning's mail, I had your letter with the
news of Father Birkenshaw's sudden and peaceful death. I agree,
it is a privilege to "see a beloved person out," as you put it. I

never had it with two such close and important people as yours were to you, but I got a taste of what lasting effects it can have through my acquaintance with Magda in her final months, and it's an experience I'm very grateful to have had.

Just as I am grateful for having had the use of your house for a year and a half. It has been a way station back to the land of the living for me. And it's been something else very important. It's hard to explain, but it has been like being given a second chance to finish my youth in a house where people close to me have lived and moved about their rooms and made their histories together in those rooms. Living in the house you two made together and shared has given me back my sense of *home*, something I hadn't had enough of when I lost mine. I was attempting to explain this to Elberta, when she bicycled over for lunch on Saturday. It was warm enough to eat outdoors, and she wanted to eat under the sycamore tree which she says you once told her was inhabited by the souls of the dead. It just occurs to me that you and I are a bit of Elberta's "home" in the same way you and Magda are part of mine. You'll be surprised when you see Elberta, by the way, she's shooting upward fast and losing her boxy shape, though she certainly hasn't lost her appetite. But when I ventured to tell her she was becoming an attractive young woman, she told me to shut up. She can still be awfully snippy and her manners certainly could use some improvement, but I'm happy to report she hasn't mentioned doing herself in once since Mamie, who is involved with a new admirer, has agreed to let her go to Emma Willard next fall.

Let me know when you'll be coming home, and I'll have my things out of here by then. (I never did get around to unpacking my thirty-two boxes of books, they're still down in your basement.) I've had adequate time to fix up the little apartment Cal and Laurence found for me back in December and it's very livable now, by New York apartment standards. Enough so that if you should want to come down to the city anytime, I can put you up on a comfortable sofa bed.

Love,
Alice

P.S. This is a postscript which I may regret later—or rather my cautious, fearful side may regret later—but while still under the influence of Magda's rousing example in that note I oughtn't to have read, I'll risk it. Do you remember that afternoon on the bus from Wells back to Bath, when you asked me if I remembered Magda's last words to me? Well, I didn't tell you everything. I told you she had asked for some books, but I wasn't sure which ones she meant. When I asked her if she meant those blue books, she scolded me: what did the colors matter? she said. Then she said—I can't remember exactly what the transition was here—she was going to leave you to me in her will. Those were her last words to me. This was the part I didn't tell you on the bus. It seemed somehow *intrusive* after you had confided to me your hopes of going back to Regina, and I felt it would be inappropriate, as if I were trying to offer myself as an alternative or something. So, for the second time in this letter, I apologize.

April 25, 1993

Dear Alice,

I received your letter and the enclosures last Thursday, but this is the first chance I've had to reply, since we've been working day and night getting furniture and medical equipment moved into the new nursing home. Father Birkenshaw jokingly called it "Home for the Terminally Challenged." He said he prayed every night he wouldn't have to go there, and with his typical strength of will he managed to escape the move by two weeks.

I go along with you completely about giving Mira Dooley only the parts you highlighted in the essay, the Magda-isms. Magda would not have wanted the essay published as it is, she made that clear in the note.

When I said I was thinking of coming back, the last thing I meant was that you should pack up your things and leave. What would be the point of that? You say Magda and I are part of your home, why can't we continue to be that for you? I see no reason why you shouldn't continue to use the house whenever you can. Why not unpack your thirty-two boxes of books and have the use of them there? You don't want to crowd up your small apartment in New York. If there's not enough shelf space, we can move Magda's books into another room. We can have additional shelves made for you as well. With my new skills in carpentry, I might attempt some myself!

Regina has been a way station for me in the same sense you mention about the house. Like you, I had some things I wasn't finished with yet. In my youth, I had idealized some aspects of the religious life and hadn't given due credit to the value of some others.

Now, through having been accepted as part of the community here, and from my talks with Father Birkenshaw, I've sorted out what I can leave behind and what I want to take away with me. There are many things I might do next, I have some pretty concrete ideas, but I'd like to have the benefit of your advice. Several days before he died, Father B. said a wonderful thing to me. We were going for one of our walks—he was such a strong personality I often forgot that I was pushing him in a wheelchair—and he said, "You know, Francis, just as the monks kept learning alive in the Dark Ages, it's going to be people like you who keep human kindness and charity alive in ours." Knowing how I admired him, you can imagine what this meant to me.

I was hoping to return in early June, if it's all right with you. I want to stay on here until we get everyone moved into the nursing home, and then I've promised to fill in for one of our cooks who's going on vacation. If I arrange a weekend flight so it wouldn't interfere with your job, maybe you would meet me at the airport? I'll of course let you know when I have definite travel plans.

Thank you for telling me what Magda said to you at the last. I can understand why you would have been reticent under the circumstances. I would have, myself. Now I must match your straightforwardness and tell you that she whispered something similar to me at the last, too, but I thought she wasn't making sense and I guess I put it out of my mind. I had actually forgotten it until I read your postscript. Serves me right, she would have said. As you can see from her note, she was always after me to keep better track of myself. But now you have given something precious back to me, not only with the note (judging from the date, March 1, I think it may have been one of the last things she was able to write), but also by your candor. For myself, I find it rather wonderful that her last words were similar to both of us. Maybe you will continue to help me recollect myself. I do hope this won't sound burdensome to you, but I would have a hard time imagining life without you as part of it. I've also come to think of you as being part of the house, and if you are agreeable, I am sure we can work something out.

My love,
Francis

March 1, 1991

Here I recline among the ruins of my mind.

Try again. Copy out where I stopped last, then try to ride on its momentum to the next thought.

It is as imitations of the spirit's variegated life that art transcends literal fact. Mundane art imitates the literal surfaces and movements of life. Visionary art imitates the underlying movement of spirit, moto spiritale. Therefore ...

Therefore what? I wrote the above only last week. Now I can't make the bridge anymore to where I was going. I can glimpse a fuzzy, shimmery outline of the kingdom where I was heading but have lost the means to get there. Like poor Moses, halted at Moab. Permitted to glimpse the promised land, but not allowed in.

Chuck it. Someone will come along and get it right. Not this essay with my name on it, but one just as good or better with someone's else's name on it. The material is there, let loose in the world for anyone with eyes to see and ears to hear. These ideas didn't originate with me and they'll be here after I'm gone.

What I take away with me, however, is mine. The broken lovely pieces that were merely mine.

Hello there, broken lovely piece. The time we went to Great Neck to stay with my mother, and she sat in her puce velvet Empire chair badly mending your trousers. You had snagged your pocket on one of her nasty aluminum screen doors and ripped them right down the side seam. Being my mother, she insisted you take off your trousers *right there*, on the spot, and so there the three of us sat in her stuffy baroque living room on that summer day in Great Neck, you in your striped undershorts, too kind to show your discomfiture, too polite to let her know you could have mended your own trousers and sewn a much better stitch. She was going on in her deliberately outrageous way, Marsha-ing me every chance she got while paying you compliments at my expense, how she never thought I had it in me to catch such a handsome lad, etc. As she progressed crookedly down the seam of your pants, she removed the pins one by one and jabbed them straight through her blouse, talking on and on, flattering you, baiting me. I watched your lovely eyes behind their new glasses grow wider and wider: you thought she was plunging the pins into her breast! And then I saw it dawn on you that it was a prosthesis, you were remembering I'd told you she'd had a mastectomy. I watched the light register on your face, then the relief, and I was almost knocked over by my sudden love for you. It struck me for the first time that I was in love with you, even if you had been so ridiculous as to want to marry me, and the realization that it was you I lived with now and not her gave me such joy that I rode it for the rest of our stay in Great Neck, even to the point of being able to playact the loving daughter.

Our urgent need to make the symbolic life part of our daily existence—

We live in and by our symbols, they bind up mundane reality for us—

Symbols make our mundane life cohere and coinhere—

A symbol is the clothing—

A symbol is not mere poetic fancy, it is the clothing of a spiritual reality in a conceptual garment so that its nature may be more readily perceived by our literal minds and thus we can see our way to choosing—

Oh chuck it, Magda, let it go, someone else will come

along and say what I've told you ad nauseam, Frannie, people must keep track of what's happening to them or they're doomed to repeat and repeat and repeat.

> Summe up at night what thou hast done by day;
> And in the morning, what thou hast to do.
> Dresse and undresse thy soul; mark the decay
> And growth of it: if with thy watch, that too
> Be down, then winde up both, since we shall be
> Most surely judg'd, make thy accounts agree.

There you are, sweet fellow, George Herbert says it better than I can, just as someone else will come along and write a better essay on the drama of the soul's choice.

Let it go, let it all go. How foolish and arrogant of me to expect that my *mind* would somehow to the very end be exempt from the ravening grin of the Gargoyle. Let it all break up in pieces and find its way into the dark stream

VIRAGO MODERN CLASSICS
&
CLASSIC NON-FICTION

The first Virago Modern Classic, *Frost in May* by Antonia White, was published in 1978. It launched a list dedicated to the celebration of women writers and to the rediscovery and reprinting of their works. Its aim was, and is, to demonstrate the existence of a female tradition in fiction, and to broaden the sometimes narrow definition of a 'classic' which has often led to the neglect of interesting novels and short stories. Published with new introductions by some of today's best writers, the books are chosen for many reasons: they may be great works of fiction; they may be wonderful period pieces; they may reveal particular aspects of women's lives; they may be classics of comedy or storytelling.

The companion series, Virago Classic Non-Fiction, includes diaries, letters, literary criticism, and biographies – often by and about authors published in the Virago Modern Classics.

'A continuingly magnificent imprint' – *Joanna Trollope*

'The Virago Modern Classics have reshaped literary history and enriched the reading of us all. No library is complete without them' – *Margaret Drabble*

'The writers are formidable, the production handsome. The whole enterprise is thoroughly grand' – *Louise Erdrich*

'The Virago Modern Classics are one of the best things in Britain today' – *Alison Lurie*

'Good news for everyone writing and reading today' – *Hilary Mantel*

'Masterful works' – *Vogue*

VIRAGO MODERN CLASSICS
&
CLASSIC NON-FICTION

Some of the authors included in these two series –

Lisa Alther, Elizabeth von Arnim, Dorothy Baker, Pat Barker, Nina Bawden, Nicola Beauman, Isabel Bolton, Kay Boyle, Vera Brittain, Leonora Carrington, Angela Carter, Willa Cather, Colette, Ivy Compton-Burnett, Barbara Comyns, E.M. Delafield, Maureen Duffy, Elaine Dundy, Nell Dunn, Emily Eden, George Eliot, Miles Franklin, Mrs Gaskell, Charlotte Perkins Gilman, Victoria Glendinning Elizabeth Forsythe Hailey, Radclyffe Hall, Shirley Hazzard, Dorothy Hewett, Mary Hocking, Alice Hoffman, Winifred Holtby, Janette Turner Hospital, Zora Neale Hurston, Elizabeth Jenkins, F. Tennyson Jesse, Molly Keane, Margaret Laurence, Maura Laverty, Rosamond Lehmann, Rose Macaulay, Shena Mackay, Olivia Manning, Paule Marshall, F.M. Mayor, Anais Nin, Mary Norton, Kate O'Brien, Olivia, Grace Paley, Mollie Panter-Downes, Dawn Powell, Dorothy Richardson, E. Arnot Robertson, Jacqueline Rose, Vita Sackville-West, Elaine Showalter, May Sinclair, Agnes Smedley, Dodie Smith, Stevie Smith, Christina Stead, Carolyn Steedman, Gertrude Stein, Jan Struther, Han Suyin, Elizabeth Taylor, Sylvia Townsend Warner, Mary Webb, Eudora Welty, Mae West, Rebecca West, Edith Wharton, Antonia White, Christa Wolf, Virginia Woolf, E.H. Young

'Found on all the best bookshelves' – *Penny Vincenzi*

'Their huge success is solid proof of the fact that literary fashion is a snare and a delusion – people like a good old-fashioned read' –
Good Housekeeping

THE ODD WOMAN

Gail Godwin

Introduced by Nicci Gerrard

Jane Clifford is in her early thirties, smart, attractive, and seemingly kitted out for life with a job as a popular teacher at a midwestern college, and an affair with a married man. But Jane knows better. And she wants more. She knows what she wants – passion, romance, 'an age of bustles and rustling silk, fine manners and literary soirees' – and what she doesn't want – to hand her life over to a man. And after a lifetime of looking to books for the answers to life's conundrums, she seems to be finding only more questions . . .

'Could be compared, in sensitivity and brilliance, to Doris Lessing and Margaret Drabble . . . Godwin's best and most ambitious book' *New York Times*

Now you can order superb titles directly from Virago

The prices shown above are correct at time of going to press. However, the publishers reserve the right to increase prices on covers from those previously advertised, without further notice.

Virago

Please allow for postage and packing: **Free UK delivery.**
Europe: add 25% of retail price; Rest of World: 45% of retail price.

To order any of the above or any other Virago titles, please call our credit card orderline or fill in this coupon and send/fax it to:

Virago, PO Box 121, Kettering, Northants NN14 4ZQ
Fax: 01832 737562   Tel: 01832 733076
Email: aspenhouse@FSBDial.co.uk

☐ I enclose a UK bank cheque made payable to Virago for £ . . . .
☐ Please charge £ . . . . . . to my Visa/Access/Mastercard/Eurocard

Expiry Date [   ]   Switch Issue No. [ ]

NAME (BLOCK LETTERS please) . . . .
ADDRESS . . . .
. . . .
. . . .
Postcode . . . . Telephone . . . .
Signature . . . .

Please allow 28 days for delivery within the UK. Offer subject to price and availability.
Please do not send any further mailings from companies carefully selected by Virago ☐